P9-DOE-216

Dear Reader,

I wrote *The Shop on Blossom Street* two years ago, and I'll admit it was one of my favorite books—mainly because I'm an avid knitter myself. If you checked out my yarn room, you'd agree. Yes, I said room. I have an entire room of my house dedicated to yarn. This is more yarn than one person could possibly expect to knit in an entire lifetime. So I can honestly say this book combined two of my greatest passions: writing and knitting.

Shortly after the book was first published, a number of wonderful surprises fell into my lap. (You can be assured there was a skein of yarn and a pair of knitting needles there, as well!) The first and most exciting was your enjoyment of the story. Like me, many of you considered Lydia, Jacqueline, Carol and Alix your friends. You wanted more and I wanted to give you more—hence the book you're holding now.

Just before *The Shop on Blossom Street* was published I was asked to be a board member for Warm Up America! If you'd like to be part of this wonderful organization, get in touch with the Warm Up America! Foundation, 2500 Lowell Road, Ranlo, NC 28054. (Or you can call 1-800-662-9999. The Web site is www.WarmUpAmerica.org.) Knitters and crocheters can submit seven-by-nine-inch patches, which will be stitched together to make blankets (or you can submit an entire blanket) for a variety of knitting charities. It's one way to reach out and lend a helping hand, and I'm honored to be able to spread the word.

As if that honor wasn't enough, Leisure Arts asked me to contribute my favorite patterns for my very own pattern book. This is like knitting nirvana. I was nearly as thrilled as the day I sold my first book. My delight at that invitation was matched only by my pleasure at meeting a number of designers and knitting gurus while collecting quotes for Lydia's chapters in *The Shop on Blossom Street* and *A Good Yarn*. I am in awe of the talented men and women I now count as friends, and grateful for their generosity.

I enjoy receiving your comments. You can write me at P.O. Box 1458, Port Orchard, WA 98366 or by logging on to my Web site at DebbieMacomber.com!

Thank you again for your continued support!

Warmest regards,

Debbie Macomber

DEBBIE MACOMBER

A Good Yarn

MIRA®

ISBN 0-7783-2295-5

A GOOD YARN

Copyright © 2005 by Debbie Macomber.

www.MIRABooks.com

Printed in U.S.A.

To Mary Colucci, Executive Director
Warm Up America! Foundation

and

David Blumenthal, President
Warm Up America! Foundation

Thank you both for bettering
the lives of so many

Peter's Socks
by Nancy Bush

Materials—Bearfoot from Mountain Colors (60% superwash wool, 25% mohair and 15% nylon) 350 yds, (320 meters) in 100 g 1 skein Moose Creek. Set of 5 #1 (2.5 mm) double point needles or size to give gauge.

Gauge—5 sts and 20 rnds = 2" over stockinette stitch before blocking.

Finished measurements after blocking—length of leg from cast-on edge to top of heel flap 8.5" (21.5 cm); length of foot from back of heel to tip of toe 10.5" (28.5 cm).

Leg

Cast on 65 sts. Divide sts onto 4 needles. Join, being careful not to twist. Begin patt—p1,* k3, p2, rep from * ending k3, p1. Work this ribbing as est for 7 more rnds. Work 1 rnd p. Rep these 9 rnds 2 more times. Cont in ribbing as est until leg measures 8.5" long. End ready to begin next rnd.

Heel Flap

K16, turn. Sl 1, p31. These 32 sts form the heel flap. The remaining 33 sts will be held for instep. Next row: *Sl 1, k1, rep from * to end, turn. Sl 1, p all across row. Rep these 2 rows until you have worked 32 rows total and have 16 chain sts down edge of flap. End having completed a WS row.

Turn Heel

Slip 1, k17, ssk, k1, turn. Sl 1, p5, p2 tog, p1, turn. *Sl 1, k to within 1 st from gap, ssk, k1, turn. Sl 1, p to within 1 st from gap, p2 tog, p1, turn. Rep from * until 1 st remains outside gap at each end. Sl 1, k16, ssk, turn. Sl 1, p16, p2 tog, turn (18 sts remain).

Gussets

K across the 18 heel sts. On the same needle, pick up and knit 16 sts down right side of heel flap. With a new needle, patt as est across instep. Pick up and knit 16 sts down left side of heel flap and knit 9 sts from heel. You will have 25 sts on first needle, 33 sts on instep, divided onto 2 needles, and 25 sts on last needle = 83 sts total.

Begin shaping the gussets. Rnds begin center of heel. K to 3 away from end of first needle, k2 tog, k1. Work across instep in patt as est. At beg of last needle, k1, ssk, k to end. Work one rnd even, keeping instep sts in patt. Cont in this manner, decreasing at the end of needle #1 and the beginning of needle #4 every other rnd and keeping patt as est on instep needle until back sts are decreased to 16 sts on each needle and you have 65 sts total.

Cont without decreasing until foot measures 3" less than desired finished length.

Toe

Work 3 rnds in St st.
Begin shaping toe:
Rnd 1—*K6, k2 tog, rep from * to 3 away from end of rnd, k 3 tog.
K 5 rnds even.
Rnd 7—*K5, k2 tog, rep from * to end. K 5 rnds even.
Rnd 13—*K4, k2 tog, rep from * to end. K 4 rnds even.
Rnd 18—*K3, k2 tog, rep from * to end. K 3 rnds even.
Rnd 22—*K2, k2 tog, rep from * to end. K 2 rnds even.
Rnd 25—*K1, k2 tog, rep from * to end. K 1 rnd even.
Rnd 27—*K2 tog, rep from * to end.

You will have 8 sts remaining.
Break yarn, and with a tapestry needle, draw yarn through the remaining sts and pull up snugly to close end of toe.

Weave in ends and block socks on sock blockers or under a damp towel.

Yarn supplied by:
Mountain Colors
P.O. Box 156
Corvallis, MT 59828
(406) 777-3377
info@mountaincolors.com

Abbreviations

Cont—continue
Cm—centimeter
Est—established
G—grams
K—knit
K2 tog—knit two together
Mm—millimeter
P—purl
P2 tog—purl 2 together
Patt—pattern
Sl 1—slip one (as to purl)
Ssk—slip, slip, knit: slip one stitch as to knit, slip the
      next stitch as to knit, knit these two slipped
      stitches together.
St(s)—stitch(es)
St st—stockinette stitch
Rnd(s)—round(s)
WS—wrong side
Yds—yards

Peter's Socks

by Nancy Bush
Translated for two circular needles by Cat Bordhi

Yarn: Mountain Colors Bearfoot (60% superwash wool, 25% mohair, 15% nylon, 100 g/ 350 yds), 1 skein in colorway "Moose Creek."

Needles: two size 1 (2.5 mm) circular needles 16"–24" in length, or size to give gauge.

Gauge: 15 sts and 20 rnds = 2" (5 cm) over stockinette stitch before blocking.

Finished measurements after blocking: length of leg from cast-on edge to top of heel flap 8.5" (21.5 cm); length of foot from back of heel to tip of toe 10.5" (28.5 cm).

Knitting in the round on 2 circular needles:
The stitches are divided between two circular needles. *Each needle knits only its own stitches. The only interaction between the two needles is to pass the yarn to the next needle when finished knitting its own stitches.* So while the first needle works its own stitches, the second circular needle rests, its stitches lined up on its cable and its ends hanging down out of the way, doing nothing at all. When the first needle is finished knitting all its stitches, the yarn is in position for the second needle to receive it and knit its own stitches, while the first needle rests. And so on.

Leg

Cast on 65 sts to the first circular needle. Slide 32 of the 65 sts onto the second circular needle, so that the working yarn comes from the end of this needle, while the first needle (with the remaining 33 sts) ends with the yarn tail. Move the 32 sts on the second needle to the middle of its cable, with the tips hanging down out of the way. Push the 33 sts on the first needle to its tip with the tail end of the yarn nearest the tip. Hold the other tip in your right hand, and prepare to knit with the yarn coming from the second needle. Being careful not to twist the cast-on sts, join by beginning ribbing pattern: *p2, k3, rep from * to end. Work ribbing for 7 more rnds. Purl 1 rnd. Rep these 9 rnds twice more. Continue ribbing until leg measures 8.5" long, ending with a completed first needle.

Heel Flap

You will work *back and forth in rows on the second needle alone* to make the square heel flap and turn the heel. The 33 sts on the first needle will become the instep and gussets, and you will resume working with them later. Begin heel flap: *Sl 1, k1, rep from * to end, turn. Sl 1, p to end. Rep these 2 rows until you have worked 32 rows total and have 16 chain sts along each edge of flap. End with a completed purl row.

Heel Turn

Continuing to work back and forth on second needle, sl 1, k17, ssk, k1, turn. Sl 1, p5, p2 tog, p1, turn. *Sl 1, k to within 1 st from gap, ssk, k1, turn. Sl 1, p to within 1 st from gap, p2 tog, p1, turn. Rep from * until 1 st remains outside gap at each end. Sl 1, k16, ssk, turn. Sl 1, p16, p2 tog, turn (18 sts remain).

Gussets

Resume working with two circular needles in the round. Still using second needle, k across the 18 heel sts. Pick up and k 16 in the 16 chains along side of heel flap. Let second needle hang, and with first needle, work ribbing as established across its 33 instep sts (the needle should begin and end with k3). Let first needle hang. With second needle, pick up and k 16 in remaining 16 chains along side of heel flap and k to end of needle. You have 50 sts on the second needle and 33 on the first. Begin shaping the gussets: *Knit instep ribbing with first needle. With second needle, k1, ssk, k until 3 sts remain on needle, k2 tog, k1. Knit 1 rnd, maintaining ribbing on first needle. Repeat these 2 rnds until 32 sts remain on second needle, 65 sts total. K all sts until foot measures 3" less than desired finished length.

Toe

Knit 3 rnds, then begin shaping toe:

Rnds 1–6: *K6, k2 tog, rep from * to 3 sts before end of rnd, k 3 tog (56 sts). Knit 5 rnds.

Rnds 7–12: *K5, k2 tog, rep from * to end (48 sts). K 5 rnds even.

Rnds 13–17: *K4, k2 tog, rep from * to end (40 sts). K 4 rnds even.

Rnds 18–21: *K3, k2 tog, rep from * to end (32 sts). K 3 rnds even.

Rnds 22–24: *K2, k2 tog, rep from * to end (24 sts). K 2 rnds even.

Rnds 25–26: *K1, k2 tog, rep from * to end (16 sts). K 1 rnd even.

Rnd 27: *k2 tog, rep from * to end (8 sts). Cut tail of yarn, and with a tapestry needle draw yarn through remaining sts and pull up snugly to close end of toe. Weave in ends. Make second sock, then block on sock blockers or under a damp towel.

For more information on knitting with two circular needles, see *Socks Soar on Two Circular Needles* by Cat Bordhi, Passing Paws Press, 2001, www.catbordhi.com. Cat is also the author of *A Treasury of Magical Knitting* and *A Second Treasury of Magical Knitting*.

Yarn supplied by:
Mountain Colors
P.O. Box 156
Corvallis, MT 59828
(406) 777-3377
info@mountaincolors.com

Abbreviations
K—knit
K2 tog—knit two together
P—purl
P2 tog—purl 2 together
Sl 1—slip one (as to purl)
Ssk—slip, slip, knit: slip one stitch as to knit, slip the next stitch as to knit, knit these two slipped stitches together.
St(s)—stitch(es)
Rnd(s)—round(s)

1

CHAPTER

"Making a sock by hand creates a connection to history; we are offered a glimpse into the lives of knitters who made socks using the same skills and techniques we continue to use today."

—Nancy Bush, author of *Folk Socks* (1994),
Folk Knitting in Estonia (1999) and *Knitting on the Road, Socks for the Traveling Knitter* (2001),
all published by Interweave Press.

LYDIA HOFFMAN

Knitting saved my life. It saw me through two lengthy bouts of cancer, a particularly terrifying kind that formed tumors inside my brain and tormented me with indescribable headaches. I experienced pain I could never have imagined before. Cancer destroyed my teen years and my twenties, but I was *determined* to survive.

I'd just turned sixteen the first time I was diagnosed, and I learned to knit while undergoing chemotherapy. A woman with breast cancer, who had the chemo chair next to mine, used to knit and she's the one who taught me. The chemo was dreadful—not quite as bad as the headaches, but close. Because of knitting, I was able to endure those endless hours of weakness and severe nausea. With two needles and a skein of yarn, I felt I could face whatever I had to. My hair fell out in clumps, but I could weave yarn around a needle and create a stitch; I could follow a pattern and finish a project. I couldn't hold down more than a few bites at a time, but I could knit. I clung to that small sense of accomplishment, treasured it.

Knitting was my salvation—knitting and my father. He lent me the emotional strength to make it through the last bout. I survived but, sadly, Dad didn't. Ironic, isn't it? I lived, but my cancer killed my father.

The death certificate states that he died of a massive heart attack, but I believe otherwise. When the cancer returned, it devastated him even more than me. Mom has never been able to deal with sickness, so the brunt of my care fell to my father. It was Dad who got me through chemotherapy, Dad who argued with the doctors and fought for the very best medical care—Dad who lent me the will to live. Consumed by my own desperate struggle for life, I didn't realize how dear a price my father paid for my recovery. By the time I was officially in remission, Dad's heart simply gave out on him.

After he died, I knew I had to make a choice about what I should do with the rest of my life. I wanted to honor my father in whatever I chose, and that meant I was prepared to take risks. I, Lydia Anne Hoffman, resolved to leave my mark on the world. In retrospect, that sounds rather melodramatic, but a year ago it was exactly how I felt. What, you might ask, did I do that was so life-changing and profound?

I opened a yarn store on Blossom Street in Seattle. That probably won't seem earth-shattering to anyone else, but for me, it was a leap of faith equal to Noah's building the ark without a rain cloud in sight. I had an inheritance from my grandparents and gambled every cent on starting my own business. Me, who's never held down a job for more than a few weeks. Me, who knew next to nothing about finances, profit-and-loss statements or business plans. I sank every dime I had into what I *did* know, and that was yarn and knitters.

Naturally, I ran into a few problems. At the time, Blossom Street was undergoing a major renovation—in fact, the architect's wife, Jacqueline Donovan, was one of the women in my first knitting class. Jacqueline, Carol and Alix, my original students, remain three of my closest friends to this day. Last summer, when I opened A Good Yarn, the street was closed to traffic. Anyone who managed to find her way to my store then had to put up with constant dust and noise. I refused to let the mess and inconvenience hamper my enthusiasm, and fortunately that was how my clientele felt, too. I was convinced I could make this work.

I didn't get the support you might expect from my family. Mom, bless her, tried to be encouraging, but she was in shock after losing Dad. She still is. Most days, she wanders hopelessly around in a fog of grief and loss. When I mentioned my plan, she didn't discourage me, but she didn't cheer me on, either. To the best of my memory, she said, "Sure, honey, go ahead, if you think you should." From my mother, this was as rousing an endorsement as I could hope to receive.

My older sister, Margaret, on the other hand, had no qualms about drowning me in tales of doom and gloom. The day I opened my store, she marched in with a spate of dire forecasts. The economy was down, she told me; people were hanging on to their money. I'd be lucky to stay afloat for six weeks. Ten minutes of listening to her ominous predictions, and I was ready to rip up the lease and close my door—until I reminded myself that this was my first official day on the job and I had yet to sell a single skein of yarn.

As you might've guessed, Margaret and I have a complicated relationship. Don't get me wrong; I love my sister. Until the cancer struck, we were like any other sisters with the normal ups and downs in our relationship. After I was initially diagnosed with brain cancer, she was wonderful. I remember she brought me a stuffed teddy bear to take to the hospital with me. I still have it somewhere if Whiskers hasn't gotten hold of it. Whiskers is my cat and he tends to shred anything with a fuzzy surface.

It was when I went through the second bout of cancer that Margaret's attitude changed noticeably. She acted as if I *wanted* to be sick, as if I was so hungry for attention that I'd brought this horror on myself. When I took my first struggling steps toward independence, I'd hoped she'd support my efforts. Instead, all I got was discouragement. But over time, that changed and eventually all my hard work won her over.

Margaret, to put it mildly, isn't the warm, spontaneous type. I didn't understand how much she cared about me until I had a third cancer scare just a few months after I opened A Good Yarn. *Scare* doesn't come close to describing my feelings when Dr. Wilson ordered those frightening, familiar tests. It was as if my entire world had come to a sudden halt. The truth is, I don't think I could've endured the struggle yet again. I'd already decided that if the cancer *had* returned, I would refuse treatment. I didn't want to die, but once you've lived with the threat of death, it loses its potency.

My come-what-may attitude disturbed Margaret, who wouldn't accept my fatalism. Talk of death unsettled her, the way it does most people, but when you've been around death and dying as much as I have, it seems as natural as turning off the lights. I don't look forward to dying, but I'm not afraid of it either. Thankfully, the tests came back negative and I'm thriving, right along with my yarn store. I mention it now because it was during those weeks that I discovered how deeply my sister loves me. In the last seventeen years, I've only seen her cry twice—when Dad died and when Dr. Wilson gave me a clean bill of health.

Once I returned to work full-time, Margaret bullied and cajoled me into contacting Brad Goetz again. Brad, who drives the UPS truck that makes deliveries to A Good Yarn, is the man I'd started seeing last year. He's divorced and has custody of his eight-year-old son, Cody. It would be an understatement to say Brad is good-looking; the fact is, he's drop-dead gorgeous. The first day he came into the store, wheeling several cartons of yarn, it was all I could do to keep the drool from dripping down my chin. I got so flustered I could hardly sign for the delivery. He asked me out three times before I finally agreed to meet him for drinks. Given my experience with male-female relationships, I was sure I'd be completely out of my element dating Brad. I would never have found the courage to say yes if not for Margaret, who harassed me into it.

I always say that A Good Yarn is my affirmation of life, but according to my sister I was *afraid* of life. Afraid to really live, to venture outside the tiny comfortable world I'd created inside my yarn store. She was right and I knew it, but still I resisted. It'd been so many years since I'd spent any amount of time with a man other than my father or my physician that I had the social finesse of a dandelion. But Margaret wouldn't listen to a single excuse, and soon Brad and I were having drinks together, followed by dinners, picnics with Cody and ball games. I've come to love Brad's son as much as I do my two nieces, Julia and Hailey.

These days Brad and I see quite a bit of each other. During my cancer scare, I'd pushed him away, which was a mistake as Margaret frequently pointed out. Brad forgave me, though, and we resumed out relationship. We're cautious—

okay, I'm the one who's taking things slow, but Brad's fine with that. He was burned once when his ex-wife walked out, claiming she needed to "find herself." There's Cody to consider, too. The boy has a close relationship with Brad, and while Cody loves me too, I don't want to disrupt that special bond between father and son. So far, everything is going well, and we're talking more and more about a future together. Brad and Cody are so much a part of my life now that I couldn't imagine being without them.

Although it took her a while, Margaret is finally in favor of my yarn store. After a shaky start, my sister is a believer. She's actually working with me now. That's right, the two of us side by side, and that's nothing short of a miracle. Occasionally we regress, but we're making strides. I'm so glad she's with me, in every sense of the word.

Before I get too carried away, I want to tell you about my shop. The minute I laid eyes on this place I saw its potential. Despite the construction mess, the temporary drawbacks and shifting neighborhood, I realized it was perfect. I was ready to sign the lease before I'd even walked inside. I loved the large display windows, which look out onto the street. Whiskers sleeps there most days, curled up among the skeins and balls of yarn. The flower boxes immediately reminded me of my father's first bicycle shop, and it was almost as if my dad was giving my venture his nod of approval. The colorful but dusty striped awning sealed the deal in my mind. I knew this old-fashioned little shop could become the welcoming place I'd envisioned—and it has.

The renovation on Blossom Street is almost complete. The bank building has been transformed into ultraexpensive condos and the video store next to it is now a French-style café, cleverly called The French Café. Alix Townsend, who took my very first beginners' knitting class, worked at the old video store, and it's somehow fitting that her first real job as a pastry chef is in exactly the same location. Unfortunately, Annie's Café down the street is closed and vacant, but the space won't be empty for long. This is a thriving neighborhood.

The bell above my door chimed as Margaret stepped inside. It was the first Tuesday morning in June, and a lovely day. Summer would be arriving any time now in the Pacific Northwest.

"Good morning," I greeted her, turning from the small coffeemaker I keep in the back room that's officially my office.

She didn't answer me right away and when she did it was more of a grumble than an actual response. Knowing my sister and her moods, I decided to bide my time. If she'd had an argument with one of her daughters or with her husband, she'd tell me eventually.

"I've got a pot of coffee on," I announced as Margaret walked into the back room and locked up her purse.

Without commenting, my sister pulled a freshly washed cup from the tray and reached for the pot. The drip continued, sizzling against the hot plate, but she didn't appear to notice.

Finally I couldn't stand it any longer and my resolve to give her a chance to get over her bad mood disappeared. "What's wrong with you?" I demanded. I have to admit I felt impatient; lately, she's brought her surly moods to work a little too often.

Facing me, Margaret managed a tentative smile. "Nothing...sorry. It's just that this feels a whole lot like a Monday."

Because the shop is closed on Mondays, Tuesday is our first workday of the week. I frowned at her, trying to figure out what the real problem was. But she'd assumed a perfectly blank expression, telling me nothing.

My sister is a striking woman with wide shoulders and thick, dark hair. She's tall and lean, but solid. She still looks like the athlete she used to be. I wish she'd do something different with her hair, though. She wears the same style she did in high school, parted in the middle and stick-straight until it hits her shoulders, where it obediently turns under, as if she's tortured it with a curling iron. That was certainly part of her teenage regimen—the curling iron, the hair spray, the vigorously wielded brush. The style's classic and it suits her, I suppose, but I'd give anything to see her try something new.

"I'm going to post a new class," I said, changing the subject abruptly, hoping to draw her out of her dour mood.

"In what?"

Ah, interest. That was a good sign. For the most part, all the classes I'd held had gone well. I'd taught a beginners' class, an intermediate and a Fair Isle, but there was one I'd been thinking of offering for a while.

"It's such a difficult question?"

My sister's sarcasm shook me from my brief reverie. "Socks," I told her. "I'm going to offer a class on knitting socks."

With the inventive new sock yarns on the market, socks were the current knitting rage. I carried a number of the European brands and loved the variety. My customers did, too. Some of the new yarns were designed to create an intricate pattern when knitted. I found it amazing to view a finished pair of socks, knowing the design had been formed by the yarn itself and not the knitter.

"Fine." Margaret's shoulders rose in a shrug. "I suppose you're going to suggest knitting them on circular needles versus the double-pointed method," she said casually.

"Of course." I preferred using two circular needles.

Margaret would rather crochet and while she can knit, she doesn't often. "There seems to be a lot of interest in socks lately, doesn't there?" Her tone was still casual, almost indifferent.

I regarded my sister closely. She always had a list of three or four reasons any idea of mine wouldn't work. It had become practically a game with us. I'd make some suggestion and she'd instantly tell me why it was bound to fail. I missed having the opportunity to state my case.

"So you think a sock class would appeal to our customers?" I couldn't help asking. Good grief, there had to be something drastically wrong with Margaret.

Personally, I was fond of knitting socks for reasons beyond the current popularity. The biggest attraction for me was the fact that a pair of socks was a small project. After finishing an afghan or a Fair Isle sweater, I usually wanted a project I knew I could complete quickly. After knitting for endless hours, I found it gratifying to watch a sock take shape almost immediately. Socks didn't require a major commitment of either time or yarn and made wonderful gifts. Yes, socks were definitely my choice for this new class. Because Tuesday seemed to be my slowest business day, it made sense to hold the sessions then.

Margaret nodded in answer to my question. "I think a sock class would definitely attract knitters," she murmured.

I stared at my sister and, for an instant, thought I saw the sheen of tears in her eyes. I stared harder. As I mentioned earlier, Margaret rarely cries. "Are you feeling okay?" I asked, just in case, keeping my voice gentle. I didn't want to pry, but if something really *was* wrong, she needed to know I was concerned about her.

"Stop asking me that," she snapped.

I sighed with relief. The old Margaret was back.

"Would you make a sign for the window?" I asked. Margaret had much more artistic ability than I did. I'd come to rely on her for the window notices and displays.

With no real show of enthusiasm, she shrugged again. "I'll have one up before noon."

"Great." I walked over to the front door, unlocked it and flipped the Closed sign to Open. Whiskers glanced up from his perch in the front window, where he lazed in the morning sun. Red Martha Washington geraniums bloomed in the window box. The soil looked parched, so I filled the watering can and carried it outside. From the corner of my eye I saw a flash of brown as a truck turned the corner. A familiar happiness stole over me. *Brad.*

Sure enough, he angled the big truck into the parking spot in front of Fanny's Floral, the shop next to mine. He hopped out, all the while smiling at me.

"It's a beautiful morning," I said, reveling in his smile. This man smiles with his whole heart, his whole being, and he has the most intense blue eyes. They're like a beacon to me. I swear I can see those eyes a mile away, they're that blue. "Have you got a yarn delivery?" I asked.

"I'm the only delivery I have for you today, but I've got a couple of minutes if there's coffee on."

"There is." It was our ritual. Brad stopped at the shop twice a week, with or without a load of yarn—more often if he could manage it. He never stayed long. He filled his travel coffee mug, took the opportunity to steal a kiss and then returned to his deliveries. As always, I followed him into the back room, pretending to be surprised when he eased me into his embrace. I love Brad's kisses. This time he started with my forehead, then gradually worked his way down my face until he reached my lips. As his mouth moved over mine, I could feel the electricity through every inch of my body. He has that kind of effect on me—and he's well aware of it.

He held me just long enough to let me regain my equilibrium. Then he released me and picked up the coffeepot. He was frowning when he turned around.

"Is there a problem between Margaret and Matt?" he asked.

I opened my mouth to assure him everything was fine, but before I could utter a word I stopped myself. All at once I realized I didn't know. "What makes you ask?"

"Your sister," he said in hushed tones. "She isn't herself lately. Haven't you noticed?"

I nodded. "Something's definitely up with her," I agreed,

remembering how she'd declined the opportunity to wage verbal battle with me.

"Do you want me to ask her?" Brad inquired, forgetting to whisper.

I paused, afraid Margaret would take offense and snap at Brad the same way she had at me. "Probably not." But then I changed my mind. My sister was half in love with Brad herself. If anyone could make it past that protective barrier of hers, he'd be the one. "Maybe, but not now."

"When?"

"Perhaps we should all get together soon."

Brad shook his head. "It'd be better if Matt wasn't around."

"Right." I nibbled on my lower lip. "Do you have any other ideas?"

Before he could answer, Margaret tore aside the curtain to the back room and glared at us. Brad and I started, no doubt looking as guilty as we felt.

"Listen, you two lovebirds, if you're going to talk about me I suggest you lower your voices." With that, she dropped the curtain and stomped into the store.

2
CHAPTER

ELISE BEAUMONT

Retirement was everything Elise Beaumont had hoped it would be, and everything she'd feared. On the positive side, the alarm portion of her clock-radio had been permanently shut off. She woke when her body told her she no longer needed sleep, ate when she felt hungry and not when the school library set her break.

Then there were the negatives. For years she'd scrimped and saved, wanting to build her own home on her own small piece of land. After months of searching, months of visiting housing developments, she found the area and the development she'd always dreamed of. It was on the outskirts of the city, and if it didn't have an ocean view, it was still beautiful, overlooking a grove of conifers. She could imagine having coffee on her small patio, watching deer emerge from the trees in the early morning. She raided her investment account and put down a large chunk of cash. She'd assumed the developer was a reputable one; to put it bluntly, he wasn't. She, along with a handful of others, had been cheated and misled. Then the company declared bankruptcy within a month, and as a result she had no home, no savings and mounting legal bills. It was a nightmarish situation that continued to get worse.

As she lay in bed, she recalled that for years she'd wanted to travel beyond the Puget Sound area, where she'd been born and raised. Well, she couldn't afford that now. But for the first time in her adult life she felt the urge to follow her creative bent. She planned to knit again and take an oil painting class. Having spent most of her career around books, she'd toyed with the idea of writing a novel. Maybe a children's story... She was open to trying just about anything—once the class-action suit against the builder was settled. Until then, she could only obsess about her lack of funds and the legal battle before her.

Her life was on hold until she was free of this mess. It was all a waiting game now as the attorneys filed the paperwork and the lawsuit worked its way through the court system. At best, it would be a year before she and the others saw even a fraction of their money. *If* they did, and that was a big if. All she could do was hope and pray that all wasn't lost.

The problems with the builder were only the start of her difficulties. Certain her house would be completed on time, she'd let go of the lease on her apartment. That had been an early mistake. The vacancy rate in Seattle was low and not only would it be difficult to find a new place, she was terrified of using the better part of her pension on an overpriced apartment. At her daughter's suggestion, Elise had moved in with her. Just for a little while, she'd promised herself. Except that it had already been six months....

No—Elise refused to spend another second thinking about this financial disaster. It only depressed her. In her eagerness to have her own home, she'd lost practically everything. At least she had her health, her daughter and grandchildren, her sanity.

"Grandma, Grandma," six-year-old John cried as he pounded urgently at her bedroom door. "Are you awake? I want to come in, okay?"

Elise slid out of bed and opened her bedroom door. Her freckle-faced grandson smiled crookedly up at her. His crop of carrot-colored hair stood nearly straight up, just the way Maverick's once had. Her youngest grandson's hair color often brought her ex-husband to mind. Elise hadn't seen him for more than brief periods over the past thirty years. How she'd ever managed to meet, let alone marry, a professional gambler was something she couldn't explain even now. He'd been her one wild, impulsive fling.

But…how she'd loved him. Elise had been head over heels for that man. They were married within weeks of their first meeting—which had happened in a grocery store, of all places. Before long, Aurora was born, but the problems had already started. At the time, Marvin "Maverick" Beaumont was working for an insurance firm, but he had an addiction to cards and gambling, and it'd nearly destroyed them both. In the end, Elise felt she had no option but to leave him. Whenever she'd threatened divorce, he'd begged her to reconsider, begged her to give him another chance, but it was the same pattern over and over until Elise finally realized she had to get him out of her life. It still hurt. She'd never loved another man with the same intensity as she had Maverick. She'd tried, but no one else had made her feel the way he had.

She'd made a genuine effort to socialize, with the hope of marrying again. The closest she came was when Aurora turned fifteen, but Elise discovered that Jules, a symphony musician she'd been dating, had a wife and two daughters living in San Francisco. Devastated, she'd avoided relationships ever since. There was something to be said for a simple life.

Looking perturbed, Elise's daughter rounded the hallway

corner. "John, I told you to leave your grandmother alone," Aurora chastised. She reached for his arm and dragged him away from Elise's door. "I'm sorry, Mom. I told the boys to let you sleep in this morning," she added, casting Elise an apologetic glance.

"It's all right, I was awake." Living with her daughter, a stay-at-home mom, and her family might not have been part of Elise's retirement plans, but for the moment this arrangement suited them both. Her furniture was in storage and her life on hold, but she had a roof over her head.

While Elise waited for the lawsuit to get settled, she paid Aurora and David rent. The amount was small at their insistence, but it was still a boon to the tight family budget. Elise also helped her daughter with the children. David, Elise's son-in-law, was a computer specialist who set up software systems for companies across North America and was often away for a week or two at a time. Elise and Aurora, always close, were company for each other, and Elise appreciated her daughter's encouragement and support.

"Can you take us to the park this afternoon?" John pleaded.

"Perhaps," Elise said, hating to refuse him anything. "I have a few errands to run this morning and I don't know how long they'll take."

"Can I come?" John was such a dear boy, anxious to go and see and do. He'd raced into the world a full month early and had yet to stop.

"No, sweetie, you've got kindergarten this morning."

His face fell instantly but he accepted her refusal with a good-natured shrug and quickly disappeared down the hallway to join his older brother.

"I thought I'd go down Blossom Street and check out that yarn store," Elise informed her daughter.

She could tell Aurora was pleased about her renewed interest in knitting. After a recent visit to her attorney's office, Elise had walked down the renovated street and noticed the yarn store, which she'd mentioned to Aurora.

Elise was pleasantly surprised by the changes on Blossom Street. For years the area had been an eyesore, with its seedy-looking establishments. The renovations weren't what she'd expected. Instead of tearing down the older buildings, the architect had refurbished what was already there and renewed a deteriorating neighborhood. The shops were appealing with awnings and flowers and sidewalk displays. The impression she'd been left with was of a warmly traditional neighborhood, a lovely little world unto itself. It was hard to believe that just a few blocks over, high-rises stretched toward the sky. Just down the hill were the huge financial enterprises, insurance complexes and other major businesses that made up downtown Seattle.

While looking in the window of A Good Yarn, Elise had noticed a sign that advertised knitting classes. She might not be able to enjoy her retirement the way she'd hoped, but she wasn't going to become a recluse afraid to spend a dime, either. Besides, knitting might keep her mind off her financial difficulties.

After a cup of tea in her room, Elise dressed for the day. She'd maintained her slim figure and chose a peach-colored pantsuit that was both stylish and comfortable. Although it was early June and sunny, the weather remained cool and she would need the matching jacket once she got outside. She pinned a small pink cameo over the top closure of her white blouse. It was the nicest piece of jewelry she owned. Maverick had given it to her before they were even married and she loved it and wore it often.

To his credit, Maverick had stayed in touch with their daughter, although not as regularly as Elise felt he should. For her own part, she wanted nothing to do with him, but she didn't begrudge Aurora the opportunity to know her father;

she never had. She considered their relationship entirely separate from her. She paused, frowning. Twice that morning she'd thought about Maverick. It wasn't as though she ever really forgot him—how could she with her grandson so physically similar—but she rarely indulged her memories of him. She didn't *want* to think about him or remember the days and nights of love.

After running a brush through her shoulder-length brown hair, she tied it back at the nape of her neck. Untouched by gray, it was her one vanity. Her hand froze as yet another memory wrapped itself around her heart. Maverick had loved her hair down. She'd worn it in a tidy bun at the library but at the end of the day, the first thing he did was reach for the pins to loosen her thick tresses. "Rapunzel, Rapunzel," he'd whisper and she'd smile…. Irritated, she tightened her lips and cast the thought from her mind.

Aurora was pouring milk into bowls of cereal when Elise walked into the kitchen.

"You look nice, Mom," she commented.

Compliments embarrassed Elise and she dismissed her daughter's words with a shake of her head.

"Have a good day at school," Elise told the boys as she opened the front door.

They watched her leave, their faces glum, as if she'd abandoned them to some malicious fate. Her grandsons were her joy but she hardly knew how Aurora managed. She marveled at her daughter's skill as a wife and mother.

Elise sometimes feared she'd failed on both counts. She was never meant to be a wife, and her two years of married life had proved as much. Aurora was the one treasure she'd managed to salvage from that shipwreck of a marriage. Her daughter, as tall as her father at six feet, was a blessing beyond compare. In more ways than Elise cared to admit, they'd grown up together. Thankfully they'd stayed close.

Maverick had faithfully paid his child support each month, and when the spirit moved him, he'd phoned Aurora from wherever he was currently living, which seemed to be in a different part of the country each time. Soon after their wedding, he'd given up any pretense of an ordinary job—although he'd been quite successful at insurance sales—and devoted his energy to gambling. Roots were a detriment to a professional gambler. And if settling down wasn't conducive to a gambler's life, a family was even less so. While Elise was in labor, her loving husband had started up a poker game in the waiting room and completely missed the birth of his only child.

Catching the #47 bus, Elise rode it down Pill Hill toward Blossom Street, getting off three stops before the Seattle Public Library, which had recently undergone a huge renovation. Through her work at the school library, Elise had met some of Washington's most influential librarians. They included Nancy Pearl, who'd organized the "If All Seattle Reads the Same Book" program. Cities, large and small, across the United States had followed Seattle's lead. Elise was delighted that this idea had become so popular. It demonstrated that the library remained an important part of the community.

Stepping off the bus, she clutched her purse close to her side. The area had once been known for its pickpockets and muggers. That didn't seem to be the case now, but one could never be too careful.

She walked past Fanny's Floral and stopped to admire a display of purple carnations. She'd never seen carnations in quite that color before and was tempted to bring home a bouquet for Aurora. She probably shouldn't waste money on flowers, but still... Well, she'd think about it.

A snoozing tabby cat was curled up in the display window of the yarn store. Elise opened the door and a small bell rang. Apparently accustomed to the sound, the cat didn't stir.

"Good morning," a pleasant-faced woman greeted her. Another, older woman stood by the counter and nodded in Elise's direction.

"Yes, it is," she said, instantly warmed by the younger woman's friendliness. This was an attractive shop, well-designed and not overcrowded with yarn. Elise liked that she could see over the top of each display case. "I've come to inquire about classes," she said, distracted by the colors and textures all around her. There were projects displayed on top of the cases, cleverly arranged on wire frames. Her eye was drawn to a sweater with a dinosaur knit into the front. Both Luke and John would love that. Perhaps one day she'd make it for her grandsons.

"We're enrolling for a sock class this week."

"Socks," Elise repeated, unsure this was a project that interested her. "I've knit with five needles before, but it's been a long time."

"These are knitted up on two circular needles," the woman told her. "Here, let me show you what I mean." She led Elise toward the middle aisle, where a row of plastic feet displayed knitted socks. The patterns were intricate—far more complicated than Elise cared to tackle. It'd been years since she'd picked up knitting needles and she wasn't eager to sabotage her efforts with a project beyond her capabilities.

She was about to say as much when the woman explained that the designs were part of the yarn itself.

"You mean I don't have to do anything but knit?"

"That's correct. The yarn is self-patterning." She went on to list the price of the class, the day and the cost, which included all the supplies she would need. "By the way, I'm Lydia Hoffman and that's my sister, Margaret. She works with me."

"Elise Beaumont," she said and smiled at both women. On closer inspection it became more obvious that they were related. The older one, Margaret, was large-boned but the other, Lydia, was petite with delicate features. Yet their faces were similar in shape, with pronounced cheekbones and large dark eyes. When she realized she was staring, she added, "I recently retired and thought I'd take up knitting again."

"That's a *wonderful* idea."

Elise smiled at Lydia's enthusiasm. Margaret's attention had returned to whatever she was doing at the counter, which apparently involved catalogues and order forms.

"A class seems like a good place to start," Elise said.

Lydia nodded. "I'm so glad you decided to stop by." She continued toward the back of the shop, where a table and chairs were set up. "If you're free on Friday afternoons, I'd like to invite you to our charity knitting sessions, too."

"Another class?" Elise could only afford one.

"Not exactly. There's no cost. A number of my regulars come here to knit for different charitable projects and organizations. You'd be most welcome, Elise." She talked about Warm Up America, the Linus Project and ChemoCaps for people undergoing chemotherapy.

"Do you supply the yarn?" Elise asked, conscious once again of her limited budget.

"As a matter of fact, I do," Lydia said. "Or at least some of it. Patrons have donated leftover yarn for the Warm Up America blankets, and anyone who purchases yarn for one of the other projects can buy it at a discount."

"Perhaps I'll do that." Elise's schedule was nearly empty and she was looking for ways to fill it. So far, she'd joined a readers' group that met once a month at a branch of the Seattle Public Library, and had volunteered to fold church newsletters. A strong supporter of the local blood bank, she'd also volunteered to handle the desk every Monday morning until noon.

"Would you like to sign up for the sock class?" Lydia pressed. "I'm sure you'd enjoy it."

Again Elise's spirits lifted at the other woman's friendliness. "Yes, I think I would." She opened her purse and removed her checkbook. "How many will be in the class?" she asked as she signed the check.

"I'd like to limit it to six."

"Has there been a lot of interest?"

"Not yet, but I only put the ad in the window Tuesday morning. You're the first person to join."

"The first," Elise repeated, and for reasons she could only guess at, being first gave her a sense of pleasure.

She decided to buy those flowers for Aurora, after all.

CHAPTER

BETHANNE HAMLIN

It wasn't supposed to be like this, Bethanne Hamlin lamented as she pulled into the driveway of her Capitol Hill home. The house, built in the 1930s before it was deemed unsafe and unfeasible to use brick on top of an earthquake fault, had been her dream home. She'd fallen in love with it the moment she saw it. The short steep driveway ended at the basement garage. Concrete steps led to a small porch, and the front door was rounded, like the door to a fairy-tale cottage, she'd always thought. A gable jutted out from the second-floor master bedroom. The window seat there overlooked the entire neighborhood. Bethanne had often sat in that window and read or daydreamed. It was in this beautiful home that she'd once lived her perfect life. Her fairy-tale life...

She turned off the engine and sat in her five-year-old Plymouth, searching for the resolve and the strength to enter her house with a smile on her face. Taking a deep breath, she slid out of the car, reaching into the backseat for her groceries.

"I'm home," she called out as she opened the front door, doing her best to sound cheerful.

She felt relief when silence greeted her.

"Andrew? Annie?" She placed the grocery bag on the kitchen countertop, filled the teakettle and set it on the burner. Before the divorce she'd never been much of a tea drinker, but in the last year she'd become practically addicted, drinking two or three pots a day.

"I'm home," she announced a second time. Again, no response.

After a few minutes, the kettle began to whistle, and she poured the steaming water over Earl Grey tea bags in the ceramic pot that had once belonged to her grandmother. Then she carried it to the breakfast table.

Sitting in the small alcove, she tried to make sense of her life. Tried to make sense of everything that had happened to her and her children over the past two years. Nothing felt right anymore. It was as if the seasons no longer followed each other in proper succession. Or as if the moon had suddenly replaced the sun... She still had trouble understanding what had happened—and why.

It'd all started sixteen months earlier on the morning of Valentine's Day. The kids were awake and banging around inside their bedrooms, getting ready for school. A little earlier, when she could hear Andrew and Annie squabbling over the bathroom, she'd thrown on her housecoat and started down to the kitchen to make breakfast. Then, as she reached the door, she'd noticed her husband sitting up in bed, knees bent, face in his hands. Bethanne's first thought was that Grant had the flu. Any other morning, he was already up and dressed for work. He loved his job as a broker for a successful real estate company. He earned enough so that Bethanne could stay home with the children; from the time Andrew was born, and Annie thirteen months later, she'd felt the children should be her career. Grant had supported her decision. He liked having her home, accessible to him and the children, and appreciated the elegant business dinners she frequently prepared for him and his colleagues.

"Grant?" she'd asked, completely unsuspecting of what was to follow.

He'd looked up and Bethanne had read such pain in his eyes that she sat down on the bed and placed her hand on his shoulder. "What is it?" she'd asked gently.

Grant couldn't seem to speak. He opened his mouth as if to begin, but no words came.

"Mom!" Annie shouted from the bottom of the stairs. "I need you."

Torn between her husband's needs and those of her children, Bethanne vacillated, then squeezed Grant's arm. "I'll be right back." Actually it took ten minutes, and both kids had left the house by the time she returned.

Grant's position was unchanged when she walked into the bedroom, his expression just as bleak.

"Tell me," she'd whispered urgently, her mind whirling as she wondered what could possibly be wrong. Grant had been to see the doctor for a physical the week before; everything seemed fine, but there'd been the routine tests. Perhaps Dr. Lyman had found something and Grant was only now able to tell her. She sat down next to him again, the mattress dipping slightly under her weight.

"It's Valentine's Day," Grant had announced in a voice so hoarse that he didn't sound like himself.

She'd kissed his cheek and felt him stiffen. "Grant, please—tell me what's wrong."

He'd started to weep then, huge sobs that shook his whole body. In the twenty years of their marriage, she could only recall a handful of times that her husband had revealed such deep emotion. "I don't want to hurt you," he cried.

"Just tell me!"

He gripped her shoulders, his fingers digging painfully into her flesh. "You're a good woman, Bethanne, but…" He faltered. "But I don't love you anymore."

At first she could only assume this was a hoax and she giggled. "What do you mean, you don't love me anymore? Grant, we've been married for twenty years. Of *course* you love me."

He closed his eyes as if he couldn't bear to look at her. "No, I don't. I'm sorry, so sorry, but I've tried. God knows I've tried. I can't carry on with this…this charade any longer."

Bethanne was dumbstruck, staring at Grant. This was the man she'd loved and slept with all these years and suddenly, in the blink of an eye, he'd become a stranger.

"What happened?" she asked uncertainly.

"Please," he begged, "don't make me say it."

"Say what?" At that moment she was more perplexed than angry. Rather than take his words personally, Bethanne immediately went into her problem-solving mode. Whatever was wrong could be fixed, the same way you'd have a broken faucet or a faulty outlet repaired. You just called a plumber or an electrician. Whatever was wrong simply needed the appropriate attention and then everything would go back to working as it always had.

"There's a reason I don't love you anymore," her husband said from between clenched teeth. He tossed aside the comforter and got out of bed. His obvious irritation took her aback.

"Grant, what's gotten into you?"

He climbed into his pants, hiked them up and closed the zipper. "Are you really this dense, or do I need to spell it out?"

In a matter of seconds he'd gone from tears to tyrant. "Spell out what?" she asked, innocently turning up her hands to receive whatever he had to tell her. She was more shocked by his rudeness than by what he was saying.

He paused, one arm in the sleeve of his shirt. He spoke

without looking at her and without emotion. "There's someone else."

It hit Bethanne then; she finally understood. "You're having an...affair?" She went numb and her mouth was instantly dry. Her tongue seemed to swell to twice its normal size, making speech impossible. In no way could this be true. She refused to believe it—Grant would never betray her like this. She'd *know* if he was cheating. Men had affairs in movies and in books. It was the sort of thing that happened to other women, other marriages, not hers. She'd clung to a surreal sense of denial for those first few minutes as he continued to dress for work.

"When? How?" she managed to stutter.

"We met at the office," Grant said. "She's another agent, recently joined the company." He sighed heavily. "I tried to make it work with you and me, but it's no good. I didn't mean for this to happen." There was a pleading quality in his voice, quickly replaced by anger. "Damn it, Bethanne, don't make things any more difficult than they already are." As if he'd planned this for days, he opened the closet door and extracted a suitcase, which he set on the bed.

"You're...leaving?"

He answered by opening his dresser drawers and lifting out his clothes. Bethanne winced as she watched him drop a stack of neatly folded undershirts on the bottom of the suitcase. Grant was extremely particular about his T-shirts, which had to be folded just so. He was meticulous about every aspect of his personal appearance and that perfectionism extended beyond his hair and clothes.

"Where...where will you go?" Her head was crowded with questions, and it seemed the most inessential ones rose to the surface first.

"I'm moving in with Tiffany," he announced.

"Tiffany?" she repeated, and why she should find humor

in the midst of the most horrible moment of her life, she would never know. All at once she was laughing. "You're leaving me for a woman named *Tiffany?*"

He glared at her as if she were truly demented and just then perhaps she was. *"Go,"* she said, almost flippantly, dismissing him with a wave of her hand. "I just want you to go."

As if to prove her point, she'd marched all the way down to the basement and collected a second, even bigger suitcase, which she hauled to their bedroom. As she climbed down and then back up the stairs, she racked her mind, trying to remember if she'd ever met this Tiffany. To the best of her recollection she hadn't. Grant's office was filled with women, but she'd never suspected he was capable of such treachery. Although she was panting by the time she'd dragged the large suitcase up two flights of stairs, she didn't pause for breath, her anger carrying her.

She flopped the empty suitcase carelessly on the bed, and a cloud of dust spread over the white comforter, which she ignored. Then she threw open the closet door, grabbed his suits around the middle and yanked them out, still on their hangers. Unceremoniously, she shoved them into the suitcase.

"Bethanne!" he shouted. "Stop it."

"No," she bellowed at the top of her lungs. Then, more quietly, she asked, "How long has this thing with you and Tiffany been going on?" When he didn't reply, she demanded, "How old is she, anyway?" Once she'd started on this line of questioning, she couldn't stop. "Is she married, too, or am I the only one being tossed aside?"

Grant refused to meet her gaze.

"A while?"

Again Grant refused to look at her as she packed his suitcases. She'd begun just throwing in his clothes but had quickly reverted to habit—folding, straightening, arranging.

"A month? Two months? How good is she in bed?"

"Bethanne, don't."

"How long?" She wouldn't stop until he told her the truth.

Grant released a laborious sigh as if her relentlessness had broken him down. "Two years."

"Two *years!*" she cried, consumed with rage. "Get out of this house."

He nodded.

"Get out, and don't come back." In that moment she meant it. But not long afterward, she'd desperately wanted him home again. It embarrassed her now to remember how frantic she'd been to win back her husband's affection. She'd been willing to do anything—see a counselor, beg, bribe, reason with him. At one point, just before the settlement hearing, she would've given up ten years of her life for Grant to return to his family.

But when Grant moved out of the house and in with Tiffany, he had no intention of returning. She'd nearly been destroyed by that. Eventually she'd had to accept it: Grant was never coming home. He didn't love her anymore and nothing she said or did would change his mind.

Her marriage was dead, and burying it had virtually obliterated her self-esteem. If not for her children, Bethanne didn't know what she would've done. Andrew and Annie needed her more than ever, and only for them did she continue.

When she'd finally made an appointment with an attorney, the man had been straightforward and helpful; what seemed like a fair financial arrangement had been settled upon. Grant refinanced the house for the third time and paid off their cars and their credit card bills with whatever equity he could extract, so they were both essentially debt-free. He was instructed to pay alimony for two years, plus child support until the children were out of high school. They would share college expenses. He hadn't been late with a check yet, but then the state made sure of that. Bethanne would have to find a job soon, but for a dozen different reasons, she delayed.

It was now six months after the divorce had been finalized, and the fog was only starting to clear. She told herself she had to live one day at a time as she learned to deal with what her family and friends called her "new reality." The problem was, she preferred her *old* reality….

Bethanne sipped her tea, which had begun to cool. She was startled from her thoughts when the door off the kitchen banged open and sixteen-year-old Annie came in, red-faced and sweating. Tendrils of wet hair pressed against the sides of her face. She wore a halter top and spandex shorts, and had apparently been out for a lengthy run. Because Annie had always felt close to her father, she'd taken the divorce particularly hard. Soon after Grant moved out, Annie had started running and would often go five and even ten miles a day. Unfortunately, that hadn't been the only change in her daughter's behavior. The new friends she'd acquired were a bigger concern.

Bethanne worried endlessly about Annie and the company she kept. The girl's anger was focused on Tiffany, and Bethanne suspected that Annie's new friends encouraged her more outrageous acts. While Bethanne was no fan of the other woman, whom she'd discovered to be fifteen years younger than her ex, she was afraid Annie might do something stupid in her zeal to retaliate against Tiffany, something that would involve the police.

Andrew had talked to Bethanne several times about various things he'd learned Annie had done. These included signing Tiffany up for magazine subscriptions, leaving her name and number with sales staff and scheduling appointments, all in Tiffany's name. However, Annie remained scornfully silent whenever Bethanne tried to bring up the subject.

"You didn't leave me a note," Bethanne chastised mildly as Annie walked over to the refrigerator and pulled out a cold bottle of water.

"Sorry," the girl mumbled unapologetically. She twisted off

the lid, leaned back her head and gulped down half the contents. "I figured you'd know. I run every day."

Bethanne did know, but that was beside the point.

"How'd it go at the employment agency?" her daughter asked.

Bethanne sighed, wishing Annie hadn't mentioned it. "Not good." She'd known this job search would be difficult, but she'd had no idea how truly painful the process would be. "When I told the interviewer about my baking skills, he didn't seem overly impressed."

"You should work in a bakery."

Bethanne had already considered that, but being around food for eight hours a day didn't appeal to her.

"Andrew and I were the envy of all our friends." Annie sounded almost nostalgic. "We had the best birthday parties and birthday cakes of anyone."

"I used to organize great scavenger hunts too, but there's little call for that these days."

"Oh, Mom." She rolled her eyes as she spoke.

"I'll look seriously once the summer is over."

"You keep putting it off," Annie chided.

Her daughter was right, but after all these years outside the job market, Bethanne didn't think she possessed any saleable skills. She was terrified that she'd end up at a grocery store asking people if they wanted paper or plastic for the rest of her life.

"I was thinking of selling cosmetics," she said tentatively, glancing at Annie for a reaction. "I could set my own hours and—"

"Mom!" Her daughter glared at her. "That's *pathetic*."

"Lots of women make a very nice income from it, and—"

"Selling cosmetics is fine for someone else, but not you. You're great at lots of things, but you'd make a terrible salesperson and we both know it. There's got to be *something* you can do. Where's your pride?"

For the last sixteen months it'd been swirling in the bottom of a toilet bowl. "I'd hate an office job," Bethanne said. She wasn't convinced she could ever adjust to a nine-to-five routine.

"You should do something just for you," Annie insisted. "I'm not even talking about a job."

Everyone Bethanne knew, including the counsellor she'd briefly seen, had told her the same thing. "When did you get so smart?" she teased.

"Isn't there anything you'd *like* to do just for fun?"

Bethanne shrugged. "You'll laugh and tell me it's pathetic."

"What?"

She sighed, reluctant to say anything. "I saw a yarn store the other day and was thinking how much I'd like to knit again. It's been years. I made you a baby blanket, remember?"

"Mom," Annie cried, flinching as though Bethanne had embarrassed her. "Of *course* I remember it. I slept with that yellow blankie until I was ten."

"I used to enjoy knitting, but that was years ago."

The front door opened, then slammed shut. Andrew, coming home from his part-time job at the local Safeway. He entered the kitchen, shucking off his backpack, and without a word to either of them, opened the fridge and stared inside. Apparently nothing interested him more than a soda, which he removed. He closed the door, leaning against it, and frowned at them.

"What's going on?" he asked, looking from Bethanne to his younger sister.

"Mom's talking about wanting to knit again," Annie said.

"It's only something I'm thinking about," Bethanne rushed to add.

"You can do it," Annie told her firmly.

"Yeah," Andrew agreed and popped the top of his soda. But Bethanne wasn't sure she could. It all seemed to require too much energy—finding a job, organizing her life, even knitting. "Maybe I will," she murmured tentatively.

"You're not putting this off the way you have everything else." Annie opened the pantry door and pulled out the Yellow Pages. "Where was that yarn shop?"

Bethanne bit her lower lip. "Blossom Street."

"Do you remember the name of it?" Andrew asked.

Annie flipped to the back of the massive directory.

"No, but listen—"

With her finger on the page, Annie looked up, eyes flashing with determination. "Found it." She smiled triumphantly at her brother, scooped up the phone and punched out the number before Bethanne could protest. When she'd finished, Annie handed the receiver to her mother.

A woman answered. "A Good Yarn," she said in a friendly voice. "How may I help you?"

"Ah, hello…my name is Bethanne Hamlin. I guess my name doesn't matter, but, well, I was wondering if you still offer knitting classes." She paused to take a breath. "I used to knit years ago," she went on, "but it's been a very long time. Perhaps it'd be better if I visited the store." Bethanne's gaze rose to meet her daughter's.

"Give me the phone," Annie demanded and without waiting for a response, grabbed it from her.

"Yes, that sounds great. Sign her up," Annie ordered. She reached for a pad and paper and wrote down the details. "She'll be there." Half a minute later, Annie replaced the portable phone.

"You signed her up for a class?" Andrew asked.

"Yup."

"I, ah…" Bethanne suddenly felt panicked about spending the money. "Listen, this might not be such a good idea, after all, because—"

Her daughter cut her off. "You'll be learning to knit socks."

"Socks?" Bethanne cried, vigorously shaking her head. "That's far too complicated for me."

"Mom," Andrew said, "you used to knit all the time, remember?"

"Socks aren't difficult, according to the shop owner," Annie continued. "Her name's Lydia Hoffman and she said they're actually quite simple."

"Yeah, right," Bethanne muttered.

"You're going, Mom, and I won't take no for an answer."

"You're going," Andrew echoed.

Apparently their roles had reversed, although this was news to Bethanne. It must've happened while she wasn't paying attention.

CHAPTER 4

COURTNEY PULANSKI

In Courtney's opinion, this entire plan of her father's was ridiculous and unfair. Okay, so she'd gotten into some minor trouble talking back to her teachers and letting her grades drop. It could've been a whole lot worse—like if the police ever found out who'd started that Dumpster fire four years ago. Who could blame her, though? Her mother had just died and Courtney was lost, angry, confused. She was doing better—not that she was over it. She'd never get "over it," despite what her more clueless friends suggested. But in time she'd straightened herself out and worked hard to salvage her high-school years and now this. This!

Her senior year of high school would be spent with her Grandma Pulanski in Seattle. While the kids she'd grown up with all her life graduated together, she'd be stuck halfway across the country. Courtney loved her grandmother, but she couldn't imagine living with her for an entire year.

There was no one else. No other place for Courtney to go while her father was in Brazil working as an engineer on a bridge-building project. Where he was going wasn't safe for a teenage girl, or so he insisted.

Jason, her oldest brother, was in graduate school and had a job teaching summer classes. Her sister, Julianna, was a college junior; she was working, too, at a vacation lodge in Alaska. Courtney was the youngest. College expenses for her brother and sister kept adding up. Plain and simple, her father needed the money; otherwise, he would've waited until Courtney had graduated from high school. Except that when she did, there wouldn't be much likelihood of getting a scholarship. Unfortunately her grades weren't the greatest and her chances of receiving an enter-college-free card were about the same as winning the lottery. In other words, her dad would be stuck paying for her, too. Spending the year in Seattle was the obvious solution.

Everything would've been different if her mother hadn't died in that freak car accident. It'd happened four years ago and still felt like yesterday.

"Courtney," her grandmother called from the foot of the stairs. "Are you awake?"

"Yes, Grandma." There was no way she could sleep in with the television blaring at five o'clock in the morning. Her grandmother needed hearing aids but refused to believe it. Everyone mumbled, according to Vera Pulanski. Everyone in the whole world!

"I have breakfast cooking," her grandmother shouted.

Courtney stared up at the ceiling and rolled her eyes. "I'm not hungry."

"Breakfast is the most important meal of the day."

She'd been with her grandmother for exactly a week and this was the seventh day in a row that they'd had this same conversation.

"I'll eat something later," Courtney promised. The thought of dry scrambled eggs made her want to gag, but that was how her grandmother cooked them. She had all these ideas from television about what was good for a teen-ager and what wasn't. Apparently, the only way to prepare anything safely was to cook the hell out of it. As a result, her grandmother's scrambled eggs tasted like rubber. Not that she'd ever eaten rubber, but she was convinced these would qualify.

"I hate to throw food away."

"I'm sorry, Grandma." With all the meals she'd skipped since she arrived, Courtney figured she should've lost weight. She hadn't. The scale had glared accusingly up at her that very morning. Fresh from the shower and completely naked, she'd stepped onto the bathroom scale, a relic if there ever was one. She'd closed her eyes, then peered down at the numbers and those ridiculously tiny lines between them. Her grandmother didn't seem to know about digital. Not only *hadn't* Courtney lost weight, but it looked as if she'd gone up a pound. She wanted to weep. Starting a new school would be bad enough, but facing strangers while she was fat was even worse.

"Courtney?" Again her grandmother yelled at her from the bottom of the stairs.

"Yes, Grandma." Vera obviously wasn't backing off this morning.

"I'm going out for a while. I need to run a few errands."

"Okay, Grandma."

"I want you to come with me."

Sighing heavily, Courtney sat up, thumped her feet onto the floor and let her shoulders slump forward. "Can I stay here?" she pleaded. After her shower, she'd put her pajamas back on, since she couldn't think of a reason to get dressed. Not a good reason, anyway.

"I'd really like it if you joined me. You spend far too much time in your room."

"All right, Grandma."

"What did you say?"

Rising slowly, Courtney went over to the doorway and shouted, "I'll be right down."

Smiling, her grandmother nodded. "Good."

Vera Pulanski was a wonderful woman and Courtney had always enjoyed her visits to Chicago. But this was different. She'd never had to live with someone this old before. Everything in the house would sell as an antique on eBay.

With a decided lack of enthusiasm, she pulled on her jeans and an oversize black T-shirt that had her dad's company logo on the front. When she'd walked down the stairs Vera smiled sweetly and stopped her on the last step. Raising her arms, her grandmother cupped Courtney's face as she studied her.

"You're a beautiful girl."

Courtney responded with a weak smile.

"You're the apple of my eye, my youngest grandchild."

"Yes, Grandma."

"I've always regretted that Ralph didn't live long enough to know you."

Her grandfather had died when Courtney was a few months old. "Me, too."

"Now, what I'm about to say is only because I love you."

Courtney bristled, bracing herself for another lecture. "Grandma, please, I know I need to lose weight. You don't have to say it, all right?" Courtney couldn't keep the defensiveness out of her voice. It wasn't as if she could avoid looking in mirrors. She was overweight and well aware of it. The weight gain had happened after her mother's death; until then, she'd been a size ten and suddenly, *poof*—she'd blown up into a sixteen. The thing Courtney resented most was being reminded of it by all those well-meaning folks who assumed it was easy to drop thirty-five pounds.

"Actually, that wasn't what I wanted to say." Her grandmother released Courtney's face. "I think you need friends."

"So do I." She missed Chicago so much, she could cry just

remembering everything and everyone she'd left behind. Even her house, which had been rented out for the year.

"You aren't going to meet anyone holed up in your room, sweetheart," her grandmother said gently. "You need to get out more."

Courtney didn't have a single argument. She lowered her eyes. "I know."

"Come with me and I'll introduce you around."

She opened her mouth to object, but knew it wouldn't do any good. Her grandmother caught her by the hand and dragged Courtney toward the kitchen. The scrambled eggs were on the table and Courtney could've sworn they were the same eggs her grandmother had cooked the day before.

"I thought we'd go to the library and then the grocery store and after that, the yarn store."

In other words, Courtney was being kidnapped.

"I'm ready now, dear, if that's all right with you."

"Me, too, Grandma." The sooner she gave in, the sooner she could get back to her room.

"Let me check to make sure the lock on the front door is turned," her grandmother said.

Actually, it was a full seven minutes before they left the house. After checking the front door, her grandmother went into the bathroom to refresh her lipstick. Then she decided she shouldn't leave the eggs out, covered them with a piece of wrinkled plastic and set the plate in the refrigerator, which confirmed Courtney's suspicions. Those *were* the same eggs as the day before.

"Are you ready now?" her grandmother asked, as if Courtney was the one holding up the process.

"Anytime you are."

"Oh!" her grandmother cried. "I nearly forgot my purse," she said, giggling. "My goodness, I might have locked us out of the house."

Finally they were outside. The car, parked in the driveway, could've been in a museum. From what Courtney's father had told her, the 1968 Ford Ranch station wagon was in prime condition. Well, it should be. The car was nearly forty years old and had only 72,000 miles on it. The door weighed a ton and creaked when Courtney opened it. Without another word, she slid onto the seat next to her grandmother.

Driving with Vera was not an experience one engaged in willingly. Once she'd started the engine, she turned to Courtney. "Look behind us. Is anyone coming?"

Courtney twisted around. "You're fine, Grandma." Then it occurred to her that her grandmother hadn't asked this out of idle curiosity. "Grandma," she said, "why didn't *you* turn around and look?"

Her grandmother squared her shoulders. "Because I can't." "You *can't?*"

"Do you have a hearing problem, child? I can't turn my head. I have this crick in my neck. It's been there for twenty years—I never had such pain. The doctor said there's nothing they can do. Nothing, and so I suffer. I don't like to complain and I wouldn't, but since you asked..."

Although the thought of being a passenger while her grandmother drove terrified Courtney, she didn't say a word. What was the point? She'd managed to avoid car trips for the last few days, but she'd realized her luck couldn't possibly hold.

Another question occurred to her. "Grandma, what would you do if I wasn't with you?" Courtney suspected, fearfully, that her grandmother would just put the car in Reverse and gun it.

Tight-lipped, her grandmother adjusted the rearview mirror, using both hands to move it one way and then the other. "That's what mirrors are for."

"Oh."

"Can we leave now?"

Her questions had clearly offended her grandmother. "Sure," Courtney said with an enthusiasm born of guilt.

Her grandmother half turned to glance at her as they reached the first stoplight. "If you're concerned about your weight, Courtney, I could help."

Courtney eyed her suspiciously. "How?"

"Exercise. I swim in the mornings and you could join me and my friends."

That didn't sound like much fun, but then exercise wasn't supposed to be. "I guess."

"What do you guess?"

"It's just an expression, Grandma. It means sure, I'd like that." This was an exaggeration in the extreme, but her grandmother was making an effort to be helpful and Courtney felt she had to respond appropriately.

Their first stop after leaving Queen Anne Hill, the Seattle area where her grandmother lived, was the library, which seemed ultramodern, especially in comparison to Vera's neighborhood. Her grandmother explained that it had only recently reopened after a renovation. While Vera picked up a reserved book—the latest hardcover romance by a local author—Courtney flipped through *Vogue* magazines, trying not to despair at all the thin, elegant models. And that was just the ads.

They drove to the grocery store next. Courtney didn't have the latest census figures for the population of the Seattle Metro area—she was convinced it had to be in the millions—but her grandmother surely knew fifty percent of them. More times than she cared to count, they were waylaid by her grandmother's friends, former neighbors, a dozen or more people from church, bridge club members.... Courtney must have been introduced to thirty people and she swore that not a single one was under seventy.

"Now Blossom Street," her grandmother said as Courtney carried the groceries out to the car. "I won't be long, I promise."

Courtney bit her tongue to keep from reminding her grandmother that this was what she'd said at the last place. Seven conversations later, they'd driven off and now Vera was working her way into the angled parking space in front of the yarn shop. She rolled an inch or so, slammed on the brake, released it enough to roll another inch, then it was brake time again. Courtney should've predicted what would happen, but it blindsided her. Her grandmother's bumper crashed against the parking meter hard enough to jolt her forward.

"Oh, darn," her grandmother mumbled.

If *darn* was the best swear word Vera Pulanski knew, Courtney would be happy to broaden her vocabulary.

Climbing out of the car, she closed the heavy door and followed her grandmother inside. Courtney immediately walked over to the cat in the window and started petting him.

"Hello, Vera. How are you?" a young, petite woman said.

"Lydia, I'm glad to see you. This is my granddaughter Courtney. Courtney, Lydia."

"Hi." Courtney raised her hand in greeting.

"Do you knit?" Lydia asked.

Courtney shrugged. "A little."

"I taught her one summer," her grandmother boasted. "She took to it right off the bat."

Courtney didn't remember it that way, but she didn't want to be rude.

"Courtney's staying with me this year while her father's in Brazil."

Not wanting to listen to another lengthy explanation of her father's important engineering role in South America, Courtney left the cat and wandered through the store. She'd had no idea there were so many different varieties of yarn. A display scarf knitted in variegated colors was gorgeous, and there was a felted hat and purse, a vest and a sweater.

"You could knit that scarf up in an evening," Lydia said, lifting the end of it for Courtney to inspect.

"Really?"

"Yes." She smiled widely. "It's easy with size thirteen needles and one skein of yarn. You cast on fifteen stitches and knit every row. It's that easy."

"Wow." Courtney had money with her, but hesitated. A twenty probably wasn't enough to cover the cost of the needles and yarn, and she didn't want to borrow from her grandmother.

Five minutes later, while Courtney was studying a display of patterned socks, Vera placed her purchases on the counter by the cash register. Courtney didn't know what her grandmother was currently knitting, but she always seemed to have some project or other on the go. She hurried over.

"Did you see the socks?" her grandmother asked.

Courtney nodded. "Those new yarns are really amazing, aren't they?"

"You could knit a pair of socks like that."

"No way."

"Would you like to?" Lydia asked.

Courtney considered the question. "I guess."

"That means yes," her grandmother translated. "Sign her up."

"Sign me up for what?" Courtney wanted to know.

"The sock class," her grandmother explained. "It's time you met people, went out, got involved."

"We'd love to have you," Lydia assured her.

"My treat," her grandmother added.

Courtney smiled, trying to show she was grateful. Actually, the idea was growing on her. She just hoped at least one other person in the sock class was under ninety years old.

5
CHAPTER

"Remember that you need *two* socks. How to achieve this feat? Knit both at the same time, and release the idea that they need to be identical!"

—Deborah Robson, knitter, writer,
publisher of knitting books
www.nomad-press.com

LYDIA HOFFMAN

I try to spend at least part of every weekend with my mother. It's been difficult for her since Dad died. Difficult for all of us. I so regret that Brad never had the opportunity to meet my father. I feel certain they would have liked each other. My dad was open and friendly, and he always found something positive in everyone he met. He had a kind word and usually a joke or two; even when I was at my sick-and-despairing worst, he could make me smile. No one told a story better than my father. I sometimes wonder if I'll ever stop thinking about him, because it seems that he's on my mind more and more instead of less.

The adjustment to life without my dad has been hardest on

Mom, though; she's aged ten years in the last fourteen months. She's emotionally shrunken—I don't know what else to call it. She's become frail and sad and uninterested in much. And she's shrunk physically, too, as if her body is reflecting her inner state, which is one of grief, of diminished expectations. In fact, at her last doctor's appointment, we learned that Mom is a full inch shorter than she was a few years ago.

The results of her osteoporosis tests aren't back yet. All at once, Mom has a number of medical problems, and I attribute this decline in her health not only to grief but to loneliness. My father was her anchor, her companion.

Although it sounds like a cliché, it seems as though part of her is missing; without him, she can't function the way she once did. I understand that, and to some degree I experience the same feeling. Dad was such a vital part of the woman I am.

When I arrived early Sunday afternoon, I found my mother in the backyard pruning her roses, fussing over them. Her flower garden is her pride, one of the few things she still cares about. She prunes the roses, she tells me, so they'll grow stronger. I consider Dad's death in the same light. Losing him helped me discern what was important in my life, what was real. Mostly, I needed to find my own path to happiness and to accept the challenges of independence. It was losing my father that gave me the courage to enlarge my life, and I did this by opening my own store—and through my relationship with Brad.

I stood in the open doorway watching her for a few minutes. Caught up in her gardening, Mom didn't hear me. She had on a big straw hat to shield her face from the sun and wore her green garden gloves. There was a bucket at her side in which she dumped the clippings. I didn't want to frighten her so I called her name softly.

"Lydia!" Mom turned toward me as I stepped out of the house. "I thought you'd be here sooner."

"So did I, but I got sidetracked after church."

"By Brad and Cody?"

I nodded. "I'm meeting them in an hour. We're going to walk around Green Lake." The three-mile stroll was good exercise and I get far less of that than I should. Brad, on the other hand, is in marvelous shape and can run circles around me. Cody has a golden retriever named Chase—because of his terrible habit of chasing after everything and everyone. Cody would probably bring his dog, but he'd been warned to keep Chase on his leash. Maybe I'd get a book on dog-training and work with Cody to teach him some basic commands. Anyway, this afternoon would be fun and I was half tempted to take my in-line skates, just so I could keep up with the two—or rather, three—of them.

My mother's hand trembled as she snipped another branch. I'd noticed the shaking more often lately. "What did you have for lunch, Mom?" I asked. Her eating habits were atrocious, and Margaret and I worried that she wasn't getting the nutrition she needed. We also worried about her medications. My fear was that some days she took more than prescribed and on others she skipped them entirely.

"What did I eat for lunch?" Mom repeated as though she needed to think about this.

"Lunch, Mom?" I coaxed gently.

"Tuna and crackers," she recalled and looked at me with such a triumphant smile that I smiled back.

Still, I had to ask, "That's all?"

She shrugged. "I wasn't hungry. Now, don't pester me by insisting I eat when I don't have an appetite. Your father used to do that. I didn't like it then and I refuse to listen to it now."

"All right, Mom." I'd leave it for now, but we'd have to check out some alternatives. Meals on Wheels, perhaps. Or a part-time housekeeper if, between us, Margaret and I could afford one. I'd discuss it with her soon.

"Next Sunday is Father's Day," Mom pointed out. "Will you take me to the cemetery? I'd like to put a vase of my roses on your dad's grave."

"Of course. Margaret and I will both come." I was speaking out of turn and hoped my sister would agree to accompany us. She'd been so prickly and out of sorts lately. The closeness we'd briefly shared had evaporated like a shallow rain puddle in the sun. Whatever was wrong, she didn't feel comfortable enough to share it with me, and frankly, that hurt. We've come a long way in our relationship, but it was situations such as this that reminded me how far we had yet to go.

As if the strength had gone out of her legs, Mom reached for a patio chair and sat down. Lifting the hat from her head, she wiped her forehead with one arm. "My goodness, it's hot."

I glanced at the temperature gauge my father had hung on the side of the house, and it read seventy-four degrees, which surprised me because it didn't feel that warm. Of course, my mother had been working outside for at least an hour, more likely two.

"Would you like to go out for dinner, Mom?" I asked, thinking that would be a treat for us both.

"No, thank you, honey. I'm not hungry. I met Dorothy Wallace at the Pancake Breakfast the Knights of Columbus held after Mass and we ate our fill."

Translated, she had one small pancake without butter or syrup, followed by a lunch of tuna and crackers, and she'd probably skip dinner altogether.

"Besides, Margaret phoned and she's stopping by with the girls later this afternoon."

Some of my worry left me. Margaret would make sure Mom had a decent meal at the end of the day.

"She enjoys working with you," my mother continued. "She's not one to say it, but she does."

I wondered if I should mention my concerns about my sister. I decided against it, although Margaret had been weighing heavily on my mind since my conversation with Brad earlier in the week. There was no need to bring Mom into this. She'd certainly mention my concerns to my sister, and that would infuriate Margaret; she would resent me for discussing her with Mom, and then I'd hear about it for weeks.

"Can I get you anything?" I asked.

Her smile was distracted. "I'd love a glass of iced tea."

I went inside and poured one for each of us, then added slices of lemon. Several other lemons had shriveled up and I tossed them without telling Mom. A quick look in the refrigerator had revealed a carton of milk a month past its expiry date and a package of liquefying spinach. I'd tossed those too. When I returned to the patio, Mom had replaced the hat and was sitting with her back to the sun.

I joined her and handed her the glass, savoring the warm sunshine against my skin, the sound of birds in the distance along with the *swish, swish* of the sprinkler watering the lawn.

"Tell me about the shop," Mom suggested. "Did you get in any new yarn this week?"

She especially enjoyed the stories about my customers; so many of them had become my friends, especially Jacqueline, Carol and Alix, my original class members. We've created a real bond, the four of us, and it's rare for me not to see them during the week. If nothing else, one or two always showed up for the charity knitting session on Fridays.

I talked nonstop for almost twenty minutes about the shop and described the three women who'd recently signed up for the sock class. The one who interested Mom most was Courtney Pulanski, the seventeen-year-old granddaughter of Vera Pulanski, a regular.

"I'm thinking of holding a potluck once a month," I said, wanting her opinion on this new idea—partly to allow her to feel involved and partly because I trusted her instincts. Over the years, she'd been a valuable sounding board to my father in his businesses.

"Do you have room at the store?"

"I think so, if I do a bit of shuffling." When I first opened my doors, there was room to set up a large table for classes, but as I'd brought in additional lines of yarn, much of that space had disappeared. Now the table, which sat six people, was surrounded by several displays.

"Are you sure you want food around all that yarn?"

My mother echoed my own reservations. "I thought we'd sit at the table where I hold my classes and put the food on a card table in the office."

My mother raised one shoulder in a half shrug. "It might work, but what would be the purpose of these monthly pot-lucks?"

Good question. "Well, I want my customers to get to know one another. Plus, when one person shows the others what she's knitted, it inspires them." It was for this very reason that I often knit up patterns for display in the shop. "You could join us, Mom," I said enthusiastically. "Margaret and I would love that." As often as possible, I try to include her. Both Margaret and I work at giving Mom little things to look forward to so she feels active and alive.

From the way Mom frowned, I doubt she heard me. "Hold a monthly show-and-tell session and keep the food out of it. If you want to eat, go to a restaurant afterward."

I liked that idea. "Thanks, Mom."

I could tell she was pleased I'd come to her for advice. I'm sure it's something she missed, since she'd so often taken that role with my father. We sat and chatted for another thirty minutes and then I left to meet Brad and Cody.

They were in the parking lot at Green Lake waiting for me, Chase tugging at the leash.

"Hi," I called as I climbed out of the car. Chase wasn't the only one eager for this outing.

Cody raced over to the car and briefly hugged me. "Can we go now?"

His father patted his head. "Okay, sport, but don't get too far ahead of us, all right? And hold on to Chase."

Cody didn't take time to answer. He was off like a rocket, boy and dog together, Cody's young legs pumping with an energy I envied.

Brad and I started walking at a brisk pace. As always on a sunny weekend day, the place was crowded with people and dogs. We passed a man with a guitar who sat on the grass strumming folk songs and a toddler chasing after a butterfly. There were a couple of canoes close to the shore. Brad and I walked side by side, keeping an eye out for Cody and Chase.

"How's your mother?" he asked, knowing I'd spent part of the afternoon with her.

Right then, I didn't want to launch into a long discussion about my anxiety over Mom. That conversation wasbest reserved for Margaret, and I'd initiate it soon. "She's about the same," I said, which was true enough. "My sister and the girls are visiting later today. Mom needs that."

"Speaking of Margaret, has she said anything to you?"

"About what?" I asked cautiously.

Brad reached for my hand and we entwined our fingers. I smiled up at him, forgetting Margaret. It's times like these, when we're feeling close and connected, that I get lost in a sensation of such bliss I can barely contain myself. Like any woman, I hunger for love, marriage, a family. Because of the cancer, I didn't think I'd ever have that chance. Every single day, I was grateful all over again for Brad, grateful to have him in my life, grateful to be loved by him despite my imperfections and flaws. He says the fact that I've battled cancer not once but twice makes me a two-time winner. I *am* a winner and I feel so incredibly blessed.

"I think I know what Margaret's problem might be," Brad said, jolting me out of my reflection.

"You do?" I was a little reluctant to talk about Margaret at the moment; I preferred to revel in my own contentment.

"Yeah. I ran into Matt at the hardware store yesterday afternoon," Brad told me.

My brother-in-law is a salt-of-the-earth kind of guy. I consider him a good balance for my sister, who usually has a pessimistic slant on things. Matt doesn't take life as seriously as she does. I find that he doesn't overreact the way she tends to and—even more appealing—he never holds grudges.

"What did Matt have to say?" The four of us had gone out on occasion, and Brad and Matt had hit if off. Margaret invited us over for dinner a few months ago, and we'd played cards until the wee hours of the morning. I'd hoped to see more of them socially, but so far we hadn't.

"He's not working."

"What do you mean, not working?" Matt had been with Boeing for as long as I could remember, probably twenty years.

"Not working as in he got laid off."

"*What?* When?"

"Three months ago."

"No." That couldn't be right. Three months? Margaret hadn't said a word about this for three months? I was in shock.

"That's what he told me. He's been pounding the pavement, looking for work, but nothing's happening for him."

My heart sank. "But I thought..." I didn't know what I thought. This was crazy. I'm Margaret's only sibling, and if she couldn't talk to me, then who could she confide in?

"Matt seemed to think I knew, so I played along."

The tingling feeling that usually precedes tears came over me. Sure enough, I felt my eyes prickling and my throat closing up.

"Are you going to cry?"

I sniffled and nodded. "You'd think she could've told me," I said hoarsely.

"At least you know why she's been so tense lately."

That didn't help. "I'd hoped my own sister would trust me, but I was obviously wrong." I swiped the tears from my eyes before they could roll down my cheeks. Now I understood, and so much of Margaret's behaviour at the shop lately started to make sense. Not only had she been moody, but she hadn't purchased new yarn in weeks, or bought anything from the French bakery across the street. In fact, now that I thought about it, I realized she hadn't spent any money at all unless it was absolutely necessary.

"I should've known," I whispered, suddenly feeling guilty. "I should've figured it out."

"How could you?"

My sister isn't the easiest person in the world to read, but in my heart I felt I should've recognized the signs. And maybe I should've paid more attention to the news; layoffs at Boeing always merited an article or two. I hadn't even noticed....

"Are you going to say anything?" Brad asked.

I considered my answer carefully. "I don't think so." For her own reasons, Margaret hadn't seen fit to share this information with me. I wouldn't force her to do so now, but I hoped that in time, she'd feel she could. Until then, all I could do was love her, be patient with her short-tempered comments and wait for her to trust me.

"You will, you know," Brad insisted softly. "I know you too well, Lydia. You won't be able to keep this buried for long. It just isn't in your nature."

I scoffed at him, but I realized he was probably right.

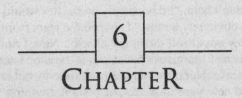

6
CHAPTER

ELISE BEAUMONT

Elise discovered that she was looking forward to starting the sock class. Without letting her daughter know, she'd purchased yarn to knit David, her son-in-law, the first pair. It was a small way of showing her appreciation for his kindness in allowing Elise to live with them during this legal mess. According to a recent update from the attorney, there hadn't been much progress yet; patience was advised. She still felt mortified that, after all her careful planning, she'd ended up living with her daughter and son-in-law, no matter how temporary that arrangement was.

The afternoon before the Tuesday class, Elise sat on the patio reading, an activity that never failed to satisfy her. Her love of books went back to when she was a child. She was an early reader, and could remember sitting in her crib with a book in her hands, utterly content. That love of books had served her well through the years.

Today she was rereading Jane Austen's *Emma*, something she did every decade or so. There were books like that, the true classics she returned to time and time again. Austen, the

Brontës, Flaubert and her favorite, George Eliot. These writers described women's lives and emotions in ways that still resonated a century or more later. She'd just reached the scene where Mr. Knightley chastises Emma when Aurora opened the sliding glass door and stepped onto the patio to join her. "Can we talk for a few minutes, Mom?" she asked tentatively. Aurora sat on the chair next to the chaise longue where Elise reclined with her legs stretched out. Her daughter held a tall glass of tea, ice cubes clinking. She was obviously nervous.

"Of course." Elise carefully inserted her bookmark and closed *Emma.* Judging by the way Aurora leaned forward, this was important.

"I want to talk about Daddy," her daughter informed her, diving headfirst into the most unpleasant of subjects.

Elise was always cautious about anything to do with her ex-husband. Maverick was a slick and dangerous man, personable to the degree that it was difficult to refuse him whatever he might want. "I suppose that would be all right." Her daughter knew the basic story of how Elise had met Maverick, fallen stupidly in love and married him. The marriage hadn't lasted eighteen months, two years on paper.

Oh, how that man could talk. Elise swore he could charm a rattlesnake. From the time she was a teenager, she'd known she wasn't a particularly attractive woman. Maverick had adamantly claimed otherwise, and being young and naive, Elise had delighted in those compliments, swallowing them whole. She'd believed him because she so badly wanted to be as lovely as he said she was. When she was with Maverick she *felt* beautiful, but it didn't take her long to realize she was living a fool's dream.

"What about your father?" Elise asked, trying to sound as neutral as possible.

"You loved him once, right?"

That was a tricky question and difficult to answer. Maverick had come into her life when she'd been at a vulnerable age, when hormones had overruled common sense. At the time, she'd believed she was in love but later acknowledged that it had been lust they'd shared and not love. Love lasts. What they shared didn't. Yet, all these years after the divorce, she still dreamed of him, yearned for him and wished with everything she held dear that their marriage had turned out differently. The relationship might have worked if Elise could have found a way to accept the man he was.

Unfortunately she hadn't and it was too late for them. Over the years he'd flitted about the country and, in her view, wasted his life. In some respects she had, too, Elise recognized sadly.

"Mom, you *did* love him, didn't you?" Aurora repeated anxiously.

"Yes, I did." So much that even now it frightened her to admit it.

Her daughter relaxed visibly. "We keep in touch, you know."

Elise was aware of that. Maverick lived among the dregs of society, as she liked to put it, making his living from card-playing and God knew what else. But apparently he was successful—enough to support Aurora all her life and through college.

Besides his regular payments and then tuition, he'd always sent extra for their daughter's birthday and at Christmas. The first seventeen years following their divorce, he wrote Aurora once a month but they were never long letters. Mostly he sent postcards to let her know where he was and if he was winning. Winning had always been important to Maverick. In fact, it was everything to him. He lived in search of the elusive jackpot that would set him up for life. To the best of Elise's knowledge, he'd never found it.

"If you want to keep in touch with your father, that has nothing to do with me," she primly informed her daughter. Elise had read those postcards, too, and wished she hadn't—

because she was afraid it meant she still cared, still hungered for what was destined never to be.

"Dad and I talk every now and then."

Elise knew that too. When Aurora was a child, she'd been so excited whenever her daddy called. As an adult, she reacted the same way. Aurora hadn't been disillusioned by her father yet, and Elise hated the thought that eventually her daughter would face the same disappointment she had. Maverick didn't intend to hurt those he loved. He was simply careless with the feelings of others; the people he claimed to love never came first with him. He just couldn't be trusted. If he said he'd be home by nine, he meant he'd be home at nine unless there was a card game going. His moods were dictated by whether he won or lost. If he won, he was elated and jubilant, swinging Elise in his arms and planning celebration dinners. If he lost, he suffered fits of anger and despair.

"He's coming, Mom," Aurora announced. She looked directly into Elise's eyes.

"Coming," Elise repeated as a numbing sensation spread through her. "To Seattle?"

Aurora nodded.

"Is there some big poker tournament taking place here?" Not that *she* was likely to know about it.

"He's coming to see me," Aurora added with more than a hint of defiance.

"How…fatherly," Elise murmured sarcastically. "Once every five or ten years he—"

"Mom!"

"Sorry." Elise clamped her mouth shut before she could say something she'd regret.

"This is what I never understood about you and Dad." Her daughter seemed to be struggling to hold on to her composure. "You make me feel like I'm being disloyal to you because I choose not to ignore my father."

"I do that?" This was a painful revelation, and Elise swallowed hard. All she'd wanted was to protect Aurora from certain disillusionment.

Aurora nodded and the tears that brightened her eyes were testament to the truth of her words.

"I'm so sorry. I never realized...I—I did that." The guilt was nearly overwhelming.

"But you do. Never once in all the years I was growing up did I hear my father say a negative thing about you. Not once, Mom, and yet I can't remember you ever saying a kind word about him."

"That is not true." Elise had tried hard to hide her feelings toward Maverick from their daughter. Surely she'd succeeded—hadn't she? Gazing into her daughter's pain-filled eyes, Elise realized that she hadn't.

Aurora's shoulders rose in a deep sigh. "Please, Mom, I don't want to argue about this."

"I don't, either." Racked with self-recrimination, Elise patted her daughter's knee. "Your father is...your father. I wish I'd given you a better one, but that's my mistake, not yours."

"See what I mean?" Aurora cried. "You don't have anything good to say about him."

"I was the one married to him, remember? I loved Maverick but we weren't meant to be together."

"I know he failed you. He admits it."

"He failed you too."

"In some ways, yes, he did," Aurora agreed, "but in other ways he was a wonderful father."

Elise understood that Aurora had to believe this. Maverick was the only father she had, and his behavior, his long absences, were all she knew. If she'd ever wondered why he traveled as much as he did, she'd never asked her mother.

"So," Elise said. The numbness had started to leave her. "Your father is visiting Seattle."

"Yes, he is." Aurora seemed to be waiting for more of a response.

"I don't have a single qualm about you seeing your father," Elise assured her. "He hasn't even met his grandsons."

"He's looking forward to that."

Again Aurora stared at Elise as if expecting something more.

"I don't have to see him," Elise said. Any encounter with him would be impossible. If Aurora wanted permission to visit with her father, then that was fine with Elise. But when it happened, Elise didn't plan to be anywhere in the vicinity. "Have him over for dinner or whatever. I'll conveniently be out for the evening or however long you need."

Maverick would thank her. Elise was fairly sure he wasn't any more interested in seeing her than she was in seeing him. They hadn't spoken in years. There'd been no reason for them to have contact, which was the way Elise preferred it.

"You won't be able to avoid seeing Dad," her daughter said, her eyes fluttering in every direction.

"What you do mean?" Elise demanded as a sinking feeling settled over her.

"Dad will be staying here."

"At the house?" Elise was aghast. This couldn't be true, but she knew from the undeniable confirmation in Aurora's face that it was. The numbness was back in full force, and spreading down to her legs. "Does he know I'm living with you?"

Her daughter answered with a nod. "I told him, but he still wants to come."

"For…how long?"

Aurora hesitated. "Two weeks."

"Two *weeks?*" Elise exploded. The book fell onto the patio floor as she sat upright. "That's out of the question! You can't possibly believe the two of us can remain in the same house— together—for that length of time." She blamed Maverick for this. He'd manipulated their daughter into agreeing to it, no doubt because he was down on his luck and penniless. Elise wanted to weep. "I'll find someplace else for a while," she murmured, thinking out loud. Really, that would be her preference, but all her things were in storage and God only knew where she could move for that short a period.

"Mom, calm down." Then, in a softer voice, she added, "Please. There's no need to overreact."

Sliding her legs over the edge of the chaise, Elise felt like burying her face in her hands, an urge she resisted. This was going to be a disaster, but her daughter didn't seem to recognize that.

"Dad's never asked anything of me before," Aurora said. "I couldn't refuse him."

"He tried the pity approach?"

"No," she snapped and seemed offended that Elise would suggest it. "He didn't. Dad has always been generous and wonderful to David, me and the boys."

"The man isn't to be trusted."

"That's only the way you view him, but to me, he's my father."

Elise felt guilty all over again. She was determined not to say another negative word about her ex-husband. "Okay, so he's going to visit for a couple of weeks."

Aurora nodded.

"And you're *sure* he knows I'm living with you?"

"Yes." From the tone of her daughter's voice, Elise suspected this was a complication Maverick hadn't expected. Well, whatever he was after, whatever he wanted, he'd have to get it past Elise—and she, thankfully, was wise to him. She wouldn't be so easily fooled.

"Where will he sleep?" The three-bedroom house was adequate in size but there wasn't a guest room. Elise had taken the third bedroom and arranged it into a tiny studio-like apartment. She had a microwave, her own bathroom, a television area complete with rocking chair, and her single bed. That was all she needed. She had privacy, a small refuge from the world, and could retreat to her room in order to give her daughter and family their own space.

"I'm putting Dad in with the boys."

That was a wise decision. Her grandsons, while an absolute delight, could be little hellions. Maverick was unaccustomed to being around children. Elise suspected he wouldn't last long sleeping in the same room as Luke and John.

"This isn't the easiest situation," Aurora continued.

Elise rolled her eyes toward the sky. "That's putting it mildly." Then she instantly felt another wave of guilt.

"I need you to work with me, Mom, not against me."

"I would never do anything to hurt you," Elise told her daughter, hiding her distress that Aurora would even imply such a thing.

"But you want to hurt Dad."

"That's not true," Elise denied hotly. "I don't have any feelings toward your father one way or the other." That was a lie and her face flushed with color as she said it.

"Mo—ther," her daughter cried, challenge in each over-enunciated syllable. "You have so many unresolved issues with Dad, it would take days to list them all."

"You're being ridiculous." Her daughter knew her well, but at this moment what mattered was maintaining a pretense of complete indifference. Somehow she'd survive these two weeks.

Aurora sampled her iced tea for the first time, her knuckles white around the glass. "I don't want to get into that with you, especially now. I need your word that you won't say or do anything, and I mean *anything,* to upset Dad."

"I would never—"

"It's crucial to keep the peace. I don't want to subject the boys to your anger toward Dad."

Elise was upset that her daughter could believe *she'd* be the one to cause problems. "You have my word I will do whatever I can to make your father's stay as pleasant as possible." If that meant hiding in her room for the next two weeks, then so be it.

"Don't promise this lightly, Mom. It's the most important request I've ever made of you."

Elise wondered again whether she should move out and save them all this grief. Sadly, she had nowhere else to go. She was stuck in the same house with the man she'd both loved and hated for the last thirty-seven years.

7

CHAPTER

"Well-fitting and carefully knitted handmade socks are the 'real' ones; the store-bought variety are just pale imitations."

—Diane Soucy, *Knitting Pure & Simple,*
www.knittingpureandsimple.com

LYDIA HOFFMAN

This was my first sock class and I was excited about our one-o'clock gathering. In the last year, I've taught several classes, and I've learned in the course of teaching that it's critical to have the right mix of personalities. I had my doubts about the women making up this class, but I didn't want to borrow trouble.

The personalities of the three women who'd enrolled for this one reminded me of my first knitting class the year before. Elise, Bethanne and Courtney had nothing in common that I could see, except a desire to knit. I'd felt the same way about the baby blanket class with Jacqueline, Carol and Alix. They were as different as any three women could be and yet we'd all forged enduring friendships in a remarkably short time. I continued to marvel over that and hoped history would repeat itself, although I didn't really expect it. Generally I'm not a pessimist—unlike my sister—but Elise Beaumont struck me as unyielding and circumspect, so self-contained. Bethanne Hamlin, judging by our brief meeting, was nervous and jittery, ready to run and hide at the slightest noise. Courtney Pulanski was a teenager. I felt sorry for her—the poor kid looked aghast when her grandmother insisted on signing her up. Unfortunately, I just didn't see these three people as a good mix.

I cast a glance toward Margaret, who was busy with a customer as I prepared for the class. This morning, first thing, I'd given my sister an opportunity to open up to me about Matt's work situation, but she remained closemouthed. I found it difficult to disguise my disappointment, but I didn't feel I could let on what I knew. Nor did I want to pressure my sister into confiding in me. My heart ached for her—and for me, too. I had a dozen questions I was dying to ask; among my other concerns, I wanted to know how my nieces, Julia and Hailey, were handling this. I've always been close to them, and I believed they would have mentioned it to me unless Margaret had forbidden it. In some ways, I could understand my sister's reluctance, but that didn't make me feel any better.

The bell above the door chimed and Elise Beaumont walked into the shop. She wasn't what I'd call a warm, friendly person, but she'd been cordial enough on our first meeting. This morning, however, she radiated displeasure. She also looked as if she hadn't been sleeping well. Had I known her longer I might have asked, but since she was a new customer, I decided against it. Oh dear, this class was *not* getting off to a good start.

"Good morning." I hoped my greeting would draw her out, but she frowned at me.

"I need to know how long this class will take."

I reached for the flyer Margaret had made on the computer and handed it to her as a reminder. "Two hours."

"I suppose that'll be all right." With a glum expression, Elise pulled out a chair and sat down at the table, placing her knitting bag in her lap.

I remembered that she'd already chosen what she'd need for the class—a self-patterning yarn in light blue with specks of gray and black. Presumably she'd be knitting her socks for a man.

No sooner was Elise at the table than Bethanne entered, dressed rather formally, in my opinion, followed almost immediately by Courtney, who couldn't have looked less formal in her jeans and oversize T-shirt. Without a word they each walked to the back of the store and took a seat at the table, as far apart as possible.

I stepped up to one end and smiled. "I see we're all here. I hope you'll enjoy learning the craft of knitting socks with circular needles. We're in for a bit of a knitting adventure, but I know you won't be disappointed. I think it'd be best if we began with introductions. Why don't you all tell us something about yourselves."

My students stared up at me; they seemed to be waiting for someone else to start. "Okay, I'll go first," I said. "I'm Lydia Hoffman, and I opened A Good Yarn just over a year ago. I love knitting, and this gives me a chance to do something I really care about. I also love the opportunity to convert others." I grinned as I said this and gestured to Courtney to go next.

The teenager straightened and glanced at the other two women. "Hi," she said and gave a short wave. "My name is Courtney Pulanski. I'm seventeen, and I recently moved in with my grandmother for my senior year of high school. My mother died a few years ago and Dad's working in Brazil as an engineer." She hesitated, then added, "That about sums it up."

"You're living with your grandmother your senior year?" Elise repeated sympathetically. "That must be difficult."

Courtney swallowed hard. "Dad agonized over the decision and so did I, but it seemed to make the most sense. I'm close to my sister and brother and we talk practically every day. Dad sends me e-mails, too, when he can, but he's been busy and, well—I know he's thinking about all of us."

Elise nodded. "That helps, I'm sure."

"It does," the girl whispered and looked down, obviously fighting back tears.

Wanting to remove the focus from Courtney, I smiled at Bethanne. "How about you?"

"Oh, hi," Bethanne said, leaning forward. "My name is Bethanne Hamlin. I'm a wife and mother of two." She stopped a moment and her distress went straight to my heart. "Actually, I'm not a wife but an ex-wife. My husband and I were recently divorced." She turned to Elise, as though anticipating a comment, and warded it off by adding, "I didn't want to get divorced. But now that I'm no longer married, my daughter insisted I needed to do something for myself." She ended on a soft, forced laugh. "So here I am."

"You've knitted before, though, right?" I asked, certain that I remembered Bethanne telling me she'd once been an avid knitter.

"I completed several projects—fairly simple ones—when the kids were young. I have the yarn and the pattern for this class, and everything's lovely, but I'm afraid I might be in over my head. Socks sound too complicated for me."

Bethanne seemed ready to give up before she'd even begun. "With only the three of you in this class, I'll be able to give you individual attention," I assured her, "so don't worry about that yet."

"But I was wondering, you know," Bethanne said hesitantly, "if I find I can't do this, what's the refund policy?"

"There are no refunds, sorry." I just couldn't afford it, and I didn't want to encourage a defeatist attitude. "Elise?" I said.

"I'm Elise Beaumont and some of you might recognize me from Harry S. Truman Elementary School, where I served as librarian for thirty-eight years. I retired a little while ago and was looking for a project that would hold my interest. I thought I'd try my hand at knitting socks." She sat back when she'd finished speaking.

I gave the three a few seconds to digest the information they'd shared, then said, "I'm glad you're all here. While this class might be small in number, I generally find that to be an advantage. Once you get into knitting socks," I continued, "you'll wonder what took you so long. They're fun, and with the circular needle method they could almost be considered easy."

My students listened as I showed them a variety of yarns available for socks, from fingering weight all the way to the Double Knit weight. I wanted to start them with a basic sock, but I explained that the designs would be as varied and as different as the yarn itself. I chose a Nancy Bush pattern. Nancy's were among my favorites and I knew my students would like them as much as I did.

"The lesson today involves the Norwegian sock cast-on," I said. "It's a bit different than what you might be accustomed to, but I have a good reason for recommending it."

"It sounds complicated," Bethanne said, watching me closely as I twisted the yarn around the needle. "I'm not sure I'll be able to do it."

"Oh, for the love of heaven, you haven't even seen how it's done yet," Elise muttered, suddenly short-tempered. "Let Lydia show us first and then you can complain."

Bethanne seemed to go deep inside herself and didn't utter another word.

"Let me demonstrate, Bethanne. It's not nearly as complicated as it looks," I said, wanting to cover the awkwardness of the moment. Whatever had upset Elise, she clearly was taking it out on poor Bethanne. From the second she'd walked in the door, I could tell she was aggrieved about something.

"My grandmother suggested I do the Knit Two-Purl Two rather than the Knit One-Purl One for a crew sock," Courtney said.

I loved Vera, the girl's grandmother, who was an accomplished knitter and one of my regular customers. I wondered why she hadn't decided to teach Courtney herself, because she was more than qualified to do so.

"What do you think?" the girl asked.

"Your grandmother's right. The Knit Two-Purl Two method gives the sock more elasticity, but we're getting ahead of ourselves here."

"Oh, sorry."

I talked for a few minutes about knitting a sock that would fit the foot properly. I also passed around a gauge to help the class figure out the proper number of stitches to cast on according to the weight of the yarn. The light, fingering style yarn required more stitches, the heavier yarns fewer.

"Is everyone still with me?" I asked.

All three nodded. I spent the remainder of the class teaching the Norwegian method of casting on and how to work with the two circular needles. Courtney picked up on everything right away. She finished first and looked up proudly while both Elise and Bethanne struggled with the needles and the yarn.

Most of my time was spent helping Bethanne. I'm sure she wasn't lying when she said she'd knit years earlier, but she could barely hold on to the yarn and needles now. I'd never met a less confident woman and I have to admit Bethanne tried my patience.

My reaction to Elise's difficulty wasn't much better. She didn't mutter an unnecessary word following her chastisement of Bethanne and I sensed she regretted the outburst. I also had the distinct feeling that she found me lacking as a teacher. It wasn't a comfortable sensation.

After they'd finished, gathered up their supplies and left, I felt as if I'd put in a full day. I was exhausted.

"How'd the class go?" Margaret asked, joining me in the back office as I made myself some tea.

"Dreadful."

"Really?"

I shook my head, not wanting to talk about it. It suddenly occurred to me that this might very well explain how my sister felt about discussing the troubles in her own life.

"I can see this isn't going to be a good class," I muttered.

Margaret was unaccustomed to a pessimistic outlook from me. "What makes you say that?"

"Just a feeling…"

"And that feeling is?"

I sighed. "Elise is cranky. Bethanne is panicky and convinced she can't remember how to knit. And Courtney is resentful."

I wondered if I was going to regret offering this class.

8

CHAPTER

After her knitting class, Bethanne waited at the white wrought-iron table outside the French bakery. Grant had reluctantly agreed to meet her, but it didn't escape her notice that he'd chosen a public place, as if he anticipated her making a scene. She had no intention of doing any such thing; all she wanted was some help and advice. She hoped they could discuss the situation in a civil manner. Surprisingly perhaps, she didn't hate Grant, and for the sake of their children, they needed to work together. Surely he recognized that, too.

Sipping an espresso, Bethanne hoped the strong hot coffee would bolster her courage. This would be an unpleasant conversation, especially when she brought up the subject of money.

Grant rounded the corner on foot and Bethanne wondered where he'd parked. She saw him before he saw her. He was a striking man, and even though he'd betrayed her in the most fundamental way, she couldn't stop loving him. It angered her that she still had feelings for him, but her love was mingled with anger and horror and disbelief. This man walking toward her now was a virtual stranger.

When Grant caught sight of her, he didn't smile; instead, he acknowledged Bethanne with a quick nod. She'd worn a black tailored blazer over a light-green silk blouse and expensive black trousers, and her hair was neatly drawn back with a large silver clip. He didn't react to her appearance at all, even though he used to admire how she looked in this outfit. He pulled out the wrought-iron chair and sat down without a smile or any indication of pleasure at seeing her.

"Would you like something to drink?" she asked, thinking this would be easier if they were both relaxed.

"No." He checked his watch. "I only have a few minutes. Now what's the problem?"

Bethanne fought back emotion at the curt way he spoke. "It's about Annie."

"That's what you said on the phone, and frankly I don't see what she's done that's so far outside of the norm. Okay, she's angry. It's to be expected and Tiff's been a good sport about putting up with the magazine subscriptions and the calls from the blood bank. You're the one who seems to think Annie's got this pent-up rage that's about to explode."

"I don't *think* it, Grant, I know it. I'm worried…even Andrew's worried. He wouldn't have come to me if he wasn't."

"Fine, so you and Andrew are worried. I don't mean to sound callous here, but I don't think Annie's that overwrought. A certain amount of animosity is normal and she'll get past that soon enough."

"But you aren't the one living with her," Bethanne argued. "I am. Yes, on the surface she seems to be adjusting, but she isn't." Grant shook his head contemptuously and she found herself growing even angrier. "When did you become an expert on the effects of divorce on teenage girls? What did you do, read a book?" It would be too much to expect that he'd talked to a counsellor.

Grant sighed and leaned back in his chair. "I know she's

taken up running, and that's a good way for her to vent her frustration," he said, ignoring her question.

"I know...I agree, but—"

"You're using the kids as a convenient way to get to me," he said, challenge in his voice.

"Get to you?" She managed not to yell. Her anger threatened to erupt but for the sake of her children, and because they were in a public place, Bethanne forced it down. She'd hoped to reach him, to show him that their daughter had a serious problem. She wasn't sure how to deal with Annie and she wanted, *needed*, his help.

"I'm supposed to feel guilty," Grant muttered. "That's what you're trying to do here. You're manipulating me, and Annie's just as bad. God knows both kids are yanking my chain. According to the terms of the divorce, they're supposed to spend every other weekend with me. They refuse, and you let them! Well, I'm sick of your games—and theirs too."

It was true; Andrew and Annie strenuously resisted all her efforts to send them to Grant's place for the mandated weekends. She couldn't *force* them to go. Not at their age.

"But, I—"

He stood as if he'd said everything he intended to say.

Bethanne knew that unless she confessed what she'd done, Grant would simply walk away. "I...I read Annie's journal." She wasn't proud of that, but instinct had told her something was wrong. The few entries she'd read had made her blood run cold. Annie had experimented with drugs and was sneaking out at night, meeting her new "friends." The boys Annie wrote about weren't the ones Bethanne had met and what went on during these secret meetings she was afraid to speculate.

Grant sat back down. "You did *what?*"

"I read her journal. Oh, Grant, you don't have any idea how furious she is at both of us. She's fooling around with...with things she shouldn't, and—"

He shrugged as if to say Bethanne should have expected this. "She'll get over it. This divorce was a shock, and we need to give her time."

"Get over it?" Bethanne repeated. Grant didn't even seem to care. The pain in her chest nearly suffocated her. She wondered if he'd always been this callous and she just hadn't seen it or if he'd changed completely in so short a time.

"It's normal in this kind of situation."

Normal? Normal that he'd abandon his family? Normal that he'd inflict this pain on the very people he'd vowed to love and cherish—and then shrug it off as if it meant nothing? Normal that in her pain and rage Annie would risk destroying her own life? Hearing Grant talk so flippantly about their daughter nearly crushed her heart.

"I suppose you're right," Bethanne murmured, and stared down at her coffee. "But I thought I should give you fair warning."

"About what?"

"Annie's little problem with hate." She'd planned to tell him that, according to Andrew, their daughter was going to step up her campaign against Tiffany, but she'd let Grant deal with it.

"Is there anything else?" he asked impatiently.

"One small thing." Bethanne circled the coffee cup with both hands and refused to meet his eyes. Discussing money with her ex-husband was distasteful.

"Yes?" he asked with a long-suffering sigh.

"Andrew has signed up for football camp." Their son was a talented athlete and Bethanne was sure he'd be offered a scholarship to either the University of Washington or Washington State.

"Yes, so I understand."

"I don't have the money for it." It was embarrassing to admit this, but she had no choice. "If you could pick up the cost of the camp, then I'll cover everything else."

"What do you mean by everything else?" he asked. "Like what?"

Already she was worried about a number of upcoming expenses—expenses she didn't know how she could meet. "I got a notice at the end of the school year that athletic fees will double in September. The school levy failed and—well, with that plus the expense of his senior pictures, I thought it was only fair that you cover the cost of the camp." She didn't bother to mention that when school started again in September, there'd also be the cost of new clothes and a hundred other related expenses.

"You can't afford the camp?"

"I can, but then there wouldn't be enough left over to make the house payment."

Grant didn't say anything for a long moment. "I was afraid of this," he murmured.

Bethanne could only imagine what he meant. "I don't intend to run to you every time I need money," she assured him.

"You're doing it now."

"Yes, but…" Surely he understood that the child support he'd been ordered to pay didn't begin to cover what it cost to raise two teenagers.

"Bethanne, listen, I can't help you. Please don't come to me again."

"But—"

"I'm giving you alimony and child support. Have you got a job yet?"

Eyes cast down, she shook her head.

"That's what I figured. Have you even tried looking?" he asked sarcastically, as if he already knew the answer. "Every penny you're now collecting comes directly from me. I don't see you making any effort to support yourself."

"I *have* tried, but I don't know what else to do, where to look." Admitting her weakness was humiliating. She longed to lash out at him, blame him, curse him, but it would do no good, so once again she swallowed what little was left of her pride.

"Start looking for a job by reading the newspaper," Grant suggested in a condescending tone. "If nothing else, you can open a child-care center at the house. You always prided yourself on being a good mother."

Bethanne used to think she was, but she'd also thought of herself as a good wife. Apparently not. She tried to shake off these feelings of failure.

"Use your natural skills," Grant went on, "in a way that isn't a constant drain on me."

She flinched at the blow his words dealt her.

"I don't mean to be ugly here, but it's time you woke up and smelled the coffee." He smiled at his own feeble joke, since she was sipping an espresso. "In two years, Annie will have graduated from high school and the child support payments will be over."

"What about college?" That had already been determined in the divorce settlement, as she had every intention of reminding him.

"We're splitting the college expenses, remember? That means not only will you need to be self-supporting, but you'll have to earn enough to pay your portion of the kids' expenses. I suggest you find yourself a career in short order."

"I know, but…"

"You always have an excuse, don't you?"

This time it was Bethanne who stood, eager to leave, to escape from this cold, selfish man who'd done everything in his power to destroy her. Now more than ever she was determined to prove him wrong.

"Goodbye, Grant. Don't worry that I'll trouble you again," she said from between clenched teeth. She glared at him, hoping he could see and feel her contempt. How had she managed to live with him all those years and not know the kind of man he was?

Bethanne left the café, but once Grant had stalked off in the opposite direction she required a few minutes to compose herself before she headed down the street to where she'd parked the car, her knitting stashed in the trunk. She'd already tried to get a refund for the class, which was an unnecessary expense, but it was too late now. The money had been spent; she wouldn't waste it.

As she reached her car, she noticed a brand-new Cadillac turning the corner. It was the style and color Grant had mentioned wanting—before the divorce. Her eyes flashed to the driver and, sure enough, it was her ex, driving a car so new it still carried the dealer's plates. He refused to help her with the cost of football camp for Andrew, but he could afford an expensive car he didn't even need.

9
CHAPTER

COURTNEY PULANSKI

"Courtney!"

Courtney heard her name being called up the stairs but, still warm and sleepy, she chose to ignore it and linger in bed.

"Courtney!" the discordant voice persisted. "You asked me to get you up, remember?"

She groaned, rolled over and opened one reluctant eye to stare at the antique clock on her bedstand. Her grandmother didn't have a digital clock in the whole house. The big hand was on the six and the little hand on the five. It was five-thirty!

"Courtney!" her grandmother shouted. "It's too hard for me to go up and down these stairs, but I will if I have to. Now get up!"

Tossing aside the warm covers, Courtney staggered out of bed and to the top of the staircase. "I'm up." She just didn't know why.

"Thank goodness." Vera Pulanski paused on the third step and looked greatly relieved to be spared the agony of the climb. "I'll be ready to leave in ten minutes."

Courtney stared blankly into space until she realized that wherever her grandmother was going, she intended on taking Courtney with her. "It's only five-thirty."

Her grandmother turned back to face her. "I know what time it is. I want to be at the pool when it opens at six."

"Oh." This was dreadful. Yes, they'd discussed swimming but Courtney had no idea that she'd have to get up at this ungodly hour. In fact, the entire discussion was a distant and rather unpleasant memory. Her grandmother had said that if Courtney wanted to lose weight, she should start exercising. She vaguely recalled that she'd agreed to give swimming a try, more to satisfy her grandmother than anything else.

Needing to hurry, Courtney dug her bathing suit out of her bottom drawer and prayed it still fit. A lot of her clothes didn't anymore, and she had to go through several contortions to zip up her jeans. Most of her shirts no longer buttoned without leaving a gap, so she wore them open over a tank top. It wasn't so easy to hide her weight gain with jeans, though, and already the stitching was threatening to rip.

"I have an extra towel." Her grandmother's voice floated up the stairs again. "Don't take any of the ones from the bathroom. They're part of a set."

"I won't, Grandma," Courtney yelled back. She stripped off her pjs and stepped into the one-piece suit, pulling it up over her thighs. It fit, but just barely. Pride demanded that she not look in the mirror. The consolation was that she probably wouldn't see anyone her age at the pool this early in the morning. She donned sweatpants and a T-shirt, slipped her feet into flip-flops and trudged down the stairs.

Her grandmother was waiting by the door and handed Courtney a towel, purple cap and goggles. "They're old," she said, referring to the goggles, "but they'll be all right until we can buy you a new pair."

"You're really into this, aren't you?" Actually, Courtney

was impressed. She hadn't known that people as old as her grandmother went swimming.

More surprises awaited her. The Olympic-length pool was in the high school. The adult lap swim session started at six and lasted until seven-thirty every morning. The lobby was filled with older people who all seemed to know each other.

Courtney walked in with her grandmother and, from the greetings she received, one would assume Vera had been gone for months. Her grandmother painstakingly introduced Courtney to her swimming buddies. A dozen names flew by so fast she had no hope of keeping track, but she did try. As much as possible, she attempted to blend into the wall. The sun might be up and shining but no reasonable person should be, in Courtney's opinion.

"So how do you like living in Seattle?" one of her grandmother's friends asked.

Courtney thought the woman's name was Leta. "Oh, it's great." She forced some enthusiasm into her voice. Well, it might be if she met someone younger than eighty. This whole knitting thing was a major disappointment, too. First, she'd had no idea the class would be so small. There were only two other women and both were way older. One was around her grandmother's age and a real biddy. She looked like she'd been sucking lemons half her life. The other woman was probably close to her mother's age—if her mother had been alive.

A sick sensation hit Courtney in the pit of her stomach as she thought about her mother. It shouldn't still hurt like this, but it did. Her brother and sister seemed to deal with the loss so much better than Courtney. No one wanted to talk about Mom anymore, and Courtney felt as if she was supposed to forget she'd ever had a mother. She couldn't and she wouldn't.

Julianna, her sister, hadn't gained thirty-five pounds the way Courtney had. In fact, her sister had lost weight. Jason thought weight was a nonissue. The one and only time Courtney had talked to her brother about her problem, he'd shrugged it off. His advice was to lose the weight if it bothered her so much. He said it like it was easy. If getting weight off was that simple, she would've done it long ago.

"We have rules here at the pool," Leta said, moving closer to Courtney. "No one's ever written them down, but it helps if you follow them."

"Okay."

"You should know the middle shower is mine. I've used it for eighteen years and if you get out of the pool first, I'd appreciate if you'd leave that shower for me."

"No problem." Courtney made an effort to remember this.

"Wet your hair before you get in the water," another of her grandmother's friends advised, joining Leta. "Drench it real good, otherwise the chlorine will ruin your hair."

"You've got a cap, don't you?" someone else asked. "I hate swimming and having my hands come up full of someone's hair."

Yuck. What a disgusting concept. "Grandma gave me a cap." She hadn't planned to use it, but Courtney could see that she was likely to get booted out if she didn't.

"How fast a swimmer are you?" Leta asked.

"Ah…"

"She should use the middle lane," Courtney's grandmother suggested. "Most of us swim in the first lane," she explained to Courtney. "The third lane is for the fast swimmers. Start in the middle lane and see how it goes."

"Okay." Courtney was waking up now, and everything was beginning to make sense. Sort of. Don't use the middle shower, but swim in the middle lane and wear a cap, but get her hair completely wet first. So far, so good.

Courtney just hoped all this exercise wouldn't make her hungry.

When the doors opened, the group flowed into the pool

area. The men turned right and made their way to one end, while the women went left toward their locker room.

Courtney followed her grandmother, Leta and the others. Vera already had her bag inside her locker when Courtney caught up to her. She took her time climbing out of her sweatpants, unwilling to have these older women view her chubby arms and legs. Her fear was that one of them—or even her own grandmother—would comment on the fact that her swimsuit was too tight.

She needn't have worried. The women were intent on getting into the water and no one gave her any attention, for which Courtney was grateful. Nevertheless, she waited until the locker room had cleared out before she stripped down to her swimsuit.

Taking the advice she'd been given, she walked over to the shower area, turned on the faucet in the end shower and stuck her head inside. She wrung out her soaking wet hair and stuffed it inside the purple cap, thankful she didn't know a soul. Anyone from home who saw her now would be hysterical.

But this was no laughing matter to Courtney. When school started in six weeks, she wanted to walk into class looking good—and she didn't care what she had to do to achieve that. If losing weight meant waking up before the birds, consorting with women five or six times her age and abiding by all the unwritten rules at the pool, then she'd do it.

Leaving the change room took courage and she made a dash from the doorway to the water, attempting to look as cool and nonchalant as possible. The shock of the pool's temperature when Courtney stepped down from the ladder nearly made her gasp. It was *cold*. The sign might say 81 degrees, but she swore it was closer to 70.

Her grandmother and friends had already begun their routines. Observing them, Courtney realized they swam in circles inside each lane—down one side and back up the other.

Several of the women were walking in the shallow end, chatting as they went, and Courtney scooted past them, keeping her arms raised and out of the cold water. When she came to the lane divider, she had no choice but to go under. Freezing! The water surrounding the *Titanic* couldn't have been this cold.

Once she was positioned in the middle lane, Courtney braced her feet against the wall and pushed off. She was panting by the time she swam to the far side and grabbed hold of the pool's edge until she caught her breath.

Her grandmother and friends had no such problem. They might be eighty years old, but not only did they swim the entire length of the pool, they didn't pause before turning and going back. Not even to breathe.

Courtney went a total of ten laps, resting after each one. When she finished number ten, she stopped long enough to adjust her goggles, even though they were fine. It gave her an excuse to take an extra breather. She was now ready to start her eleventh lap and felt downright proud.

Her grandmother had explained that sixteen laps was half a mile. In that case, half a mile in the water was a hell of a lot further than on land. Doing a quick calculation, she decided she'd already swum three-quarters of half a mile. This was great!

As soon as she got back to the house, Courtney planned to weigh herself. After such an intense workout she had to be down. It would be a relief to see that thin dial move in the opposite direction for once.

"Time to get out," her grandmother told her before she could start the eleventh lap.

"I want to do a couple more," Courtney protested.

"Not on Wednesdays. The swim team comes in at seven."

A chill that had nothing to do with the water went through Courtney. "Swim team? Please tell me this isn't the high-school swim team."

Her grandmother lifted the goggles from her head and stared at Courtney in puzzlement. "Is that a problem?"

Of course it was a problem. It was bad enough to expose her body to her grandmother's friends, but she was horrified at the thought of anyone from the high school seeing her *like this*.

What a disaster. To complicate everything, she hadn't even brought her towel out from the locker room. She glanced through one of the large windows enclosing the pool. Just as she was about to leap out of the water and run for it, the foyer door opened and a line of impossibly thin girls filed in. Courtney didn't dare look at the guys who followed. The girls on the swim team were intimidation enough.

She froze, unsure what to do. If she climbed out now, she'd expose her too-tight swimsuit and her fat to all those girls. They'd certainly notice someone her age with all these old ladies.

"Courtney," her grandmother said loudly, standing on the deck. "It's time to get out."

"I know." She sank to the bottom of the pool and sat there for a moment, wishing she could just disappear.

Eventually she was forced to climb out of the water and reveal herself to the world. She kept her gaze on the floor as she shuffled into the locker room, now crowded with stick-figured teenagers.

For two weeks Courtney had been dying to meet someone her own age—but not like this, when she was practically naked and at her worst. These swim-team girls didn't have an ounce of extra weight on them. They were perfect.

Head lowered, Courtney hurried to her locker.

"You need to shower," Leta said, stepping up next to her. "I'm finished, so you can use the middle one."

"I'll shower once I get home," Courtney muttered. She grabbed her towel, wrapping it around her as if she were in danger of freezing to death.

"You *should* take a shower," her grandmother's friend continued. "Get that chlorine off you."

No way would Courtney strip off her swimsuit in the shower, especially now.

She happened to glance up just then and saw two girls with their heads together, whispering. They looked directly at her. Sure as anything, Courtney knew they were talking about her. Turning her back, she buried her face in her hands. One day in the not-too-distant future, she'd see these very girls in the high-school halls.

10
Chapter

"To grow as a knitter, don't be afraid to take chances. Knitting is a far safer sport than sky-diving. Very little is ever irrevocable!"
—Lucy Neatby, Tradewind Knitwear Designs, Inc.,
www.tradewindknits.com

LYDIA HOFFMAN

By Saturday it was all I could do to keep quiet when it came to dealing with Margaret. I was hurt and angry that she'd been so secretive about Matt for all these weeks. Now that I did know, I found myself watching her more closely. The longer she kept up this charade, the more offended I got.

Saturdays were generally my busiest day of the week, but sales tended to slow down toward the end of the month, just before payday.

"Do you have any special plans for the fourth?" I asked Margaret when there was a lull shortly after noon.

"Not really." She didn't exhibit a lot of enthusiasm one way or the other. "What about you?"

"Nothing definite yet." Brad and I hadn't made any formal plans, but I wanted to suggest we drive to the ocean, have a picnic and watch the fireworks there with Cody and Chase. The last time I visited Ocean Shores, a resort town about three hours away, I'd been a teenager. I remembered that it'd been shortly before they discovered my first brain tumor. The trip was one of the last carefree times I'd had that summer and for years afterward.

"We'll probably just have a barbecue in the backyard and watch the fireworks on TV," my sister added.

I stared at her. I couldn't help it. Seattle had two incredible fireworks displays every year. The first was at Myrtle Edwards Park on the waterfront and the second at Lake Union's Gas Works Park north of downtown. The fireworks on the lake were timed to patriotic music—a stirring experience and one that always dramatized for me what we were really celebrating.

Margaret lived on Capitol Hill, not far from Blossom Street, which was a perfect location for viewing the Lake Union display. I couldn't believe that she'd choose to sit in front of her television rather than stand outside her front door.

"What about Julia and Hailey?" I adored my nieces, aged fifteen and ten, respectively. We'd grown even closer in the past year, when my rather tense and complicated relationship with their mother had begun to relax. I used to think Margaret tried to keep the girls away from me out of spite, but in retrospect I understood that she was protecting them. She was afraid of letting her daughters love me too much, for fear I'd get sick again. If I lost my battle with cancer and died, my nieces would be devastated.

Margaret focused on busywork, reorganizing one of the yarn bins. "The girls already have plans."

"Oh."

"Julia's going to Lake Washington with friends and Hailey's going camping with the neighbors."

"So it'll just be you and Matt?"

Margaret shrugged, her back to me. "Looks that way."

I waited a moment, then decided to say something. I'd drop a hint to see if she responded. "Brad said he ran into Matt recently."

Turning slowly, Margaret studied me and seemed to be searching for some clue that I'd learned the truth. "Matt didn't mention it."

"No need, I suppose," I said casually.

"Probably not," my sister agreed.

"Will you invite Mom over?" I asked next. I hated the thought of her spending the holiday alone. We'd somehow gotten through the year without Dad and all the terrible firsts that accompanied the death of a family member. The first Thanksgiving and Christmas were the worst for me, followed by Valentine's Day and then the Fourth of July.

"I didn't say anything to her. What about you?" Margaret was hedging, and I could see that she'd rather I dealt with Mom.

"Do you want me to talk to her?" I asked, which was another way of saying I'd be responsible for keeping our mother occupied over the holiday.

"That would be best," my sister said.

I found it an effort not to point out that it would make more sense for Mom to join Margaret and Matt. A backyard barbecue would be ideal for her and a lot less strenuous than a trip to the ocean, if that was indeed what Brad and I decided to do.

"She'll have a better time with you," Margaret murmured apologetically.

Finally I couldn't stand it any longer. "You could have told me, you know," I said softly, hoping to broach the subject of Matt's unemployment in a nonconfrontational manner.

"Told you what?"

I couldn't understand why Margaret continued to maintain

the pretense. "That Matt's been out of a job for months. I'm your sister—you should be able to talk to me."

Margaret glared at me but didn't say a word.

"Is it some deep, dark secret you're ashamed of letting anyone know?" I cried, unable to conceal the pain and anger I felt.

"This is Matt's business and mine. It's none of your concern."

I reached for my knitting and sat down. Knitting is a great tension reliever for me. My hands were moving quickly as I worked on my current project, a sweater I wanted to put on display.

"There isn't anything I don't tell *you*," I reminded her. The past year I'd shared everything, and I do mean everything, with my sister. I'd confided my fears, my joys, my hopes, my…my soul. My knitting increased in speed, keeping pace with my outrage.

"This is different," Margaret returned evenly. She picked up her crocheting, jerking it so hard the ball of cotton yarn fell to the floor. Scrambling to pick it up, she tucked it under her arm and started in with the hook, her fingers moving as quickly as mine.

"How's it different?" I challenged.

"It's not me, it's Matt."

"He told Brad. Your husband felt comfortable enough letting Brad know, but my own sister didn't tell me." I felt a sense of betrayal, even more so now that Margaret's attitude was out in the open. She hadn't shown the least bit of remorse, although I'd hoped she would admit how much she'd wanted to talk to me. Apparently that had never been the case.

"Who Matt tells is his business." Margaret's eyes were focused on her project, a poncho for Julia. Her hand flew as she worked, her concentration fierce.

"Exactly." I tugged viciously on the ball of yarn, yanking it out of the wicker basket. It went tumbling to the floor.

Margaret scooped up the pretty blue yarn and placed it in

my basket, and as she did I noticed that her hands were shaking. I resisted the urge to touch her, to let her know I cared and that I wanted to help if I could. I would've done it but I feared her rejection, feared she'd turn away from me again, and I couldn't have borne that.

"Finding out about Matt's job explains a lot," I said, continuing to knit although I knew I'd have to unravel every stitch. I slowed down as I gathered my thoughts. I'd given up paying attention to the pattern and was working the design by memory. Knitting right now wasn't a good idea because I was bound to make errors, but I needed something to occupy my hands.

"What do you mean, explains a lot?" Margaret echoed, her tone hostile.

"Your attitude at work, with me and with other people."

"You don't know what you're talking about."

I wasn't choosing my words as carefully as I should, but I went on, anyway. "You've been prickly and abrupt with the customers."

"If you don't want me working here, all you have to do is say so," Margaret snapped.

"Why does it have to be like this with us?" I pleaded. "I'm your *sister.*"

"You're my employer."

"I'm both, but I've never felt it was necessary to draw any lines." Apparently she did. "I asked you recently if everything was all right and you assured me it was."

"Like I said, my life is none of your business."

I blinked back tears. "If that's how you feel, then fine."

"Whatever!"

I'd heard my two nieces respond in just that way countless times and always been amused, but I wasn't now. Stuffing the half-knit sweater back into the wicker basket, I bolted to my feet. "I'm your sister," I said again. "Isn't it time you started treating me like one?"

To my absolute horror, Margaret covered her face and burst into tears. I watched her, aghast, hardly knowing what to say.

"Margaret?" I whispered. "What is it?"

My sister whirled away and rushed to the back room.

Despite the two customers who'd just come in, I followed her. Thankfully they didn't need yarn or attention just then, because I would've abandoned them. Margaret was my first priority. Once again risking her rejection, I placed my arm around her. To my surprise, she turned to me and rested her head on my shoulder.

"I wanted to tell you," she sobbed.

"Why didn't you?" I didn't understand it. I was afraid I'd failed her in some way, but had no idea how.

"I…couldn't."

"Yes, you could."

"Matt is feeling wretched…. He always believed he'd retire from Boeing. He's been with the company all these years."

"I know," I said soothingly. "I'm so sorry."

Margaret straightened and wiped the tears from her cheeks. "I was afraid you'd give me that Mary Sunshine routine of yours, and I just couldn't deal with it."

"The what routine?"

"You know—your 'everything will be better in the morning' speech."

I stared at her blankly.

"All you need to do is think happy thoughts, and all your problems will go away," she went on in an insulting saccharine voice.

Sometimes the truth is painful to hear and this was one of those times. Had Margaret come to me a few weeks earlier that *is* what I would've said. Well—not exactly, but something along those lines. Being positive and hopeful, choosing happiness: that was the approach I tried to bring to my life these days. Without intending to, I'd probably sounded glib to Margaret as I burbled on about my own contentment.

"What can I do to help you?" I asked.

She shook her head. "Nothing. All I really want you to do is be my sister. I don't want advice. I don't want you to worry." She tried to smile. "I'm doing enough of that for everyone."

"There must be some way I can help," I insisted. I was beginning to think I'd already failed on all counts, but I was determined to try.

Margaret's teary eyes met mine. "You could listen."

I nodded and we hugged. "Why don't Brad and I join you on the fourth," I suggested. "We'll have a barbecue together."

Margaret managed a quavery smile. "As you might've noticed, I'm not much fun to be around lately." ·

"We'll make the best of it. We're family."

Fresh tears filled her eyes. "Thank you," she whispered.

I hugged her again, grateful we'd talked, and sorry I'd delayed it so long.

CHAPTER 11

ELISE BEAUMONT

Elise was as ready to see Marvin "Maverick" Beaumont as she could be. He was due to arrive that afternoon. Her daughter had been fussing with the house for days, cooking and cleaning as if she were expecting royalty. All this special attention irritated Elise no end. At any other time and for anyone else, Elise would've been just as involved, elbow-deep in the preparations. To be fair, she'd helped some, mostly by keeping the boys entertained so Aurora could do her straightening, vacuuming and polishing.

"Mom," Aurora cried in a panic, rushing into the spotless living room where Elise was reading to her grandsons. "Where did you put the vanilla?"

Sighing, Elise set aside *The Hobbit.* "It's in the cupboard next to the stove, right-hand side."

"It isn't there!" More panic.

"Aurora," Elise said with infinite patience as she made her way into the kitchen. "It's exactly where I said it was. Look again." To prove her point, she opened the cupboard, extracted the small bottle of vanilla and handed it to her daughter. "What are you baking?"

"Carrot cake—it's Dad's favorite."

Elise had baked it for Maverick years ago and passed the recipe on to Aurora. As a matter of course, she no longer baked or ate carrot cake because—well, because of the memories. He'd always been so grateful, so loving afterward. Those were the times she most yearned to forget. Over the years, she'd clung to the disappointments and the worry because that made it easier to justify the divorce. But Elise had loved that man, loved him until she was sure she'd lose her mind if she stayed married to him.

"Thanks, Mom," Aurora said, and held her gaze a moment longer than necessary. Sighing, she added, "I know this is difficult for you."

"Don't worry," Elise said. "I'll stay out of your father's way as much as possible. All I ask is that you not try to drag me into this reunion." The next few weeks would be uncomfortable, but she suspected he'd be just as eager to avoid her.

"I won't, I promise."

"Thank you." With that Elise returned to the living room where Luke and John were wrestling on the newly vacuumed carpet. They'd already knocked over a stack of magazines, which she quickly righted. "Boys, boys," she cried, clapping her hands. "Settle down." Her grandsons reluctantly obeyed. John climbed into her lap and settled in the crook of her arm as she reached for the book. At six he wouldn't do this much longer, and she treasured these special moments.

Predictably, Maverick arrived an hour late with all the fanfare of Hannibal crossing the Alps. Voice booming "Hello," he came through the front door pulling his suitcase, arms laden with gifts. Luke and John were instantly at his side screeching and leaping up and down, seeking his attention and, of course, the gifts.

It'd been…twenty years since Elise had last seen him. He'd planned to attend Aurora and David's wedding, but his flight was cancelled because of a winter storm. Elise had always wondered if it was the blizzard or a poker game that had changed his plans. Both Luke and John were born in the middle of important poker tournaments; he'd sent huge floral arrangements at their births, as if that would make up for his absence.

Elise had intended to retreat to her room when he arrived, but she found herself rooted to the spot, unable to look away. Maverick's red hair was shockingly white now. He had a well-trimmed beard, also white. He'd maintained every inch of his six-foot frame and seemed to be in good health. Elise faltered, resisting the magnetic pull she'd always experienced whenever he was close. She'd learned in the most painful manner that Maverick was not to be trusted, least of all with her heart. Yes, she'd loved this man, perhaps still loved him, but he was wrong for her. That was an undeniable, irrevocable fact, one she didn't dare ignore.

The next minute, Maverick was hugging both boys and Aurora. He made a production of doling out his gifts, as if it were Christmas morning and he was Santa. The boys dropped to the floor and tore into their packages, while Aurora carried her smaller box into the living room. She sat sideways in the recliner and opened the lid. Elise admitted to being curious, so she lingered in the hallway.

"Oh, Daddy," Aurora said in a soft voice. Elise watched as her daughter lifted out a single teardrop-shaped black pearl on a long gold chain. "It's beautiful…just beautiful." Her voice caught, and looking up at her father with adoration, Aurora whispered, "I'll treasure it always."

This was better than any jewelry he'd ever given Elise. Not that it mattered. Seeing how generous he was now, she could tell that Maverick was on a winning streak. Easy come, easy go. And it went with surprising ease, as Elise remembered all too well.

Against her will, she found her gaze drawn to his. Neither spoke for the longest moment. She felt an odd sensation as they stared into each other's eyes—as if the years had disappeared and they were young again. In his she read such regret that she stepped involuntarily toward him. So time had brought disappointments to him as well as her.... It wasn't something she'd expected to see.

Maverick broke the silence first. "Hello, Elise," he said quietly.

She inclined her head toward him, refusing to let him mesmerize her so soon after his arrival. "Marvin."

He grimaced. "Maverick, please."

"Maverick, then." She knew he hated his given name although she'd never understood why. She'd married Marvin, loved Marvin, but he'd never been content to be that man. Instead, he'd sought out glamour and glitz and the instant gratification of a gambling win, and in the process destroyed their lives together.

"I would've brought you a gift, but I didn't think you'd accept one from me."

"I appreciate the thought, but you're right. A gift wouldn't have been appropriate." That was true, although she couldn't help wondering what he would have chosen for her.

"You look good," he said as his gaze slid up and down her trim body.

Despite herself, Elise raised her hand to her hair, as if to check that it was still in place. His compliment flustered her, but she managed to regroup enough to say, "You too."

"Grandpa, Grandpa, want to see where you're going to sleep?" Luke asked, tugging at Maverick's arm.

"I sure do," he said, suddenly turning away from Elise. He lifted John into his arms as Luke raced ahead, and the three of them moved down the hallway.

"This is our room," Luke said, opening the first door on the right.

"And that's Grandma's room." John pointed to Elise's, which was almost directly across from it.

"And that's the bathroom for the boys." Luke hurried over to the third doorway.

"Grandma has her own bathroom, and we're not supposed to use it no matter how bad we have to go," John explained. "Mom said."

Maverick chuckled.

"Grandpa, Grandpa, you know that dangling thing in the back of your throat? Did you know if you pull on it you barf?"

"John Peter Tully, what a thing to say," Elise chastised, but stopped when Maverick threw back his head and bellowed with laughter. Leave it to a man to find the topic of vomit amusing.

"You get to sleep on the bottom bunk, and Luke and me are gonna share the other one," John explained and dove onto the mattress. "Mom changed the sheets."

"That's 'cause John still wets the bed."

"Do not," John screamed, leaping off the bed and swinging wildly at his older brother.

Elise started to move into the room to break up the fight, but Maverick quickly took control, pulling the boys apart. He immediately got them involved in showing him the rest of the house. Seeing that she wasn't needed, Elise retreated to the security of her own bedroom.

Forty-five minutes later, she sat with her feet up, watching television and knitting. Her mind wasn't on the news, but on her family; she felt irritated that she'd allowed Maverick to isolate her from those she loved most.

Someone knocked politely at her door and Aurora stuck her head inside. "I hoped you'd join us for dinner," she said with a pleading look. "David made a point of being home early tonight, and it would mean a great deal to me."

Elise would rather avoid this "welcome" dinner, but there was little she could refuse her daughter, who'd been so wonderful to her throughout this legal mess. "All right."

"Thank you." Gratitude glistened in Aurora's eyes.

To the best of Elise's memory, this was the first time Aurora had shared a meal with both parents at the same table. That was a sad commentary and, for her daughter's sake, Elise wished her marriage had ended differently. She didn't consider herself an emotional woman, but she found Aurora's happiness at something so simple poignant enough to bring her to tears.

When Elise finally entered the dining room, David had arrived home from the office and was pouring wine for the adults. Elise had a good relationship with David; as far as she was concerned, he was a model husband. She would be forever grateful that Aurora, unlike her, had had the sense to marry a decent, reliable man who actually worked at a real job.

Aurora was still bustling about the kitchen and Elise joined her. While David and Maverick chatted, drinking their wine, the women carried the salad, sliced roast, mashed potatoes and gravy to the table.

"It's a feast," Luke announced grandly.

"Just like Thanksgiving, except without the turkey," redheaded John added, dragging his chair closer to the table. "I get to sit next to Grandpa."

"Me too," Luke insisted, and it seemed the boys were on the verge of breaking into another fight. Once more Maverick smoothly ended the conflict by promising to sit between them.

Despite Elise's worries, dinner was a pleasant affair. Maverick entertained them with tales of his travels. He'd been all over the world, from Alaska to Argentina, from Paris to Polynesia, touring the places Elise had only read about in books. One day she'd see them, too, she told herself, but the likelihood of that dimmed with every message from her attorney.

Before dessert was served, Elise arranged the dishes in the dishwasher and made the coffee. As soon as she could, she'd return to her room and her knitting. Knowing Aurora would want to spend time with her father and husband, she carried the coffeepot to the living room, where the others lingered.

"Come on, boys," she said to her grandsons. "I'll help you get ready for bed."

This elicited the usual whines and groans.

Elise had expected that. "I'll read you another chapter from *The Hobbit*."

The whines dwindled somewhat.

"Let me read to them, Elise," Maverick offered.

Elise was perfectly happy to let him assume the task but felt she should warn him. Once she started reading, it was difficult to stop. The boys wanted to hear more and more. They always bombarded her with "Another chapter, Grandma," or "Please, just to the end of the page." They begged and pleaded, and she could never say *no*. It was sometimes a full hour before she turned off the lights. Still, she took satisfaction in knowing that her grandsons had learned to associate reading with pleasure and hoped that books would remain as important to them as they'd always been to her.

"Elise?" Maverick asked again.

"By all means." She left the small party and hurried to her room. With one ear on the television and the other focused on the room across the hall, she waited for the sure-to-follow battle, grinning wickedly to herself. Maverick was learning a valuable lesson about being a grandparent.

When she didn't hear any squabbling, she lowered the volume on her television.

Nothing.

Frowning, she rose and opened the door a crack. She heard Maverick's rich baritone voice as he read animatedly and with emotion. He was good; she'd give him that. There wasn't a sound from the youngsters. No doubt they were enthralled by the reading as much as the story.

In spite of what Aurora thought, Elise wanted her daughter to have a good relationship with her father. True, her feelings on the subject were mixed. Although Maverick had promptly paid child support and always kept in touch, he'd made no effort to be a constant part of their daughter's life. She didn't understand why he'd decided it was so important to make contact now.

Elise returned to her rocking chair and twenty minutes later she checked again, her ear at the door. When someone knocked, she nearly leaped out of her skin. With one hand over her startled heart, she opened the door to discover Maverick standing in the hallway.

She gasped. "The boys?" she managed to utter, expecting him to ask her advice on how to coax them to sleep.

"Out like the proverbial light," he said with a shrug.

Impossible! Luke and John didn't go down without a fight. It was part of their nightly ritual. She realized she was frowning again.

Maverick's mouth twitched with a smile. "I read them one chapter and John wanted a second."

She nodded. That was their usual pattern.

"The kid's got a real dramatic streak," he said.

Elise forced back a smile.

"He said 'Grandpa, I beg of you, I beg of you.'"

"Did you give in?"

"Yes—but I made them promise they'd go right down, and they did."

"Count your blessings."

For a moment she was lost in him. Then, with a jolt of dismay, she recognized what she was doing. Resolutely, she lifted her chin and looked him square in the eyes. "Was there something you wanted?"

He hesitated, and she could see he was stifling a grin. He'd always been able to see straight through her. "Just to tell you good-night and that I enjoyed being with you again."

Elise wanted to groan. How was it that a man she'd been divorced from for more than thirty-seven years still had power over her? She loathed her own weakness, loathed her inability to forget how much she'd loved him. "Th-ank you," she managed, stumbling over the words.

To her astonishment, Maverick pressed his hand to her cheek, his touch soft. His blue eyes brightened with intensity. Elise's knees felt as if they were about to buckle and her mouth fell open.

"You've always been the most beautiful woman I've ever known."

Her heart hammering inside her chest, Elise stepped back, breaking the contact. Otherwise she didn't know what she might have done…

"Good night," she whispered and while she had the strength, she closed the door. Old feelings, it seemed, died hard. She reminded herself that she couldn't relax her vigilance with this gambler she'd once married. Not for a minute. Not for even a second.

12

CHAPTER

BETHANNE HAMLIN

Bethanne's meeting with Grant had been a week ago, and she was still so angry that she hadn't slept an entire night since. The selfish bastard wasn't willing to spend three hundred dollars on his son. Bethanne knew the reason. Grant didn't have the courage to say it, but she knew.

This was payback. When Grant moved out of the house and in with Tiffany, their then-sixteen-year-old son had confronted his father and told him exactly what he thought of Grant's behavior. Grant hadn't taken kindly to Andrew's honesty, and their relationship had been strained ever since.

"You okay, Mom?" Annie asked, entering the kitchen.

"Fine," she snapped, then smiled sheepishly. "Sorry, I was lost in thought."

Annie flopped down at the kitchen table beside Bethanne, who sat there with a cup of tea. "Thinking about Dad?"

She didn't bother to deny it. "He's been on my mind lately."

"Mine too," Annie admitted. "I can't believe he's still with *her.*"

Annie never mentioned Tiffany's name. She was always *her* or *the bitch*. Her daughter's own relationship with Grant was confused. Annie loved her father and had been close to him, and longed to be close once again, but she felt hurt and betrayed. She was also unsure where she stood with him. Grant gave her the minimum of attention and expected Annie to be the one to call him, which she did on occasion. But the brunt of her daughter's anger was directed toward Tiffany because Annie believed the other woman had stolen Grant from his family. Bethanne didn't take that anger lightly, especially after flipping through Annie's journal, but she didn't know what to do about it, either. She prayed that eventually her daughter's bitterness would fade.

It was times like this that she missed her mother most. Martha Gibson had died suddenly of an aneurysm the year Annie was born, and Bethanne's father had declined physically and emotionally after that. He lived in a retirement community in Arizona, but it was up to her to maintain contact.

"I think they might be getting married," Annie murmured, her voice barely audible.

"Is that so?" Bethanne tried not to reveal any interest, but her head was spinning. If anyone in the family was likely to learn of Grant's wedding plans, it would be her daughter. He might not talk to Annie much, but he talked to her more than to Andrew or Bethanne. *Married.* That explained why her ex had turned into such a miser. She'd bet every penny left in her bank account that he was buying Tiffany a huge diamond and planning the honeymoon. At least Tiffany was getting one; Bethanne never had. Grant and Bethanne got married while in college, and there'd been money for no more than a wedding night in a three-star hotel on the Oregon coast. Monday morning they were both back in school.

"I hate *her*, Mom. I know you said I shouldn't, but I can't help it. If it wasn't for *her*, Dad would be with us and everything would be like it used to be." Annie's voice cracked with the intensity of her emotions.

"I know," Bethanne whispered, fighting her own anger, "but if it wasn't *her,* it probably would've been someone else." This insight had been a small epiphany for Bethanne during the divorce proceedings. Her attorney had been going over the settlement, and it was all Bethanne could do to concentrate when the truth suddenly dawned on her. *It wasn't her fault.* She'd been a good wife and a good mother. She'd remained faithful and loving. Not once in the entire twenty years of her marriage had she even considered cheating on Grant. Her whole life had been about family. Without resentment or complaint, she'd cooked her husband's meals, cleaned his home and raised his children. She'd been a hostess for his parties, which were legendary.

Their huge Christmas, Super Bowl and Fourth of July parties, in particular, had been favorites with their friends, and Grant had loved playing host. It didn't matter that she'd done all the work, they were a team.

No, she wasn't to blame for the mess he'd made of their lives and she refused to accept the guilt. Sitting in her attorney's office that day, she'd recognized Grant's actions for what they were. Blaming her was Grant's way of justifying his lack of loyalty and fidelity, his failure as a husband and father. It obviously assuaged the guilt he was unwilling to feel. For a time *she'd* assumed that responsibility, certain she must be the one who'd failed. He wanted her to think she'd become so wrapped up in the children's lives she'd abandoned him. She hadn't, and she wouldn't listen to those cruel voices in the back of her head ever again. Voices that echoed his…

"Mom, Mom," Annie said, reaching across the table to touch Bethanne's forearm. "You're spacing out on me."

"Oh, sorry."

"How was the sock class?" Annie asked, apparently trying

to turn Bethanne's mind in another direction, away from the darkness that had overtaken her.

"Really great." The second class had gone much better than the first. They'd no sooner sat down at the table than Elise apologized for what she called her "crankiness" the week before. She explained that she'd received bad news and hadn't had time to digest it before the class. She was very sorry if she'd offended anyone.

Bethanne had her own confession to make. She told the others why she'd been tense the week before—that she'd been hoping to get out of the class because she regretted having spent the money. She no longer felt that way. She was still worried about finances, but Annie was right; she needed something for herself. Something completely unrelated to everything else in her life.

Even Courtney seemed to be in a better mood. She'd announced proudly that she'd lost two pounds. At first Bethanne thought the teenager meant she'd lost the weight knitting, which seemed peculiar, but then she realized Courtney was saying that knitting had kept her out of the kitchen.

The two-hour class had sped by, and Bethanne felt wonderful afterward, grateful she hadn't dropped out. She'd made progress on her socks—or the first one, anyway—and had truly enjoyed the companionship of the other women.

"I knew you'd like it." Annie's eyes flashed with triumph.

The phone rang and her daughter leaped up in her rush to answer. "Hello."

Annie's eyes zeroed in on Bethanne.

"Yes, she's here." She held the phone against her stomach. "It's for you." She hesitated, then whispered, "It's a man."

Bethanne rolled her eyes. "It's probably the guy at the bank, phoning to tell me I've overdrawn the checking account again." She'd already done that twice, and it was embarrassing in the extreme.

Annie brought her the phone.

"This is Bethanne Hamlin," she said, trying to sound brisk and professional. According to the check register, she should have at least fifty dollars in that account, but she hadn't gotten it to balance since she'd opened it. Math had never been one of her strengths.

"Bethanne, this is Paul Ormond."

She felt as if all the oxygen had been sucked out of her lungs. Paul was Tiffany's ex-husband. Tiffany had filed for a divorce at the same time as Grant. Apparently they'd coordinated when to file, and she could imagine the two of them traipsing down to the courthouse, giggling and holding hands. Paul and Bethanne had been the spouses left behind to deal with the emotional devastation of the affair and its aftermath.

"Hello, Paul," she said with difficulty. She'd met him only once, briefly, but she'd considered calling him a couple of times. She'd wanted to ask if he'd known about the affair before his wife told him. Had Tiffany done it on Valentine's Day, like Grant? In the end, Bethanne hadn't bothered.

"I was wondering if we could talk," Paul said.

"Sure. I mean, that would be fine," she said awkwardly.

Her answer was met with silence.

"Do you mean now?" she asked.

"No," he said quickly. "How about later this afternoon? After five?"

"Okay." Her social calendar was empty. This had been a shock to Bethanne. Her friends had rallied around her and supported her through the divorce, but they no longer invited her to socialize with them. Most events in their circle were geared to couples, and as a newly single woman—an unwillingly single woman—she'd become an outcast. Besides, she suspected Tiffany had taken her place at some of those dinners and parties. Just when she most needed her friends, they'd disappeared.

"Would you be willing to have dinner with me? My treat." He sounded hesitant, as if he expected her to decline.

"That would be nice," she said impulsively. "Where would you like to meet?"

"Anthony's, say around six. I'll make the reservation."

The waterfront restaurant wasn't far from Pike Place Market and was well known in the area as one of the top seafood places.

Bethanne thanked him and ended the call, both puzzled and pleased. This wasn't a date, but it was as close to one as she'd come in the last twenty-two years.

"Who was that?" Annie asked when Bethanne replaced the receiver.

For some reason, Bethanne was reluctant to explain. "An old friend," she finally said.

"He wants to take you out?" Annie asked, as if this were beyond imagining.

"Do you think I shouldn't go?" Bethanne instantly assumed she'd made a mistake in agreeing to meet Paul.

Annie shrugged. "I don't know. Why ask me? Who's the adult here, anyway?"

"You're right," Bethanne said. "I'm the adult and I'm meeting…an old friend."

When it was time to leave, both Annie and Andrew were gone for the evening, so Bethanne propped a note for them on the kitchen counter, the way they did for her.

She had to find parking downtown, because she couldn't afford the lot prices. Fortunately, she located a place three short blocks from the restaurant. When she walked toward Anthony's, Paul Ormond was already there, standing outside waiting. He waved at her as she approached.

Paul was around thirty-five, she guessed, with dark hair and eyes, a pleasant face and a bit of a paunch. If she remembered correctly, he worked in the downtown area for an international shipping firm. He wore a suit and tie. Bethanne was surprised that the lovely Tiffany would have married such an ordinary-looking man. The impression she had of "Tiff" was of a status-conscious woman, to whom a husband's appearance would be almost as important as her own.

"Thank you for coming," Paul said as he opened the door to the restaurant. When he stepped forward and announced his name to the hostess, they were immediately seated.

They both ordered a glass of wine and Paul stared out the window at Puget Sound. "I imagine you're wondering why I called you," he said after several minutes of silence. Oddly, Bethanne didn't feel uncomfortable, nor did she feel her usual urge to make small talk.

She nodded. "I was kind of curious. The divorces have been final for quite a while now."

"It doesn't feel that way to me."

"Me neither," she admitted. "I—" She started to tell Paul that Grant had refused to pay for Andrew's football camp. It didn't matter, she had to remind herself. It just didn't matter.

"When did you find out about the affair?" he asked.

She was embarrassed to tell him the truth. "Not until Grant told me. You know how they say the wife's always the last to know. What about you?"

"I knew almost from the first," he said, "but I couldn't make myself believe it."

"How long were you and Tiffany married?"

"Six years," he said. "Four good ones, at any rate. Then she met Grant." He shook his head. "I think I guessed what was going on when she wanted to delay having a family."

Bethanne knew from what Grant had told her that there were no other children involved. The whole thing was bad enough without hurting more innocents.

She took a sip from her glass of chardonnay, then another. "Annie told me this afternoon she thinks they're getting married."

Paul arched his eyebrows. "I suppose that's inevitable."

Although her appetite had vanished with talk of the affair, Bethanne opened the menu. "I don't know if I'll ever get over it," she whispered.

"Please don't say that," Paul begged. "I was hoping, you know, that everything was better for you."

"It *is* better," she said valiantly, "it's just that…I don't feel it yet." If being alone hurt this badly all these months after the divorce, she couldn't imagine that pain would ever go away.

"Your husband and my wife were cheating on us," he said with sudden anger. "So, why are we the ones feeling bad?"

It wasn't fair. She was the injured party; Paul, too. While Grant and Tiffany were free of their responsibilities and probably partying every night, Bethanne was dealing with children whose security had been shattered, an aging house and more emotional pain than any one person should be expected to bear.

"I told myself they have to live with what they've done," Paul said, "but that's little comfort."

"It's no comfort."

Paul opened his menu, too. "I was thinking—"

"Do you mind if we don't talk about the divorce?" Bethanne asked abruptly. "We're supposed to be getting on with our lives. Let's order dinner, okay?"

Paul nodded. "Have you decided what you want?"

"Just an appetizer. The smoked salmon, I think. And maybe a cup of chowder."

He called over the waiter and they placed their orders, with Paul choosing the chowder and a small dish of seafood pasta. "So, are you?" he asked. "Getting on with your life, I mean."

"I'm really trying."

"How?" he asked, and at her startled look, he added, "The reason I want to know is that I need help. I guess I was hoping you were doing better than I am and might have some words of wisdom to share."

"I…I joined a knitting class."

Paul grinned, and when he smiled he was almost boyishly handsome. "That's more of a women's thing, I think."

"Plenty of men knit, too."

"They do?"

She shrugged. "That's what I've heard."

"I've taken up golf, but so far I don't show any real knack for it."

Another silence, as they concentrated on their chowder, which had just been delivered. They both murmured appreciatively. It truly was delicious, and Bethanne found herself automatically deconstructing the ingredients, the way she used to when she was married and always searching for new recipes. Unexpectedly, that made her feel better, not worse, as if she'd recovered a small part of the woman she used to be.

She tried her smoked salmon. Good, but she wouldn't have served it with the curried mayonnaise. Too many strong flavors.

Time to wade back into the conversational waters. "Have you started dating again?" she asked.

He shook his head. "What about you?"

Smiling, she pointed to him. "You're my first dinner date in twenty-two years."

"You're my first date in seven."

"Is that cause for celebration?"

Paul chuckled. "I think it is." With that he gestured to the waiter and they ordered a second glass of wine.

Paul might not be the most attractive man she'd ever met, especially compared to Grant, but Bethanne was struck by how genuine he was, how generous and caring. Even though he was in as much pain as she was, he'd told her he was sorry that his wife had been the one to break up her family.

"Is there anything I can do for you?" he asked, as they walked out of the restaurant.

Bethanne had only one burning need. A job. "Do you know anyone who'd be willing to hire me?"

"For what?"

She sighed. "At this point, I'd do just about anything."

"Do you have computer skills?"

"Well…" The truth was, she didn't. Bethanne knew her way around the Internet, but mostly because her kids had shown her. She could manage basic word processing programs, but anything beyond that and she was at a loss.

"Maybe you should get some training," Paul suggested.

He was right, but she hated the thought of it. This adjustment, trying to find employment after so many years out of the job market, was almost as difficult as the divorce.

Paul insisted on walking her to where she'd parked her car. "I had a good time tonight, Bethanne, thank you."

"Thank *you*." They exchanged handshakes. "If you ever need someone to talk to, give me a call."

He perked up. "You wouldn't mind?"

"Not in the least."

Bethanne listened to the radio on the drive home. It was almost ten by the time she pulled into the driveway. She hadn't even made it to the house before the front door was thrown open and her children stood in the entrance glaring at her.

"Just exactly where were you?" Annie demanded.

"We were worried sick," Andrew said.

Bethanne stared back at them in complete shock. "I beg your pardon? Annie, I told you I was seeing an old friend."

"But you didn't say you were going to be this *late!*" Annie cried in disgust.

"We talked and…and the time flew," Bethanne answered before she thought better of it.

"I can't believe you'd do this," Andrew muttered.

"What?"

"After everything you've said to us about knowing where we are and who we're with." Andrew shook his head.

"This is totally bogus," Annie muttered.

"Could you please let me in?" As they moved aside, she said, "I left you a note."

"I know, but you didn't give us the guy's name or tell us where you went. I'm not sure about this, Mom," Andrew tried to explain. "It just doesn't seem right that my mother's the one on a date."

"It shouldn't be such a big deal," Annie said, speaking more thoughtfully now. "But it doesn't *feel* right."

"It doesn't for me either," Bethanne agreed. "However, this is my new reality." For the first time, she could say those hated words without flinching.

"So we should get used to it?" Andrew asked.

Bethanne nodded. Her children had nothing to worry about; she was their rock, their security. Their *mother.* That wouldn't change no matter what their father did.

13

CHAPTER

COURTNEY PULANSKI

If Courtney could trust her grandmother's antique scale, it showed that she'd lost four pounds. Five if she balanced on one foot and stared straight down at the dial. This was the first time in months that she'd managed to stay on any formal eating program. She felt good, really good.

The exercising helped, she was sure of it. Her sister had e-mailed and suggested a low-carb diet, but Courtney preferred to make up one of her own. It was a very simple concept: she didn't eat anything that started with the letter P. That included pasta, peanut butter, pizza, popcorn and just about everything else she'd craved in the last four years.

She routinely heard from Julianna, who e-mailed her from Alaska every day. Julianna's stories about life at the summer lodge—her coworkers, the guests, the wildlife—were endlessly entertaining. Jason sent her encouraging messages once or twice a week, and Courtney was grateful for them. She wrote both Jason and Julianna long e-mails in exchange. She hadn't mentioned her P diet but she boasted proudly, at least to her sister, about each pound lost.

Her father was in regular contact, too. This job in Brazil demanded a lot of his time, but she could tell he was trying hard to be there for her. She loved him for it. Now that she'd finished feeling sorry for herself, she realized how difficult this situation was for him. He desperately missed his children and talked constantly about when he'd return home. This year was destined to be the longest of all their lives.

The only problem with living in Seattle was that Courtney still hadn't met anyone her age. After that one disaster, when she'd run into all those sleek-bodied girls from the swim team, she'd avoided the pool on Mondays and Wednesdays—which was when the team practiced.

She swam laps three mornings a week and biked on the other days. She'd even biked to her last knitting class, although her grandmother was convinced it wasn't safe to ride a bicycle in Seattle traffic. It hadn't been easy to go the full three miles, and she'd felt justified in congratulating herself. Riding a bike up the steep Seattle hills was a challenge. She figured Lance Armstrong would've been out of breath, too. At one point she'd had to stop, climb off her bike and walk when it became too much for her. Her new goal was to make it all the way up Capitol Hill without stopping. That would take practice, but she knew she'd eventually manage it.

"Are you going out again?" her grandmother asked when Courtney bounced down the stairs. She had on her shorts and T-shirt and held her helmet by the straps.

"I won't be long, Grams." Last week *Grandma* had gotten shortened to *Grams*. She'd decided that *Grandma* seemed kind of juvenile; besides, it was just too much of a mouthful.

"You be careful," Vera cried, glancing away from the television screen long enough to warn her.

"I will, I promise."

"When will you be back?"

Courtney glanced at her watch. "Give me an hour, okay?"

Grams didn't answer and Courtney suspected she hadn't heard her, which was often the case. Placing the helmet on her head and donning her gloves, Courtney went out to the garage, where she kept her bicycle.

She was on the ten-speed and wheeling along at a fast clip, the wind in her face, when she noticed a familiar figure in the parking lot of the Safeway grocery store. Bethanne saw her at the same time and raised her hand in greeting. Courtney would've biked past with only a wave but Bethanne called her over.

Courtney rode into the lot and approached Bethanne, who had obviously been shopping. A good-looking young man with broad shoulders and short dark hair had pushed her cart next to her car, ready to load the groceries.

"Hi," Courtney said, a bit winded. She reached for her water bottle and took a swig.

"Courtney, I want to introduce you to my son, Andrew. He works here part-time—as you can see." She gestured at his employee vest with its store logo.

At the last class she'd mentioned her children but Courtney hadn't paid that much attention. Bethanne had two, she remembered—a boy and a girl.

"Hi," Andrew said without any real enthusiasm.

"Hi." Great, she would meet him when she was all sweaty and hot and wearing shorts. She preferred to keep her legs covered and did most of the time.

"Courtney's in my knitting class," Bethanne explained to her son. "She's the girl I told you about the other day. She'll be starting her senior year at Washington High this September." She turned to Courtney and added, "Andrew will be a senior, too."

"At Washington?"

He nodded.

"Didn't you say you had an extra ticket to the Mariners'

game this evening?" Bethanne asked her son, and then before he even had a chance to answer, she said, "You should invite Courtney. She hasn't met many kids here, and it would be a great way for her to get to know your friends."

"You don't need to do that," Courtney rushed to tell him, embarrassed that Bethanne had put her son in such an awkward position.

"You want to come?" Andrew asked her.

"I guess." Although she sounded like it was no big deal, it was. Inside she was doing cartwheels but she dared not let it show.

"You'll pick her up, won't you?" Bethanne said.

"If I can have the car." From his tone, taking the car had been a contentious issue.

Bethanne grinned. "All right, all right, you can have the car."

Andrew got Courtney's address and phone number, and promised to call later in the afternoon once he was off work.

Courtney was so excited she couldn't bike home fast enough. Andrew was totally cool and cute and just the kind of guy she'd hoped to meet. The game was hours away but she had a thousand things to do first.

By the time Courtney got back to the house, her grandmother had lunch on the table. She grabbed an apple, bit off a huge chunk and raced up the stairs.

"Hey," Grams shouted after her, "where are you headed?"

"I met someone. Bethanne's son." When Vera looked a little puzzled, she added, "Bethanne? From the knitting class?" Courtney took a deep breath. "I'm going to the Mariners' game this evening."

"That isn't for hours yet."

"I know," she yelled from the top of the stairs, "but I need to shower and everything. Oh Grams, what should I wear?" Silly question. Grams was sweet, but she knew next to nothing about fashion. "Never mind," Courtney said, "I'll figure it out."

After her shower, Courtney changed clothes about fifteen times, weighing herself with each outfit and then doing a complete and thorough evaluation in front of the mirror. In the end she decided on jeans and a white tank-top with a yellow flowered overshirt. She weighed more in this outfit than one of the others, but the yellow shirt made her eyes darker and set off her dark-brown hair. It was her best choice.

Andrew phoned at five and said he'd be by in thirty minutes to pick her up for the six o'clock game. Courtney didn't want to appear too eager by waiting outside, but she didn't want him to have to come inside and get her, either. This wasn't like a date or anything. She compromised by watching for him out the living room window. As soon as he pulled up in front, she kissed her grandmother on the cheek and dashed out the door.

"Have a good time," Grams called after her.

"I will." This was so much better than sitting in her room or surfing the Internet for hours. And television in the summer was just plain bad.

Andrew leaned over and opened the passenger door for her. "Hi," he said, again without a lot of enthusiasm.

"Hi! Thanks for including me."

Courtney was already in the front seat before she realized someone else was in the car. "Hi," she said, twisting around as she grabbed the seat belt.

"That's Annie, my sister. She'll be a junior this year. Annie, Courtney."

Courtney's automatic smile faded as she recognized Andrew's sister. Annie was the girl from the swim team who'd been staring at Courtney and whispering with her friend. All she could do was hope that Annie didn't recognize her with her clothes on. Apparently she didn't, because she made no reference to that day at the pool.

"Andrew and Mom forced me into going to this game with him," the girl muttered.

That was in case Courtney assumed Annie had joined them for the fun of it, she suspected.

"How long have you been in Seattle?" Andrew asked after casting his sister a hard look.

"A couple of weeks. I'm living with my grandmother." Courtney talked about her dad's work situation for a few minutes, and the importance of this Brazilian bridge. She said her brother was in graduate school and her sister in college and working in Alaska for the summer. She told them that she'd hated to leave Chicago and her friends. She was sure she'd given them more information than they wanted, but it was just so good to be with her own kind.

"Are your parents divorced?" Annie asked from the backseat.

Courtney went still. "My mom died in a car accident four years ago."

"Bummer," Andrew said sympathetically.

"Yeah." All of a sudden, she didn't have anything more to say and Andrew and Annie didn't, either. The silence in the car seemed to vibrate.

"I wish Dad had died." Annie spoke in a low voice.

"Don't say that," Andrew barked.

"I mean it!" Her anger was explosive.

"Our parents were recently divorced, but I suppose Mom mentioned that," Andrew said by way of explanation.

"Just in the first class." The other thing Courtney knew was that Bethanne needed to find a job.

"Our father's a jerk!" Annie said in a near-shout.

"My sister didn't take it well," Andrew added under his breath.

"I can hear you," Annie snorted from the backseat.

They parked on a side street and climbed out of the car. Annie stared at her and Courtney held her breath, praying the other girl had forgotten where she'd seen her. No such luck.

"I know you," Annie said, eyeing her.

Courtney's heart fell. "Maybe you saw me when your mother came to knitting class," she suggested hopefully, but a sinking feeling in the pit of her stomach refused to go away.

"I know," Annie said triumphantly. "You were at the swimming pool, weren't you? The early-morning session with all the old ladies." Then she leaned close and said in a loud stage whisper, "You don't need to worry about running into me again. I quit the team last week. Mom doesn't know yet and Andrew won't tell her because we have a deal."

Andrew's gaze narrowed on his sister.

"He wanted to be sure I came along when he took you to the game," Annie gleefully reported. "He was afraid his girlfriend would find out."

"Shut up, would you," Andrew snapped at Annie. He threw Courtney an apologetic glance.

"It's not a problem," she assured him, and it wasn't.

CHAPTER

"There's magic in pulling loops through loops, whether between the limbs of a knitted tree house, or shaped to fit the geography of a foot."
  —Cat Bordhi, author of *Socks Soar on Two Circular Needles, A Treasury of Magical Knitting & Second Treasury of Magical Knitting.*
                              www.catbordhi.com

LYDIA HOFFMAN

I could hardly wait for Brad to make his neighborhood deliveries and come to the store. I've read my share of romance novels, so I can say with authority that if ever there was a romantic hero, it's Brad. Because I've lived with cancer from the time I was sixteen, I've been absorbed by threats and fears. But despite my terrible scare last year, my life had never been better and for someone like me that's a little frightening—as though feeling confident and happy is testing fate, somehow.

I think I mentioned that Dr. Wilson found something on a routine checkup and I was convinced the cancer was back. My attitude was fatalistic. It was during this time that I broke up with Brad. Without giving him a reason, I shoved him out of my life with the flimsiest of excuses. He didn't walk away easily. I loved how he fought for me, how he stood by me until I made it too painful for him to stay. Then, naturally, I learned I was fine, but at that point, I couldn't blame Brad for not wanting anything more to do with me. Thankfully he was willing to listen when I came to my senses. Once again, I had Margaret to thank; without her encouragement I don't know what would've happened. That was all in the past now, and I felt so grateful to have Brad in my life.

On the phone the night before, he and I had talked about our Fourth of July plans. He wanted to wait until he saw me before we confirmed the barbecue at Margaret and Matt's. I always get as excited as a kid about this holiday. Mostly I was looking forward to being with Brad and Cody—and away from work, because I could use the break.

The shop had been so busy lately, which was good but physically draining. I was on my feet a solid eight hours every day. Margaret did as much as she could, but she was preoccupied with the situation at home and hadn't been as much help. She tried, though, and I was doing my best to be supportive and understanding.

My Friday knitting sessions were consistently productive; Jacqueline, in particular, came every week and spent hours knitting squares for Warm Up America. Granted, she had the most free time, since Alix was working and Carol was staying home with little Cameron. Still, Jacqueline's generosity with her time and money impressed me.

Then there was my sock class. The women were an interesting mix and I was getting to know them. They were loosening up a bit, and that was a good sign. I love the way knitting brings people together. As diverse as these women seemed to be, in personality, in background and in age, they were beginning to enjoy each other's company. The class got off to a difficult start because Elise was so short-tempered that first day, but her apology went a long way toward smoothing things over and I was grateful. The tone of the class was set by Elise, I noticed. She's a natural leader, and while I wish I could've been the one dictating mood, I wasn't.

Just after ten, I saw Brad's truck in front of the shop. I waited for him to stroll through the door and address me as "Beautiful." It's part one of our private ritual—which then moves into my office for part two, a little kissing and caressing. I preferred to do that away from Margaret's interested eye.

Not that it mattered. She was late—again. It had become almost normal for her to show up thirty minutes after I opened for the day. I didn't want to nag her but I found it irritating that she'd grown so slack about her responsibilities. Eventually I'd need to speak to her about it, but now wasn't the time.

The bell over the door chimed and I relaxed. Everything was better when I could spend a few minutes alone with Brad.

"Hi," he said, wheeling the boxes of new yarn toward me.

"Hey, what happened to 'Morning, Beautiful'?" I teased. "Did I sprout big ears overnight or something?"

"Or something," he murmured.

"Brad? Is everything all right?" He wasn't his usual cheerful self, and that had me worried. I could see everything wasn't all right; I didn't really need to ask. The way he refused to look at me was answer enough.

"Everything's fine—I think." But he hesitated.

"Is it Cody?" I asked, immediately concerned.

"No, no, Cody's fine."

I love Brad's son. Every now and then, Cody would slip and call me Mom, and I loved the sound of it. If things went as I hoped, I'd soon be his stepmother.

"Tell me what's wrong," I insisted.

"It'd be best if we talked later," he said.

"About what?" I wasn't going to let him walk out the door without explaining.

Brad heaved a sigh and seemed to wish he was anyplace in the world but my yarn store. We'd been involved with each other for a year, and in all that time I'd never seen him like this.

"Forget this later business. Just tell me," I said again.

"I can't be with you on the Fourth," he blurted out.

My disappointment was sharp, but I tried to hide it. "Oh. Any particular reason?"

He seemed to pretend he hadn't heard me and unloaded the dolly, stacking the boxes next to the cash register. Out of habit I signed my name on his automated clipboard.

"Brad," I said urgently. "Whatever it is can't be *that* bad."

He straightened, and I don't think I've ever seen him more serious or less sure of himself. "You'd better sit down."

"No." I adamantly refused. "I'll stand. Just say what you have to say." I could feel a numbing sensation starting in my feet and working its way up my ankles and calves. I think it was then that I knew. I could almost predict what was coming. I've had this kind of conversation twice before; both times, the men who'd claimed to love me decided it was over. Back then, I didn't blame either of them. Loving me was a bad bet, since my prognosis wasn't all that good. Twice, I'd faced the possibility of death, and I couldn't expect them to face it with me. But now...

Brad rubbed his hand down his thigh and swallowed hard. "I can't be with you on the Fourth because Cody and I will be with Janice."

I barely had a chance to digest this before he muttered, "Janice phoned a couple of days ago and asked if we could talk."

I knew Brad had worked hard to maintain a good relationship with his ex-wife. The breakup of their marriage had been her idea, and she'd been perfectly content to let Brad retain custody of their son.

"So you and Janice talked?" I asked when he wasn't forthcoming with details. "Apparently she had a great deal to say." From the tightness around his eyes and mouth, this appeared to be an understatement.

Brad's shoulders rose in a deep sigh. "She's done a lot of thinking in the last few months and realizes she made a mistake when she left Cody and me."

"A little late for that, isn't it?"

Brad didn't answer right away "She wants another chance."

I laughed, hardly able to believe Brad would seriously consider taking back his ex. "I'd say that's mighty convenient, wouldn't you?" I recognized instantly what was happening, even if Brad didn't.

"What do you mean?" he asked, his gaze flying to mine.

"Did you happen to mention that you've asked me to marry you?" I couldn't feel anything other than cynical about this. Of course Janice wanted him back! She was about to lose him for good.

Brad shook his head, but my guess was that Cody had told his mother about our plans to be married. "She knows," I told him, "and she doesn't like it. She's toying with you. Now that we're talking marriage, she can't stand the thought of you and Cody with anyone else." Even if Janice didn't want to be married to Brad, she didn't want me or any other woman to have him, either.

Brad motioned helplessly with his hands. "She seemed sincere and genuinely regretful. If it was an act, then she should get an Oscar nomination."

Naturally Brad wanted to believe that; his ego required it. Any man's would. "Well," I said, confused about what this meant for Brad and me. He didn't seem to know himself. "Are you saying you don't love me and that you were just killing time until Janice came to her senses?"

"Of course not!" he asserted.

"*Do* you love her?" I asked.

"No," was his immediate reply, followed by a brief pause. "I loved Janice when we were married and I still loved her when she walked out on me. But I don't anymore—my feelings for her are gone. The truth is, she's Cody's mother and my son needs her."

"What exactly does that mean for us?"

He shoved his hands in his pants pockets. "I don't know."

"It looks like you're about to retract the proposal," I said, striving for a bit of humor, "and if that's the case, you'll have one hell of a fight on your hands, fellow."

He almost smiled. "I'm not, but I'm going to ask you to do something I have no right to ask."

I could predict what that would be. "You want me to voluntarily step aside and give Janice an opportunity to lure you and Cody back? Sorry, Brad, I can't do that. You either love me or you love her."

"I don't love her." His eyes pleaded for understanding. "It's more complicated than that."

"No, it's not," I argued. "Are you going to be at her beck and call for the rest of your life?"

"No! Anyway this isn't about me, it's about my son."

"It's too late for Janice," I said. Surely he could see my position. Surely he knew he was ripping my heart out.

He didn't answer for a long, long time. "I owe this to Cody. He loves his mother and wants us to be a family again." Brad closed his eyes, as if he couldn't bear to see the pain he was inflicting on me. "I'm so sorry, Lydia. I'd give anything not to hurt you."

"But I love Cody, too!" I cried. The numbness had attacked my entire body now. I could barely function as I turned away.

"I know you do, and he loves you."

"But I'll never be his mother," I said in such pain I thought

I'd be physically ill. Janice would always be the woman he'd loved first, the woman he loved best. Hard as I tried, I would only be a shadowy imitation. Squaring my shoulders, I turned back. Brad hadn't moved. "I…I guess you're glad I delayed our wedding plans, aren't you?"

"No," he breathed. "Lydia, please, try to understand. I don't want this—I didn't ask for this."

We stood there, he and I, and the room seemed to grow smaller and smaller around us.

Pride demanded that I do my best to put a good face on this, although it took every ounce of resolve I possessed. "Seeing that you've made your choice, all I can do is wish you, Janice and Cody a good life."

He didn't respond.

"I can't play this game, Brad. I won't play it."

"This isn't a game."

"But it can be. It will be. After a while, Janice will realize she's made yet another mistake and she'll want her independence once again. Only I won't be here."

"What are you saying? All I'm asking—"

"For whatever reason, you want to give Janice another chance," I broke in. "For Cody's sake or your own, I'm not sure. That's your decision, but I can't let you in and out of my life on her whim."

"I don't know what's right anymore," he shouted.

"I don't, either," I told him. "But apparently I'm second-best now." It was difficult to maintain my composure. "Does she want to move back in with you? Is that it?"

"No." Brad shook his head. "She'll keep her place and I'll keep mine. We haven't made any other decisions. I couldn't do that until I talked to you."

This was supposed to cheer me up? If so, it hadn't worked. Brad was obviously deluded about his ex-wife's motivations. I knew Janice loved Cody. We'd talked several times, Janice and I, over the past months, and she'd made it perfectly clear that despite her maternal connection with Cody, she didn't want the demands of a husband and family. I was completely dumbfounded by this sudden change of heart.

"I love you," I said, and my voice trembled so badly it was hard to speak, "but I can't and won't play tug-of-war with Janice over you and Cody. You can't ask me to share your life one minute, and then the next want me to step aside while you test the waters with your ex. I don't know what you expect me to say."

He didn't respond but I could see that his teeth were clenched, his jaw rigid. "I'll do what I can to switch routes so we won't have to see each other."

"Thank you." I was surprised by how calm I sounded, because on the inside I was crumbling.

"I'm sorry, Lydia."

I looked away, unwilling to let him witness the pain I was in.

The man I loved turned and walked out of my life. The instant the door closed, I fell into a chair and covered my face with both hands. I took deep, shuddering breaths as I struggled to make sense of what had just happened. Moments earlier, I'd been anticipating our Fourth of July barbecue with Cody.... My heart froze as I realized anew that not only was I losing Brad, I was losing Cody. Sweet Cody, who'd taught me so much about love and what it meant to be a mom.

The bell jingled with irritating gaiety. I dropped my hands and plastered a smile on my face, which became a frown when I saw it was Margaret. I said the first thing that came to mind. "You're late."

"I know," she said, without explanation.

"If you're going to work for me, then I'd appreciate if you could make an effort to be here on time," I snapped. "Just because I'm your sister doesn't mean you can show up for work whenever you like."

Margaret's jaw sagged at the unexpectedness of my attack. "Okay, message received."

I stood and retreated to the back room but the trembling in my hands refused to stop. I had to pull myself together, or I'd be an emotional wreck. Unfortunately it was probably too late.

"Did you get out of bed on the wrong side this morning?" Margaret asked, following me.

I attempted to pour a cup of coffee and couldn't. Setting the pot back on the burner, I turned to face my sister, certain I'd gone completely ashen.

"Lydia," she whispered, looking shaken when she saw me. "What happened?"

I opened my mouth to speak but the words wouldn't come. Instead, a low moan escaped and then my body was racked by gut-wrenching sobs. So much for regaining my composure.

Margaret's arms were around me in a flash, and it was a good thing because I was on the verge of collapse.

"Lydia, Lydia, what happened?" She paused, staring at me. "Is it Brad? I saw him outside and he didn't say a word to me."

I couldn't make myself speak. It felt as if this was the end of the world—my world, anyway. I'd been so happy, so excited. For the first time since I was a teenager, I felt truly alive and *normal.* I'd found love—only to discover how fleeting it can be.

"I...need to go upstairs," I whispered after I'd pulled myself together enough to speak. "Can you handle the store for a while?"

"Of course."

"Thank you." I retrieved Whiskers from the front window and by chance looked out to see Brad sitting inside his truck. He had doubled over, his forehead pressed against the upper curve of the steering wheel.

Margaret came to stand behind me. She placed her hand on my shoulder and then glanced out the window.

"You and Brad?" she asked gently.

I nodded. "He's going back to his ex-wife."

Margaret turned me in her arms, and hugged me close and hard. "I'm so sorry," she whispered and I'm sure she was but not nearly as sorry as me.

15

CHAPTER

ELISE BEAUMONT

Elise wasn't in the best of moods when she returned from her knitting class. Her nonexistent class. She'd arrived at A Good Yarn to find that Lydia had fallen ill and the class had been cancelled. Margaret had tried to be helpful, but apparently she wasn't much of a knitter and had never made socks. She did say Lydia would extend the class by one week, which was only fair. Elise, however, had made a considerable effort to get to the yarn store on time and was sorely disappointed.

By way of apology Margaret had offered Elise, Bethanne and Courtney a thirty percent discount on anything they wanted to buy that day. Elise wasn't buying anything. She didn't need yarn, she needed help with the socks and was annoyed that she'd have to wait until the following week to continue.

"You're home early," Aurora commented when Elise walked into the house. Her dour look must have conveyed her mood because her daughter frowned. "What happened, did the class get cancelled?"

"Yes, and I wanted to learn how to turn the heel." She

hadn't mentioned that the socks were a gift for David. She wished now that she'd lingered downtown and perhaps visited a friend or gone to the library. Instead, she'd rushed back to the house as if she had nothing better to do.

That sudden desire to return home worried Elise; she was afraid she was succumbing to Maverick's effect on her. She did everything she could to maintain the distance between them, but it wasn't easy. After all, they slept across the hall from each other and shared one if not two meals a day.

Maverick didn't lose an opportunity to sweet-talk her. Oh, Elise recognized it for what it was. This was simply a form of entertainment to him. She was a challenge, and he was determined to win her over, just to prove he could do it. He might view himself as an irresistible force, but Elise was equally determined to remain an immovable object. She absolutely would not fall under his spell—unlike her daughter and everyone else in the household.

"I'm glad you're here," Aurora said under her breath. "Dad volunteered to watch the boys for me while I run some errands, but I'm afraid they might be too much for him."

"You want me to help?"

Aurora's eyes softened with gratitude. "If you would, Mom, that'd be great."

Elise longed to refuse, but didn't feel she could. Maverick would surely welcome this as another chance to exercise his considerable charm. That man would try to talk his way into heaven, and was probably counting on doing exactly that.

"I'll let Dad know you're here," Aurora said, hugging Elise. "Thanks, Mom."

Elise went to her room, but kept the door open, which she often used to do before Maverick's visit. Heaven only knew how long he intended to stay. He'd said two weeks; he'd been here one week already and hadn't given any indication that he was ready to head out. Each day was agony. She wanted him gone so she could relax and not have to stay constantly on guard.

Sorting through her dirty clothes, Elise carried her whites to the laundry room off the kitchen. She loaded the washing machine and waited until she heard the water running before she left.

As she walked into the living room, she saw Maverick standing there, a boy under each arm. Luke and John squealed with delight and he growled playfully, but stopped abruptly when he saw her. "The boys want me to take them to the park."

"Then I think you should," she said formally.

"I will if you come along."

An automatic protest rose. But before she could utter a word, Luke and John begged her to accompany them. She felt she had no choice, particularly since she'd promised Aurora she'd help out with the kids. "All right, I'll grab my sweater."

"It's not cold," Luke told her.

Today was unseasonably cold for the end of June, but perhaps to a child who raced and played it was pleasant enough. Elise, however, required a sweater.

Maverick and the children were waiting out front for her. Elise called Aurora, who had a cell phone, and explained that they were all walking to the park, which was two blocks away.

The park was little more than a playground with a few pieces of equipment, an abundance of dwarf cherry trees, several well-maintained flower beds and a few benches. The boys loved the swing set and the slides. As soon as they got close, Luke and John tore off across the freshly mowed lawn toward the play equipment.

Maverick followed Elise to a nearby bench. She planned to sit and wait quietly until the boys wore themselves out. She didn't care what Maverick did and wanted to groan out loud when he settled down next to her. He watched the kids play, laughing aloud a couple of times and shouting encouragement. She had to acknowledge that he was an excellent grand-father. Although he'd had very little experience with chil-dren—as far as she knew—he seemed to have a natural affinity for them. Women too, she reminded herself.

"Don't you envy all that energy?" he asked casually.

"Oh, yes." She would answer his questions but had no in-tention of starting up a conversation.

Maverick didn't say anything for a minute or so, which for him must be some kind of record. That man could talk more than anyone she'd ever known.

When he finally did speak, she wished he hadn't. "I was surprised to find you living with Aurora."

She frowned and gathered the sweater more tightly around her. He knew before he'd arrived that she was living with their daughter and her family. "What you really mean is that you're wondering why an independent woman like me is pinching my pennies." She hadn't heard from the attorney in a couple of weeks now and was beginning to fear she'd never get her money back. Thinking about the situation made her feel angry and ill, so most of the time she tried to put it out of her mind.

"All right," he agreed, "I am wondering. What happened?"

"I…I'm in the middle of a class-action lawsuit with a de-veloper. I bought a piece of land and put money down on a house after touring the model home. Then the development company went belly-up." The bile rose in her throat as she re-layed the details of this disaster. "Trust me, dealing with at-torneys and lawsuits isn't how I thought I'd be spending my retirement."

It was embarrassing to admit how foolish she'd been in not investigating the project thoroughly before she wrote the check. If she had, she would've discovered that the developer was in a financial mess.

"You can't get the money back?" Maverick asked.

"I'm trying, along with the other people he swindled," she snapped, angry that he wouldn't drop the subject. "What I didn't lose on the house, the attorney's fees are eating up. Now, if you don't mind, I'd rather not discuss this further."

"Sorry."

"Me, too."

"Is he wanted by the police?"

She wished he was; then perhaps there'd be some recourse, but there wasn't a damn thing she could do except join the others in a lawsuit. "No. It was incompetence, not outright fraud. In the end, I have no one to blame but myself." Maverick didn't need to tell her she'd been naive and trusting—Elise was well aware of that fact.

"Is there anything I can do?"

His offer touched her. She didn't want his kindness or his understanding, and at the same time she craved both. "I should've brought my knitting," she declared with such urgency that Maverick stood, seemingly ready to retrieve it on her behalf.

"Do you need it?"

She shook her head. "It helps calm my nerves, that's all."

He sat back down. "I'll go get it if you want."

"No, no, it's all right. Just don't be kind to me, Maverick. I don't want you to, so please don't."

A scowl darkened his features, and then he seemed to go from anger to gentleness in one blink of his eyes. When he looked at her again, his expression was tender. "I love you, Elise."

Now she was the one who vaulted to her feet. "Don't you *dare* say that to me! Don't you dare!"

"I mean it."

"Don't, Maverick, please don't. Did you love me when you spent the rent check on a double or nothing bet? Did you love me when there wasn't enough money to buy milk for the baby?"

He went very still, then whispered. "Yes, I did, but sweet-heart, it was a good bet. I couldn't lose. And I didn't."

Elise groaned inwardly. "You say you loved me but you loved gambling more."

"I did." He patted the bench, silently inviting her to sit down.

She waited a moment and then gave in. Maverick Beau-mont had always been her weakness, but she was older and wiser now and not as easily swayed. Or so she told herself.

"Do you still love gambling as much?" she asked, curios-ity forcing her to ask.

He hesitated. "I'm going to tell you something. You might not believe it, but I swear to you it's true. I've given it up. I was good at it, Elise, really good. I made a name for myself but it means nothing to me now. What's important is my fam-ily. I'm through with cards."

She smiled and resisted the urge to remind him how often she'd heard that before. "You're right. I don't believe you."

"That's why I'm in Seattle."

"There are plenty of casinos around here."

"I won't be in any of them. I'm looking for a place to buy close to Aurora so I can spend time with her and my grand-sons. I missed out on so much while my daughter was grow-ing up, and I feel that God's given me a second chance with these boys. I'm different now, Elise. I swear to you I'm a changed man."

"I'm sorry, Maverick. As much as I want to believe you, I can't."

It was as if he hadn't heard her. "I've got my eye on a condo. I put down earnest money, but the unit won't be available until August first. Aurora told me I could stay as long as I needed, and David agreed. Once everything's been worked out with the title company and the place is vacant, I'll move in."

Elise wasn't sure she should let herself trust him. She wanted to believe what he said, but he'd made so many promises before. His intentions always started out good, but after a week or two of staying away from the gaming tables, he'd find a poker game and be willing to wager their food money on a roll of the dice. She'd seen it far too many times.

"Grandma, Grandpa," Luke cried, running toward the park bench at breakneck speed.

John followed a few paces behind. "We're ready to go back to the house."

This was a pleasant surprise. Generally, it took the boys an hour or more to wind down enough to even consider returning home.

"We want to play that game you taught us," Luke said, grabbing hold of Maverick's arm.

Elise's suspicions rose. "What game?"

"It's with cards," Luke explained.

A fierce anger gripped her and her heart began to race.

"Excuse me?" she said to Maverick. "With cards?"

"It's a Texas game," John told her excitedly.

"Texas Hold 'em," Maverick said, and had the decency to glance sheepishly in her direction. "Now, Elise, don't go looking at me like that. It's a harmless game."

She placed both hands on her hips and glared at him. "Do you mean to tell me you're teaching our grandsons how to gamble?"

He didn't deny it.

She should have known...should have known.

16

CHAPTER

COURTNEY PULANSKI

After the evening's inauspicious beginning, the Mariners' game with Andrew and Annie Hamlin had turned out to be fun. Courtney had met five of Andrew's friends, and they'd all seemed friendly. The one person who'd been standoffish and distant, not to mention rude, had been Annie. It was more than obvious that she didn't want to be at the game and had somehow been thwarted by her mother and brother from doing something else. She'd ignored both Andrew and Courtney and had barely spoken a word the entire evening. Which was why Courtney was rather shocked when Annie phoned on Friday afternoon and invited her to a movie that night.

"Yeah, sure I guess," Courtney said. It wasn't like she had any other plans. And a movie was certainly preferable to her other option—playing bingo at the VFW Hall with her grandmother. "What did you want to see?"

Annie seemed unprepared for the question. "I don't really care, do you? I just need to get out for a while."

"No, anything is fine." But a nice romantic comedy would suit her; Courtney was in the mood to laugh.

After some perfunctory chitchat, they arranged a time and place to meet. Precisely at seven, Courtney's grandmother dropped her off at the entrance to Pacific Place, near the Pottery Barn, on her way to bingo, and Courtney waited outside until Annie arrived. Bethanne waved at Courtney as Annie jumped out of the car and slammed the passenger door.

The smile on Annie's face faded as soon as her mother's car was out of sight. "You can split now if you want."

"Split?"

"I only needed you so Mom would think I was going to the movie."

Courtney didn't know whether to feel hurt or offended; what she didn't feel was surprised. "Where *are* you going?" she asked.

"I'm meeting friends."

The message was clear: Courtney wasn't one of those friends. Fine, but she had no intention of wandering around town all by herself. "Can I come?"

Annie gave her the once-over, then shrugged. "Okay, but not looking like that."

"What's wrong with what I'm wearing?" Courtney asked defensively.

Annie shrugged again. "Nothing, I guess, but you need more makeup."

"Sure, fine." Courtney had plenty in her purse.

"Follow me," Bethanne's daughter said, turning abruptly. She walked into Pacific Place.

Given no choice, Courtney followed her, weaving through the throng of Friday-evening shoppers. They passed a kiosk selling designer cosmetics, which Annie stopped to admire. "You'd look good with this lipstick," she said, twisting open a display tube of bright purple. She checked the price, raised her eyebrows and put it back.

Courtney started to examine several little pots of eye glitter but didn't get a chance to see much. Annie had already walked away. Once again, she had to rush in order to catch up. Pacific Place was bright, noisy, crowded with shoppers jostling packages and bags.

Courtney realized Annie was headed for the ladies' room. Once inside, Annie stepped into a stall while Courtney stood in front of the sink. She set her purse on the counter and pulled out her cosmetics bag. She was stroking on more eye shadow when Annie left the stall in what appeared to be a completely new outfit.

The other girl's blouse had been replaced by a scanty halter top, with her breasts spilling out over the top. The jeans were now a thigh-high, skin-tight denim skirt.

"Shocked?" Annie asked and laughed. "Mom would be, too, if she saw me." Her eyes narrowed as she studied Courtney. "You won't tell her, will you?"

The question was accompanied by a glare that promised to make trouble for her if she refused. "I won't tell."

"Promise?"

Courtney nodded.

Annie's face relaxed in a smile. "Good. Here's a gift for you." She tossed Courtney the tube of purple lipstick she'd been looking at only moments earlier.

Courtney caught it just before it hit the floor. She was stunned; she could've sworn she'd seen Annie return it.

"It's a skill I have," Annie explained.

Courtney hoped she wasn't around when this little kleptomaniac got arrested. She couldn't, wouldn't, keep the lipstick herself. After her mother died, she'd been shoplifting at an expensive clothing store. Security had called the police and, worse, her father. Nothing was worth risking that humiliation again. Or the guilt… She'd never forget the sorrow and disappointment on her father's face.

When Annie wasn't looking, Courtney threw the tube in the garbage.

Staring into a mirror, Annie teased her hair, reapplied her makeup with an expert hand and moved toward the door. She sighed when Courtney didn't immediately follow her. "Are you coming or not?"

Hurriedly, Courtney stuffed her cosmetics bag inside her purse and started after the other girl, wondering where Annie was going now. It didn't matter. Courtney decided she had to go with her. She didn't know what Annie was up to but felt responsible. Maybe because of Bethanne; she wasn't sure. Or maybe it was simply because she recognized the signs—an unhappy, self-destructive girl intent on finding trouble.

They left Pacific Place and walked a few blocks north. Annie chatted along the way, talking about music and school, and she seemed almost grateful for the company. When the Space Needle came into view, Courtney realized they were close to the Seattle Center.

Several kids had already assembled in a parking lot not far from the Center. A tall thin boy with long, greasy hair climbed out of his car, a beat-up old hatchback, when Annie approached.

"Who's she?" he asked, gesturing toward Courtney, whom he eyed suspiciously.

"That's Courtney," Annie said. "She's cool."

"Hi." Courtney raised her hand.

"I'm Chris," he said as he grabbed Annie around the waist and pulled her against him.

This guy gave Courtney the creeps, but he and Annie obviously had some kind of relationship.

"You got the stuff?" Annie asked.

He nodded.

"Then what are we waiting for?" she said with a saucy laugh.

From the way the two of them acted, whispering and laughing together, Courtney assumed they were about to take off without her. They were both inside the vehicle when Chris leaned over the backseat and opened the rear passenger door.

"Get in," he said. "If Annie says you're cool, you're cool."

Courtney reluctantly clambered into the backseat; the moment she'd gotten into the vehicle, Chris roared out of the parking lot. "Where are we going?" she asked, searching for a seat belt. There didn't seem to be one.

"It's better if you don't know," Annie told her.

They drove for a while, taking various back streets, and went up and down several others. Although she tried to keep track, Courtney got too confused. She did figure out that they must be somewhere near the waterfront because she saw warehouses and heard a blast from an incoming ferry. By now it was after eight.

Chris parked and Annie slid out of the front seat. "Come on," she shouted to Courtney.

"Where are we?" she asked.

"A rave."

"What?"

"You don't know what a rave is?" Annie sounded incredulous.

"Sure I do," Courtney said, but she'd never been to one. They were illegal in Chicago and probably Seattle, too.

"You ever done ecstasy?" Chris asked, looping his arm around Annie's neck.

Courtney stood back and shook her head.

"Don't worry about it," Annie assured her. "I'll get you some."

"No, thanks… I, uh, think I'll just watch the first time."

Annie glanced at Chris, who shrugged. "No problem."

The warehouse was dark and the music so loud it was actually painful. After a few minutes, Courtney's eyes adjusted and she strained to see what was happening around her. Couples were dancing, some frenetically. Other people were on the side, guzzling drinks—bottles of water, it looked like, and beer. They seemed oblivious to what was going on around them. A fog of smoke hung over the room, and Courtney recognized the pungent scent of marijuana.

Almost immediately Annie and Chris were on the dance floor. Courtney kept an eye on her. She knew Annie was angry and probably depressed; she'd seen it the night of the base-ball game. She'd gone through a difficult time herself after her mother died. Her grades fell and she'd started hanging around with the wrong crowd, getting into minor kinds of trouble. Only she'd been younger, so boys hadn't been as much of an issue. And she'd smartened up before things could escalate—to raves and drugs. Still, she'd done some pretty stupid stuff that she regretted now and she didn't want Annie to go through what she had.

Moving as far back as she could, while still watching Annie, Courtney nearly stumbled over a man squatting in the corner. Her eyes widened as she saw him insert a needle into his arm. After injecting the drug—heroin? She didn't know—he leaned his head back, then slumped to the ground.

Annie staggered off the floor. "Dance!" she demanded of Courtney. "Don't be such a drag."

"Okay." Courtney moved closer to the dancers and lifted her arms up and down like a monkey. She felt stupid, awkward and out of place. Julianna would have her head on a platter if she ever learned about this. Forget her dad; Courtney's big sis-ter would be furious. But Courtney was stuck now and had no idea where she was or how she'd ever find her way home.

Annie was acting weird, weirder than before. She and Chris were deeply absorbed in each other. The music was loud and the entire place seemed to reverberate with it. Despite the darkened room, Courtney saw Annie's purse slip from her shoulder to the floor and ran over to grab it. Neither Annie nor Chris appeared to notice.

The more she watched the other girl, the more concerned she became. Annie was high. Out of control. She was fling-ing herself around the dance floor, clutching at Chris, sweat-ing profusely. Nearly desperate, Courtney dug around in

Annie's large purse, past the discarded clothes, until she found a cell phone. Annie needed help. She might not appreciate the interference, but Courtney felt she had to do something and fast. Scrolling down the address book, she paused at the second name. She had to phone either Bethanne or Andrew. Annie was more likely to forgive her for contacting her brother. She hit the key and pressed the phone to her ear, struggling to hear above the din of the music.

It rang four times before Andrew answered. "What?" he demanded irritably.

"Andrew, it's Courtney."

"Why are you calling me from my sister's cell?"

"Annie's in trouble and I don't know what to do." She didn't want to overstate the problem, nor did she feel she should downplay it.

"Where are you?"

"I don't know," she shouted, struggling to be heard. "We're somewhere on the waterfront, in a warehouse. It's a rave. Oh, no!"

"What?"

Courtney hurried back to the dance door. "Annie's topless," she said in horror. "She's doing drugs. Ecstasy, I think." She walked toward the doors, where it was marginally quieter.

"Is she with Chris?"

"Yes." Courtney had left the building now and was surprised to see that it was completely dark out.

Andrew swore. "I think I know where you are. I'll be there as soon as I can."

Relief washed over her.

"Stay with Annie," he instructed her.

"I will."

"And Courtney, listen." He hesitated. "Thanks." He clicked off, abruptly ending the conversation.

Courtney ran back inside and frantically searched the room until she found Annie. She had her legs wrapped around a man, her head thrown back and her arms flaying about to some earsplitting tempo. Chris was with another girl, a spike-haired brunette, and although Courtney couldn't be sure, it looked as if they were in the middle of sex. Courtney turned away, unwilling to watch. She alternated between rushing outside to flag down Andrew and checking on Annie. An eternity passed before she saw Andrew pull up outside the warehouse in Bethanne's car.

"Where is she?" he shouted, running toward Courtney. He carried a plaid blanket he'd obviously brought with him.

"Inside. She's with some guy I've never seen before." She didn't want to say it, but she was terrified of what Andrew would find when he located his sister. In all likelihood, Annie would never forgive her. Still, Courtney was convinced that Annie didn't know what she was doing, or with whom.

"Wait here," he told her, his eyes hard.

Although it was difficult, she did what he asked. She feared Andrew might need help, that Annie would fight him and others might get involved. She conjured up such frightening scenarios that by the time he appeared, carrying his sister, Courtney was ready to phone the police.

"Is she all right?" Courtney asked anxiously. Annie seemed half-unconscious, her head lolling back. She was wrapped in the blanket, and Courtney admired Andrew's thoughtfulness in bringing it.

His mouth in a tight line, Andrew nodded. "Help me get her in the car," he ordered.

Working together, they got Annie into the backseat. Courtney reached into Annie's purse, producing the blouse she'd worn earlier in the evening, and managed to push Annie's arms through the sleeves. The girl offered no help and stared up at them, dazed and senseless. Once Courtney had buttoned it, Annie fell across the backseat. Andrew lifted his sister's legs so that she was completely prone and draped her with the blanket.

"Did you have fun?" She raised her head enough to ask Courtney in a slurred voice.

"Oh, yeah," Courtney muttered, and climbed into the front seat next to Andrew.

"Lie down and shut up," Andrew told his sister.

She started to groan when they took off. Courtney thought she heard sirens in the distance; whether they had anything to do with the rave or not, she didn't know.

"What's wrong?" Courtney asked. She didn't need to clarify her question. Andrew knew what she meant.

"Annie and my dad were close," he said from between gritted teeth. "My sister hasn't adjusted to the divorce, as you could no doubt tell on Monday night. It's like she's trying to make my parents regret what they did. The thing she doesn't understand is how badly she's hurting herself."

"I don't want her to get angry with me."

"She won't," Andrew promised.

"How can you be so sure?" Courtney believed she understood his sister far better than Andrew would ever know. Annie felt as if she'd lost her father; Courtney knew what it was like to lose a parent. Her own life had changed irrevocably the minute her mother died. Nothing was or would ever be the same again. She wouldn't walk into the house after school and hear her mother's voice. There wouldn't be any more of the special traditions Courtney treasured. The world had become a smaller place, a crueler place, without her mother. She didn't criticize Annie for using drugs. Courtney had chosen another addiction to dull her pain—food. It'd taken her four years to find the resolve to break free of this self-imposed punishment.

Courtney turned toward him. "I want to talk to Annie later, all right?" she said.

Andrew looked away from the road long enough to make eye contact with her. "She needs professional help."

"I know." Courtney just hoped Annie got that help before it was too late.

CHAPTER 17

"Most of us knit these garments for someone special. In doing so, we let our love and loving thoughts for one another grow, a single stitch at a time."
—Eugene Bourgeois, The Philosopher's Wool Co., Inverhuron, Ontario. www.philosopherswool.com

LYDIA HOFFMAN

Somehow I made it through the Fourth of July, thanks to my family. Matt and Margaret were so good to me, and Mom only asked about Brad once. I don't know what Margaret said, but his name was conspicuously absent from our conversations for the rest of the day.

Mom seemed especially quiet and even a bit confused. I spent as much time with her as I could, talking to her about the garden, the yarn shop, a TV show we'd both seen. My thoughts were with Brad, though, and with Cody. I experienced my grief as physical pain, as an ache in my chest—I think that's what people mean when they talk about a broken heart. I wanted to scream at the injustice of it: that Janice was with them and I wasn't. I tried hard to remember that Cody needed his mother.

After our barbecued chicken, coleslaw and corn—an all-American feast—I brought out a box of assorted pastries from the French Café. I'd included some cream puffs and napoleons, which were Alix's specialties. I hoped to see her on Friday at the shop. Once we'd finished dessert I took Mom home; she was too tired by then to wait for darkness to fall and the fireworks to begin.

We gathered, Matt, Margaret and I, to watch the fireworks, and as they burst over the Seattle skyline, tears rolled down my cheeks. I'd hardly ever felt more wretched or alone.

I wasn't good company. It'd been almost two weeks, and I knew I could make it if I didn't think about the future, if I coped with one day at a time. If I could get through today, I told myself, I'd find the courage to confront the next day and the next.

It didn't help that Brad continued to work the same route. Tuesday morning he told Margaret he'd requested a transfer but had been denied. I believed him. Last year, when I'd ended our relationship, he'd applied for—and received—a transfer and then later, when things were settled between us, he'd requested his old route back. Now the powers that be were obviously tired of this. So we were stuck seeing each other on a regular basis.

After weeks of depression over Matt's unexpected job loss, Margaret seemed to have cheered up considerably. I didn't know if this was an act for my benefit. In any case, I chose to believe that because Margaret loves me, she was trying to bolster my mood and create a supportive environment. I valued her support and this new tenderness.

I also needed Margaret as a buffer between Brad and me. He'd been in the shop four or five times since our last conversation and, thankfully, my sister was available to deal with him. This saved me, because I wasn't ready to pretend our relationship was merely casual. I couldn't speak to him without letting my emotions show and that would've humiliated me all the more.

Besides Margaret, one of my few comforts during this bleak time was the charity knitting group. They came Friday afternoons to work on a number of projects. When I first suggested this idea, my original class decided that they'd knit patches for Warm Up America. The nine-by-seven-inch pieces are crocheted together by Margaret to form blankets. This is her contribution to the effort. The patches make for an easy project, and each requires only a small commitment of time. Jacqueline, Carol and Alix lead busy lives, so this worked well for them. They also liked the idea of being involved in the same projects.

Elise wanted to come, but hadn't yet. I'd given her some donated yarn and she was knitting a blanket for the Linus Project at home. Alix had knit a couple of blankets for them, too, between classes at the Seattle Cooking Academy and her parttime job at the French Café.

Margaret was in the store when all three of the women from my original class showed up on Friday afternoon. She'd become as fond of them as I had. The first to arrive was Jacqueline.

"I'm back," she announced as she swept into the shop. Jacqueline was always one to make an entrance. Margaret and I have come to love the way she broadcasts her arrival, although at one time it annoyed me. As always, Jacqueline looked like the society matron she is, every hair in place. She once told me never to discount the effectiveness of a good hair spray. I would've laughed if she hadn't been serious.

I've given up trying to keep track of all the traveling Jacqueline and Reece do. In the past year, they'd been on a cruise in the Greek islands, a walking tour of England's Lake District and most recently they went salmon fishing in Alaska.

That, according to Jacqueline, was a longtime dream of her husband's. To my utter amazement, she loved it and even brought me some smoked salmon.

"How are you?" Jacqueline asked, gazing into my eyes. She didn't wait for a response before pulling me into a tight hug.

"I'm okay," I lied.

She took her place at the table and brought out her knitting. Her patch was knit in super-wash, hand-dyed wool at fourteen dollars a skein, but that was Jacqueline. Price was rarely a consideration. And in her generosity, she always bought her own yarn for the charity projects, rather than accepting donated leftovers from me.

"I see I'm the first one here," she said, looking around. This was unusual in itself. "Well, I've got great news and I'll tell you first." She smiled widely. "Tammy Lee's pregnant again! Reece and I are beside ourselves."

I remember how she'd once objected strenuously to her southern daughter-in-law and called her "white trash" and a "breeder." My friend had experienced a change of heart, largely due to Tammy Lee's patience and her loving personality—as Jacqueline's the first to admit. Jacqueline adores little Amelia and I was sure she'd feel exactly the same about this new baby.

"It's a girl and she's due in February around Valentine's Day." Her eyes lit up. "Isn't that *perfect?*" She smiled again. "I want to look through your baby patterns later. There's knitting to be done!"

As we laughed, the door opened and Carol came in. I was mildly surprised to find she was by herself.

"Where's Cameron?" I asked. The baby had been a miracle, one that had happened last year. Carol and Doug had tried desperately for a baby through in vitro fertilization. They had their son now, but he'd been adopted—truly a child of their hearts. That was thanks to Alix, whose roommate had been secretly and unhappily pregnant.

"Doug has the day off, so Cam's with his daddy," Carol explained as she sat down next to Jacqueline. They exchanged greetings and she took out her knitting. It was wonderful to see her. With a toddler underfoot she couldn't participate every week. If she did stop by, it was during Cameron's naptime. She'd park the stroller by the table and stay only until her son woke up. Her child was the delight of her life; he brought her the greatest happiness imaginable. She'd told me that she and Doug were closer than ever, both of them completely dedicated to Cameron. I wanted to tell her to hold on to this joy, to cling to it, because—as I'd learned two weeks ago—happiness can disappear all too fast.

Carol's knitting needles clicked rapidly as she worked on her section of the blanket. She was a fearless knitter who loved a challenge. I'd showed her the two-needle technique for socks and she'd basically taught herself the rest. "I heard from my brother the other day," she said, frowning. "He's remarried."

"You mean he didn't invite you to the wedding?"

"No. He let us know after the fact."

From the way she said it, I knew Carol was disappointed in him. She'd confided in me earlier about Rick, and I gathered he was a self-indulgent and rather immature man. An airline pilot, he was a little too apt to engage in dalliances with flight attendants and other women he met on his travels. That had, of course, ruined his marriage to a woman Carol liked.

"I hope this marriage lasts longer than his first one," she added. "Doug and I mailed them a gift. We rarely hear from Rick these days." In other words, she wasn't running to the mailbox looking for a thank-you card.

She was about to say more when the door opened again and in walked Alix.

"Whuzzup?" she cried to a chorus of greetings. Alix is…unique. When she first signed up for the class, I was afraid I'd be dealing with a felon. The first thing Alix did was tell me she'd be knitting the baby blanket to satisfy her court-ordered community service hours. Next, she wanted to know if that would count toward anger management. Despite some awkward moments early on, we've all come to treasure her. Time and love have worn away the rough edges of her personality. Last year she started dating Jordan, a youth minister she'd known since grade school. I knew the two of them were getting serious, and it wouldn't surprise me if Alix announced their engagement in the near future.

Alix looked me in the eye. "I know about Brad. I could have him hurt if you want."

I didn't know if she was joking or not, so I laughed, or tried to. I told her the same thing I did Jacqueline. "I'm okay."

"You sure?"

I swallowed hard and nodded.

Alix pulled out a chair and sat down with her needles and yarn. I sat at the end of the table, resuming a ChemoCap I'd begun the week before. Smiling at my friends, I tried to imagine the Warm Up America blanket they'd construct. Jacqueline with her lavender-and-pink super-wash wool patches; Carol's patches in a nice Paton's baby-blue yarn left from a sweater she'd knit Cameron; and Alix's variegated green-and-yellow blend, leftovers one of my other customers had donated.

"I made a genoise this morning," Alix said proudly. "Those are really hard to do—very delicate. It turned out perfectly. And it sold right away."

"That's wonderful," Jacqueline exclaimed. "I want to order one for a business dinner we're having next week."

"For you—it's free. I'll make it at home." Alix continued to live in the housekeeper's quarters at Jacqueline and Reece's place. She'd originally been hired to help with the housework, but with school and her job, it'd become too much for her. Jacqueline had hired someone else who came in during the days to do the housekeeping, but Alix was still staying with the Donovans to watch the house whenever Jacqueline and Reece traveled.

"Just think of it," Alix said, "I get my first real job as a pastry chef, and wouldn't you know, it's in the same spot I worked before. Only this time it's not a video joint, but a classy café."

"And Reece and I didn't have a thing to do with her getting that job," Jacqueline reminded everyone. "Alix was hired for her skills."

"You bet I was. Anyone who tastes my éclairs and cream puffs would know it, too."

"Don't mention those éclairs," Jacqueline pleaded, briefly closing her eyes. "I'm on a new diet and I'm avoiding desserts—except at dinner parties, of course."

"Speaking of diets," I said, changing the subject, "I've got a teenager in my sock class, Courtney, who's knitting in an effort to lose weight." I laughed as I said it. "How it works, she says, is that while she's knitting, she's not in the kitchen hauling food out of the fridge. And she's definitely lost a few pounds."

"Hmm," Jacqueline murmured. "It's worth considering. Keep us posted."

"Courtney's a high-school senior," I said. "Does anyone remember meeting Vera Pulanski? This is her granddaughter."

Jacqueline nodded. "Vera gave me her scarf pattern."

"Courtney's living with her this year."

"How's she doing?" Alix asked. "That's tough, moving around so much. I should know."

"So far, so good," I assured her.

"Did anyone else interesting sign up for your classes?" Carol asked, finishing her row.

I hesitated before mentioning Bethanne. "A divorced woman who hasn't quite found herself." I couldn't help worrying about her. Bethanne had talked about needing a job, but apparently nothing I or any of the other women suggested was suitable. She seemed depressed to me, lacking direction and purpose. All that kept her going was her two teenage children, who'd be out of the house within a few years. Bethanne would be completely alone then.

"There's Elise, too."

"She's the retired librarian?" Carol asked.

"Yes." I put aside the ChemoCap and cast on stitches for a new patch in an acrylic and wool blend, a sample one of the reps had given me. "I thought she was a bit of a prude when we first met, but I've changed my mind. I think she's simply...self-contained. I got the impression she doesn't have many friends."

"Did you tell her about my Birthday Club?" Jacqueline asked. "She's welcome to join."

I should've guessed that my friend, the social butterfly, would be willing to draw Elise into her circle. "I don't think she's part of the country club set," I protested.

"That doesn't matter. It's a good excuse to go out once a month and celebrate. And if nobody in the group has a birthday that month, we choose a celebrity or a famous writer. So in June, we toasted Judy Garland *and* Dorothy Sayers. We have a lot of fun." She giggled like a schoolgirl, silly and joyous. Sometimes it was difficult to remember that this was the same stuffy socialite who'd walked in my door a year ago. I attributed the transformation to the fact that my friend had rediscovered her love for her husband and become close to her daughter-in-law.

"I'll tell Elise," I said, but I'd feel a little uncomfortable doing it. Elise was a difficult woman to read. She was guarded and didn't share much about her life, as if she was afraid to let people know who she was. However, she brightened whenever she mentioned her daughter and grandchildren.

During the last class, she'd been even more withdrawn

than usual. When I tried to get her to enter into the conversation, she'd smiled weakly and apologized for being out of sorts. She'd actually revealed something about herself that day. Her ex-husband was visiting, she told us, and had announced he was moving to the area. Elise didn't appear pleased at the prospect of sharing her family with a man who'd been absent for most of his daughter's life.

The bell chimed and because it was Friday, I half feared it might be Brad. I'd leave Margaret to deal with him; she'd been busy with customers all afternoon. She seemed to sense that I needed this break, this time surrounded by friends. I sighed with relief when I saw Elise. "I was just talking about you," I said and greeted her warmly.

She looked shyly around the table. I introduced her, and Jacqueline was quick to move her knitting bag, clearing a space in the chair next to hers. "Lydia said you recently retired. I'd say it's high time you joined the Birthday Club." She paused. "When *is* your birthday?"

"January." Elise seemed uncertain about Jacqueline's invitation. "At my age, I don't think it's a good idea to make a fuss about getting older."

Jacqueline smiled. "Are you kidding? Every new year is a reason to celebrate. You'll love it, I promise. Our next meeting is Thursday lunch and I'll come and get you. Life is meant to be lived, that's what I say."

"I—I won't know anyone. And...what about the cost? How much is it?"

"You'll know me," Jacqueline insisted. "And your first lunch is my treat, since we missed your real birthday." When Elise continued to object, Jacqueline spoke in a decisive tone the rest of us were familiar with. "You're coming, understand? I won't listen to a single argument."

"I suppose that would be all right," Elise said, but she didn't sound confident that this would be a pleasant experience.

I was smiling, genuinely warmed by my friends. The bell chimed again and when I looked up there was Brad. Just as I'd feared… The happiness drained out of me but I need not have worried.

Margaret's gaze went straight to me from across the room. "I'll take care of this," she muttered.

Alix frowned and leaned forward to whisper, "I can still have him hurt. I know people. You say the word, and it's done."

I still hadn't decided whether or not she was joking, but I couldn't keep my eyes away from Brad. I shook my head. He looked as miserable as I felt. "That won't be necessary," I assured Alix. He was hurting enough already. We both were.

18
CHAPTER

ELISE BEAUMONT

Elise's book club met at two o'clock on the second Monday of every month and she loved it. The group was sponsored by the Seattle Public Library, and Elise had promised herself she'd participate after she retired. She also planned to join Jacqueline's Birthday Club at least once, and was determined to enjoy herself.

The July book discussion revolved around the book *Girl In Hyacinth Blue* by Susan Vreeland. It had been lively, and Elise left the meeting feeling invigorated. The group had brought a variety of perspectives to the novel, including some she hadn't previously considered.

The bus dropped her off a half block from home. The house was quiet when she walked in and she tried to remember what Aurora had said about her plans.

The minute she walked in the door, Luke and John always demanded her attention. The silence this afternoon was disorienting.

"Aurora, I'm back, and it was the best meeting yet," she

called. "I—" She paused in midsentence when Maverick stepped out of the kitchen wearing an apron and wielding a tomato-smeared wooden spoon.

"Aurora and the boys are out for the afternoon," he explained. "Last-minute plans."

"Oh." Her excitement evaporated quickly.

"I'm cooking," he explained, although that was obvious. "Lasagna to be exact—it was always your favorite of my dishes."

Elise imagined he'd dirtied every single pan and bowl. She remembered how he could wreak havoc in an orderly kitchen. "Does Aurora know about this?" she asked sternly. He expected her to comment on the fact that he was supposedly doing this for her benefit, but she wasn't saying a word.

"Aurora suggested it."

Elise wondered about that, but couldn't very well argue with him.

"You will join me for dinner, won't you?" he asked, smiling at her in a way that made refusing him difficult. "It'll probably be just the two of us."

Despite herself, she was tempted, but common sense overruled that brief thought. "Thank you, but no," she returned stiffly. "I had a snack this afternoon at my book club."

"What did you read?" he asked, delaying her in the hallway when he knew very well she wanted to escape.

"A book."

He chuckled as though he found that amusing.

"I'd like to go to my room now, if you'd kindly move aside."

"I'm just putting the lasagna in the oven. Dinner will be ready in an hour."

"When will Aurora and the boys be back?" she asked, instead of arguing.

"She couldn't say for sure. Eight o'clock, she figured. She's meeting her friend—Susan?"

He made it a question, apparently unsure of the name.

"Susan Katz has been Aurora's best friend nearly her entire life." Her voice hummed with indignation. Had Maverick taken more than a casual interest in their daughter, he would've known that. "Susan has two little girls around the same age as Luke and John. Did they go to Lake Washington?" It was a favorite summertime activity for them.

"I think so."

That told Elise her ex-husband was right—her daughter and grandsons wouldn't be home until late. With busy schedules and complicated lives, it was difficult for Aurora and Susan to coordinate time together. They'd probably stop somewhere for dinner on the drive home.

"David's out of town until Wednesday," she murmured.

"I know," he said. "It's just you and me."

"No," she took delight in informing him. "It's just you. I'm not hungry. I intend to spend the rest of the evening in my room. Apparently you weren't listening."

His smile faded. "No." He sounded discouraged. "I guess I wasn't."

Elise almost felt sorry for him. She was relieved when he turned away and went back to the kitchen. Feeling guilty at having dampened his spirits—and feeling angry about feeling guilty—she continued down the long hallway to her sanctuary.

An hour later, Elise sat in front of her television, half watching the evening news. Her fingers moved nimbly as she worked on her charity knitting project. She'd knit fifteen patches for the Warm Up America blanket, plus a blanket for the Linus Project, and kept herself busy with that while she waited for the next sock-knitting class.

Binding off the patch, she was about to reach for the remote control when her stomach growled. Those snacks she'd mentioned—a few carrots and celery sticks from the veggie tray and a small piece of cheese—had long since disappeared. Whether she wanted to admit it or not, she was famished.

As if this message had somehow been telegraphed to Maverick, he chose that precise moment to knock at her bedroom door. Once she'd called out, he opened it.

"I was hoping I could get you to change your mind. It's no fun eating alone."

The scents emerging from the kitchen, fresh basil and oregano blended with the enticing aromas of garlic and tomatoes, were her undoing. "I suppose I could manage to eat a bit." This was fair warning to keep food in her room for future emergencies, she told herself.

"You won't be sorry," Maverick promised gleefully. He led her into the dining room, and it was as if he'd planned this meal just for her. Fresh white daisies adorned the center of the table. There were two place settings, opposite each other, and he'd used Aurora's loveliest china and crystal. He'd already poured the wine. A merlot, she suspected, remembering his preferences. Although it'd been years since they'd dined like this, she remembered his every like and dislike. Elise recalled, too, that Maverick had cooked for her the night he proposed. Not lasagna that time but linguine with a shrimp and crab cream sauce. Oh, this was ridiculous! Why was she still thinking about a meal she'd had decades ago?

Maverick pulled out the chair to seat her. "You were very confident, weren't you?" she said stiffly, looking at her filled wineglass.

"I was more confident about the scent of my cooking."

She didn't want to be with him like this and yet she did— and it was more than the empty sensation in her stomach. Spending this kind of time with him was dangerous. Well, she knew that, but she was here now, and hungry, and she might as well have dinner.

Maverick brought a Caesar salad, redolent with garlic, into

the dining room. When he was seated again, he lifted his wineglass. "I'd like to propose a toast," he said.

"That isn't necessary," she said and heard the tremor in her voice. "This is thoughtful of you, but it's dinner and nothing more. There's no romance between us, and one meal isn't going to resurrect long-dead feelings."

Maverick arched his eyebrows. "Long-dead?"

"We've been divorced more years than I care to think about," she felt obliged to remind him. If he wasn't counting, she was.

"A toast," he continued, ignoring her outburst. "To Elise, the love of my life."

She pushed back the chair, ready to walk away. "Don't," she warned him. Her throat thickened with resentment. How dared he say such a thing to her!

He lowered his wineglass as if nothing was amiss, and reached for his fork. Since—apparently—he intended to behave himself, she reached for her own. Although the lump in her throat made it difficult to chew and swallow, the effort was worth it. Maverick possessed many talents but he excelled in the kitchen. He could have been a noteworthy chef had he followed that path. Instead he'd chased after a pot of gold, collecting nothing except dust and false dreams along the way.

When they'd finished their salad, he removed the plates and served the lasagna. It tasted as heavenly as it smelled, and Elise savored every bite, eating far more than she normally did.

They ate in silence until he finally spoke. "There's something we should discuss."

"I can't imagine what," she replied primly.

To her astonishment, he relaxed in his chair and broke into a smile.

"What's so amusing?" she demanded.

"I used to love it when you got all uppity."

"I beg your pardon?" She already regretted agreeing to dinner. Would she never learn?

"You used to do that," he said, motioning toward her with his hand, "when we were married."

"Do what?"

"You'd get that haughty look on your face—the same look you have right now." He grinned triumphantly. "I loved it. Still do."

She scraped up the last forkful of noodle, sauce and melted cheese, not deigning to respond. In another minute, she'd retreat to her room....

"I used to time myself—see how long it would take me to get you to smile."

"Damn it," she sputtered, outraged by his remark. Everything, *everything,* was a challenge to him. A game.

"Don't you remember," he teased, his eyes sparkling. "I used to wrap my arms around you from behind and kiss you till—"

"You did no such thing." She remembered all too well, but chose to push those memories away. During their marriage, Maverick always got what he wanted—always won his little games—by using her love for him. Taking advantage of it, of her.

"Oh, you remember," he whispered. "You do."

"I've done my best to forget," she said without emotion. "You might not believe this, but living with you had very little to recommend it."

His smile faded and he sobered. "No one is more aware of that than I am."

"Nothing's changed," she said. "You might claim you've given up gambling but you can't do it. The allure is still there."

"Not true."

"Not *true?* You can't stay away from the cards."

"I can play," he said calmly. "I don't need to gamble."

Elise shook her head. "That's like an alcoholic claiming he can go into a tavern and not be tempted." Considering that he was teaching their grandsons poker, he was being more than a little unrealistic about his ability to control his gambling.

"I mean it, Elise. It's over. I refuse to squander the rest of my life on a roll of the dice or the luck of the draw. I want my family and I want you."

Shocked by his words, Elise nearly spewed wine across the tablecloth. With a supreme effort she swallowed. "You're too late," she told him. "Thirty-seven years too late."

"I think," he said as he saluted her with his wineglass, "that I'm just in time."

19

CHAPTER

BETHANNE HAMLIN

Bethanne turned off the vacuum cleaner and listened. Sure enough, the phone was ringing. She debated letting the answering machine pick up, but she'd left job applications at a number of businesses and didn't want to miss a call from a prospective employer.

Hurrying into the kitchen, she drew in a calming breath and grabbed the receiver. "This is Bethanne Hamlin," she said in her most professional voice.

"We need to talk."

Deflated, Bethanne leaned against the kitchen wall. She didn't want to deal with her ex-husband again. Their last meeting, at the café on Blossom Street, had left her reeling with resentment and anger. "Hello, Grant, how unpleasant to hear from you," she murmured sweetly.

"I'm coming over."

She bit back the words to tell him *she* would choose the time and place of their next meeting, but it would do little good. After twenty years of marriage she knew Grant's moods. She could tell from his tone that he was furious and wouldn't be put off.

"Fine," she said curtly.

"I'll be there in ten minutes."

"Fine." The unnamed problem was apparently urgent enough for Grant to take time off in the middle of the day—something that hardly ever happened. She hung up and returned to her vacuuming.

Exactly seven minutes after his call, she heard the knob twist and then a heavy fist pounding against the front door. Grant mistakenly assumed he had the right to walk into her home. Well, she'd fixed that. After the divorce was final, Bethanne had changed the locks, and it gave her a sense of satisfaction to thwart him now.

"Did you think I intended to break in?" he snarled when she unlocked the door and stepped aside to let him into the house.

"I wasn't about to give you the opportunity," she snarled back. She wanted him to know that he was only there now with her express permission.

Grant charged into the kitchen, then whirled around to face her. "Did you put Annie up to this?" he demanded, his eyes spitting fire at her.

"To what?"

"You know what I'm talking about." He glared at her, fists clenched at his sides. "Where is she anyway?"

"If you're referring to our daughter, all I can tell you is that she's out." Bethanne folded her arms over her chest and relaxed, leaning her hip against the kitchen counter. She'd tried to warn him, had done her level best to let him know what she'd discovered. Grant had dismissed her worry, as he so often had in the past. In her view, that meant any mischief Annie had visited on Tiffany was his problem, not hers.

"You knew—and you didn't say a word!"

"What are you talking about? I warned you about the way

she felt—the way she still feels." She sighed with exaggerated patience. "If you recall, I mentioned that I'd read Annie's journal." Bethanne didn't know what her daughter had done on this particular occasion, only that Annie festered with rage.

Grant started to pace. "All you said was that she's angry."

"Correction," she snapped. "That was all you *let* me say. As I remember the conversation, you brushed aside my concern and said Annie would get over it in time." She sighed again. "What did she do?"

"You don't know?"

Bethanne shrugged. "She's hurting and she blames Tiffany. I assume she had some bedwetting information mailed to her." She'd read that in the journal and been privately amused. There'd been plenty of other items Annie had requested in Tiffany's name. Immature and annoying behavior, yes—but what had really shocked Bethanne was the pure hatred her daughter felt for the other woman. Her words were full of spite and anger, to the point that Bethanne knew something had to be done. Annie refused to discuss it, and Grant refused to listen. Bethanne had made an appointment with the therapist she'd seen briefly after Grant's defection; she wanted to talk about the situation, get some advice, maybe arrange for Annie to see her, too.

"Having all that crap sent to the apartment is mail fraud, and it isn't a laughing matter. But that's not the half of it. She's gone way over the line this time."

"How unfortunate you have to deal with more junk mail than usual," Bethanne said sarcastically, knowing it was a childish response. "My sympathies to you both."

Grant scowled at her. "I can't thank you enough for your support," he muttered. "Especially since I've spent the last hour dealing with Tiff who's hysterical because someone poured sugar down her gas tank."

"No," Bethanne gasped.

"One guess who's at the top of the suspect list."

"Oh, no." This was much worse than Bethanne had expected. Grant was probably right, too—it was a step up from requesting nuisance mail, but exactly the type of revenge Annie could wreak.

"That's a serious offense," he said. "We haven't talked to the cops yet, but—"

"Would you really prosecute your own daughter?" Grant had sunk lower than she'd ever thought he would, but she'd never dreamed he'd turn Annie over to the authorities.

"It isn't me she's doing this to, it's Tiff."

Tiff, it was. Poor, poor Tiff. "Then perhaps you should have *Tiff* discuss the matter with Annie and work this out."

"That's not all," he shouted. "Annie's done her best to make Tiffany's life and mine a living hell. You don't even want to know about the horrible garbage she's sent via the Internet. Why can't you control your daughter?"

"Listen. Annie's your daughter, too, and her secure and happy life was uprooted because her father's brains are located below his belt buckle."

"Damn it, Bethanne, I don't have to put up with that kind of verbal abuse from you. We're divorced."

"Fine, then," she said, gesturing at the front door. "Get out of *my* house."

"The only reason you have this house is because I gave it to you."

"*Gave* it to me?" she cried, outraged he'd even suggest such a thing. "Gave it to me mortgaged to the hilt. There's not a penny's equity in this place, thanks to you."

"But who's making the payments?" he challenged. "Don't forget I'm the one signing those alimony checks—which allow *you* to keep this house. And that reminds me, do you have a job yet?" This was asked with such blatant sarcasm, Bethanne cringed.

She closed her eyes and tried to control her anger. She didn't want to argue with Grant. There was no point.

"All right, all right," he said, apparently reaching the same conclusion. "I didn't come here to fight. We need to develop some sort of plan to deal with Annie's problem. This can't go on."

"She isn't angry with *me*. You deal with her." She wasn't being flippant. Annie's pain was caused by her father. Bethanne was making an effort to help, but anything she could do seemed more like damage control. Grant had to take some responsibility here.

Grant splayed his fingers through his hair. "I'm afraid Annie might do something to physically hurt Tiff," he mumbled and shook his head. "I can't believe this is happening."

"You're worried about *Tiffany?*" Bethanne exploded.

"Damn straight I am. Someone who'd deliberately sabotage her car is one step from doing something physically aggressive."

"What about Annie?" Bethanne asked, shocked that he could be so self-absorbed. "Aren't you worried about *her?* Doesn't she deserve any concern?"

"Of course I'm worried, but I can't deal with her. She hates me. At least that's the impression she's given me. If you know something I don't, then I'd appreciate being filled in."

"That's the problem," Bethanne said in a shaky voice. "She desperately loves you and believe it or not, Annie needs her father. It was one thing to divorce me, but you weren't supposed to divorce your children. When was the last time you talked to your daughter? You used to at least call her every week or two. I understand that's stopped. Why? When did you last have a conversation with her—or Andrew, for that matter? Need I remind you these are *your* children, too?"

He looked down at his shoes. "I've been busy and—"

"Busy?" she cried. "Do you honestly expect me to consider that a valid excuse?"

"I don't need you as my conscience. Besides, Annie and Andrew refuse to have anything to do with Tiff. They won't even come to the condo because she might be there."

"Talk to Annie," she advised, setting her pride aside long enough to plead with him. "Call her up and take her to lunch. She needs assurances that you still care about her and that you want to be part of her life. But only if you're sincere. Don't just pay her lip service—that'll do more harm than good."

He nodded like a petulant child. "All right. I will. I'll call her in a couple of days." He hesitated, then gave her a wry smile. "Thanks, Bethanne."

She shrugged. "You're welcome."

"How's Andrew?"

Bethanne resisted the urge to roll her eyes. "Ask him yourself."

Grant cast her a chagrined look. "He wasn't keen to have anything to do with me, with or without Tiff around."

"Show up for a few of his football games in September, and my guess is he'd be willing to remember you're his father again."

Grant seemed to consider that. "Maybe I will."

In other words, if it didn't interfere with his schedule and he had nothing better to do.

She waited, thinking it was time he left, but Grant lingered as if there was something else on his mind. "I understand you and Paul Ormond recently got together," he finally said.

"Who told you that?"

He offered her a half smile. "Word gets around. A guy from the office—you don't know him—saw the two of you at Anthony's the other night. What's that about?"

"How did he know me?" she asked curiously.

"I had your picture on my credenza."

Past tense, she noticed. The irony of the situation didn't escape her. For two years he'd snuck around behind her back, having an affair, and not once had she gotten wind of it. But she had one date in twenty-two years, and someone reported it to Grant.

"Are you and Paul an item?" he asked.

Bethanne stopped herself just in time. It wasn't any of his concern who she saw—or dated. Nor did he need to know that Paul had phoned two or three times since and encouraged her in her job search. They were simply friends, but she'd never had a male friend before.

"That's between Paul and me."

"In other words, I should mind my own business."

"Yes," she said, smiling gleefully. "I think you put it very well a few months ago. I have my own life now, Grant, and it *is* my life."

CHAPTER 20

COURTNEY PULANSKI

Courtney felt wretched. An enraged Annie Hamlin sat in the middle of Courtney's bed. She'd ranted for a good five minutes without taking a breath, still angry almost two weeks after the rave and everything that had happened.

"You had no right to contact Andrew," Annie finished, whispering fiercely, apparently afraid of being overheard.

Courtney didn't bother to tell her not to worry, that her grandmother was half-deaf. "I didn't do it because I *wanted* to, you know."

"Andrew says I should thank you, but you can forget that." She glared at Courtney as if she'd purposely set out to ruin Annie's life.

"Fine. I'll forget it."

"I should've known you'd be a goody-goody type."

"Think what you like, Annie," she said, unwilling to let the other girl attack her. "But maybe it wouldn't do you any harm to hear what I have to say."

"About what?"

Courtney sidestepped the question and got directly to the point. "I know what you're feeling."

She shook her head. "No, you don't. You can't know."

"My mother died and—"

Annie's gaze narrowed. "Am I supposed to feel sorry for you?"

"No. Now shut up and listen! Your father walked out on you and what you feel isn't that different from what I felt when my mom was killed."

"I wish my dad was dead."

Courtney grabbed the other girl's shoulders and her fingers dug into Annie's arms. "No, you don't! You're angry and the pain is ripping you up inside, but you don't wish that. You can't. My mother is dead and I'd give *anything* to have her back. Dead is forever, you understand? You haven't got any idea what it's like to have your mother alive and laughing one day, and then on some slab in a morgue the next. You can't possibly know what *that's* like." Tears clouded her eyes. "It's been four years, and I think about her every single day. Some days it's every single minute. My mom didn't want to die, you know. She was meeting a friend for lunch and a truck blew a tire and swerved onto the other side of the road." She rarely talked about the accident, rarely mentioned it to anyone, but Courtney felt it was vital that Annie understand what she was saying. Courtney had argued with her mother, too. She'd been furious with her a dozen or more times in that last year, but—as she'd just told Annie—she'd give anything she had now, or ever would, to have her mother back.

"Don't tell me what I feel," Annie shouted, twisting free of her grip.

Courtney no longer cared if Grams was listening to the conversation. She tried another way to reach Annie. "I used to pretend my mom was still alive."

"This is supposed to make me feel better?"

"No, it's a reality check."

"I can't deal with any more reality than I already am. I just want my life back the way it used to be, with my mom and dad and—" She bit her lower lip and her eyes filled with tears. "I've got to go." In a flash Annie was off the bed. She grabbed her purse. "Just don't do me any more favors, all right?"

"Whatever," Courtney muttered. She felt like a failure. It was a risk to contact Andrew that night, and Annie didn't seem to appreciate how difficult the decision had been. Her only reaction was embarrassment, and that had turned to anger at Courtney. If it hadn't been for her, Andrew would never have known she was at the rave. On the other hand, Annie could've been in serious trouble. Kids had died from ecstasy; Courtney had heard of cases in Chicago.

"Courtney," Grams shouted from the bottom of the stairs.

"Yes," she shouted back, lazily unfolding her legs and moving off the bed.

"Is everything all right up there? Your friend left in a mighty big rush."

"Everything's fine," Courtney assured her.

"It's good that you have a friend," Grams said smiling up at her. "I'm heading out to the Missionary Society Meeting. Do you want to tag along?"

"Would it be okay if I took my bike out instead?" She really didn't enjoy sorting and packing clothes to ship to China. Perhaps in a few years chatting with Grams's friends would be stimulating, but currently Courtney found it uninspiring. All they talked about were their aches and pains.

"Where are you going?" Grams asked.

After three years during which her father had given her practically free rein, being accountable to her grandmother was a drag. "I thought I'd stop off at the yarn store and deliver those patches you knit." That was a destination and a purpose Grams would approve of.

"Oh, sure, that'd be fine. Say hello to Lydia for me."

"Will do."

Grabbing her helmet and gloves, Courtney bounded down the stairs. The frustration she felt was nearly overwhelming. She'd tried to do the right thing for Annie and those insults were all the thanks she got. Biking might give her a chance to vent her annoyance.

It didn't help that Courtney saw she'd gained a pound when she stepped on the scale that morning. After a solid week of denial, she should've lost at least that much and instead she'd gained.

"What time will you be back?" Grams wanted to know as Courtney came through the kitchen on her way to the garage.

"Soon."

"You've got money with you?"

"Yeah." She didn't bother hanging around to listen to any other questions. She wanted to escape and longed to feel the wind on her face and the sun on her neck as she pumped those pedals. The hell with Annie. She'd tried to help, tried to talk to her; she'd told her more than she'd ever shared with anyone about her mother, but it'd been a waste of time.

Courtney was breathless when she reached Blossom Street. As she turned the corner, A Good Yarn came into view and so did the French café on the other side of the street. The front window had a display of pastries.

Slowing the bike, she coasted to a stop outside the yarn store. Forcing her eyes away from the bakery window, she glanced into the front window of the shop and noticed Whiskers curled up, fast asleep. Lydia was busy with a customer; Margaret was, too. Even if Courtney did go directly inside, neither would have time to talk to her. Her gaze eagerly returned to the bakery.

Just last week Bethanne had talked about the chocolate

éclairs and how delicious they were. Lydia had taken up the subject, raving about the croissants, but those éclairs were her favorite, too, she'd said. She made it sound as if she ate them by the dozen. If so, she hadn't gained an ounce.

Courtney had practically starved to death all week and she'd *gained* weight. It was hard enough to stay on this P diet; not seeing results was a case of adding insult to injury. Or was it the other way around? She could never remember.

She peered inside the yarn store again and then looked over at the bakery. The pastries weren't the only thing Lydia had bragged about. She'd made sure everyone knew that a girl from her original knitting class was one of the bakers. Her name was Alix, and she'd made a big deal about how it was spelled with an *i* instead of an *e*.

Alix baked in the morning and waited behind the counter some afternoons. She also attended class at the culinary institute, so she must be good at making those delectable-sounding treats. The five-dollar bill in Courtney's pocket felt like it was on fire. Éclairs didn't start with the letter P. Okay, *pastry* did, but she was willing to overlook that minor detail.

Driven by her desire to taste something sweet, Courtney walked her bike across the street and parked it against the side of the building. The girl behind the counter didn't seem the knitting type. Then Courtney read her name tag. Alix with an *i*. Yup, just like Grams always said, appearances could be deceiving.

"You're Alix?" she asked.

The other girl nodded. "Do I know you?"

"Probably not. I'm in one of Lydia's knitting classes."

She immediately brightened. "You wouldn't happen to be Courtney, would you?"

Surprised, Courtney nodded. "Lydia mentioned me?"

"Yeah. Do you know what's going on with her and Brad?"

Courtney raised her eyes from the glass case, where the

chocolate éclairs oozed rich custard and sat on a platter decorated with a paper doily. "Going on?" she repeated.

"Yeah, since they broke up."

"I don't know any more than you do."

"I hope they patch things up." Alix sounded genuinely concerned.

"How much for one of the chocolate éclairs?" They weren't all that big, so perhaps she should order two.

Alix told her, and Courtney calculated how much it would cost for two, with tax. Plus a Coke, and not the diet variety, either. She was sick of drinking sugar-free soda. If she was going on a sugar high, then she might as well go the whole way. Why cheat herself out of a soda?

"Lydia said you've been losing weight. My hat's off to you. It's hard," Alix said softly.

Courtney nodded.

"I make a mean low-fat, sugar-free chocolate latte."

Courtney's mouth was watering for that éclair. "A latte?" She paused to consider her choices and realized she was being offered far more than an incentive to stay on her eating plan. Friendship had no calories, and it was the special on Alix's menu.

"I'll take that latte," she said with as much enthusiasm as she could manage.

Alix smiled. "Good. I'll make my best one ever."

Courtney sighed with relief. Without Alix's encouragement she probably would've given in and ordered the éclairs and eaten them so fast they'd disappear before she'd even tasted them. Then, they'd reappear on her thighs.

"Thanks," she said when Alix handed her the latte. "I appreciate the help."

"Anytime. Come back whenever you want. And if you find out anything about Brad and Lydia, let me know, all right?"

"Will do," Courtney promised. Her first sip of the latte was divine. This was just as good as Alix had promised. And *latte* didn't start with the letter P.

CHAPTER 21

LYDIA HOFFMAN

Tuesday morning when Margaret showed up for work, I knew right away that something was wrong. I hoped my sister would tell me. No matter what, though, I was determined not to pry it out of Margaret. Our relationship had been less strained, but I suspect that was primarily because of the situation between Brad and me.

We'd arrived at an unspoken agreement. I didn't inquire about Matt's job search and she didn't mention Brad. It was an uneasy truce. I knew she was curious and no doubt concerned; I felt the same way about her. I kept quiet about the fact that Brad had phoned me one evening. When his name came up on Caller ID, I didn't pick up. I couldn't. It occurred to me later that the call might be from Cody, and in some ways, that would've been even more difficult. I hadn't guessed how much I'd miss him.

With the passing of time, I'd begun to understand what Brad had meant about giving his son a family. As much as I love Cody, and I do, I had to accept that I'll never be his mother. Brad loves him, and despite his feelings for me or for that matter Janice, his son had to come first. I could only love and admire him more for the strength of his devotion to Cody.

When Brad divulged that he was talking to Janice, I was too hurt and angry to appreciate his sacrifice. But I came to realize that this wasn't about Brad and his ex-wife, it was about Cody. It'd always been about Cody. Brad loves me, yet he was willing to let me go in order to give Cody back his mother.

Strangely, Brad's efforts to reconcile with Janice helped me grasp the depth of my own father's love for me. Dad made sacrifices daily; sacrifices I came to expect because I was so sick and so needy. Not until he died did I appreciate everything my father had been to me.

I would've loved to discuss Brad and Cody with my dad. He was always so wise and loving; he would've known just the right thing to say. Even now, I'd give anything to hear his voice again, to feel the comfort of his presence.

"Looks like we need to order more sock yarn," Margaret said, breaking into my thoughts.

"Already?" The self-patterning yarn seemed to go out of the shop almost as fast as it came in.

My class was going well. I'd wondered if holding it on a Tuesday afternoon was a mistake. It's the first day of my work week and there always seemed to be a hundred things that required my attention. But I decided it was actually an advantage; the small class size meant I could develop real relationships with all three women, just as I had in my original class.

During one class, Elise described the awkward situation with her ex-husband. Frankly, I was surprised she'd told us that much. She'd always been so restrained. I can't tell you how shocked we all were when she revealed that Maverick was a professional gambler. The minute *that* was out, the conversation became lively indeed. What an interesting combination! A librarian and a gambler. This was the stuff of romance novels—but unfortunately there hadn't been a happy ending for Elise.

Bethanne Hamlin had ex-husband problems, too. But she was growing more self-confident every week. We could all see it; I'd say it even showed in her knitting. She was experiencing some difficulties with her teenage daughter, but she'd only touched on that subject briefly. I thought she might be afraid of saying too much because of Courtney, who'd become friends with Annie.

Speaking of Courtney—we all loved her. What a charming girl and such a typical teenager. She talked about her father a great deal and was as excited to get an e-mail or a letter from him as she would an invitation to the senior prom. I was grateful she seemed to be making friends. Although she didn't say anything about it, I had the feeling she liked Andrew Hamlin, Bethanne's son. Andrew was the school's football star, the quarterback, and I was sure he could date just about any girl at Washington High. I also figured Courtney probably didn't stand much of a chance with him. He'd want slim, trim and stylish—the cheerleader type. Courtney was losing weight, but she still had a few pounds to go.

On Tuesday, just before one, I heard the bell over the door and immediately glanced up to see Bethanne walk in. She hadn't even reached her seat before she pulled out her half-knitted sock and held it up for inspection.

"Notice, I successfully turned the heel," she announced. "I feel like I should get a gold star for this. It took hours."

"Then you did it wrong," Margaret offered from the other side of the shop.

I was irritated by her comment, but smiled encouragingly at Bethanne. "It gets easier the more often you do it, so don't worry."

"I'm not worried. Well, I was at first because it just didn't look right, but I followed the instructions and everything came out looking exactly the way it should. I knew one thing—I wasn't giving up until I got it right."

"Good for you!" I said, resisting the urge to hug her. I really was very proud of Bethanne. She'd come a long way in this class and I wasn't just talking about knitting.

"I wish I could do as well in my job search," she murmured dejectedly.

Elise arrived moments after Bethanne, and they sat across from one other and compared socks. Elise had knit socks before and turned the heel, but never on two circular needles, which requires a different technique.

"This is a lovely job," I said, studying Elise's work. Every stitch was perfectly formed. I felt she was a very purposeful knitter—and I had the impression that was exactly how she went about her life, too.

Courtney was the last one to get there. She rode her bike and parked it outside the shop, chaining it to the light post. I could tell she'd lost more weight. I wanted to say something about how good she looked, but I was afraid my compliment might embarrass her.

"Sorry I'm late," Courtney said, bursting into the shop like a sudden squall. She removed the helmet and shrugged off her backpack as she took her seat. Within a minute or two she was set up with her knitting, ready to learn.

"How did everyone do?" I asked. We'd already reached the most difficult stage of knitting socks and that was the gusset. In my opinion, the technique has been simplified by the two-needle method, but there are still knitters who prefer the four or five double-pointed needle approach. I know that socks can also be knit on a single 40-inch needle in what is known as the "magic loop" method; personally, I'm most comfortable knitting and teaching with the two circular needles.

I carefully examined everyone's half-completed first sock and found that my students had done very well. We always went through this procedure, almost a little ritual, even if I'd already seen their work. There was something satisfying about it, maybe because of the way it formally acknowledged everyone's effort. Sitting with them, I described the next step of the process, then left them to knit.

"I just wish getting a job was this easy," Bethanne commented, knitting the stitches from one needle to the other.

Elise looked at her. "I've been giving this matter of a job some thought. Where have you applied?"

"Everywhere," she cried, and her voice fell with discouragement. "Everywhere I can think of," she amended. "The truth is, I hate not being available for my children."

"Your children are old enough to be on their own, aren't they?" Margaret said, feeling free to leap into the conversation despite helping a paying customer. "I've got two daughters," she continued, oblivious to my frown, "and I leave them."

Bethanne considered that for a moment. "Do you feel good about it?"

Margaret shrugged. "Actually, their father's home this summer and I'm glad of it. We'd both rather he was working, but he's been able to spend time with the girls and gotten much closer to them."

"Well, to be honest, I'm afraid to leave Annie alone," Bethanne said. I saw Courtney give her a quick glance. "Annie's not...quite herself and...well, after the upheaval in their lives, I'd rather be around to keep an eye on her. It isn't

that I don't *want* to work—I do! But at the same time, I want
to give an employer my best and I won't be able to do that if
I'm constantly worried about what's happening at home."

I remembered how hard Brad found this situation as a single father. Cody was eight this year, and he hated the idea of
going to day care, but he was too young to be on his own.

"So, Elise—you said you'd been thinking about this?"
Bethanne murmured.

"I have."

"I've given it my best shot," Bethanne said, shaking her
head. "I've applied for everything from waiting tables—I'm
so grateful they didn't hire me—to a receptionist for a dentist. And just about everything in between."

"You really weren't interested in that job at the dentist's
either, were you?" Elise asked.

"Not really."

Elise laughed. "That's what I thought. No one will hire you
with that attitude."

"But I need a job—and soon—otherwise I'm going to end
up homeless," she said grimly.

I knew that must be an exaggeration; still, I understood how
worried she was about finances. I wished there was enough
business so I could hire her myself, but there wasn't and I
couldn't.

"Every time we talked about this, you said your only real
skill was throwing parties, especially kids' birthday parties."

There'd been various discussions about the parties
Bethanne had planned for her children through the years. She
obviously did have a knack for it.

Bethanne nodded, with a woeful shrug. "Unfortunately, no
one's going to hire me to do that."

"Don't be so sure," Elise said.

Bethanne's eyes widened. "What do you mean?" she asked
breathlessly.

"My grandson's birthday is coming up soon," Elise continued. "My daughter's a talented woman, but she doesn't have a creative bone in her body. I'd like to hire you to help her with Luke's birthday party."

Bethanne immediately sat up straighter. "You mean to say you'd actually *pay* me to do this?"

"Within reason, yes," Elise assured her. I gathered Elise didn't have much extra cash, so I found this extremely generous.

"I have lots of wonderful ideas for little boys." Bethanne was excited now. "What does Luke like?"

"Currently, it's dinosaurs."

"Perfect. I'll get dinosaur eggs, fill them with prizes and bury them. The boys can go on a dig, if that won't damage your daughter's lawn or garden. Otherwise I'll simply hide them."

Elise smiled. "That sounds good. And I'll find out if it's okay to bury the eggs."

"I know!" Bethanne said happily. "I could make a dinosaur cake, too—it can't be that hard. Luke's probably way beyond Barney, but I'll bet he'd enjoy a purple cake."

Last year about this time, I'd knit Cody a sweater with a big dinosaur on the front and he'd loved it so much, he'd slept with it on. The memory brought a twinge of pain that I did my best to ignore.

"I'd be happy to help with the party," Bethanne said, but then her enthusiasm dwindled. "It's just that I don't think I'd be able to support myself by throwing kids' birthday parties."

"Don't be so sure," Elise said again.

"Amelia's about to have her first birthday, and I know Jacqueline's hoping to make an event of it," I threw in for good measure. "I'm sure if you approached her with a few ideas, she'd hire you."

"Do you really think so?" Bethanne looked around the table for encouragement. Everyone nodded and made encouraging remarks—even Margaret.

"I know so." I'd never seen Bethanne more animated. Jacqueline had the money to pay for something really special, too. "Call her. I'll give you her number."

"I will," Bethanne promised. Her needles clicked energetically as she started describing possibilities for little Amelia's party. "How about a teddy bears' picnic? Or a storytelling party? Or—"

Margaret walked over with the phone number written on a sheet of paper. My sister is nothing if not efficient.

"I can help you," Courtney offered. "I mean, if you need an assistant, and Annie and Andrew are busy. Most days I have a bunch of free time and you wouldn't have to pay me or anything."

Bethanne's eyes filled with tears. "That is so sweet of you."

"Honestly, I'm glad to do it."

Bethanne glanced from one woman to the next. "Thank you all so much. Especially you, Elise. You've given me a wonderful idea and I just love it. This is something I'm really, really good at, and I know I can make it a success." Impulsively she put down her knitting and sprang up to hug the older woman.

I was delighted by her brand-new confidence and wanted to cheer her on. "I was impressed with the music video party you threw for Annie when she turned twelve," I said. Bethanne had told us about this a few weeks ago. "I can just imagine how much fun those girls had dressing up as their favorite rock stars and then having a video made of them singing to a karaoke machine. What a wonderful keepsake."

"Or the pirate party for Andrew when he was seven," Courtney added. "It was so clever to actually bury treasure at the beach."

"It was fun drawing up the treasure maps," Bethanne said, smiling. "One for each boy. The treasures were quite elaborate, too. I'd collected junk jewelry, and bought chocolate coins and eye patches. It was a great party. In fact, it was that party that made me realize how much I enjoyed this. Over the years, I've helped some of my friends with their kids' parties, but I never dreamed anyone would actually *pay* me for doing it."

"That was Andrew's favorite party, he says. I mean, he still talks about it." Courtney grinned. "I wouldn't have minded a party like that myself."

Elise nodded. "And it's absolutely perfect for little boys."

"Thanks." Bethanne nodded. "Grant got involved, too. He bought a huge toy parrot and dressed up as Long John Silver."

I could see that remembering her husband in those better times was making her feel nostalgic.

"I think Elise might really be on to something here," Margaret said. "There's a market for this kind of—"

The door opened, interrupting her, and in walked a distinguished-looking older gentleman. I don't get many men in the shop. There are definitely male knitters, but most of the yarn I sell is to women.

Elise raised her head up when the bell chimed and went pale. "Maverick," she whispered.

"Hello, everyone," he said without the least hesitation. He seemed completely at ease in the shop, although not all men are comfortable in such a female environment. "I'm here for Elise." He looked in her direction and I noticed the way his eyes softened. "I was in the neighborhood and figured I'd give you a ride home."

"I—I'll be a while yet," she said, blushing. Flustered, she dropped a stitch and then did a marvelous job of picking it up again.

I enjoyed watching the two of them. They might be divorced, but it was plain they still had strong feelings for each other. This was an intriguing development—and not something Elise had mentioned. I suppose I'd had an image of a professional gambler and to be honest, Maverick didn't fit the picture. With his white hair and beard, my first thought was that he resembled Charlie Rich, the country singer. On closer examination, I saw that he was taller and more solidly built.

"Don't rush on my account," Maverick told her. "I'm parked outside. I'll wait there."

Elise gazed down at her knitting. "Ah…okay."

The class continued for another fifteen minutes and then gradually, one by one, my students left, chatting about next week's session. I found it interesting that the entire group had decided to knit socks for men. Bethanne's were probably for her son. Courtney had said hers would be a gift for her dad. And Elise? My guess was that her ex-husband would receive them.

"That was a wonderful suggestion Elise had for Bethanne," I commented to Margaret as I straightened the class area. I still felt good about what had happened; it seemed like a step toward real friendship.

Suddenly I saw that my sister was crying.

"Margaret?"

She brushed the tears away, obviously upset and embarrassed that I'd seen them.

"What is it?" I asked, despite my earlier resolve. "Tell me."

"We got a notice in the mail yesterday," she said in a voice so low I had to strain to hear. "Matt didn't know I saw it. He takes care of all the bills, and I just assumed we were managing all right. I've cut back as much as I can. I know he has, too, but apparently… Oh, Lydia, we're so far behind on the mortgage payments that we're in danger of losing the house."

"Oh, no." Every penny I had was invested in the store or I would've immediately offered to help.

"I tried to talk it over with Matt. I know he was just trying to protect me, but—but I'm his wife. He *should* tell me. When I told him that, he said I had enough on my mind without worrying about this too."

"How much do you need?" I asked.

"The letter said we had until next Monday to come up with ten thousand dollars."

"Oh, Margaret. I'm so sorry, I had no idea."

"I know, I know... Matt says everything will work out, and...and I'm sure it will. I didn't mean to burden you with our problems—it's just that it was such a shock...."

Although Margaret tried to sound hopeful, I didn't have a good feeling about this. My sister was about to lose her home and I couldn't do a thing to help.

22

CHAPTER

ELISE BEAUMONT

Elise was deep in thought as she tore lettuce leaves for the dinner salad. Her grandsons were at the small neighborhood park with Maverick. Luke and John dragged him there every chance they got, and he was always agreeable. If he'd been half as good a husband and father as he was a grandfather, the marriage might've lasted.

Although she hated to admit it, Elise had begun to enjoy Maverick's company. Relying on him for anything, even casual friendship, was dangerous, as she very well knew. In fact, no one knew that better than she did. But over the last few weeks, he'd managed to break down her determination to avoid him. Little by little, he'd erased her resentment and doubt. He'd done it not with extravagant promises or declarations but through his actions—especially in the way he loved Aurora and his grandchildren. He respected Elise's feelings, never argued with her or defended himself. He seemed sincere. She didn't *want* to trust him, knew she shouldn't allow him into her life, but nevertheless found herself drawn to him.

The timer in the laundry room went off and Elise dried her hands before transferring the freshly laundered clothes from the dryer to a clothes basket. Aurora was meeting with Bethanne about Luke's birthday party. She'd loved Elise's suggestion about hiring Bethanne and insisted on paying the cost herself. She and Elise had engaged in a good-natured argument about it and finally decided Elise would pay for the cake.

Realizing Aurora would be pressed for time, Elise had started dinner. She'd already prepared the sauce and grated cheese for a family favorite that went by the rather inelegant name of "spaghetti pie."

In a few minutes she'd folded her grandsons' play clothes. Rather than leave them in the laundry area, she carried them to the boys' room. Since Maverick's arrival, she'd stayed away from that room. If she wanted him to respect her privacy, then it was important she afford him the same rights.

She opened the top dresser drawer and discovered that Aurora had given it to Maverick. Instantly she closed it and found that the second and third drawers were for Luke and John's clothes. She quickly and neatly put away the shorts and T-shirts. Elise knew what she should do next—turn around and walk away. But she couldn't resist…. She'd noticed the edge of a picture frame in Maverick's drawer. It was none of her business whose picture it was or why he'd buried it at the bottom of a drawer.

Turning swiftly, she started toward the door, then pivoted back, heart pounding. On the small table next to the bottom bunk, she saw a book Maverick was currently reading, and a coffee cup. But no photographs.

Suddenly she couldn't stand it any longer. Why torment herself like this? One peek would tell her whose picture it was, and her curiosity would be satisfied. Sliding open the drawer, she stared down. The edge of the frame stuck out from under his T-shirts. The frame itself was silver and slightly tarnished.

One look, she decided again. Okay, it would be a violation of his privacy, but a minor one. Not that she usually approved of such…such subjective morality. No, she'd be honest about this. Looking at the photograph was wrong. But she was going to do it, anyway. She wouldn't touch it. All she'd do was lift the shirts. Knowing Maverick, it was probably a picture from some blackjack tournament he'd won.

Pulse hammering, she lifted the shirts with one finger— and froze. Her lungs refused to function. The photograph was of her.

He'd taken the picture shortly after she'd learned she was pregnant with Aurora. They'd been walking through a nearby park, and he'd snapped it just as she turned from examining a rosebush. Her eyes shone with love and excitement. This was before the disillusionment had truly taken hold, before she'd been forced to face the truth about the man she'd married. But at that moment, her heart full of happiness unlike any she'd known before or since, he'd captured her image. She'd been a woman in love, a woman dreaming of the future, of her baby, of being a family.

Elise stared at the woman in the photo and bit her lip, surprised by the flood of memories. Of emotions.

"Do you remember when I took that?" Maverick asked, standing just inside the bedroom.

Elise gasped, leaping back from the chest of drawers, hand flying to her heart. She was shocked that she hadn't heard him enter the house. Even more than shocked, she was embarrassed that he'd caught her looking at her own photo. Hidden in *his* drawer. In *his* room.

"I…I apologize," she murmured, unable to look at him.

"For what? Snooping?"

Mortified, she kept her head turned away and nodded. "I…I should never—I am so sorry. I can only imagine what you must be thinking."

"You didn't answer my question."

All she wanted was to escape. "I don't recall your question."

"I asked," he said slowly and deliberately, "if you remembered when I took that picture."

Rather than answer verbally, she nodded.

"I've carried it with me all these years," he said quietly. "But then it started to fall apart so I bought this frame."

"Oh."

"I wanted you with me."

"We're divorced," she reminded him sharply. She didn't want to remember what it felt like to abandon herself to loving him. She was acutely aware of how close he was, only footsteps away. She smelled the scent of his aftershave, the same brand he'd worn when they were married. She didn't recall the name but the fresh, woodsy smell wafted toward her like an aphrodisiac. Against her will, she swayed closer, afraid for those few seconds that she'd collapse at his feet.

Maverick walked into the room and stood before her. "I told you this already," he said. He placed his index finger under her chin and raised her head until their eyes met. "I loved you then. I've loved you all this time. I love you now."

The thickness in her throat made it impossible to speak, so she shook her head.

"I know," he whispered, "It wasn't enough—it *isn't* enough. But it's all I ever had."

She realized he would have kissed her if not for the arrival of Luke and John. The boys burst into the room like a tornado touching down, all arms and legs, fighting and furious. Apparently they'd gotten into a squabble while putting their bikes in the garage.

With obvious reluctance, Maverick broke away from her and immediately took charge of the situation. Elise used the opportunity to escape. Returning to the kitchen, she gripped the counter with both hands, breathing hard. Her ex-husband had been about to kiss her, and that was shock enough, but knowing she would've let him made her knees go weak.

Thankfully, she had something to occupy her hands. Elise finished the salad and vigorously stirred the tomato and meat sauce simmering on the stove. She then put on a large pot of water to boil the spaghetti noodles. Everything would go together in a casserole dish, along with the grated cheese.

When the garage door closed twenty minutes later, she sighed with relief; either Aurora or David was home.

It was her daughter who stepped in from the garage. When she saw that Elise had begun dinner, Aurora let out a cry of delight.

"Oh, Mom, thank you so much!" She hugged her mother tightly.

"Thank me for what?" she asked. "Dinner? I try to help as much as I can." As she spoke, she drained the spaghetti and assembled the ingredients, stirring in the cheese last.

"No, I mean, yes, thanks for that, but Mom, *thank you* for telling me about Bethanne. She's fabulous! She had a dozen different ideas, but we're going with the dinosaur motif." Beaming, she hugged her again. "Until I talked to her, I was planning to take everyone out for pizza and ice cream, and that would've been fine. But for the same amount of money, Luke is going to have a spectacular party that he'll always remember."

Elise's instincts had been right. Busy parents would be willing to pay for a party that was different and specially designed around their children's interests.

"Gayle from across the street went with me and she booked a party, too, even though Sonja's birthday isn't for another month."

"That's wonderful." Elise smiled broadly. Opening the oven door, she slid the round casserole dish inside.

"What's up?" Maverick asked, coming into the kitchen. His gaze went directly to Elise.

"One of the women in my knitting group needs a job. It's complicated," she said, not wanting to go into the long drawn-out story of why it was so important that Bethanne find employment.

"Gayle was so excited she called three friends on the drive home," Aurora explained.

"I'm so pleased," Elise murmured.

"You should be. Bethanne told me this was all your idea."

Elise blushed, and wanting to deflect the attention, said, "Dinner's almost ready."

"What are we having?" Luke asked suspiciously. He was the finicky eater in the family.

Maverick peered into the oven and turned to face his grandson. "It looks like worms and blood to me."

"Maverick Beaumont!" Elise cried, horrified he'd say such a thing.

Luke's eyes widened with delight as he raced into the other room to share the news with his brother.

"Better known as spaghetti pie," Maverick informed his daughter.

"Oh."

Elise smiled and admired Maverick for being so clever.

"I'll set the table," he offered.

"It's early yet," Aurora said. "Why don't you and Mom collect a bouquet of flowers from the backyard and I'll use them as a centerpiece. My roses are beautiful this summer."

Any other time, Elise would've objected and either given the task to Maverick or insisted on cutting the flowers herself. She should have then, but she didn't.

Together they went into the backyard, where Aurora's roses bloomed against the high wooden fence. For their first anniversary David had given her an antique rosebush and year after year it had flourished. Now, on this July afternoon, the fragrance of roses perfumed the air.

Elise inhaled deeply. "I'll get the—"

Maverick stopped her by taking her hand and entwining his fingers with hers. "Let's just stroll around the yard for a few minutes. Would that be all right?"

"Yes," she said, barely recognizing her own voice. "That would be fine."

But it was more than fine.

23
CHAPTER

BETHANNE HAMLIN

"The thing is," Bethanne said excitedly, reaching for another tortilla chip, "Grant was right."

Paul frowned. "Right about what?"

"About how I should find a way to support myself. He won't be financially responsible for me much longer, as he's frequently pointed out. A couple of months ago, he told me to use my God-given talents to find a job. He was talking about childcare and so on, and he meant it sarcastically. At the time I was so furious with him I couldn't see straight, but you know what? He was right."

Paul grinned, and once again Bethanne was struck by the fact that while he wasn't a handsome man, he was an appealing one, easy to talk to and be around. They'd met for dinner after her first major birthday party, for Elise's grandson. Because there'd been so little time, she'd had to arrange the party quickly, but everything had fallen nicely into place. The little boys had loved the dinosaur egg hunt, not to mention games like "pin the tail on the dinosaur," which she'd created herself with Annie's help.

"Did I mention I got three new bookings from Luke's party? I'm also going to do one—a really elaborate one—for a lady I met at the yarn store. They all want 'my special touch' for their kids' parties," she said. She dipped her chip in the thick salsa before bringing it to her mouth. The most thrilling part of all this was that with her clients' deposits, she had enough money for Andrew to attend football camp. She'd nearly burst with pride when she handed it over to him.

"I believe you did say something about upcoming parties." Paul raised a salsa-laden chip.

"More than once?" She had the feeling she'd probably repeated the same information a dozen times, but she couldn't help it. This was the most wonderful thing to happen to her in…years.

"As the kids got older, Grant used to think all the fuss I made over birthday parties was a waste of money," she explained. "Who would've guessed his wife would make a career of it." She stopped herself. "Ex-wife," she corrected. She sighed. "Will I ever get used to saying that?"

"I don't know. I haven't yet."

She refused to let that one slip destroy her mood. "I was really glad you phoned."

"I wanted to see how everything went with the party."

"I'm so happy and excited, and this…this is just great. I love Mexican food."

"Me, too." He reached for his margarita and licked the salt from the edge of his glass before taking a sip.

The sight of his tongue unnerved her. Bethanne immediately looked away, then chided herself for being silly. But perhaps it was a natural reaction. It'd been so long since she'd made love, she could hardly even remember.

"Do you miss…" She hesitated to say it aloud, so she leaned toward him and whispered. "Sex?"

"Sex." Paul's eyes narrowed. "What's that?"

They both laughed as if it was the funniest thing they'd heard in ages.

"Really," she pressed. "I want to know."

He nodded. "Big time. What about you?"

She nodded, too. She couldn't ask that question of anyone else, and it made her appreciate their friendship even more. They felt safe with each other; safe in speaking honestly about their anger and pain. There was something healing in that kind of openness.

"How are things with Annie and Andrew?" he asked, deftly changing the subject.

Bethanne was on her second margarita, which she knew had loosened her inhibitions, probably past the point of decorum. "I've had some long conversations with Annie since I learned she put sugar in Tiffany's gas tank." At first Annie had tried to deny it, but when she broke down and admitted what she'd done, they'd clung to each other, Bethanne's heart breaking for her daughter.

Annie had agreed to see the therapist, and after two visits, felt she had a better perspective on the family's situation and her own feelings. There'd been several tearful discussions between mother and daughter. Annie seemed better now, more like her old self, and Bethanne sensed that her daughter could move forward, with or without her father.

"Has Grant had a chance to talk to Annie?" Paul asked.

Bethanne had mentioned his most recent visit, although she'd left out his inquiry about her relationship with Paul.

"He phoned the house." Bethanne shrugged. "I don't know what he said, but Annie was on and off the phone in about two minutes, so it couldn't have been much of a conversation."

"From what I understand, the insurance paid for the damage to Tiffany's engine," Paul told her.

"Did she contact you?" Bethanne asked. Paul rarely mentioned his ex-wife.

"No, but our agent told me about it. It's a good thing Tiff continued the coverage for vandalism."

Bethanne nodded. She wouldn't put it past Tiffany to have Annie arrested; even worse, she wasn't sure Grant would stand up for their daughter. Yes, Annie had been wrong and she needed to accept the consequences of her actions, but Bethanne couldn't bear the thought of her daughter being prosecuted. At the therapist's suggestion, Annie had written Tiffany a letter of apology and Bethanne hoped the matter would end there.

The waitress came by, and Bethanne ordered the fajita salad, while Paul chose the chicken enchilada plate. He waited until she'd left the table before resuming the conversation.

"How's Annie now?" he asked.

"She's dealing with a lot," Bethanne replied. "She's coming through it, though, and I think the worst is over, but it's been a difficult time for her."

"She needs a friend," Paul said. "Someone who really understands."

"I agree, but—" Bethanne stopped in midsentence. "Yes. She does."

Paul laughed softly. "You've got that look in your eye."

Bethanne sat back in her chair. "She already has one. Only, my daughter is a lot like her mother and isn't always aware of what's right in front of her."

"You seem to be full of good news tonight," he teased.

She giggled. "I'm full of something, all right." Suddenly she reached across the table and grabbed his hand. "Oh, my goodness," she cried, shocked into momentary silence.

"What?" Paul asked in concern.

"Paul, I just realized that I'm *happy.* I'm actually happy. I didn't think I'd ever feel this way again, but I do. I really do."

Paul nodded thoughtfully.

Bethanne leaned toward him. "Has it happened for you yet?"

He didn't meet her eyes.

"Be honest," she told him.

"Not yet," he admitted with a faint smile, "but I can feel it approaching."

"Good." She felt better knowing that he was hopeful enough to anticipate the return of joy.

"Seeing you makes me happy," he confessed.

"Thank you." Bethanne sipped her margarita and sighed. "That's sweet."

"I think about you a lot, Bethanne. About us both."

"Us." She choked a little as she swallowed her drink.

"What would you think of the two of us dating?"

She frowned. She'd never asked, but assumed she was older than Paul, possibly by as much as ten years. "I...I like you as a friend, Paul, but as for this dating idea—I don't know. I'm afraid it might change our whole relationship and I wouldn't want that. I want things to stay the way they are."

He shrugged with apparent nonchalance. "That's all right."

"Don't take offense, please. I couldn't bear it if you did. You're my friend and I treasure our times together, but..."

"Just think about us dating, all right?"

"Okay, but... Okay, okay, I'll think about it."

"Good." He appeared to relax then. "I'm glad, Bethanne. You're exactly the kind of woman I can imagine myself with."

She glanced around to make sure no one was listening in on their conversation. "This is because I asked you about sex, isn't it?"

"No," he said abruptly. "This has to do with the fact that I really enjoy being with you. Not you, the ex-wife of the man my ex-wife left me for, but *you*, the person I've come to know and trust."

"Oh." After two margaritas, she found it difficult to frame a response.

"That surprises you?"

"No." Bethanne answered from her heart. "The truth is, I find your interest a very big compliment. For now, I'm more comfortable just being friends, but I'm willing to see where things go."

"You're a beautiful woman, Bethanne," he said in a serious tone.

"That's the lack of sex talking," she teased.

"Hmm—that could easily be fixed," he joked back.

Bethanne giggled. "I think it's time we cut off the margaritas."

Paul smiled. "Let's not be hasty. The conversation's just getting good."

24

CHAPTER

COURTNEY PULANSKI

It'd been a pleasant surprise to hear from Annie, especially after the way their last meeting had ended, with Annie storming out of Courtney's bedroom. Courtney had wanted to ask Bethanne about her during knitting class. She hadn't, because she didn't want to put Annie's mother on the spot.

Courtney was afraid for the girl, afraid of what she might do. She'd tried to talk to her, to help her, and explain that she understood—she'd gone through this horrible emotional pain herself. But Annie had made it abundantly clear that she wasn't interested.

Then, on a Monday afternoon, after no contact in almost two weeks, Annie had phoned and invited Courtney to her house. Her grandmother dropped her off at the Hamlins' on her way to the church, where Vera volunteered at the library once a month. Before she moved to Seattle, Courtney had assumed her grandmother sat in front of the television and knit most afternoons. Boy, had she been wrong. Vera was at the pool four mornings a week and ate a robust breakfast. Then she worked in her yard and garden. She probably spent as many hours doing volunteer work, including various church committees, as she would've spent on a full-time job.

As Grams drove off, Courtney stood on the sidewalk and examined Annie's house. She immediately liked the brick structure with its steep front steps, rounded door and the gable that jutted out over the small porch. It reminded her of homes in some Chicago neighborhoods.

Homesickness rushed through her. Chicago was where she had friends, where everything was familiar. Courtney hated having to rebuild her life in her senior year of high school. She'd worked for eleven years to reach this point, and she'd looked forward to being with her friends, some of whom she'd known nearly her entire life.

She found it hard not to feel sorry for herself, but Courtney knew, and had long ago accepted, that this sacrifice was necessary. Julianna had recently reminded Courtney that next year, when she left for college, she'd be experiencing the same kind of dislocation, so in essence Courtney was simply making the move a year earlier than she normally would. She'd be that much more prepared for college, Julianna said, and Courtney appreciated her sister's insight. She relied on the contact with her family, especially Julianna, to ward off feelings of isolation.

Annie opened the door before Courtney had even rung the bell. "I saw your grandmother pull up," she said. She wore tight shorts, a loose T-shirt and big fuzzy slippers.

And she wasn't smiling. Their conversation had been short, and she wondered if it'd been prompted by Bethanne or if Annie was sincere about wanting to see her. At the time, Courtney had been too grateful to question the other girl's motives.

"How's it going?" Courtney asked, walking into the house.

"All right, I guess." Annie turned and headed up the stairs.

Courtney followed her, although she wished she could look around a bit more. The house was beautiful, with cream-colored walls, furniture upholstered in dark reds and greens, shining wood floors, simple but expensive-looking area rugs. Fresh flowers graced the mantel. As she'd expected, Bethanne had gorgeous taste.

Photographs lined the wall, and she paused long enough to look at the family portrait, obviously taken in better times. Andrew resembled his father, with deep blue eyes and a strong square chin, and Annie took after her mother. "Where is everyone?" she asked, trudging up the carpeted stairs.

"Out," Annie responded. "Why? Is that a problem?"

Courtney decided to ignore the lack of welcome. "It's fine with me."

"Good." Annie had reached the top of the stairs and frowned when she saw Courtney regarding the framed portraits. "I told Mom to throw those away, but she wouldn't do it."

The glass in the most recent family photograph was cracked, and Courtney wondered if Annie had tried to destroy it. "There's pictures of my mother all over our house in Chicago, too." Or there had been before the house was rented. "I used to come home, all excited about something, and rush into the house. Then as soon as I saw Mom's photo I'd start to cry." Talking about it still had that effect on her, and she turned aside to blot her eyes with her sleeve.

Annie didn't respond for a moment, and when she did speak, her voice was barely above a whisper. "When Dad first left, I thought for sure he'd be back. I hated him for leaving us. I wanted to…to punish him, and at the same time, I wanted him here, the way he'd always been." She looked away as if she'd said more than she'd intended.

"I didn't cry at my mom's funeral," Courtney confessed. "Everyone was sobbing and carrying on. Even my dad broke down." It was difficult to tell anyone this, even now, but she felt Annie would understand.

"Why not?" Annie asked.

"I think I must've been in shock. So many people came to the funeral and there was all this talk about how good Mom looked. She didn't look good—she looked dead." Her voice cracked as she said this and she lowered it, not wanting Annie to hear how emotional she got talking about her mom. "I wanted everyone to go away. I didn't want all those people around me. That night—" she paused, swallowing hard "—after everyone left and we'd gone to bed, I couldn't sleep. Then it hit me. We'd just buried Mom. This wasn't like some TV show. She was gone. I couldn't stand it. I started to scream."

Annie stared at her. "You must've felt bad," she said quietly.

"I did. So bad." Courtney nodded. "I couldn't stop. I screamed and screamed. Everyone came rushing into my room, and all I could do was scream. I wanted my mother. I wanted her with me. I felt like *I* was the one who died, not her. I wished it was me."

"What did your dad do?"

"Dad held me." Tears streaked her face and once again she wiped them away.

"Then Jason and Julianna sat on my bed with Dad and me, and we all cried together. Up until then, I'd been the youngest, you know? Julianna and I weren't that close—Jason and I weren't, either—but we became real brother and sisters that night. Our whole family changed. We're all so close now." She was embarrassed to have said this much.

Annie looked as if she didn't know what to say.

Courtney wanted her to realize that while she'd lost her father, he was still a part of her life, and she should be grateful for that.

"My room's over here." Annie gestured down the hallway.

Courtney gave the photos one last look and followed her slowly up the rest of the stairs and into the bedroom.

Annie was sitting on her bed when Courtney came in. Discarded clothes littered the floor and the dresser was piled with CDs, books, makeup and magazines. A picture of a boy was stuck in a corner of the mirror.

Courtney walked over to study the snapshot. Another one she hadn't initially noticed was taped to the bottom edge of the mirror. It was of Annie and the same boy at a school dance, standing beneath an archway of white and black balloons. Annie wore a pink party dress with a matching floral shawl and her date had on a suit.

"That's Conner," Annie whispered, her voice quavering. "We broke up a couple of months ago. He said I'd gotten to be a drag."

"He's cute." Courtney assumed Annie still cared about him, otherwise she wouldn't have kept the photos.

Annie shrugged. "He's all right."

"Do you ever see him anymore?"

"Once in a while. He's going out with someone else now, but he's on the football team with Andrew, so it's unavoidable, you know? You like my brother, don't you?"

Courtney whirled around at the unexpectedness of the comment and felt color flood her face. "I—I think he's nice." She was afraid to say more, for fear it would be misconstrued. Andrew was cute and popular and, according to Bethanne, one of the school's star athletes. Probably every girl there was already in love with him. Courtney didn't figure she had a chance, and she accepted that. She wouldn't waste her time pining over a lost cause. If she was lucky, maybe they could be friends....

Annie heaved a sigh. "Speaking of my brother, he said I had to thank you for what you did that night. He's right. I...I wasn't *really* angry at you afterward."

"I know. You were angry with yourself more than anything. You got in deeper than you meant to, and then it was too late."

Annie stared down at the floor. "I'm sorry about your mom," she said. "But my dad—it's not the same. My dad *wanted* to leave. Your mother didn't. He walked away, and now it's as if Andrew and I are nothing more than…than collateral damage. All he cares about is *her.*" Annie's face was red as she spit out the words.

Courtney resisted the urge to squeeze her hand, knowing the other girl might reject her comfort. After a moment, she added, "Your father's gone and your entire life's been turned upside down. My life was too, Annie. It might not seem the same, but in some ways it was. I wouldn't be living in Seattle if my mother hadn't died, and my dad wouldn't be in South America risking his life, either."

"If my father could keep his pants zipped, my mother wouldn't be out singing 'Happy Birthday' to a bunch of brats and—" Annie began to sob, then jerkily moved her hand across her cheek. "I don't want to talk about my dad, all right? I hate him and it doesn't matter."

"We can talk about anything," Courtney told her.

Annie seemed to relax, as though she was relieved to change the subject. "The thing is, I actually think it's cool what my mom's doing. She always loved putting on parties, and she's really enjoying this. And you know what? She's making money. We're getting a lot of phone calls, and Andrew and I help out whenever we can. I have a surprise for her. Want to see?"

"Sure," Courtney said.

Annie leaped off the bed and sat down at her desk, turning on her computer. "Come and look," she said, glancing over her shoulder.

Courtney stood behind Annie as she brought up a graphic arts display. It featured balloons in one corner and a brightly decorated cake in the center, under a banner that read PARTIES BY BETHANNE, Birthdays a Specialty. Below that was their phone number.

"What do you think?" she asked. "It's for a business card."

"It's great!"

"I wasn't sure about the balloons, but it needs something there, don't you think?"

Courtney examined it again and disagreed. "Take them out," she suggested.

With a click of her mouse, Annie deleted the balloons. She cocked her head to one side and nodded. "You're right. It looks cleaner without the balloons. Besides, Mom said someone phoned and asked about an adult birthday party and I think balloons are more associated with kids, don't you?"

Courtney nodded. "This whole party idea has taken off, hasn't it?"

Annie smiled. "It's been really wild around here. Andrew and I thought Mom should have her own business cards. I guess she'll need a Web site next." She returned her attention to the screen. "Anything else I should change?"

Courtney studied the graphic for another couple of minutes. "You might want to use a different font," she suggested, "one of the less fancy ones. This one's pretty but it's kind of difficult to read. Try Comic Sans or Verdana. Or maybe Georgia."

Annie made the changes, deciding on Comic Sans, and sat back to examine the effect. "Hey, I like that."

So did Courtney. "This is really nice—you doing this for your mom, I mean."

"She asked me to work at one of her parties this weekend," she said, still focusing on the monitor.

"Are you going to?" Courtney didn't mention that she'd volunteered, too.

"Yeah, I guess. She said you might be there."

"I was thinking about it."

"I'll do it if you will," Annie said and looked up, grinning.

A warm feeling touched Courtney. "Does this mean we're

friends?" she asked. It was an awkward question, but she needed to know.

Annie seemed to seriously consider it. After a moment she said, "I'd like that. And I know I already said this, but Andrew's right—I do owe you. He says you saved my ass." Her voice fell to a whisper. "So…thanks."

"It's okay." Courtney dismissed her gratitude. "I did some pretty stupid stuff myself after Mom died. One day I started a fire behind the grocery store. I can't even explain why I did it." She lowered her head. No one knew about that, not even her sister. "I was hurting so bad. It was stupid, and if anyone ever found out, I'd probably still be in some detention center."

"You didn't go to a rave, though, did you?"

"No, but I was younger than you. Trust me—I got into my share of trouble."

Annie's responding smile was weak, and she bit her lip. "According to the therapist I saw, what happened to us is pretty common. I'm not alone. Families split up, fathers walk away, and the kids just have to cope. I'm not very good at that. And…and I thought my father loved me."

"I'm sure he does." Courtney felt confident of that, although she could tell it was hard for Annie to believe.

"Maybe," Annie agreed reluctantly. "But he loves *her* more. It's all right, though—I'm dealing with it." Tears sprang to her eyes and she tried to blink them away.

"Can you print out that design?" Courtney asked, hoping to distract Annie. She pretended not to notice she was crying.

"Good idea." Annie turned back to her computer, reached for the mouse and clicked on the printer icon. The printer started to hum, and they both stared at it as a sheet of paper slowly emerged.

Courtney picked it up and studied the design. "It looks fabulous."

"You think so?" Annie asked. "I mean, I think it does, but it has to be perfect, you know? It has to look professional."

"It does. Your mom's going to flip when she sees it."

Annie's smile was bright with unshed tears. "Thanks, Court."

Court—that was what her friends in Chicago used to call her. For the first time since she'd left home, she didn't have that empty feeling in her stomach.

"Hey, what are you two up to?" Andrew asked, leaning against his sister's door.

He looked really good. He must've just returned from football camp because he carried his gym bag, which was unzipped. His cleats were on top.

"I designed Mom some business cards," Annie told him.

Courtney handed him the printout.

"Hey, this is good!"

"Don't act so surprised," his sister snapped.

His eyes met Courtney's, and he grinned. "You two want to go out for pizza?"

"You buying?" Annie asked.

"Sure. I got paid this week." He gestured at Courtney. "Can you come?"

"I'd like to." One slice of pizza and a small salad would be fine. She'd enjoy her friends' company and eat a reasonably healthy meal.

She was no longer trying to fill the hollowness inside.

25
CHAPTER

"Knitters just naturally create communities of friends and newfound friends at work, after work, or on the Internet, sharing their passion for knitting."
—Mary Colucci, Executive Director,
Warm Up America! Foundation

LYDIA HOFFMAN

I'd been spending a lot of time outside the shop, talking to the loan managers at three local banks. I had to do *something* to help Margaret, but because of my medical history I was afraid I'd be refused a loan. My suspicions were right—until I talked to a wonderful manager at the third bank I tried. My business had been open for a little more than a year, I was showing a profit, and my latest checkup with Dr. Wilson had revealed that I was cancer-free. Seattle First, a small neighborhood bank, looked everything over and agreed to give me the loan. This was a red-letter day in my life as a businesswoman. I was able to apply for and receive a loan! Definitely cause for celebration.

Margaret knew nothing about what I was doing. She made an effort to put on a brave front, the same way I did when it came to Brad. Matt still didn't have a job in his field. He'd worked as an electrical engineer for Boeing, but I wasn't really sure what he did. He'd recently found a job painting houses; I knew he hated it, but it brought in a paycheck, and with the little bit I paid Margaret they were managing to stay afloat. Except for their missed mortgage payments...

I signed the loan papers the first Monday in August. The summer was flying by, and I hadn't accomplished any of what I'd hoped. Earlier in the spring, Brad had promised to build me additional shelves for the yarn. We'd spent a few very satisfying Sunday afternoons working everything out on paper, measuring and designing the cubicles so they'd fit properly. I'd looked forward to helping him build them; so had Cody.

I needed new shelves, but that would have to wait, along with an idea I wanted to borrow from another store. In almost every yarn shop, space is a major consideration. There are so many new yarns and hand-dyed wools available that displaying them could be difficult. The particular store I'd visited in the north end of King County suspended hanks of brightly colored hand-dyed wool from the ceiling. It was clever and effective, and I'd hoped to do the same thing in a small section of A Good Yarn. Brad had said he'd place the screws in the ceiling for me.

I was perfectly capable of doing that on my own, but I hadn't done it. For some reason, I didn't seem able to move forward. Every improvement Brad and I had discussed, I'd put off. I just didn't have the heart for it.

Once I'd deposited the check in my account and had a cashier's check made out to Margaret, I drove to my sister's house. We'd talked briefly on Sunday and I'd casually asked her if she had any plans for today. Nothing much, she'd told me.

Margaret was outside watering her flower beds when I

parked on the street. Absorbed in thought, she apparently didn't hear or see me.

"Hey, big sister!" I called out in order to get her attention.

She started at the sound of my voice, and her hand jerked, sending a spray of water onto the sidewalk. "What are you doing sneaking up on me?" she snapped.

"I need to talk to you about something."

"This couldn't have waited until Tuesday?"

"Not really."

Margaret is always gruff when she's upset. Over the past year, I'd learned a great deal about her personality. She'll never be a vivacious, friendly sort of person, and I don't think she really knows how brusque she often sounds. She'd been a big help to me—still is—and while I pay her a salary, she could make a higher wage elsewhere. I wanted to do something for her and Matt, just…just because she's my sister. Just so she'd know how much I love her.

"Do you need anything?" Margaret asked, eyeing me suspiciously.

"A glass of iced tea would be nice."

Margaret hesitated before agreeing with a sigh and a nod of her head. She walked over to the side of the house, turned off the water and marched up the porch steps.

I followed her into the house and immediately saw the cardboard boxes cluttering the living room.

"We can't make the payment deadline, so there's no use pretending we can," Margaret said before I could ask. "We have until Friday before the bank files an eviction notice. It's bad enough to lose the house, but I don't want to drag my family through the humiliation of being evicted."

In the kitchen, too, I saw a number of boxes stacked in the corner. I was grateful I'd managed to get the loan when I did.

"I probably shouldn't worry about watering the yard," Margaret commented, "but I had to get out of here for a while." She took two tumblers from the cupboard. "It's just too depressing."

"I thought it was best to talk to you right away," I said, leading carefully into the reason for my visit. "Instead of waiting until morning," I added.

"Talk to me about what?" Setting the glasses on the table, Margaret sat down across from me.

"You know how much I appreciate the fact that you're working with me," I said.

"But?" she said cynically.

"But nothing."

Her eyes widened. "You aren't going to fire me?"

"Why would I fire you? I *need* you. No, I'm here to help."

Again Margaret had a suspicious look. "Help me do what? Pack up our belongings?"

I decided it was pointless to discuss this when I was sitting with a cashier's check in my purse. I opened my handbag and handed it to Margaret.

My sister took the check, read it, then frowned across the table at me. "Where did you get this money?" she demanded. "You went to Mom, didn't you?"

"No," I said. One thing my sister had in abundance was pride. She'd absolutely insisted Mom not know about this. I'd kept my promise and hadn't breathed a word to our mother.

"I got a bank loan," I said, unable to squelch my glee. "Think of it, Margaret. This is a huge step forward for me. A bank was willing to lend me money." I couldn't keep the excitement out of my voice. "That says something, doesn't it? They seem to think I'm a good risk."

My sister held the check with both hands as if she were afraid to release it. "What did you tell the bank?"

"They didn't ask too many questions." A slight exaggeration. I'd been drilled by one officer and then another, and I'd filled out as many forms as if I were being admitted to the hospital.

"You used the shop as collateral?"

I nodded. "It's all I have." That was true. My entire future, all I have and all I ever hope to have, is tied up in my yarn store.

Margaret's eyes filled with tears and she tried twice before she was able to speak. "I can't let you do this."

"Too late. It's already done." Knowing Margaret, I'd expected an argument. That was one reason I'd had the cashier's check made out in her name. "You're going to take that check, Margaret," I said using my sternest voice, "and give it to the mortgage company first thing tomorrow."

"I...I don't know how long it'll be before I can pay you back," she muttered.

I should have explained this earlier. "It isn't a loan."

"What do you mean?"

"I'm giving you the money."

Stunned at first, Margaret said nothing, then shook her head. "I—I don't know what to say."

"I mean it. The money is a gift." I'd thought very carefully about this. If I made the ten thousand dollars a loan, it would always come between us. My relationship with my sister was too important to risk problems over money. As far as I was concerned, this was the best way to handle it.

"I'm paying you back every cent," my sister said, still on the verge of tears.

"Margaret," I said, stretching my arm across the table to take her hand. "I repeat—the money is a gift."

"One I fully intend on repaying with interest once Matt's back on the job."

I could see that arguing with her was pointless. "Do whatever you feel you have to, but this isn't a debt or a loan or anything. It's a...a gift of love, from me to you. One day, who knows, I might need your help. I have in the past." Maybe not financial support, but emotional. "Don't you remember last year when I had that cancer scare? You were with me every single day. I couldn't have made it through that time without you. Now it's my turn."

Big tears finally spilled down her face and she struggled to speak. "Thank you," she managed in a hoarse croak.

I finished my iced tea and went home with a good feeling, grateful for the opportunity to help my sister. Although my store is officially closed on Mondays, I'm almost always there. I use Mondays to clear off my desk, process paperwork, place orders and get caught up on business.

Whiskers greeted me as I came into the shop, weaving between my legs and making a general nuisance of himself. My cat objects to being alone for long periods. I'd been away for a good part of the morning, and Whiskers wasn't happy with me. I crouched down and petted him, running my hand along his fur from ears to tail. He purred his appreciation as I murmured endearments.

That was when I saw the business-size envelope on the floor, some distance from the mail slot. Someone had apparently slipped a letter under my door. I couldn't imagine who or why. I straightened and walked over to pick it up.

Almost immediately I recognized Cody's printing. LYDIA was penciled across the front, with the *Y* and *D* almost double the size of the other letters.

Heart pounding, I tore open the note. It was a simple message. I MISS YOU. CAN I SEE YOU SOME TIME? Without meaning to, I crumpled the paper in my hands. Since my last meeting with Brad, when he'd announced that he was going back to Janice, I hadn't said a word to him. Not a single word. He'd come into the shop any number of times on business, but Margaret had always been there to run interference.

I doubted Brad knew anything about this note. He'd abided by my wishes and not contacted me. I suspected even more strongly that the one time Brad's name had come up on my

Caller ID, it hadn't been Brad at all, but his son. Cody hadn't phoned since, probably on strict orders from his father.

As I looked out the window, I noticed the UPS truck parked across the street. He wasn't inside. Before I could change my mind or reconsider the wisdom of what I was about to do, I unlocked the door and walked outside to see him. I wasn't sure where he was making his delivery, but I knew that sooner or later he'd reappear.

I surveyed the neighborhood and was about to cross the street when he stepped out of the floral shop next door to me.

"Brad," I said, stopping him. "Could we talk for just a moment?" I made an effort to sound unaffected.

He seemed surprised, but nodded. "Sure."

There were many things I wanted to say. I longed to tell him that I understood why he'd decided to try again with Janice. And—more than that—how much I loved him and Cody, how desperately I missed them both. But I didn't. "I got a note from Cody."

"What? When?" He sounded shocked, distressed—and hopeful—all at once.

"I found it this morning." I looked down for fear of what he'd read in my eyes. "He wanted to know if he could talk to me sometime."

"He misses you," Brad murmured.

"I miss him, too." And I missed Cody's father, but I didn't mention that. "I know this is hard on him and I…I don't want to confuse Cody or upset Janice, so if you think it's best if I don't call him, I'll understand."

Brad's eyes held mine. "I appreciate that."

My heart felt like it was about to break. "You don't want me to talk to Cody?" My disappointment obviously showed, because Brad quickly shook his head.

"If Cody wants to talk to you and you're willing, then I can't see that it would do any harm."

"Thank you," I whispered, overwhelmed and grateful. "Please recognize that I want Cody to have his family intact. When you first came to me, I was angry and hurt, but I'm over that now—over you." This seemed to be my day for exaggeration. I was far from over Brad, but I had to pretend otherwise.

He hesitated, as if he didn't know what to say.

"I'm dating again and…well, the two of us ignoring each other like this is silly." The dating part was an outright lie. I was nowhere near ready for a new relationship.

"Anyone I know?" Brad asked.

I shook my head, unwilling to lie further. I'm not very good at it—and it's not really a skill I hope to develop. I knew that if he questioned Margaret she'd cover for me, but I doubted he'd approach her; she'd been curt with him ever since our breakup. "If Cody wants to phone, please let him."

This time, Brad didn't meet my eyes. "He's been asking to, but I wasn't sure…"

"Like I said, I don't want to make Janice uncomfortable."

"I doubt she'll mind."

I gave him a slight, though genuine, smile. Being separated from Cody had been so hard, and the opportunity to at least speak to him lightened my heart. "I'll look forward to hearing from him, then," I said, as if we were no more than business acquaintances. That was all we ever would be, now that Janice was back in his life.

"Have a good day," he said automatically—as if I were just like any other customer.

"Thanks," I whispered, returning to the safety of my yarn store. Not until I turned the lock and retreated to my office did I realize how badly my hands shook.

This had been an eventful Monday for me. I'd received a bank loan, helped my sister and lied to the man I loved.

26

CHAPTER

ELISE BEAUMONT

Elise had never learned to drive. A driver's license was good for ID purposes, but hardly necessary. Seattle had perfectly good public transportation. The bus generally got her wherever she needed to go, and on rare occasions, Aurora would drive her or she'd take a taxi.

That all changed with Maverick's arrival. He was more than willing to drive her anywhere she wanted. Then he'd wait for her with limitless patience. For the past two weeks, he'd sat outside the yarn store while she attended her knitting class. She spoke so often about Bethanne, Courtney and Lydia that he knew almost as much about her friends as she did. She shared her concerns about Bethanne's job and her hopes that Courtney's senior year would be a good one. She'd also told him about Jacqueline, with whom she'd now attended two Birthday Club lunches.

"Let's go for a ride," he suggested Friday afternoon when they'd finished lunch.

Aurora, David and the boys were on a rare family outing to the Woodland Park Zoo. It was just the two of them, Maverick and Elise.

"A ride where?" she asked. No longer did she avoid his company and, in fact, she often sought him out. No longer did she instinctively distrust him—although she never forgot that he was a gambler. She didn't like it, feared he wouldn't be able to keep his promise, but decided to enjoy whatever time she had with him before he gave in to his compulsion again.

She did love to hear his stories, though. While she didn't approve of gambling, she had to admit the tales of his exploits intrigued her. He'd been all over the world, to Europe, to Australia, to the Caribbean. He'd gambled in many of those places, but he'd also experienced real adventures—a boat trip down the Nile, driving through the Australian Outback, being briefly—and erroneously—arrested in Paris. He'd met famous people and told her anecdotes about them. Elise found she could listen to him for hours. She envied, just a little, his emotional extravagance. Unlike Maverick, Elise had always been cautious and frugal, with her money *and* her life.

The ideal way to live, she thought, was probably a combination of his approach and hers....

"I was thinking it might be nice to take a drive to the mountains," Maverick said. "It's been years since I went up to Mount Rainier."

Elise frowned. "It's a little late in the day for that, don't you think?"

"Nah. Come on, Elise, aren't you bored sitting around the house knitting?"

She bristled. "I happen to enjoy my knitting, thank you very much."

"Bring it with you. You can knit in the car, can't you?"

"I...I suppose." Suddenly, she didn't *want* to yield to his plans. She no longer seemed to have any resistance to him, and that frightened her. "I believe I'll pass, but thank you for thinking of me," she said stiffly.

Maverick grew quiet then, his disappointment unmistakable. He washed his lunch plate and tucked it inside the dishwasher. Then he disappeared for a few minutes, returning with a spy novel he'd been reading, and sat down in the family room off the kitchen.

As she wiped the counters, Elise glared at him. She refused to let him manipulate her.

"You can go without me, you know," she told him.

Maverick lowered his book and glanced at her over his reading glasses. "I know." He went back to his novel, apparently engrossed in the plot.

With Maverick reading, Elise walked down the hallway to her room and reached for her knitting. She was finished with the first sock and working on the second one. On Tuesday she'd purchased yarn for another pair of socks; these, she'd knit for her daughter.

She finished two complete rounds until, with a disgusted sigh, she set her knitting aside and marched into the family room. "Oh, all right. I'll go."

His face broke into a broad smile. "I hoped you'd come around."

He'd blatantly used guilt to get his own way—and she'd let him. He was quite a master of manipulation; with barely a word, he'd coerced her into doing exactly what he wanted.

Within ten minutes, they were in the car and on their way out of the city, heading toward Mount Rainier National Park. Although Maverick had suggested it, Elise didn't bring her knitting. She had enough to concentrate on.

Maverick was a fascinating conversationalist, able to talk about anything, able to switch topics instantly. This was a gift she didn't have and one her ex-husband often used to ensnare his opponent on the other side of the gaming table. At least, according to his stories...

"I want you to tell me what happened," he said as they continued down the two-lane highway that led to the park.

"If you're referring to the debacle with the house, then let me inform you, the subject is closed." She couldn't bear the idea of exposing her foolishness to his scrutiny.

"Will you be okay financially?"

"Of course I will, once the lawsuit is settled." She felt irritated that he was asking her these awkward questions now, while she was virtually his captive. The only thing she could do was change the subject. "I don't remember the last time I was up in Paradise," she murmured, staring out the window. Maverick was a skillful driver and the scenery was breathtaking.

"I do," Maverick said, shooting her a look. "I'll bet you remember, too. We were on our honeymoon."

She swallowed tightly. Time to change the subject again. "You were gone this Wednesday. For several hours."

"I had personal business and before you ask, I wasn't gambling. You have my word on that."

She shouldn't have brought it up, and regretted that she had.

"Paradise was a misnomer," she said after a stilted pause. "Our honeymoon was ruined by those dreadful mice."

Maverick burst out laughing.

"It was no laughing matter," she said with a shudder. Maverick had managed to get them reservations in the National Park's beautiful and romantic lodge. In the middle of the night, Elise had awoken to a faint scratching sound. Her mistake was turning on the light. To her absolute horror, she saw five or six deer mice crawling in Maverick's overnight bag. She'd let out a scream that had startled her husband—and probably half the lodge—into sudden wakefulness. Maverick had peanuts in his suitcase and the mice had gone after those, carrying them out one by one in what was practically an assembly line.

The following morning Elise had complained to the man at the registration desk about the unsanitary conditions and the fact that there appeared to be an infestation of mice. He'd informed her that the lodge was prohibited by federal law from killing any of the wildlife in the area—including mice. The only place they were allowed to set traps was in the kitchen.

"Remember how I distracted you?" Maverick asked in a sultry voice.

Leave it to a man to mention sex. Or to hint at it, anyway. She refused to give him the satisfaction of a reply.

"You remember," he said, his amusement obvious.

"I most certainly do not." She hugged herself even tighter.

He laughed at her stubborn refusal to admit the passion they'd shared. "How long has it been, Elise?"

She shifted uncomfortably in her seat. "Longer for me than for you, no doubt."

"Don't be so sure."

She turned around to glance at him. "You can't fool me, Maverick. I was married to you, remember? I know you. You had an extremely healthy sexual appetite."

"After we split up, you used to let me come to your bed."

Her face went instantly crimson. "That was a mistake." The year following their separation and divorce, he'd showed up at the apartment every few nights and talked his way into her bedroom. Then he'd abruptly stopped and Elise knew why. He'd found some other woman who welcomed him. One who was happy to overlook his flaws and take what he offered without questions or recriminations.

"It wasn't a mistake on *my* part," he said.

"Do you mind if we talk about something else?" she asked in a bored voice.

"You used to be such a prude—until I got you between the sheets." He shook his head. "I guess you still are a prude."

"Stop it right this minute! Or I swear I'll…I'll open this door and jump out of the car."

"Well, that got a reaction, didn't it?" He chuckled softly.

"I'm sixty-five years old and I find this discussion embarrassing."

"I'm not dead yet, and I doubt you are, either," Maverick said smoothly.

Elise was determined not to answer.

They drove in silence after that and then, for no apparent reason, Maverick started laughing. Despite everything, Elise grinned. Then Maverick reached over and gave her hand a gentle squeeze.

The rest of the afternoon was delightful. They drove through Rainier National Park and dined on steak and baked potatoes in the lodge.

The house was dark and quiet when they finally returned. Worn out from an entire day at the zoo, Luke and John were sound asleep. Aurora and David must have been tired, too, because not a sound came from their part of the house.

Maverick escorted Elise to her bedroom door. "Thank you for a wonderful afternoon and evening," he whispered.

Elise kept her gaze averted. "Dinner was lovely." Everything about the day had been lovely. "Just...thank you." About to turn away, she didn't expect him to kiss her. But he did. He leaned forward and pressed his mouth to hers. His lips were warm and moist and his arms slid around her waist, pulling her close. When he ended the kiss and released her, Elise's knees nearly buckled.

"Good night, Elise," he whispered, touching her face as if memorizing the feel of her skin.

She mumbled a reply that was completely unintelligible and nearly fell into her room. Her hands shook as she undressed and carefully hung up her clothes.

The tap on her bedroom door came just as she'd finished brushing her teeth.

She closed her eyes, swaying, not sure what to do. She

could ignore him and go to bed—or she could open her door. Deciding quickly, she walked to the door.

As she'd expected, Maverick stood in the hallway. His eyes met hers in the light from her room. "Are you going to let me in," he asked, "or turn me away?"

27

CHAPTER

BETHANNE HAMLIN

"I don't mind helping you, Mom, but I've got a life too," Annie muttered as Bethanne carried party supplies out to the car. The trunk was nearly full.

Annie followed her with a china tea set for an Alice in Wonderland party. The birthday girl was turning nine and *Alice's Adventures in Wonderland* was one of her favorite books. Bethanne had designed an entire birthday party around that theme, including games, prizes and finger foods. Since her first dinosaur party for Elise's grandson, she'd come up with dozens of new party ideas.

"What are you going to do once school starts?" Annie asked, unwilling to drop the subject.

That was a good question. Bethanne had come to rely on her children and on Courtney for help with these events. Following football camp, practices had begun a few weeks earlier, and Andrew was busy most days. Annie was busy a lot of the time, too. To date, Courtney had been her most reliable helper. Thankfully her children didn't expect or want to be paid, and Courtney, too, refused any monetary compensation. Bethanne was grateful for their generosity, and since she was just getting this operation underway, every cent she could, she invested in the business.

"School starts in two weeks," Annie reminded her.

Bethanne closed the trunk. "I know." She could've done without that reminder. School was looming, and she'd truly be on her own with the business then. She could probably get help with the actual parties, but she'd have to complete the preparations herself. Still, all the work was worth it; giving Andrew a check so he could attend football camp had been the highlight of her summer. Nothing could diminish the sense of pride and accomplishment she'd felt.

"Andrew will be totally engrossed in football, so you won't be able to rely on him," Annie went on, oblivious to everything else.

As much as possible Bethanne would book parties around her son's games. She wanted to attend every one she could.

"And I'm on the swim team again."

"When did that happen?" Bethanne kept her voice carefully neutral. She'd been disappointed when her daughter dropped out of the swim team, and she was delighted that Annie had rejoined it. Yes, it did seem that the old Annie was back. According to Grant, the harassment against Tiffany had ceased. Painful as this period had been, Annie appeared to be past it.

"I called the coach and he said he'd welcome me back, but I have a lot of time to put in if I'm going to catch up with the other girls."

This was why Annie had been gone so much recently, Bethanne realized. Her daughter hadn't informed her about the swim team, and Bethanne didn't really understand why. Maybe Annie had wanted to wait, make sure it all worked out.

"I think swimming is a good idea," Bethanne said.

"What are you going to do?" her daughter asked. "When we're back in school and doing all our extracurricular stuff?"

"I'm thinking about it."

"How many parties have you got booked for September?"

"Annie, please," Bethanne cried. "I have to leave now if we're going to pick up Courtney, otherwise we'll be late."

"Mom, you need a *plan*."

"We can talk about it on the way," she said, hurrying inside for her purse and car keys. She didn't miss Annie's exasperated expression.

Annie was already in the front seat and buckled up by the time Bethanne returned.

"Well?" Annie demanded as Bethanne backed out of the driveway.

"I'll hire someone."

"Who?"

"Courtney." The girl was trustworthy and a natural with kids, and she seemed to have more free time than her own children did. Bethanne would insist on paying her.

Annie and Courtney had become good friends, just as she'd hoped. She had no idea what they talked about, but it wasn't unusual for them to spend two and three hours at a stretch in Annie's bedroom. Bethanne would've guessed they didn't have much in common, but apparently she was wrong.

"Courtney!" Annie exploded right on cue. "I was afraid you'd say that."

"Is something wrong with Courtney?" she asked mildly, reviewing her party list. Food, dishes, decorations, costumes… Eventually, she'd like to upgrade to a party van, too. She'd need the extra space, plus she could have her logo and phone number painted on the side.

"Mom," Annie continued, "you *can't* hire Courtney."

"Why not?" Bethanne asked, stopping for a red light.

"It isn't fair to her! This is her senior year and she's in a new school. She wants to join the yearbook staff. Did you know she was chosen to be yearbook editor at her high school in Chicago?"

Annie said this in awe. Bethanne suspected that her daughter was less impressed by the fact that Courtney was yearbook editor than by her willingness to walk away from the honor for her family's sake.

"Courtney came to Seattle and she doesn't know anyone," Annie went on.

"She knows you and Andrew," Bethanne countered.

"Andrew is so self-absorbed he isn't going to be much help to her," Annie said with a dismissive gesture. "Mom, if you ask Courtney, I know she'll say yes, so you *can't* ask her. It would be completely unfair. Courtney needs a chance to make friends, and to do that she needs time. Besides—" she gave an exasperated sigh "—she's already off on the wrong foot."

"What do you mean?" The light changed, and Bethanne drove through the intersection.

"Didn't you hear?" Annie cried as if this were a disaster of catastrophic proportions. "Courtney registered for classes without talking to me and it's *awful*. She signed up for all the wrong ones. She's in first-period PE!"

As Bethanne recalled, there'd been some discussion about this during their most recent knitting class. Courtney didn't have a lot of options in registering for her classes. After the basic requirements were met, the only electives left were the least popular ones.

"Okay, I'll find someone else to hire," Bethanne said. "Not Courtney." Privately, she thought Courtney should make the decision about whether or not to accept the job herself. On the other hand, she didn't want the girl agreeing to it out of a sense of obligation or friendship, and Annie was probably right in thinking that would happen.

"Thanks, Mom."

After a few minutes' silence, her daughter said, "I phoned Dad last night."

"Oh." That was unexpected, but Bethanne knew better than to reveal any emotion. Annie wouldn't have mentioned the call if there wasn't something she wanted her mother to know.

"We talked."

"I'm proud of you," Bethanne said, and she meant it. The fact that Annie had reached out to him revealed a new maturity in her daughter. "I want you to have a relationship with your father."

Annie laughed softly. "Dad's still pretty mad about some of the stuff I pulled. I told him to get over it."

That was a fitting comment, since Grant had said virtually the same thing about Annie during that conversation at the French Café.

"I bragged about how successful your party business is."

"Thanks," Bethanne said, grinning at her daughter. She was curious to know whether Grant had commented on her business accomplishments, but she wouldn't ask.

"*She's* still upset about what I did to her car, even though the insurance company covered it."

"I'd rather not discuss that," Bethanne said. "That's in the past, you've apologized and it'll never happen again."

"Yeah," Annie said on the end of a sigh. "But about Tiffany—well, there's no easy way to say this."

"Then just say it," Bethanne advised.

"She and Dad are flying to Vegas this afternoon to get married. They've got everything arranged with one of those wedding chapel places. He seemed to think I should know. I guess because he wanted me to tell you."

She'd known it would happen sooner or later, but still…

"Are you okay?" her daughter asked, watching her closely. Her sweet face was tense with concern.

"I'm fine." And she was, although there was regret and

melancholy mingled with her acceptance. "What's going to be different?" she asked with a nonchalant shrug. "He's been living with Tiffany ever since he moved out."

"I just wanted to make sure you weren't going to freak out."

"How do *you* feel about it?" Bethanne asked.

Annie took a moment to consider the question. "It's sad, you know. It's like Dad isn't even part of my life anymore. I don't even see him because *she* refuses to let me in the house. As if I'd *want* to visit," she scoffed. "You know, Mom, I don't really care."

"I don't either," Bethanne murmured. "But it's important that you maintain a connection with your dad. Your relationship with Grant has nothing to do with Tiffany—or me."

After the party, she had an overwhelming urge to talk to Paul, but she waited until Andrew and Annie were out for the night. They were attending a rock concert at Key Arena—some rapper whose lyrics Bethanne couldn't make out. From what she knew of rappers, that was probably for the best.

Paul answered on the second ring. "I was going to give you a call," he said. He sounded genuinely pleased to hear from her.

"Would you like to come over for dinner?" She wanted to see him although she didn't intend to cook. "I'm going to order pizza."

"Perfect. I'll rent a movie," he said, then hesitated. "Now tell me what's wrong."

"How do you know something's wrong?"

"I can hear it in your voice."

"Really?"

"Bethanne, you're avoiding the subject."

"You might want to wait until you get here."

"No," he insisted, "tell me now."

She sighed. Grant hadn't had the courage to tell her; instead he'd done it through their daughter. Even then, Annie had been the one to phone him, otherwise none of them would've known until after the fact.

"Tonight, while we're eating pizza and watching a DVD, Grant and Tiffany will be in Vegas. Three guesses why."

"They're getting married."

"Bingo."

Paul didn't comment for a long moment. "I'll bring the wine."

"Make it a big bottle," she said.

28
CHAPTER

COURTNEY PULANSKI

Courtney arrived for her orientation class at Washington High School early on Monday, August 15. She'd already received her class assignments, and according to Annie, she'd failed miserably in choosing her electives. She was doomed to become a social outcast if what Annie said was true.

She spent the morning at the high school. The purpose of the orientation was to ensure, among other things, that she'd be familiar enough with the building to make her way from class to class on the first day of school. The summer was almost over, and Courtney prayed the year would pass just as quickly.

At noon, once she was finished with orientation, she headed home. Grams had volunteered to drive her, but Courtney had refused, taking her bike instead. It was parked behind the building, close to the football field. When she went to retrieve it, she noticed the football team practicing. She stopped and decided to watch for a few minutes. Annie had boasted that Andrew played quarterback, although it was hard to recognize him beneath all that equipment.

The three of them had gone out for pizza that one night, but Andrew didn't stay with Annie and Courtney long. Very soon after they'd arrived at the restaurant, Andrew had run into a group of his friends and abandoned the girls. Not that it really mattered… She'd seen him a few times since, mostly at Annie's place, but she doubted she'd said a dozen words to him.

Sitting in the stands, Courtney saw Andrew throw a pass deep into the end zone. The receiver leaped into the air and miraculously came down with the football. Excited to have scored the touchdown, Andrew raced to the end of the field and threw his arms around the receiver.

A whistle blew and the team formed a huddle around their coach. After a couple of minutes, all the players sent up a cheer and trotted toward the locker room.

Andrew had removed his helmet and was talking to a friend when he glanced up into the stands. He must have seen her because he stared as if trying to determine whether this was someone he knew.

Courtney felt uncomfortably conspicuous. She waved and stood up to leave.

Andrew started toward the chain-link fence, obviously intending to speak to her. Embarrassed now, Courtney walked down the steep concrete steps and met him at the fence.

"I didn't recognize you at first," he said.

"I wasn't sure that was you, either." Courtney smiled, happy just to see him. She hoped he'd notice the fact that she'd lost weight—almost fifteen pounds. She was beginning to discern a difference in how her clothes fit.

"They had orientation for new students this morning," she explained, nervously pointing at the building behind her. She had to make clear to Andrew that she hadn't come down here because of him. She liked him—okay, *really* liked him—but she didn't want him knowing it.

"Yeah, the school always does that."

"My bicycle's back here."

He nodded, apparently disinterested. "Have you got your class assignments yet?"

Courtney told him what she remembered.

"I'm in second period Honors English," he said.

"You are?" This was good news as far as Courtney was concerned. She'd know at least one person in that class. To hear Annie talk, she'd gotten the very dregs of the elective courses.

Another player shouted at Andrew, and he looked over his shoulder. "Be there in a minute," he shouted back.

"You'd better go," she said.

"Yeah," he agreed. "Listen, I haven't had a chance to tell you, but I'm grateful you called me that night about Annie. She's feeling a lot better since she started hangin' with you."

"Thanks. I needed a friend, too."

They exchanged goodbyes and see-you-laters. As Andrew walked away, a blond girl raced onto the field. She gave a loud shriek, and when Andrew turned, she leaped into his arms, wrapping her legs around his waist. Although Andrew was sweaty and hot from practice and still in his uniform, she planted an openmouthed kiss on his lips. Naturally, the girl was thin and beautiful.

Courtney turned away to find a second girl almost directly behind her.

"Oh. Hi," she said, giving Courtney a look that would have frozen motor oil.

"Hi." Despite the chilly greeting, Courtney felt this was her opportunity to make friends. "I'm Courtney Pulanski."

"Shelly Johnson. I'm with Melanie."

It seemed Melanie was the one with a lip lock on Andrew.

"I'm a friend of Andrew and Annie's," she said, hoping this would smooth the way for her. They were basically the only teenagers she knew. She'd met a lot of people since she'd arrived in Seattle, but most of them collected social security. Bethanne and Lydia were two exceptions, but Bethanne was probably close to her father's age, and Lydia had to be at least thirty.

"Yeah," Shelly said with the same lack of welcome. "I've heard about you."

This was interesting. "Really?"

"Uh-huh."

Courtney thought giving the other girl some background might warm her reception. "I recently moved here from Chicago."

"Will you be going to this school?"

Courtney nodded. "It's my senior year."

"Same as Andrew," she said, and her gaze narrowed suspiciously, as if she was trying to read Courtney's intentions toward Annie's brother.

Courtney wanted it understood that she didn't consider herself competition for Melanie. "I'm actually more Annie's friend than Andrew's," she murmured.

"Uh-huh. Just so you know, Mel and Andrew have been dating for a year. Mel's the head cheerleader and she'll probably be Homecoming Queen. It's *perfect* because Andrew's for sure gonna be King."

"Perfect," Courtney echoed. It was all so perfectly perfect. She didn't understand how she could be deemed a threat to this perfect romance.

As soon as she could, Courtney left and biked back to her grandmother's. She felt a surprising sense of energy as she rode, although she was definitely out of sorts.

"I have your lunch ready," Grams told her when she walked

into the kitchen. A bowl of soup waited on the table, along with a tray of sliced carrots and celery.

"I'm not hungry," Courtney snapped, stomping toward her bedroom.

"Courtney Pulanski, there's no need to get snippy with me," her grandmother said sternly.

Courtney was instantly contrite. "I'm sorry, Grams."

"What's wrong?"

Courtney shook her head, not knowing what to say. She could hardly even put words to what she felt. It was that familiar ache of loneliness, that sense of not fitting in. She missed her friends and her family and her old high school. More than anything in the world, she just wanted to go home.

"Maybe you're tired?" her grandmother suggested.

A nap was her grandmother's solution to just about every problem. That or a bowel movement. Rather than respond, Courtney continued up the stairs to her room.

Once inside, she closed the door and logged onto the Internet. Her spirits lifted immediately when she saw an e-mail from her father. He sounded well, which was a huge relief. She felt a constant, nagging worry about him. She'd heard far too many stories about kidnappings in South America to be comfortable with her dad working there. She answered his e-mail right away and described the orientation class, exaggerating her enthusiasm for the start of school. Courtney didn't want her father to be concerned about her, didn't want to add to the burdens he already carried.

After reading her other mail—from Julianna and two of her Chicago friends—she lay down on her bed and stared up at the ceiling, assessing her chances for success this year. At the moment everything seemed bleak.

It was the way Melanie had looked at her, Courtney decided. Andrew's girlfriend had given her the eye as she claimed possession of Andrew. She viewed Courtney as an unknown and unwelcome threat. Funny how much you could derive from a single look.

Shelly, the friend, didn't even pretend to be friendly. Their entire conversation had been an attempt to gain information so she could assure the perfect "Mel" that Courtney was a nobody.

Courtney did wonder why Annie had never mentioned Melanie. Maybe she didn't like her brother's girlfriend. Or maybe it simply hadn't occurred to her.

"Do you want me to bring you your lunch?" her grandmother shouted from the foot of the stairs.

Courtney reluctantly slid off the bed and stepped out into the hallway. "Grams, I told you, I'm not hungry." And the last thing she wanted was for her grandmother to climb the stairs. Vera had made her feelings about that quite clear.

"You should eat something."

"I will later."

Her grandmother's face darkened. "I'm worried about you."

"I'm all right."

"Did someone upset you?"

Courtney slowly came down the stairs, her hand on the railing. "It doesn't matter."

Her grandmother looked as if she didn't believe her.

"Maybe I'll have some soup, after all," Courtney said, and Grams brightened.

"I want to hear about your classes." She bustled into the kitchen, with Courtney following.

They sat at the table and chatted while Courtney ate her tomato soup and carrot sticks.

"Leta thinks once you're settled in school, you should join the swim team," Courtney's grandmother said in an encouraging voice. "We all agree you're like greased lightning in the water."

Courtney hid a smile. She'd become a more skilled swimmer through the summer, but it wasn't any wonder Grams thought she was fast, considering her competition was a group of eighty-year-olds.

"Think about it," Grams urged.

"I will," Courtney promised.

29
CHAPTER

"You can do it. It's only one stitch at a time."
—Myra Hansen, owner, Fancy Image Yarn,
Shelton, WA.
www.FancyImageYarn.com

LYDIA HOFFMAN

I was looking forward to my next sock class—although it was technically my last. Elise, Bethanne and Courtney had each completed one pair of socks using two circular needles and had already started on a second. Once again I was enthralled with the way three women, from dissimilar backgrounds, could be brought together by the simple enjoyment of knitting. I'd been a silent witness to it all, and marveled anew at how their lives had become entwined.

Elise was the one who'd suggested Bethanne start her own party business, and Courtney had become a special friend to Bethanne's daughter, Annie. Best of all, they'd become friends to each other. And to me…

Margaret had been in good spirits ever since the worry of

losing their home had been removed. I didn't know what she'd told Matt about the money, but it didn't matter. Not once had she brought up the subject of the ten thousand dollars, and frankly, I was relieved. I'd gladly make those loan payments and never say a word. My family had sacrificed so much for me through the years that it felt good to be giving something back. To Mom, who needed my time and attention more than ever, and to my sister.

Elise arrived for class first, and I noticed the white Lincoln Continental parked in front of the shop with the distinguished older man sitting behind the wheel. I found her ex-husband's devotion rather touching, and there was a certain reassurance in knowing that love can be renewed—not that I expected any such thing in my own life.

I love Brad and Cody; time wouldn't change that. Cody and I talked once or twice a week. He told me his dad said he could phone me anytime he wanted. He rarely mentioned his mother, as if he knew talking about Janice and his dad was painful to me. The only concrete information I'd learned was that his mom still had her own place. I figured that probably wouldn't be for long.

"Good morning, everyone," Elise said. She positively glowed—there was no other word for it.

I had to stop what I was doing and look again. "You're in a good mood," I commented.

"My daughter said the same thing."

"I see Maverick's here," Margaret announced, looking out the display window.

Elise blushed with pleasure. "I told him it's utter nonsense to sit outside and wait, but he says he doesn't have anything better to do. He reads the newspaper." She sat down at the table and brought out her knitting. "I ended up giving him the socks I knit, so once I finish these for Aurora, I'll make a pair for David."

"Was Maverick surprised?" It wasn't any of my business, but I was curious. The first socks I'd knit with the circular-needle method were for Brad. He'd nearly worn them out, so I'd knit several more pairs. I wonder if he still wore them. If Janice knew who'd made those socks, she might ask him to throw them in the garbage. Or do it herself, I thought darkly.

Elise was explaining that Maverick loved the socks and yes, he'd been completely surprised, when the door opened and Bethanne breezed into the shop.

"I'm not late, am I?" she asked. "I get so involved with what I'm doing that I lose track of where I need to be." She hurried to the back of the shop, where Elise sat by herself.

Bethanne had changed so much since that first class in June. She was confident, optimistic, *happy*. There was a mystery man in her life, too. She'd mentioned his name in passing, Pete or Paul, but I'd forgotten.

Courtney was almost directly behind Bethanne. I was concerned about her; for the past two weeks she'd been quieter than usual. I knew she was feeling stressed about starting a new school and I hoped the transition would be smooth. I wouldn't broach the subject, but if she wanted to bring it up, I'd be ready and willing to listen.

"This is officially our last class," I said and to my delight the announcement was greeted with boos and jeers. "Would you like to continue?" All three instantly agreed, which was exactly what had happened with my original class. "Then I propose that we turn this into a knitting support group." I'd been thinking about beginning a new one, and this was the perfect opportunity. "I'll let the other classes know, so we might have a few other knitters joining us now and then." I explained that they'd continue meeting each week—same time, same place. They were welcome to bring in whatever they wanted to knit and I'd be available to help anyone who had a question or a problem. I no longer charged for this, because I'd seen the benefits of having people come to the shop on a regular basis.

"That sounds ideal," Elise said, speaking for the group. "I've enjoyed this class more than I can say."

I suspected she was so in love with her ex-husband that the whole world seemed shiny and bright. I didn't know whether there was any kind of arrangement between them. Maybe they were just living in the present, not worrying about the future.

"I'll come every week I can," Bethanne assured the others. "The only reason I couldn't is if I have a function, but I can't imagine there'll be too many birthday parties on weekday afternoons."

"Me neither," I agreed. "You've finished your socks, right?"

Bethanne nodded.

"You gave them to your son?"

Color crept up her neck and invaded her cheeks. "Actually, no. I gave them to a…friend."

Margaret walked over to the table, carrying a stack of pattern books. "Paul?"

Bethanne nodded. "Don't look at me like that. We're just friends. He's the ex-husband of the woman my husband left me for." There were a few gasps. "His ex-wife and my ex-husband are married now," she said matter-of-factly, "and we get together once in a while to talk things over. How we feel about it and all that."

"When did they get married?" Courtney asked and seemed surprised.

"Just recently. It wasn't unexpected, but it helps to have someone to discuss this with. Paul's great." She took a deep breath. "He's a few years younger and well, he'd like us to have a more…romantic relationship. I promised to consider it, but in the end I decided we'd be more valuable to each other as friends. I told him the only way I'd go out with him was if his mother came along to chaperone."

Elise and Courtney laughed.

"I'm encouraging him to see someone closer to his own age."

"What about you?" Margaret asked. "Are you ready to date?"

Bethanne shook her head. "Not yet. Dating means I'd have to shave my legs and wear panty hose. That's more bother than it's worth at this point."

"You don't shave your legs?" Courtney asked with an appalled look. "I do practically every day."

"Annie, too." Then Bethanne shrugged. "I got out of the habit in my thirties."

"What about you, Court?" I asked, feeling comfortable enough with the teenager to shorten her name. "Will you be able to join the support group?"

"I'll come until school starts," she said, "and I might even be able to come after that, but I'd need to discuss it with my advisor. I think my Tuesday schedule should be okay."

"Hey," Elise said, "who says we have to meet at the same time? We could make it after school, instead, and then Courtney could join us for sure. Does that work for everyone?"

An immediate chorus of agreement followed. "Three o'clock it is," I announced.

The bell chimed and one of my all-time favorite knitters came into the shop. "Jacqueline!" I cried, cheered to see her. It'd been a couple of weeks since we'd talked. She was a regular at the Friday charity sessions, but she'd been on a trip with her husband.

"I'm back from New York City and here for a yarn fix," she informed me. Everyone at the table knew Jacqueline, so introductions weren't necessary.

She had that look in her eye, a look I recognized. Those of us who are addicted to yarn seem to share it. Jacqueline was among my best customers; she could afford to buy as much yarn as she wanted and she did, without restraint. She'd told me recently that Reece had set aside a room in their house for her yarn stash. I envied her all that space. Jacqueline had every intention of knitting each skein—once she found the project best suited to it. I, too, had a million projects waiting. We both had more yarn tucked away than we could possibly knit in an entire lifetime, or even two.

Jacqueline sat down next to Elise and admired her work. She tended to dominate the conversation, but no one really minded. Her enthusiasm for yarn and knitting was contagious.

The phone rang and my ever-efficient sister answered it. I wasn't paying much attention but when she replaced the receiver and walked over to the table, where I sat with the class, I noticed the color had drained from her face.

Margaret placed her hand on my shoulder. "It's Mom," she managed to say. "We need to get to Swedish Hospital right away."

"What happened?" My heart was instantly in my throat.

"She collapsed—the neighbor found her on the patio. No one knows how long she was there."

I leaped up from the chair, ready to rush out, when I realized I had a store full of customers. Several women were browsing among the yarn displays and one was flipping through patterns. Not to mention my class...

"Go," Jacqueline insisted. "I'll mind the business until you get back. Just go."

"Can I do anything to help?" Elise asked.

"Me?" That was Bethanne.

"I can stay, too," Courtney said.

I was overwhelmed by gratitude for their kindness and compassion. "Thank you. Thank you all so much." These women were more than my customers and my students. They were my friends.

Margaret had her purse by the time I went to collect mine. When I came out of the office, Brad had just arrived with a delivery. He stood near the door.

"We have to leave," Margaret was telling him as she

signed for the yarn. "It's Mom. She's been rushed to the hospital."

He looked at me, frowning with concern. "Is she going to be all right?"

"I don't know," I told him. "I don't know anything yet." I couldn't control my reaction, my need for comfort, for *him*. I reached out to Brad. I needed his arms around me one last time, for courage and strength. He seemed to understand that intuitively, and when I moved toward him, he drew me into his embrace.

"We have to go," Margaret said in a low voice.

He released me, and I thanked him wordlessly, then rushed out of the store.

The staff at Swedish was wonderful, although it took what seemed like hours before we were able to talk to anyone. I berated myself over and over for not being more available to my mother. She was never demanding of my time and grateful for whatever I gave her. I did visit two or three times a week, but clearly that wasn't enough.

Margaret saw her as often as she could, too. But Mom needed more than scattered visits from her two daughters. I was nearly choking on guilt and so, I suspected, was my sister.

Margaret hated being inside a hospital. It was because of the smell, she said, which immediately made her feel anxious. I'd spent practically my entire youth in one and had grown so accustomed to it that I no longer noticed. Margaret had a firm grip on my arm, and for once she was relying on me.

We were asked to wait in a sitting room until the doctor could update us on Mom's condition. The chairs were comfortable, and a television was on, playing a soap opera—ironically it was *General Hospital*. I didn't pay attention, didn't hear a single word. My mind whirled with guilt and fear and recriminations. I was certain I'd failed my mother and that everything was somehow my fault.

A physician appeared and, as if our movements were synchronized, Margaret and I stood simultaneously.

The doctor came straight to the point. "Your mother is in serious condition. She's in a diabetic coma."

This was a shock to both of us.

"We've got her stabilized and I expect her insulin levels to even out, but this is a disease that is not to be taken lightly."

"No one in the family is diabetic," Margaret said. "We had no idea Mom could come down with this."

"She lives alone?"

We both nodded.

Again the physician was straightforward. "Well, I'd suggest you investigate placing her in assisted living."

He wanted us to take our mother out of the only home she'd known for the last fifty years. I didn't know if I could do that—but I realized we had no choice.

30
CHAPTER

ELISE BEAUMONT

The house was quiet when the light tap sounded at Elise's bedroom door. She was waiting for Maverick. She was so in love with this man that she'd lost all sense of propriety. She knew what he was, knew it to the very depths of her heart, but now—just like all those years ago—it didn't seem to matter.

The knock came, and she opened her door to let him in. He pulled her into his arms and they kissed. They'd made love just once—the night after their excursion into the mountains—and when it was over, they'd both cried, holding each other in the aftermath of passion. Their first sexual reunion had been a combination of excitement, embarrassment, fear and anticipation. They'd felt awkward with each other, but they'd also experienced tenderness and joy. They'd spent most nights together since then, simply holding each other close. After sleeping alone all these years, Elise hadn't thought it possible to bring a man to her bed, a single bed at that. Anyone seeing them cramped against the wall would've found the sight comical, she was sure. She fell asleep in his embrace and then in the early hours of the morning, Maverick slipped back into the boys' room.

No one was the wiser. At least, not as far as she knew. She suspected David and Aurora had guessed, but neither mentioned it. Elise pretended her daughter was oblivious to the late-night shuffle between Maverick's room and hers.

"This is silly, you know," Maverick murmured, pulling back the sheet so they could get into bed together. He let her go first and then followed.

"What's silly, our being together?" He was right, but she found it alarming that he'd admit it.

"Our being together is the only thing *right* about this situation," Maverick insisted in a husky whisper. "What's wrong is sneaking around in the middle of the night. Good grief, Elise, I'm sixty-six years old. The last time I did this, I was a teenager."

"Stop!" she said, giggling.

"Don't tell me *you're* accustomed to this."

"Of course I'm not!"

"Then let me make an honest woman of you."

Elise slid under the sheets until she was down far enough to rest her head against Maverick's shoulder. "Are you suggesting we…get married? Again?" While it might sound appealing, she wasn't convinced that was really the solution.

"Do you want to live in sin?"

"I…I don't know." She'd had her freedom for the past thirty years. "Can I think about it?"

"Yes." He rubbed his leg against hers. "I love you, Elise. I've always loved you."

She believed Maverick did love her, but that didn't mean she could trust him. If she was a gambling woman, she would've bet that, given the opportunity, he'd be back at the gaming tables.

Maverick kissed the top of her head. "I talked to the real

estate agent about the apartment complex this afternoon," he whispered.

He'd left the house after lunch and been gone almost four hours. He never told her where he went, but this wasn't the first time he'd mysteriously disappeared. Elise had her suspicions, but didn't press him for details. Some things it was better not to know.

But it was too hard not to say *something,* not to ask for even a hint. "You were away for a long time," she murmured.

"I know. You're worried, aren't you?"

"Should I be?"

"I wasn't gambling."

Elise closed her eyes. She struggled, once again, to take him at his word. Too often, she'd looked the other way rather than confront the truth. It distressed her to realize that nothing had really changed about him—or her—in all these years.

"I swear to you I wasn't," he reiterated.

"Okay." She placed her arm around his middle. He'd been her one folly in life. She knew what he was when she'd married him the first time. Her love hadn't changed him then and it probably wouldn't now.

"The deal went through on the condo."

"Oh."

"I'm moving in next week."

She didn't know how to respond, unwilling to reveal her disappointment or her sudden feeling of loss.

"I've stayed longer than I should have," he whispered. "I never intended to intrude on Aurora and David for more than a couple of weeks."

He didn't want to overstay his welcome any more than Elise wanted to burden her daughter and family. But there was nowhere else for her to go. She was beginning to think she might never get her money back. The courts moved so slowly that by the time the case was settled, she'd be dead and buried, she thought cynically.

"I'd like you to move in with me," he said, his voice a throaty whisper.

"I'm…not sure." The temptation to give in was stronger than anything she'd felt in years.

"We don't need to remarry if you don't want."

"Do you?" she asked.

"More than you'll ever know." He tightened his hold on her. She lay there quietly, comforted by his arms around her, and eventually realized he was asleep.

It was a long time before Elise managed to doze off. In the morning when she woke, he was gone. Aurora was already up and in the kitchen, dressed in her housecoat. Elise poured herself a cup of coffee. She knew David had left for work; he was usually on the road by seven. The house remained quiet. Before long, the boys would be up and so would Maverick. Elise savored these few minutes alone with her daughter.

"Mom," Aurora said tentatively. "Did you know Dad's moving?"

Elise nodded. "He told me…last night." Embarrassed, she kept her back to Aurora as she added cream to her coffee, stirring more than necessary.

"You and Dad seem to be getting along quite well."

"Uh… We are."

"It's all gone so much better than I expected."

"Yes, but then your father always was a charmer," Elise said tartly. She turned around and her face heated up at Aurora's speculative look. "Oh, all right, if you must know, your father and I are sharing a bed." Elise didn't understand what possessed her to blurt it out like that. It made their love sound sordid and wrong, when sleeping with Maverick was the most natural thing in the world.

Aurora tried to hide her amusement by taking a sip of coffee. "It's no secret. David and I guessed right away."

This was embarrassing. Might as well go for broke. "He wants me to marry him."

"Will you?"

If she knew the answer to that, she wouldn't be discussing it with her daughter. "I...I'm not sure what to do. Your father—well, you know your father."

"I don't, Mom, not really. I have an image of him, but what Dad's really like...I guess it's somewhere between reality and my fantasy."

"He's been here all these weeks."

"Yes," Aurora said with a deep sigh. "He's been wonderful with the boys. They adore him and I do, too—but then I always did."

"I know," she whispered. There'd been a time when Elise had resented her daughter's love for her father, but no more. "I've made so many mistakes in my life," she confessed. "I don't want to make another one."

"Follow your heart, Mom," Aurora said quietly. "Follow your heart."

31

CHAPTER

BETHANNE HAMLIN

Bethanne was almost afraid of her newfound happiness. Her fledgling business showed real promise. With every birthday party she designed, she booked two and often three more. But Annie was right. She couldn't continue to do this without paid employees and additional help. With school starting in a few days, she wouldn't have any choice but to hire an assistant.

What she needed, according to Paul, was a start-up business loan. He seemed so confident she'd get one that her doubts fell away. Because she'd never established credit on her own or even filled out a loan application, he'd promised to look everything over before she visited the bank.

They were meeting Monday at noon on the Seattle waterfront at Myrtle Edwards Park. She'd packed a thick deli sandwich, fruit and a drink as a small thank-you for his thoughtfulness. She was too nervous to eat and intended to go directly to her local bank following their meeting.

She had a picnic table staked out early and sat there, enjoying the late-summer day. The sun's reflection on the water made it a deep greenish-blue and the wind off Puget Sound was fresh with the briny scent of the sea. A Washington State ferry could be seen leaving the dock, heading for either Bremerton or the town of Winslow on Bainbridge Island.

Bethanne rarely had reason to take the ferry, but in the painful aftermath of divorce, she'd taken one to Bremerton. She'd stood outside in the coldest, wettest part of the winter, tears streaming down her cheeks. The wind and the rain pummeled her, and she prayed with desperation that she'd catch cold and die because death seemed preferable to this horrible pain. How grateful she was now that her prayer hadn't been answered. It felt as though the sun was shining on her life these days.

She didn't see Paul until he stepped up to the table. "You're certainly preoccupied," he said with a smile.

"Paul," she gasped. Impulsively she reached out and hugged him—and was shocked when he wrapped his arms around her. They talked almost every day and saw each other two or three times a week. He'd become her confidant and her friend, and they relied on each other for moral support. She didn't want that to change, and she'd assumed he understood her feelings. Gently she disengaged herself.

"How's my favorite party girl?" he teased.

"I'm great—I think." She'd know more after he reviewed her loan application. "I brought you lunch," she announced and pointed to the small cooler she'd carried from her car.

"You didn't need to do that," he protested, slipping into the seat across from her.

"I know, but I wanted to thank you for everything you've done."

"Like what?"

"Paul, don't you know?" She couldn't believe he was unaware of how much he'd helped her in the past few months. He'd been her friend when she'd badly needed one. He'd been a major source of encouragement when she'd started her party business. Most importantly, Paul had showed her she was alive again when the divorce had nearly destroyed her. Paul, and her friends at A Good Yarn, had shaped the new Bethanne. The new, improved Bethanne, with dreams and courage and a promising future. She told him all this, and then couldn't seem to stop talking.

"Okay, okay." He laughed and held up both hands. "I didn't have a clue I was such a hero."

"You *are*. You're my hero."

He sobered then, the laughter vanishing from his eyes. "And you're mine."

The intensity of his look made Bethanne uncomfortable, so she opened the small cooler and brought out the thick corned beef sandwich she'd prepared. "Here, I'll get this ready while you read over the loan application."

"Okay," he said agreeably.

As she set up his lunch, Bethanne noticed that her hands were shaking. The last few times she'd been with Paul, she'd recognized the subtle changes in their relationship. The sexual tension between them was all too evident, and that frightened her more than applying for the bank loan. As much as possible, she wanted to keep this relationship safe. She feared that acting on sexual impulses would ruin the friendship, and Bethanne couldn't bear that.

She spread out a napkin and peeled the wrap from around the sandwich while Paul scanned the loan application.

"You didn't work after you were married?" he asked, glancing up.

"Well, I did until Andrew was born. I have it down there." She pointed out where her previous employment was listed on the application. She'd worked in a boutique, doing the display windows. She'd enjoyed her job for the two years she'd worked there.

"That was more than eighteen years ago."

"I know, but if you take a look at the volunteer work I've done, I think it shows I'm qualified and responsible."

Paul nodded.

Bethanne relaxed. "Okay, be honest now," she said. "If you were a bank officer, would you give me the loan?"

His hesitation was enough to make her heart stop. "Paul?"

"You said you wanted me to be honest."

"Yes." She wouldn't have it any other way.

"It's going to be a hard sell. There are disadvantages—and advantages. The fact that you've never had your own credit is a negative. So is the fact that you haven't had a paying job in the last eighteen years."

"What can I do to make the loan application more attractive?" she asked.

"Show the bank your business records for the work you've done this summer."

Bethanne was afraid he'd say that. She wasn't much good at this sort of thing and really needed to take a class to learn basic accounting. All her receipts were crammed in a shoebox. Perhaps Andrew and Annie might be able to help. She recalled that her son had taken a bookkeeping class as a junior, but he was so busy these days with football and his part-time job. And now school was starting again.

"Well, well, well. What do we have here?" That ironic male voice was easily recognizable to Bethanne.

She smiled serenely. "Hello, Grant."

Her ex-husband stared at Bethanne and Paul. He didn't look good; his shirt was wrinkled—not badly, but it wasn't pressed the way she used to do it. Grant had always been meticulous about his appearance. He needed a haircut, and that was another surprise. He used to have regular appointments. Bethanne knew, because she was the one who'd set up those appointments. They'd been apart for two years, so one would think he'd manage to survive without her by now.

"You know Paul, don't you?" Bethanne said casually, gesturing toward Tiffany's ex-husband. Paul lowered his sandwich to the napkin, looked up at Grant and nodded.

"I believe we've met," Grant muttered.

"I understand congratulations are in order," Bethanne said, hoping to cover the awkward silence. "Annie told me you and Tiffany recently got married. Congratulations."

He nodded. "Thank you."

"I hope you're very happy," Bethanne said sincerely. A short while ago, those words might have been filled with sarcasm, but they weren't now. She felt no animosity toward Grant. She'd once loved him, heart and soul, but he'd betrayed that love and whatever she'd felt for him had been destroyed. That didn't mean—or it no longer did—that she wanted vengeance. Or that she begrudged him happiness just because he hadn't found it with her. The moment she'd realized that, she'd finally released him and the bitterness that surrounded their divorce.

"I see Paul's lucky enough to have you packing his lunch these days," Grant said. He looked longingly at the sandwich. "You made the best corned beef sandwiches I ever tasted."

"I'm helping Bethanne with some paperwork," Paul explained.

Bethanne wanted to elaborate, but stopped herself. This really had nothing to do with Grant. Other than the fact that he was the father of her children, they had little in common any more. The twenty-year history they shared had become irrelevant.

"I see." Grant offered them both a weak smile.

"It's a lovely afternoon, which is why Paul suggested we meet in the park," she added.

Grant seemed uncomfortable. "I saw you here and thought I'd drop by and say hello." He turned to Paul. "Good to see you again."

Bethanne doubted he really meant that. She studied Grant

and instinctively knew he wasn't happy. "Is everything okay?" she asked and immediately wished she hadn't. Even if there was a problem, he wasn't likely to talk about it in front of Paul.

"Everything's just great," he said but his words rang hollow. The two men stared at each other.

"Andrew said you paid for his football camp." Grant turned his attention back to her.

Bethanne hadn't realized Andrew was speaking to his father. This was a good sign, and she was encouraged that father and son had made an effort to overcome their differences.

"You challenged me to find a way to support myself," Bethanne said with a laugh, "and I have. If nothing else, I should thank you for that."

He nodded as if accepting her appreciation. "I'm glad it's working out for you," he said without irony.

"It is." She tried to resist the urge to brag but didn't quite succeed. "I have six parties booked for this week and more calls coming in every day. Annie and a friend of hers created business cards for me, and the kids have been my assistants."

"Great. A family effort."

"In more ways than one."

"I wish you every success," Grant said. Without another word, he walked away.

Paul glared after him.

"Paul, Paul, Paul," she whispered and touched his arm. "You've got to let it go."

He sighed heavily. "I don't know if I can."

"You can and you will," she assured him. "It just takes time."

He relaxed somewhat, but Bethanne could see he was still agitated by the encounter.

"The only reason I believe it's possible," he said thoughtfully, "is because I see it in you. Did I ever mention how much I admire you?"

She grinned. "Once or twice."

"I'm afraid this will upset you, Bethanne, but it's the truth—I'm falling in love with you." He reached for her hand. Bethanne closed her eyes. She loved Paul, but not in that way. This was something she didn't want—or need.

32
CHAPTER

ELISE BEAUMONT

Now that Maverick was living in his condominium, Elise missed him. She'd made the difficult decision to remain where she was for now, but she was miserable without Maverick. She missed everything about him. It'd been that way after the divorce, too. The scent of him, the feel of him, the incredible joy of watching him with their infant daughter...

The ache inside her seemed to grow day by day. And yet it wasn't as if she didn't see him. Maverick was at the house almost daily for one reason or another. Each and every visit, he attempted to lure her to his home, to convince her he was a changed man and that she could trust him. So far she'd resisted, but her resolve was weakening. She could feel it crack under the pressure of her own needs, but she dared not give in.

Elise half-expected Maverick this morning. He knew as well as she did that Aurora intended to take the boys shopping for school clothes. The house would be theirs if they chose to take advantage of it.

Half an hour after her daughter left, Elise was anxiously

pacing the kitchen. When the bell rang, she dashed to the front door and threw it open. Maverick was right about her—in one area, especially. Elise had a thriving sexual appetite. She'd supressed it all these years but, beginning the night he had told her he was leaving, she'd given it free rein. She liked nothing better than to take her ex-husband to bed in the middle of a hot afternoon. Her cheeks flushed at the thought. If anyone ever learned about this secret part of her nature, she'd die of mortification. She'd simply die.

She loved how much Maverick loved her. All they needed was each other. And yet...could they *live* with each other?

Elise was afraid that joining her life with his would end the same way it had before. It was inevitable that he'd succumb to his compulsion to gamble again, and she couldn't handle that.

Despite her hopes, it wasn't Maverick at the door. "Bethanne!" Elise held open the screen door. Something must be very wrong, because her friend was so pale. "Come in, come in."

"I hope you don't mind me just showing up like this."

"Of course not." Elise led the way to the living room. She offered to make coffee or tea, but Bethanne declined with a quick shake of her head.

Bethanne sat down on the sofa, plucking a tissue from her purse. "I promised myself I wouldn't cry and look at me. I haven't said a word and I'm already an emotional wreck."

Elise sat across from her. "Start at the beginning. Tell me exactly what happened."

Bethanne bit her trembling lower lip. "I—I've been to six banks now, and each one rejected my loan application." While Elise listened, Bethanne reviewed the first five banks and the rejections, which were all because she was considered a poor loan risk.

"Then I talked to Lydia, and she mentioned a neighborhood bank that gave her a loan recently. She told me there were things about her history that made her look like a poor risk, too.

On paper, anyway. But you and I both know that Lydia's a fabulous businessperson. She has more financial sense in her little finger than I do in my entire body. But I'm willing to learn."

"Of course you can learn," Elise assured her. She couldn't remember ever seeing Bethanne this upset—not even when she'd first talked about the divorce. "Did you apply with this bank Lydia recommended?" she asked.

Bethanne nodded. "At Lydia's insistence, I used her as a reference." She stopped talking long enough to blow her nose. "I just heard back from them yesterday afternoon. After a lot of debate, they decided to refuse me the loan. Elise," she cried, "I don't know what to do."

If Elise had the money herself, she'd lend it to her. In some ways, she felt responsible; she'd been the one to suggest the party business and she was proud of Bethanne's success.

"How can I help?" she asked.

Bethanne took a moment to collect herself. "Just by listening to me," she whispered, unable to keep the emotion out of her voice. "I…I admire you so much and I'm so grateful I met you."

"Me?" Elise blushed at the praise. All she'd ever done was encourage Bethanne. Elise had been a single mother herself, and knew the hardships that entailed.

"Oh, Elise, you're such a good friend."

Now it was her turn to tear up. Naturally, she'd had friends through the years, but she'd come to realize that those relationships were superficial. There was no real grief in leaving them behind. Somehow, it was different with the knitting group. Her reserve had slowly begun to dissolve; she even found herself talking about Maverick. Of course, she hadn't shared the fact that they were sleeping together—that was far too intimate a detail—but she wouldn't be surprised if her friends had guessed. Until this summer she'd hardly ever mentioned his name.

"I found out something wonderful about Lydia," Bethanne

said. "One time she told me she didn't owe a single penny to anyone. She was proud of that. All the yarn in her store's paid for and—until she got this loan—she was pretty well debt-free."

Elise nodded; she approved of doing business on a pay-as-you-go basis. Far too many young people got caught in the credit trap. It was too easy to use a credit card and pay later. Except that the debt always grew so much faster than anyone seemed to expect. She'd seen it with her own daughter and son-in-law, warned them as gently as she could and then shut up.

"I didn't want to ask Lydia why she needed a loan. But later Margaret pulled me aside and said Lydia had given the money to her."

Elise couldn't hide her surprise. Not at the fact that Lydia had given her sister money, but that Margaret would freely volunteer this information.

"I think she felt sorry for me and wanted to encourage me and I think—I think she wanted me to know what a wonderful sister she has," Bethanne said.

"Margaret needed the money?"

Bethanne nodded. "She told me her husband's been out of work for the last six months and they'd gotten behind on their house payments."

"God bless Lydia," Elise whispered.

"And she's hurting so badly," Bethanne added.

"And now her mother's in a nursing home."

"It's come to that?" The last Elise heard, Margaret and Lydia were researching assisted living facilities.

"She shouldn't be there more than a week or two," Bethanne said, "but it's expensive, even as an interim solution."

"This doesn't seem to be a good time economically for any of us, does it?"

"I just hope I can survive for the next few months."

"You're going to be fine," Elise told her. "This business is just too promising to be ignored for long."

"Do you really think so?"

"I know so."

Bethanne stared down at the carpet, then sighed deeply. "I so badly want to believe you."

"Did you get someone to help you with the bookkeeping?" Elise asked, moving on to practical matters.

The younger woman nodded. "Paul's been going over everything with me."

The doorbell sounded and before Elise could answer, Maverick strolled into the room, looking about as debonair as she'd ever seen him. Her heart skipped a beat. His gaze went from Elise to Bethanne and back again.

"I can come another time," he said.

An automatic protest rose in her throat, but she needn't have worried.

"No, please don't. I should go," Bethanne insisted. "I came because I had to talk to a friend. All I really needed was for Elise to tell me I'm not a failure."

She stood and Elise led her to the front door. Before Bethanne left, they hugged. "Call me anytime, understand?"

Bethanne nodded. "Thank you so much for listening."

"Anytime," she repeated.

"I'll see you Tuesday." And then Bethanne was gone.

Elise turned to find Maverick standing in the foyer watching her.

"Is everything all right?" he asked.

"She's been rejected for six bank loans and is about to give up."

He frowned. "You've been very good to her."

Elise dismissed his words. "She's been wonderful to me."

Maverick slowly advanced toward her. "You're one hell of a woman, Elise Beaumont." He slipped his arms around her waist and brought her close with a gentleness that melted her worries.

"Oh, Maverick…"

He kissed her and whispered promises that made her knees weak.

"Come home with me," he pleaded. "You won't be sorry."

She refused with an adamant "No."

"Elise, I need you with me."

"I can't." The minute she was in his apartment he'd find a way to convince her to move in. She loved him. Despite his flaws and weakness, she loved him.

But she still wasn't sure she could trust him.

33

CHAPTER

COURTNEY PULANSKI

The second-period bell rang, and the high school erupted into chaos as students poured out of their classrooms. Courtney *thought* she knew her way around the building. During the orientation session, she'd paid close attention to where her classes were scheduled, but now she felt hopelessly lost.

The one bright spot in the day, she hoped, would be Honors English, because she knew Andrew Hamlin was in the class. Not that she expected him to speak to her or anything. But at least he'd be a familiar face.

The bell rang again, and the halls were suddenly deserted. Courtney pressed her books to her chest and looked around, completely disoriented. Eventually the hall monitor found her and pointed her in the right direction. Knowing she was already late, she ran down one corridor and then another to Honors English.

The class had already begun when she opened the door and attempted to slip inside unnoticed. That would've been asking too much, she realized, when she discovered the entire class watching her.

"Sorry," she mumbled at the teacher. "I got lost."

"Do you think you'll be able to find your way tomorrow?" Mr. Hazelton asked sternly.

She nodded, kept her head lowered and found an empty seat as far back in the room as she could. Once she was settled, she searched the class for Andrew and saw that he was three rows to the left of her, near the front.

Forty-five minutes later, the bell rang and Courtney checked her schedule to confirm that this was her lunch hour. She dreaded going into the cafeteria. In Chicago, she would've been eating with her friends, laughing and exchanging gossip. Here, she'd stand out like a searchlight in fog. The new kid. Friendless and alone.

She dawdled until the classroom was empty, then gathered up her things and headed out. To her astonishment, Andrew was waiting by the door.

"How's it going?" he asked. His books were tucked close to his side; Courtney immediately noticed how tanned he was—and how cute.

"About as well as can be expected," she told him. It seemed everyone was moving in the same direction, and Courtney followed the flow. So did Andrew. She stopped at her locker long enough to drop off her books. She was gratified that Andrew chose to wait for her again. "I certainly know how to make a grand entrance, don't I?" she said wryly.

Andrew grinned, which made him even more appealing, and Courtney forced herself to glance away. "I haven't seen Annie yet."

"She was looking for you earlier."

That was encouraging.

"How'd you get to school?"

It was embarrassing to admit she'd taken the bus. Her grandmother had needed her car and besides, Courtney had never driven it. All summer she'd used her bicycle for transportation and it'd worked out great. But things were different now. Only nerds rode bicycles to school. So it was either walk or take the bus. Given those choices, she'd opted for the school bus but had been the only senior on board.

"The bus," she whispered.

"I'd offer to drive you, but I have to come in early because of football."

He'd do that for her?

"Mom dropped Annie off," he explained.

"I can't ask my grandmother to do that."

He nodded in agreement. "Let me work on it. I know a guy who doesn't live that far from you. If you were to offer Mike gas money, he'd probably be willing to pick you up."

Courtney smiled delightedly, relieved and a little astonished at her good fortune. This was a perfect solution and she'd pay whatever his friend wanted. Not only would she avoid the humiliation of the bus, she'd have an opportunity to make a friend.

As they entered the cafeteria, she expected Andrew to join his friends. Instead, he got in the lunch line behind her.

"You're looking great, by the way," he said.

She'd worked hard this summer and it felt so good to have him, of all people, notice how much weight she'd lost. "Thanks. You are, too."

"It's football," he explained. "I bulk up every year." He slid his tray behind her as they advanced in the line. "I'll talk to Mike and get back to you tonight."

"Cool."

She chose a chef's salad with low-fat dressing and skipped the soda, selecting bottled water instead. If there was an award for righteousness, she should receive it.

"Courtney," Annie shouted and hurried over to her as soon as she'd finished paying for her salad. "Come and meet my friends."

"Sure." She started to walk away and realized she'd abandoned Andrew. Turning back, holding her tray with both hands, she said, "I'll talk to you later, all right?"

"Later." He nodded, sauntering across the room to join a group of seniors.

"He's going to find someone to give me a ride to school," Courtney told Annie, nearly bursting with the news.

"Mom said he should," Annie informed her. So much for that, Courtney thought, squelching her disappointment. Bethanne was responsible for this. Well, it shouldn't matter. Instead of obsessing about the fact that Andrew hadn't come up with the idea himself, Courtney should be grateful—and she was. Just not as happy as she'd been before.

"Annie!" a girl called out. "Over here."

Annie hesitated, and when she turned toward the other girl, Courtney sensed reluctance. Courtney followed her to a table occupied by two heavily made-up girls. They had various body parts pierced and were dressed mostly in black leather. Courtney felt completely out of place; for their part, Annie's friends eyed her as if she'd descended from outer space.

"This is Courtney," Annie said, introducing her. "We met over the summer. Tina and Shyla." Annie gestured first to one and then the other.

"Hi," Courtney said.

"Hi." Shyla smiled; Tina didn't.

"You trying out for the cheerleading squad?" Tina, the girl dressed entirely in black, asked. Her nose was pierced in five places.

That these friends of Annie's figured Courtney was skinny enough to make the grade was a compliment, but she knew they didn't mean it that way.

"Not really."

Annie frowned at the other girls. "Courtney's my friend. Come on, guys, she's new here."

Tina turned her gaze from Courtney and stared at Annie. "We haven't seen much of you lately."

"I've been busy, you know," Annie said.

"With Courtney?" Shyla asked.

Annie's eyes narrowed. "Yeah. What about it?"

"Maybe it's time you decided who your friends are," Tina suggested, "because it's either her kind or us. If you want to be the cheerleader type, just say so."

"Maybe I do," Annie muttered. "Come on, Courtney, let's get out of here."

Annie marched off, and once again, Courtney followed. She could almost feel the daggers. She didn't want to get caught alone in the girls' room with those two anytime soon.

"You were never really one of us, you know," Tina taunted.

Annie ignored her and led Courtney across the cafeteria.

They found a recently vacated table, where Courtney set down her tray. "Annie, I'm sorry."

"Don't worry about it. I've outgrown them, anyway." But she looked more than a little perturbed.

"I don't want to be—"

She wasn't allowed to finish before Annie snapped. "Don't take it personally, all right? This isn't about you."

Courtney shrugged, unsure what to say.

Annie frowned as the two of them sat alone at the end of a table. After they'd eaten their salads, Annie took out an apple and munched on that, but they barely exchanged another word.

"I'll see you later?" Courtney asked when the bell rang.

"I guess." Annie didn't sound too enthusiastic about it, though.

When Annie left, Courtney returned her tray to the kitchen area, where she saw two other girls with their heads together, whispering and looking at her. She recognized Shelly and Melanie, Andrew's supposed girlfriend and her sidekick. She wanted to wave and let them know she realized they were talking about her, but decided it was better, not to mention easier, just to ignore them.

The rest of the afternoon was uneventful. She wasn't late for any other classes and that, at least, was an improvement. Still, her stomach was in knots when school was over and she headed to the bus line. She hoped the ride situation would work out with that friend of Andrew's.

As she climbed onto the bus, Courtney saw Annie with the two discontented girls from the cafeteria. They stood in a tight circle talking. No one was smiling.

"You getting on or not?" the guy behind Courtney asked when she paused on the steps.

"Sorry," she murmured, hurrying into the bus. As she took her seat, she looked out the side window and saw Andrew talking to Melanie. He had his arm around her waist and she was gazing up at him with wide-eyed wonder. It was enough to make Courtney puke. Leaning against the window, she closed her eyes. She'd do her best to get through this year; there was no other alternative.

She had no expectations and apparently no friends.

34
CHAPTER

ELISE BEAUMONT

Elise's disillusion came soon after school started for her grandsons. She'd expected it all along, knew Maverick wouldn't be able to stay away from gambling. The entire time he'd been in Seattle she'd been waiting, listening, expecting the worst. If she was surprised by anything, it was that Maverick had held out as long as he did. She learned the truth the day her book club met.

"Your father said he'd be by to drive me to the library this afternoon," Elise told Aurora after she'd waited as long as she could. Until now, Maverick had always been punctual. She'd known it was a mistake to rely on him, but it had been too hard to resist. Now she had to scurry in order to make the book club meeting.

"I'm sure he has a perfectly good explanation," her daughter said, ever eager to defend her father.

Still the niggling doubts had begun to form. Maverick mysteriously disappeared for several hours once a week. He swore he hadn't been gambling, but he hadn't felt inclined to enlighten her as to where he spent his time, either. She hadn't pressed him; she knew it was because she was afraid of what she'd find out.

Elise had other worries, too. Aurora had been acting differently toward Maverick. She hadn't been able to put her finger on exactly how the father-daughter relationship had changed, but it had. She'd noticed it a few weeks ago—whispered conversations, intercepted glances, a sense of confidences shared. Elise felt excluded, although she tried not to.

Aurora offered to drive her, but Elise declined. "I'll take the bus. It's not a problem," Elise murmured. Her daughter was right about Maverick. He probably did have a credible excuse, only Elise supposed that was exactly what it would be. An excuse. A lie...

"I'm sure Dad'll be there to pick you up," Aurora said as she walked Elise to the front door.

She nodded, but she suspected otherwise. During the bus trip, she tried—unsuccessfully—to forget her fears. She got off automatically and transferred to the second bus. After all these years of traveling by Metro, Elise knew the schedules as well as her own address.

She arrived late, and the meeting itself was a blur. By the time the group broke up, she knew it had been pointless to attend. She hadn't been able to concentrate, and contributed little to the discussion.

Her doubts and suspicions regarding Maverick were simply impossible to ignore. She knew his history, and yet she'd so badly wanted to believe him that she'd played a dangerous game of pretend. Loving him again had come so easy—too easy.

On the short walk to the bus stop, she passed a number of card rooms. She passed them whenever she took this route but had never before felt even the slightest inclination to glance inside. But now the need to find Maverick consumed her. She wanted to burst into these places, slamming open the doors, hoping to catch him in his lie. But through sheer willpower, she resisted. That was a degrading thing she'd done early in their marriage, dragging their infant daughter into bowling alleys and taverns, looking for Maverick. Praying she'd find him before he lost the money they needed for rent.

The memories bombarded her, and when she stepped off the bus late that afternoon, she was emotionally exhausted. She wasn't surprised to see Maverick's car parked in front of the house. She made a decision then: she couldn't do this anymore.

He didn't meet her eyes when she walked in the door, which was another sure sign he'd been up to no good.

"Hello," she said stiffly.

"Elise." He cast a look toward their daughter, who promptly left the room. "I figure you and I should talk. I apologize for not being here to take you to your readers' group." He paused for a few seconds. "I'm sorry."

"Yes, I knew you probably would be," she said, setting her purse on the small table in the hallway. Her throat was dry as she walked into the kitchen and took a pitcher of iced tea from the refrigerator. Hand trembling, she reached for a glass.

"I'm hoping we can talk about this," he said, standing not more than two feet behind her. When she glanced around, she saw that he'd folded his hands like a repentant child.

She shrugged as if it was of no importance. Compared to missing their daughter's childhood—missing their entire marriage, for that matter—this was minor.

"You were counting on me," he said.

"The bus was fine."

"Come on, Elise." He held out his hands. "I hate it when you're angry with me. I'm not a grade-school child who's come to you about an overdue book. I'm your husband."

"Ex-husband," she reminded him.

"All right, so we're divorced, but—"

"You were gambling this afternoon." It wasn't a question.

She *knew,* and she suspected that was where he'd been every week, although he'd denied it.

"Would you *listen* for once?" he demanded.

"No. There's nothing more to be said. You made your choice all those years ago, and you've made the same choice again. Gambling is more important than me, than our marriage, more important than anything. I'm not surprised. Why should I be? It's only history repeating itself." Putting down the glass after a single swallow, she walked through the hallway to her room.

Maverick followed her, leaping back as she shut the door. Despite her anger, Elise hadn't intended to slam it in his face. She leaned her shoulder against it, feeling too weak to stand without support.

Maverick paced outside in the hallway; she could hear the sound of his footsteps. "All I ask is that you listen. Please, honey, just listen."

She closed her eyes. He hadn't called her honey since before the divorce.

"I love you, Elise. I know you don't believe that, and I don't blame you, but it's true."

The declaration was all too familiar. Unable to stop herself, she jerked open the door. "I do believe you love me," she said with great calm, "but you love cards more." She watched Maverick's face twist with pain and feared it was a reflection of her own. Unable to look at him, she gently closed the door.

"No, no, you've got to believe me," he pleaded. "I'm doing this for you."

Elise stood facing the door. That, too, was a common excuse of his. It was never for him, never about what *he* wanted. He'd squander what little they had on the promise of more. Except that promise had almost always proved to be empty.

Granted, he'd obviously made a certain amount of money through the years—to meet his child support obligations, to travel—but she was sure he'd lost far more than he'd ever won. That was the pattern with gamblers.

"This afternoon I *was* playing poker," he confessed. "I wanted to talk to you about it first, but I knew you'd be upset. You get this…this look and it rips me up inside. Makes me feel like I've disappointed you again. I couldn't bear to see it."

It hadn't stopped him, though.

"I wore the socks you knit me and felt close to you the entire time I was playing. They brought me luck."

Elise wished she'd given those socks to David the way she'd originally intended.

"I won the tournament, Elise," he said triumphantly.

She refused to answer him. Winning was possibly the worst thing that could've happened. It only made the situation worse. Maverick would feel encouraged. He'd wager more and more until he'd lost everything, including his pride. In those early years, she'd seen him down on his luck too many times, sick at heart, emotionally depleted.

"Don't you want to know how much I won?"

"No!"

"It was my lucky socks," he shouted through the barrier of the door.

Refusing to listen, she turned on her television, blocking out anything else he had to say. She didn't notice when he left, but she checked ten minutes later and he was gone.

Aurora watched her closely as Elise entered the kitchen. She put on a fine performance, if she did say so herself. Thankfully Maverick was out of the house, but she guessed he'd be back for dinner.

"Dad asked me to talk to you," Aurora said. Elise was setting the table for their evening meal. She included a place for Maverick; her daughter would ask too many questions if she didn't. David was in the family room reading the paper and the boys were playing in the backyard.

"He's gambling again," Elise told her, in case Aurora hadn't figured it out.

"I know."

"How long has this been going on?" She was suddenly afraid that her daughter had been in on the deception.

Aurora looked at her. "As far as I know, this was the first time since he got here."

"Listen to me, Aurora," Elise said frantically, clasping her daughter's shoulders. "Your father has a gambling addiction."

"He's a professional gambler." Aurora's voice was unemotional. "Yes, I agree, he can get carried away, but he loves it."

Elise hated that her own daughter couldn't or wouldn't recognize the problem. "Gambling is a disease—not unlike being an alcoholic or using drugs—and it's just as destructive to a marriage and a family." She wanted to remind her that Maverick's love of gambling had destroyed their own family, but she bit back the words. She'd said what she needed to say.

"He isn't as bad as you make him sound," Aurora insisted.

Not wanting to argue, Elise dropped her hands. "He's your father and you love him. I'm not going to say anything against Maverick—except to plead with you to open your eyes and admit the truth."

Aurora's gaze implored her. "He loves you, Mom, he really does."

She swallowed the lump in her throat. "I know." Maverick did love her as much as he was able to love anyone—but it wasn't enough. It hadn't been enough thirty-seven years ago and it wasn't enough now.

"He promised me he'd stop as soon as this tournament is over," Aurora said.

Elise had heard all that before, too. "And you *believe* him?" If this wasn't so tragic, she'd laugh.

"Yes, I do. He's—" Aurora bit her lip.

"He's what?"

"He's doing this out of love for you. To help you. That's what he said."

Elise burst into such loud, derisive laughter that David, who'd turned on the evening news, glanced over his shoulder.

"Then advise him not to love me so much," she whispered. "Furthermore, I don't want or need his help. Can't you see that's only an excuse?"

"Oh, Mom."

"I think it might be best if we didn't discuss your father again." She spoke as if this had been a pleasant everyday conversation.

"You're not going to talk to him?"

"No. I'd appreciate if you'd let me know when he'll be at the house, because I'll make a point of staying in my room or not being here."

"Mom, don't do this."

Elise was saddened to see her daughter hurt. Aurora might be married and a mother herself, but that little-girl part of her continued to search for a happy ending. Like every child, she needed her father and craved the security of knowing that her parents loved each other.

"Grandma, Grandma," Luke shouted as he ran in from outside.

"What is it?" Elise asked, crouching down so they were at eye level.

"Did you hear?" he cried. "Did you hear?"

"Luke…" Aurora warned.

"It's okay. Grandpa said I could tell if I wanted to."

Elise frowned up at her daughter. She'd wondered if Aurora was holding something back, but hadn't been sure what.

"Grandpa's going to the Carry Bean for a poker tournament!"

Elise blinked. "The Caribbean?" she asked Aurora as she

straightened. Maverick had already broken his promise. One moment he swore he was through; the next, he booked his passage to play in another tournament.

35

CHAPTER

"Knitting is just the best ever hobby! Creative, therapeutic, stress-busting, relaxing and rewarding, it's the perfect way to both express your creativity and to gently unwind. Make it part of your everyday life."
—Kate Buller, Brand Manager, Handknittings.
(Rowan Yarns, Jaeger Handknits, Patons, R2)

LYDIA HOFFMAN

Margaret had been working a lot of hours at the shop while I made the arrangements for our mother's continuing care, since I'm the one with the most experience in dealing with medical bureaucracy. I needed to get the paperwork set up at the nursing home first and then I'd organize her finances so Mom could make a smooth transition to the assisted living complex we'd found.

This time-consuming work gave me a new appreciation for everything my parents had gone through when I was first diagnosed with cancer. Hours of sorting through bank statements, old receipts, insurance information. Hours spent on the phone and in meetings. Hours on the computer. Hours—

days—away from the shop. Then there was the time I spent with the real estate agent and cleaning Mom's house before we listed it. That couldn't be put off. We needed the money to finance her care.

It wasn't until Friday afternoon as I counted out the money from the till that I realized my gross intake for the second week of September was almost half of what it'd been for any week in August. A quick check of my nightly deposits showed a substantial decrease in revenues. I'd known that spending so much time away from the shop would be detrimental to business, but I had no idea it would have this much impact.

Margaret just isn't a natural salesperson, nor does she share my appreciation for yarn. I knew all that, but I couldn't ask anyone else. She's familiar with the shop and my regular customers in a way no one other than me is. And she's my sister.

While I tallied the figures again, a sense of doom came over me. I had loan payments now, and they made a significant dent in my income. I'd wanted to repay the bank as quickly as possible, so I'd asked for an eighteen-month payment schedule. I could always go back to request an extension, but it wouldn't look good if I had to do that after only the second payment. Although nothing was said, I had the impression this shortened loan period was one of the reasons the bank had agreed to give me the money.

I sat at my desk, feeling sick to my stomach. The summer months are usually slower, but my sales had doubled from the previous year. Now, not only did they seem to be slipping, I had a huge financial obligation to worry about. There were cost-saving options, such as decreasing orders, but I didn't want to do this. Part of my success, I believed, was that I carried a wide range of yarns from the inexpensive to the more exclusive.

I was so preoccupied with these worries that I didn't hear the knock at the shop door until the pounding grew louder.

Leaping out of my chair, I hurried into the main part of the store; normally I'd simply explain that we were closed, but right now I didn't feel I could turn down a single sale.

However, it wasn't a customer. Brad stood at the door with his hands cupped around his face, peering inside. As soon as he saw he'd gotten my attention, he backed away from the glass.

The last time we'd talked had been almost a month ago. I'd had brief conversations with Cody but they seemed as painful for him as they were for me. When I'd talked to Cody at the end of August, his mother must have been standing close by, because he sounded tentative and cautious, almost as though he was afraid of saying the wrong thing. He hadn't called me since.

Unlocking the door, I sighed. I didn't have the physical energy or emotional resources to talk to Brad, so I decided not to allow him inside. Instead, I stood in the opening and waited.

"Hi," I said, hoping I'd found the right tone to convey my feelings.

"Hi," Brad said, hands in his uniform pockets. "Hadn't seen you at the store in a while."

I could've stated the obvious and told him I hadn't been at the shop more than an hour or so each day, but that seemed unnecessary. I didn't respond.

"Margaret said you found a place for your mom?"

He made it a question. I answered as if it was. "We're planning to move her next week." If I could finish all the paperwork, arrange for all the necessary medical records, finalize the sale of Mom's house and complete my dealings with her lawyer and her bank.

"How are you holding up?" he asked.

"I'm okay." I didn't want Brad's sympathy; his concern would be my undoing. I was tempted to ask about Janice, but didn't. If they were getting along well, I didn't want to hear

it. At the same time, I didn't want to know if their reconciliation wasn't working out. Just then, at the end of a
long day in an emotionally crowded week, I couldn't deal
with another crisis. "How's Cody?" It hurt my heart to ask
because I missed him so much—missed our talks, missed
hearing about his dog and the tricks he'd taught Chase. Difficult though our conversations often were, I needed them. I
loved that child.

"He's doing great," he said quickly, which I suppose was
Brad's way of informing me that his happy little family was
flourishing.

"Give him my love, would you?"

"Of course. I've been worried about you," he added as he
stared down at the sidewalk.

"Worried about me?" I asked, forcing surprise into my
voice. "Whatever for?"

He looked up, wearing a crooked half smile. "I know you,
Lydia. When you're under stress, it shows."

"How would you know? You haven't seen me in weeks."

"I *have* seen you—I just haven't made a point of seeking
you out. You're tired and—"

"Yes," I said, cutting him off. I didn't need Brad Goetz to
tell me what I already knew.

"Let me take you out for a drink," he suggested.

I shook my head. "No, thanks."

"I know you're dating someone else now, but this is just as
friends."

Actually, I could hardly believe Margaret hadn't enlight-
ened Brad, hadn't told him I'd lied about meeting someone
new. I'd done that out of pride, and I regretted it.

"Why not?"

"I have one hard and fast rule when it comes to men," I said,
smiling as I spoke. "I avoid the married ones."

"Janice and I are divorced."

"Are you or are you not reconciling?" I snapped. Damn it, he couldn't have it both ways.

He didn't answer at first, then muttered, "Janice and I are talking."

"In that case, having a drink with me would be inappropriate. I appreciate the offer, Brad, but...I don't think so."

Brad said goodbye rather abruptly and left. I stood in the doorway, my arms crossed, and watched him walk away, feeling empty and alone. I closed and locked the door again, then returned slowly to my office.

When someone tapped on the door ten minutes later, I half suspected Brad had come back. I turned and retraced my steps to peer through the glass.

It wasn't Brad. Instead, Alix Townsend stood on the other side. She held a plate of chocolate éclairs, which guaranteed I'd open the door.

"Hi," she greeted me cheerfully as I let her in.

I'd dropped in at the charity knitting session that afternoon and she hadn't been there, so I'd guessed she was working at the café. Her classes were usually in the morning.

"I saw you and Brad talking just now. You don't have to tell me what happened unless you want to—but I thought these might help."

I hid a smile. Brad might have succeeded in getting past my threshold if he'd brought chocolate.

"I don't have any worries a chocolate éclair won't cure," I said, leading the way to the office. "I've got coffee on, if you're interested."

"I'd love a cup." Alix followed me into my tiny office, where she settled on a corner of my desk, moving papers aside and making herself at home. I didn't mind. That was Alix—why sit on a chair if there was a desk? Why walk if you could run? I loved her exuberance, her loyalty and her frequently unconventional behavior.

I poured her a mug and felt slightly guilty because it looked so dark. I hoped it wasn't bitter.

"So Brad came to see you," she said, unable to hide her curiosity, after all.

In retrospect, my attitude toward him seemed coldhearted. Unkind. Part of me wanted to call him back, to begin the conversation all over again. I wouldn't, though. Leaving things as they were was for the best. "Lydia?" Alix asked. She reached out to touch me.

I nodded. "Yes, he did."

"Anything happening?" Although she'd brought the éclairs for me, Alix scooped one off the plate and took a bite. When the custard filling oozed out from the sides, she grabbed a tissue from the box on my desk.

"Nothing really. How about with you and Jordan?"

Alix raised her eyebrows. "You're changing the subject." She picked up the plate and offered me an éclair.

I didn't need a second invitation. "I know. I don't want to talk about Brad, that's all."

"He doesn't want to talk about you, either," Alix informed me. "He makes a delivery to the café every now and then, and he's his old chatty self until I mention your name. Then he shuts up tighter than a coffin."

I didn't like the image. "We both have our reasons."

"So it seems." She hopped down from the desk. "Gotta go. Jordan and I are seeing a movie with the youth group tonight. I just thought I'd come over and say hello."

"I'm glad you did," I said. I walked her to the door, unlocking it and letting her out. As soon as she was gone, I relocked the door, found Whiskers waiting for me and headed up the stairs to my apartment—first remembering to turn off the lights and retrieve Alix's plate. I could've been having a drink with Brad, I mused nostalgically, but for emotional protection, I'd decided on my own company.

I'd spend the night with my television, my cat and my éclairs.

Whiskers meowed as though to remind me I wasn't alone. He was absolutely right.

36
CHAPTER

BETHANNE HAMLIN

Bethanne had three parties scheduled that week and she'd carefully gone over the budget for each. Finances would be tight until her alimony check arrived and she received full payment for the parties. Paying for all her supplies out of her dwindling checking account meant she'd have very little cash until the weekend, which meant, in turn, that she'd have to delay buying groceries. She didn't dare use her VISA to buy party stuff; she'd reached her credit limit. Still, she could manage until she deposited the various checks. The problem was, she found herself writing checks and hoping they wouldn't clear for a few days. It was a complicated balancing act, since her expenses still exceeded her income.

Unfortunately, Annie and Andrew constantly needed money for one thing or another. Their school expenses were legitimate and she couldn't defer them. These amounts, plus household bills and business costs—a balancing act, indeed.

The phone rang, and although she hoped it was another party booking, Caller ID showed that it was her bank. She grabbed the receiver, praying that somehow the loan officer had recognized the error of his ways and was calling to offer her a loan.

A few years ago, Grant had taken her to Vegas and they'd brought travelers' checks that equaled more than what she wanted to borrow now. Vegas? The trip was a complete surprise and Bethanne had been so pleased and excited. In light of what she'd learned since, she suspected Grant had arranged it out of guilt.

"Hello," she answered in her most cheerful voice. "This is Bethanne."

Her smile quickly died as the bank manager explained that a check she'd written to the local service station had bounced. In the past, the bank had provided overdraft protection, for a fee, to cover small amounts, but wouldn't any longer. In addition, the service station charged a seventy-five-dollar fee for bounced checks.

"Seventy-five dollars," she cried, outraged at the unnecessary expense. "You've got to be kidding!"

"I assure you I'm not."

"How…much is this going to cost me?" A tank of gas was normally about twenty-five dollars; now there were bank fees, penalties and the seventy-five bucks the service station had heaped on.

The total was staggering. "*How* much?" she cried.

"When would it be convenient for you to make a deposit?" the bank manager asked.

"I—I—" She didn't have it; she simply didn't have it. The only thing left to do was take a ring or two down to the pawnshop and see what she could get. "I'll bring some money this afternoon," she said meekly, feeling chastised.

The manager wasn't an ogre—he was only doing his job—but Bethanne was in a panic. She rushed upstairs to her jewelry box and sorted through what she had, which wasn't much.

Why, oh why, hadn't Grant given her a diamond bracelet instead of that stupid trip to Vegas? A bracelet she could cash in, but the trip had been a waste. Grant lost all the money they'd taken with them. That hadn't stopped him from returning, she noted bitterly. He'd married Tiffany in Vegas. Bethanne found herself hoping he'd lost big—in more ways than one.

This negative thinking wasn't good for her, but she felt desperate. Other than pawning her jewelry, she had very few options. Annie and Andrew had bank accounts and could probably lend her what she needed. She supposed that was better than asking Grant. But…she couldn't do either of those things. The bank could repossess the house before she'd approach her ex-husband for another dime. Asking family, especially her kids, or her friends was out of the question. She had her pride—and, apparently, very little else.

After much deliberation, Bethanne chose her wedding band—it wasn't doing her any good in a jewelry box—and a small sapphire ring, plus a pair of gold earrings. Surely that would give her enough to at least cover the check, the fees and the penalties.

She was sickened by how little money she got for all three, but it was enough to pay the necessary minimum at the bank. This had been a valuable lesson. She couldn't write checks for money she didn't have, no matter how soon she'd have it.

As she walked out of the bank, she nearly collided with her ex-husband in the parking lot. Her face instantly went beet-red, as though Grant could read on her forehead the reason for her visit.

"Bethanne," Grant said, taking her by the shoulders in order to steady her.

"Grant." She wasn't sure how to respond. "Hi…I was just—" She closed her mouth, refusing to embarrass herself. This wasn't his concern.

"You're looking good," he said, stepping back to admire her.

The new hairstyle had been an extravagance she regretted. Annie and Courtney had talked her into it. The stylist had done wonders with her hair and suggested she color it. When Bethanne explained she couldn't possibly afford that, the two girls had insisted they could do it.

They'd selected one of the more expensive brands—another ten bucks—in a deep brunette with auburn overtones. Considering that she'd put herself in the hands of teenagers, it'd turned out surprisingly well.

"Thanks," Bethanne said casually.

"What are you doing here?" Grant asked.

As if that was any of his business. "Making a deposit. What about you?" He didn't need to know the details, but at least she'd told him the truth.

"A withdrawal," he said, and he didn't sound too happy about it. "Switching money from savings to checking."

"For little ol' me?" she asked in her most saccharine drawl.

"Actually, no," he said, frowning.

"Could it be that your new wife is straining your finances?" she asked, not hiding the gleam in her eyes.

Grant snickered. "You don't know the half of it."

He didn't sound like he was joking, which should've pleased her, but Bethanne was bothered by the dark circles under his eyes. "Is everything okay with you, Grant?" she asked. His well-being no longer had anything to do with her, and yet she couldn't prevent the automatic rush of concern.

"Would it make you happy if I said it wasn't?" He didn't give her a chance to answer. "As a matter of fact, I'm blissfully happy."

Bethanne hadn't realized what a poor liar he was and wondered why she hadn't seen through him during the years he'd been having that affair. She supposed it was because she hadn't *wanted* to know. "I'm sorry, Grant," she said. She was sincere.

He shrugged in an offhand way.

It was ironic, really, that they'd have their first decent conversation in a parking lot months after their divorce.

"So how's the relationship with the Boy Toy?" he asked. "Or is it the Toy Boy?"

"Do you mean Paul?" she said sharply. So much for decent. "It doesn't bother us that I'm older, anymore than it bothers you that Tiffany's fifteen years younger," she said. "Besides, I can see anyone I choose. You didn't want to be married to me, and Tiffany didn't want to be with Paul. He and I have a lot in common."

"You got the new hairstyle for him, didn't you? Are you trying to look younger?"

"Not really."

"Oh."

"I'd better get back to the house," she said, eager to leave. She thought of mentioning the Homecoming Dance at the end of the month but decided against it. Grant would learn soon enough that their son had been voted part of the Homecoming Court.

Grant nodded, hands in his pants pockets. "It was good to see you, Bethanne." He offered her a slight smile. "I do mean that."

"Thanks. It was good seeing you, too."

Bethanne started toward her car, but stopped to look back. Grant was still standing in the same spot, staring after her.

She almost gave him a friendly wave. She didn't wish her ex-husband ill. Okay, sometimes she did, but she'd also made real progress toward forgiveness this summer.

She hated being alone, but in reality nothing had changed. Grant might've been living at the house two years ago and sharing her bed, but he'd been emotionally involved with another woman. And that meant he hadn't been fully committed to his family—as he'd proven since.

Yes, her financial situation was uncomfortable, but she

was a fast learner. Yes, she was bound to make mistakes, but she had a new life and a good friend in Paul. She was close to her children.

The odd man out was Grant, who seemed to have some regrets. He'd hinted at it, then claimed, rather unconvincingly, that he was happy. She doubted he'd tell her the truth.

CHAPTER

37

COURTNEY PULANSKI

Courtney hadn't heard from her father in a week. She was growing frightened; that just wasn't like him. He might go a day or two without e-mailing her, but never a week. While Ralph Pulanski, Jr. had been silent, the e-mails had flown between Courtney, her sister and their older brother. They were as worried as she was. The three of them clung to each other.

Courtney hid her fears from her grandmother as much as she could. Grams was doing a lot of knitting these days—to comfort herself, Courtney figured. Mostly she and Grams said reassuring things to each other, like "I'm sure he's fine," and "Maybe his computer broke down."

Jason had tried to reach their father through the construction company that employed him, but he'd learned nothing concrete. According to the executive Jason had talked to, the area was known to be secure and there was no reason for alarm. The company would try to get in touch with him; that was as much as they'd promise at this point.

Julianna, who was back at school and on a tight budget,

broke down and phoned Courtney. They talked for twenty minutes.

"I miss you so much," Courtney told her sister, struggling not to weep. She clutched the telephone receiver to her ear, as if that would bring Julianna closer.

"How's school?"

Her sister *would* ask. "It's okay." Courtney tried to brush off the question because they had bigger concerns than her inability to make friends, other than Annie Hamlin, and her sense of being alone.

"Don't give me that," Julianna said sternly in a voice so like their mother's that it took Courtney's breath away. "I want to know how you're *really* doing."

"Awful." It was the truth. "I thought if I lost weight I'd be instantly popular," Courtney confessed. "I thought boys would be asking for my phone number, but it isn't like that at all." Of course, there was only one boy who interested her, and that was Andrew Hamlin. Unfortunately, he had a long-standing girlfriend.

Annie claimed Melanie was living in a dreamworld, and Andrew was no more going steady with her than he was with Britney Spears. The evidence, which Courtney had seen for herself, said otherwise.

"Twenty-five pounds is a lot to lose, and I'm proud of you. You feel better, don't you?"

"Health-wise, you mean? Yeah, I guess." She did feel better now that those pounds were off. She, too, was proud of that accomplishment, but she'd hoped for certain things that hadn't come to pass. In fact, everything remained exactly as it was before. When you came right down to it, all that had changed was the number on Grams's antique scale. Oh, and some of her pants were looser around the waist.

"Call if you need me," Julianna said. "I mean it, Court."

"Okay. Keep in touch about Dad."

"I will," her sister promised.

Courtney was grateful for her sister's call. She wished they could talk regularly. Although Julianna was older and had been away from home for nearly three years, she was close to their dad. Caught up in her own woes, Courtney hadn't spent enough time considering her sister's feelings.

Wednesday morning, eight days since her last communication with her father, Courtney didn't feel like going to school. Grams said she understood, but encouraged Courtney to go anyway.

"You won't resolve anything sitting by the phone all day," Grams said with perfect logic.

After sleeping fitfully for two nights, Courtney had hoped to rest, but she knew her grandmother was right. While she might not have made a lot of friends yet, she was better off at school than hanging around at home, waiting and worrying.

Mike, Andrew's friend, picked her up to drive her to school. Courtney paid him ten dollars a week and appreciated not having to take the bus. The only problem was Mike himself, who seemed inordinately shy. He rarely said a word, either on the way to school or on the way home. At first she'd tried to carry the conversation, but after a week of minimal responses, she'd given up.

Wouldn't you know it? This was the morning Mike discovered he had a tongue.

"Did you hear from your dad?" he asked as she climbed into his fifteen-year-old Honda.

"Not yet."

"Are you worried?"

"What do you think?" She didn't mean to be sarcastic, but that was a stupid question if she'd ever heard one.

"I think you're worried," he concluded.

Courtney closed her eyes and leaned her head against the

passenger window, just praying there'd be an e-mail from her father when she got home from school.

"Are you ready for the English test?" he asked next.

She straightened abruptly. "There's a test?" Preoccupied as she'd been with her father, she hadn't paid attention. "On what?"

"Poetry."

She groaned. Perhaps if she showed up at the office and claimed she had the flu, they'd believe her and let her go home.

Home. No matter how hard she tried, she couldn't think of her grandmother's place as home. It was Grams's house, not hers.

Mike parked and they walked wordlessly into the school. Once in the building, they went their separate ways, Mike to the left and Courtney to the right. She had, at best, five minutes to leaf through her book of poems and her English notes before the bell rang. Dickinson. Whitman. Who else?

She stood outside her homeroom, leaning against the wall, as she flipped desperately from one page to the next.

"Hi." Andrew sidled up to her, books under his arm.

Surprised, Courtney nearly dropped her own book. "I didn't realize we had a test today," she declared, her nose in the book as she tried to take in as much information as possible.

"In what?"

"English—poetry. Nineteenth-century American. I think." He didn't seem to know about it, either.

"Mike told me."

"That explains it," Andrew said. "He's in regular Senior English, we're Honors. Mr. Hazelton didn't mention a test. I don't even think we're studying the same material."

A wave of relief washed over her. "Thank you, God." She raised her head toward the ceiling.

"And they say school prayer is dead," Andrew teased.

She smiled.

"How're you doing?" he asked.

They stood there for a few minutes before going to their homerooms. Rather than discuss her worries about her father, Courtney merely shrugged. "How about you?"

What a dumb question. She realized it as soon as the words were out of her mouth. Andrew had just been named part of the Homecoming Court, exactly as Shelly had predicted. As head cheerleader, Melanie had also been a nominee. On the afternoon before the big game, the king and queen would be chosen at a school assembly. Again according to Shelly, Melanie and Andrew would take the prize.

"I'm fine," Andrew said. He didn't seem that excited about his nomination. "What about your dad?"

"He's still missing," Courtney blurted out. She couldn't hold it in any longer. "Andrew, I'm so worried! I don't know what I'd do if something happened to my dad." Tears sprang to her eyes and she tried to hide them by staring down at the floor.

To her shock, he placed his arm around her shoulders. "Don't worry. Everything's going to be all right."

"No, it isn't," she cried, sobbing openly now. "I need my father." He, more than anyone, held the family together. He was her father and she'd already lost her mother, and if her father was dead she couldn't bear it.

"I know, I know," he murmured.

She looked up at him with wet eyes, unable to speak.

"If anything happened to my mother," he went on, "I'd feel just like you do right now, but I will tell you this. No matter what happens, you'll find your way through it. Isn't that what you told Annie?"

Courtney sniffed and nodded. She grabbed a tissue from her purse and blew her nose, embarrassed by all the attention they'd attracted. It didn't seem to bother Andrew, though, and she pretended it didn't bother her, either.

"That was good advice," Andrew said. "Annie was close to

losing it when you signed up for that knitting class with my mom. I'm so glad you did, because she needed a friend. She's still got a few problems, but she's so much better now, thanks to you."

Courtney was too stunned to respond.

"I didn't thank you properly, but maybe I can help you with your dad. Do you think it'd be all right if I came to your grandmother's house after football practice?"

It required a monumental effort to simply nod. The final bell rang for homeroom.

"Gotta go," Andrew said. "See you later." He hurried down the hall.

Courtney dashed into her own classroom, marveling that one person could experience so many emotions in such a short time.

As soon as Mike dropped her off at Grams's after school, Courtney raced upstairs to her computer and logged on.

"Any word?" her grandmother shouted from the foot of the stairs.

Her heart fell when she hurriedly scanned her in-box. Nothing from her father. "No," she called back, dispirited.

The phone rang and normally Courtney would've answered it, but she wasn't in the mood to talk to anyone. Not even Andrew. Despite what she'd said about getting through whatever you had to, she didn't think she could. She *couldn't* lose her father. There weren't enough chocolate chip cookies or skeins of yarn or comforting words to see her through that.

"Yes, yes, of course, I'll get her right away." She could hear her grandmother's voice. "Courtney, phone," she yelled even as Courtney walked down the stairs. "Someone wants to talk to you." Smiling, she held out the receiver.

The minute Courtney heard her father, she burst into tears of joy. The phone connection wasn't the greatest as her dad poured out his story of being stranded in the jungle for five days with no way to get in touch. There'd been torrential rains while they were surveying but he was safe. He was sorry to have caused his family so much worry.

The tears had yet to dry on her cheeks when Andrew arrived. Courtney was on the phone with Julianna and had just finished talking to Jason.

"I have company and I need to go," she told her sister, glancing self-consciously at Andrew. He stood awkwardly in the living room, being fussed over by Grams.

"Boy or girl?" Julianna pressed.

"It's a B," she muttered.

"Andrew?"

"Yes," she hissed. It was clear she'd told her sister far more than she should have.

"Then get off the phone and entertain your company," Julianna teased.

Grams was a gracious hostess. She'd seated Andrew on the sofa and chatted away with him as though he was a longtime family friend.

Courtney walked shyly into the room, and Grams smiled over at her. "I was just telling Andrew that you heard from your father."

"I was talking to my sister." Embarrassed, she pointed to the ancient black phone at the foot of the stairs.

"Is this the young man you mentioned?" Grams asked, lowering her voice as if Andrew couldn't hear the question. "The one you're knitting the socks for?"

Courtney wished she could snap her fingers and vanish, like the witch on that old TV series Grams sometimes watched. Her face felt hot and she glared at her grandmother.

"She knit a lovely pair for her dad," her grandmother was saying. "Those were navy blue, but these are green and—" She looked quizzically at Courtney. "Oh, dear, was that supposed to be a surprise?" Getting up with uncharacteristic agility, Grams scurried to the kitchen.

Andrew stood, his eyes holding hers. "You're knitting me socks?"

Courtney nodded. "I'm just finishing up the gusset on the second one, but it's nearly done."

"That's the coolest thing anyone's ever done for me. It's really...sweet."

Sweet. He thought of her as *sweet*. That was the last thing Courtney wanted.

38
CHAPTER

ELISE BEAUMONT

Bethanne's invitation to visit was a welcome reprieve in the middle of Elise's week. Bethanne had asked if she'd help check her budget. Elise was no expert, but she was willing to do what she could. She was also grateful for an excuse to get out of the house.

Neither Aurora nor David ever mentioned Maverick in her presence. Unfortunately her grandsons, oblivious to the tension between their estranged grandparents, dragged his name into practically every conversation. Maverick was playing in some poker game in the Carry Bean, as the boys called it. She wished him well, but she couldn't be part of his life. Their second attempt at being a couple was as much of a failure as the first. No, it was over for good.

The bus dropped her off a block from Bethanne's. She liked the other woman and found that they had more in common than anyone might expect. As divorced mothers, they'd been left to deal with the children and the house and everything else. Well, no need to dwell on that old history now, she decided.

The Hamlins' neighborhood was a busy one, and the house itself was charming. Elise walked up the steps and rang the doorbell, admiring the garden as she did. She'd just leaned over to take a closer look at a huge, coppery chrysanthemum when a smiling Bethanne opened the door. A pot of tea and a plate of brownies waited on the kitchen table.

"Thank you for doing this," Bethanne said, handing over a spiral notebook. "I asked you because this whole party business was your idea and…well, because you seem so clear headed and sensible to me." She sighed. "I've gone over these figures a dozen times and after a while, everything starts to blur."

"I know what you mean."

Bethanne had listed her monthly expenses in one column and the total alimony and child support she received from Grant in another. On a separate page, she'd set out the anticipated income from the parties she'd booked, including the deposits already paid, and the costs for each.

Elise looked over all the lists and glanced up to see Bethanne watching her. "You need to charge more for your parties," she said decisively. Before Bethanne could protest, she asked, "What's your hourly wage?"

"I—I don't know. I just add twenty percent to the cost of each party and that's what I charge."

Elise shook her head. "That's not near enough. Don't forget, you're putting your creative genius behind each event."

"Creative genius," Bethanne repeated. "Oh, I like the sound of that."

"It's true." Elise refused to diminish Bethanne's talent. "You're offering something unique. No party is like any other. Each one's exclusively designed around the child's interests. But if you feel you might be pricing yourself out of a job…"

"I do," she murmured. "People can't afford to pay me an outrageous fee on top of all their other expenses."

"Then standardize the parties. Make up a list of your favorites, the ones you've already created, and offer those when people call to inquire. Establish a price for each one, and give them the option of a standard party or a customized one."

Bethanne's eyes lit up. "Of course...of course. I should've thought of that." She smiled. "I can buy supplies in bulk and save money that way, too. Not to mention time."

"You might also contract with a local bakery, for the cakes."

They looked at each other and both spoke at the same moment. "Alix."

"Alix," Elise repeated, "would be perfect. Plus she'd be bringing business into the French Café and that's a feather in her cap."

"Fabulous." Bethanne jumped up and gave Elise an impulsive hug. "Thank you, thank you, Elise. *You're* the real genius here."

Elise smiled with pleasure. Before she left, she reminded Bethanne to pay herself better. "Start with twenty dollars an hour," she said. "And your hours should include your preparation time, plus cleanup and driving."

Bethanne promised she would.

Later, on the bus ride home, Elise felt the satisfaction of having helped a friend. But it wasn't a one-way street by any means; she'd learned from Bethanne too. The younger woman's lack of bitterness and anger toward Grant impressed her. When Elise had commented on her calm acceptance, Bethanne said she considered it a gift that had come to her because of the divorce.

In Elise's view, divorce didn't mean anything except gut-wrenching emotional agony. But Bethanne had found nuggets of wisdom buried in the pain and suffering Grant's betrayal had brought into her life.

When Elise entered the house, she thought no one was home. Then she heard the sound of the television. Since it was a bright, sunny afternoon, she couldn't imagine why the entire family would be staring at the TV.

"What's going on?" she asked, as she stood just inside the family room.

"Shh." Luke beckoned her in. "Grandpa's on TV," he whispered.

"Mom." Aurora glanced over her shoulder. "Sit with me. Dad's playing poker on national TV."

"No, thank you." Elise whirled around so fast, she nearly lost her balance. Television or not, it didn't matter. Gambling was gambling. There'd be no stopping Maverick now that he'd made it all the way to national television. He'd live on that high for months to come, thinking he was invincible—that he couldn't lose.

"Mom?" A short time later, Aurora tapped gently on her bedroom door. "Can I come in?"

"Of course." Elise was determined to say something about allowing the children to…to *admire* their grandfather when it was obvious he had a problem.

"You looked upset when you got home."

Elise had made no effort to hide her feelings, but the entire family had been so absorbed in watching Maverick that it surprised her anyone had noticed.

"Dad—"

"It would be best if we didn't discuss your father." She'd said this before and needed to say it again. Only a couple of hours earlier she'd marveled at Bethanne's attitude toward Grant. Elise wanted to find that same kind of peace with Maverick, and hadn't.

Aurora sat on the edge of Elise's bed. "I think we should discuss Dad one last time."

Elise's nod was reluctant.

"Don't you want to know if he won or lost?"

"Not really." She reached for her knitting, needing something to occupy her hands.

"He wore his lucky socks."

"There is no such thing as luck." Aurora was more like her father than Elise had known. "They're simply hand-knit socks," she said, more sharply than she'd intended.

"Dad didn't want you to know." Her daughter spoke in a voice so low Elise had to strain to hear.

Frowning, she paused in her knitting and raised her head. "Know what?" she asked.

Aurora clasped her hands together and stared down at the carpet. "He's dying."

"What?"

"He has a rare form of leukemia. Don't ask me to repeat the medical name, because I don't know if I can even pronounce it. Those afternoons he was away? He was going in for blood transfusions. He only has about a year left. Two years possibly, but no one's placing any bets." She smiled sadly when she realized what she'd said.

"Dying?" It felt as if Elise's heart had stopped beating.

"He came to Seattle because he wanted to get to know me and the family while he still could." Tears shone in her eyes. "He didn't gamble until that one day, when he entered the poker competition. He swore to me he hadn't, and I believe him."

"But why did he do it then?" Elise demanded. "And don't tell me it was for my sake, because I refuse to believe it."

Aurora shook her head as if she didn't know what to say. "That's what he told me."

"Dying," Elise repeated slowly. Everything became very clear to her in those few moments. Her mind scanned the last months. She should've understood that something was wrong; in his whole life, Maverick had never been content to sit and do nothing, yet he'd spent hours sitting in the car, waiting for her. She'd accepted that without question, as she had his sudden need to see his daughter.

"A year…"

Aurora nodded. "He loves you, Mom. He's told me that a dozen times, and I know it's true."

Elise swallowed the thickness in her throat. "I love him, too."

"I know."

Without invitation Luke wandered into the bedroom, feet dragging. He fell into his mother's lap, sighing dejectedly.

"What's the matter?" Elise asked.

"You don't know?" he exclaimed. "Grandpa lost."

Elise stretched out her arms to her grandson, and Luke slid away from his mother and walked over to her. Holding the boy close, she shut her eyes and mused that her ex-husband was no luckier in cards than he was in life.

CHAPTER 39

BETHANNE HAMLIN

On a Friday evening in mid-September, when both Andrew and Annie were busy with school activities, Paul phoned and suggested a movie. Bethanne agreed, although he wanted to see a fast-paced action-adventure she normally wouldn't have chosen. Whenever there were violent scenes Bethanne had to close her eyes. But every time the hero seemed to be facing certain death, he managed to escape. Still, the loud pounding music heightened her anxiety. Could things possibly end well?

During a brief lull in the action, she thought about Grant. She hadn't told Paul—or anyone—that she'd run into him in the bank parking lot. The episode had an almost unreal quality to it.

Bethanne realized with a sense of something approaching sorrow that the affair—and the divorce—had cost him dearly. His children were, for all intents and purposes, estranged from him. Annie talked to her father now and then, but her attitude was more insolent than it should have been. Andrew was still refusing to have much to do with him, despite a couple of attempts by his father to patch up the relationship.

Bethanne hoped that in time Andrew would find it in his heart to forgive Grant.

Bethanne experienced a familiar sadness over the loss of her marriage. Grant had changed, but she didn't know when those changes had taken place, hadn't even recognized what was happening. The man he was now wasn't the man she'd married or the husband who'd stayed with her in the labor room and walked the floors when the children were sick. Perhaps she'd contributed to whatever went wrong. That wasn't something she'd been willing to acknowledge before. Caught up in her own small world, involved with their children, perhaps Bethanne hadn't paid enough attention to her marriage. Eventually she and Grant had become strangers to each other.

Glancing over at Paul, she discovered he was studying her instead of watching the screen. "You okay?" he whispered.

She nodded, but could tell he didn't believe her. They went for coffee following the movie—which did end happily. At least the hero had survived.

They sat across from each other in a booth at Denny's, and the waitress smiled admiringly at Paul as she brought their coffee. There was a lot to admire, to find attractive about him. The waitress's smile clarified what Bethanne had been feeling lately.

"You seem to be deep in thought," he said.

"Well, I've been doing a lot of thinking."

"About what?" Paul asked absently as he reached for a sugar packet. He looked up as he stirred it into his coffee.

She shrugged and experienced a brief surge of sadness. "You're not dating anyone, are you?"

"You mean besides you?"

"Yes," she said. "No. I mean, we're not dating. We're seeing each other as friends."

"Why the frown? I thought that's what you wanted."

"We've got a problem, Paul." She decided to be direct.

"We've come to rely on each other. I consider you safe and I'm fairly sure you feel the same way about me."

He seemed about to argue with her, but had the good sense to wait.

"If we don't do something soon, there's a danger of us becoming so emotionally dependent, we'll pass up other opportunities, with other people." Although she made it sound like a possibility, Bethanne feared it was already a reality, especially for him. "I don't want that to happen."

"I don't, either," he agreed, but with reluctance.

"It's time we went out into the dating world without training wheels." Bethanne tried to make a joke of it. She wished she'd thought this through more carefully.

The waitress refilled their coffee and Paul reached for his, sipping it pensively. "Is there someone you want to get involved with?"

"No, but this isn't about me."

"Then what *is* it about? I don't understand, Bethanne. I hoped—I hoped we could become more than friends, damn it," he said, sounding frustrated. "I was afraid of this. You're worried about the age difference, aren't you?"

"No—okay, a little, but that's not the point. Much as I care about you, I don't think our relationship is emotionally healthy."

"What's wrong with it?"

She didn't want to repeat everything she'd already said. "Let's stop relying on each other for a while. I'm not doing you any favors. You should be seeing other women, finding someone who can be everything to you."

"I'll be the judge of that," he argued. "You're the one person who understood how I felt when Tiffany left me. We're the injured parties, and it's only natural that we'd have a lot in common. Now you're saying we should walk away from all that."

"I'm not explaining myself well."

"Yes, you are. I'm getting the message loud and clear. You want us to stop seeing each other but I don't understand why, especially now. It's…it's like before."

"I'm not Tiffany!"

"Then why do I have this knot in my gut? Why do I feel the same things I did when she told me she was in love with another man? This is just another rejection."

"No, it's not." She'd done a terrible job of conveying her feelings. "I want us to stay friends. I also want you to get out there and date someone else."

"Why?" he demanded. "I like you."

"I like you, too. But I think we should stop seeing each other for a while."

She smiled and reached across the table to squeeze his hand. "You're a wonderful man, Paul, and I can't tell you how much I appreciate everything you've done for me. But it's time for us to let go a little. To explore relationships with other people."

"This *isn't* a rejection?" he asked sardonically. "It sure as hell sounds like one."

"Being more independent doesn't mean we can't talk or give each other emotional support. I want us to have a healthy relationship. I want us to be real friends." Bethanne glanced around the Denny's, afraid their conversation was entertainment for half the restaurant. She leaned toward him. "I want you to date a wonderful woman who's crazy about you."

"I thought that was you."

Bethanne sighed. "You don't know how easy it would be to fall in love with you. I'm halfway there already."

Her words obviously pleased him, as some of the intensity left his face. "What's stopping you?"

"My conscience," she told him. "I'm not the right woman for you."

"Let me be the judge of that," he said again, just as stubbornly.

"The thing is, there's a corollary."

He scowled, then slowly said, "In other words, I'm not the right man for you, either."

She nodded. "I should've said something earlier, but I didn't have the courage to let you go. Your friendship's been really important to me." She paused to take a deep breath. "I hope you'll find a woman you'll have children with. You'll make a terrific father." Both Andrew and Annie, who'd met him a number of times, thought the world of him.

"Fine, but I still plan to see you. And call you." He would, too, especially at first, but when he opened his eyes to other relationships those calls would probably become farther apart. If that happened, it would be hard.

"You were absolutely wonderful for my self-esteem," she told him, feeling almost tearful. "After Grant left, I was convinced no man would ever find me attractive again."

"I did," he said, then added softly, sweetly. "I do."

"Thank you for that."

"Will you see other men?" he asked. "Because I'm not going out into the great unknown all by myself."

Bethanne managed a smile.

"I imagine that, given time, I will," she said. "But I don't think I'm ready just yet." She'd take it slow, get on her feet financially, build her business. That was her first priority, aside from taking care of her children. One thing she'd learned through all of this was that she didn't *need* a man in her life. After twenty years as Grant's wife, she was finding her own identity. That might be a cliché these days, but like all clichés it was based in truth.

Part of that new identity was seeing herself as a businesswoman. Two days earlier, she'd been contacted by a friend of a friend who wanted to know if Bethanne did catering. She didn't, but she knew someone who did. That conversation gave her an idea. Bethanne was good at organizing parties and social events. So far, all she'd booked were children's birthday parties, but she wanted to expand, do more, connect with other professionals. The possibilities were endless and would be beneficial for all concerned. She might even end up becoming a wedding consultant. What was a wedding except one big party?

"I'll date someone else if you will too," Paul agreed after a lengthy silence.

That was all the assurance Bethanne needed. "I think that would be wise for us both."

Like a youngster with an assignment, Paul propped his elbows on the table and said, "Any suggestions where to start?"

Bethanne smothered a giggle. "What about your office?"

He shook his head. "Everyone there's already married."

"I'll bet someone you know has offered to set you up with a blind date."

Paul dismissed that idea with a shake of his head. "No, thanks."

Bethanne didn't blame him. "I saw one of those decorator pillows once that read *I've had so many blind dates I need a Seeing Eye dog.*"

They both laughed, but Paul quickly sobered. "I don't think I'm going to find anyone who can make me laugh the way you do."

"Well, try," she challenged, rather than allowing the compliment to sway her.

"What about you?" he asked. "When you decide you're ready, where are you planning to meet single men? Clubs?"

"Oh, hardly," she said, dismissing his comment with a wave of her hand. "I don't have the shoes for it." He laughed, as she'd wanted him to. "I'll keep my eyes and ears open. Eventually I'll meet someone, through a friend or my business or just by chance."

"But you aren't looking now?"

"No! Not yet."

"Maybe you should." His smile was infectious. He turned, craning his neck to take a good look around the restaurant.

"Paul! You're being ridiculous."

"Am I?" he teased. "What about that guy over there—the one with the baseball cap?"

"Paul, stop it," she hissed, keeping her voice low. "Stop it right this minute. Unless you want me to introduce you to a couple of women." Turnabout was fair play, so she caught their waitress's eye. The young woman picked up a coffeepot and brought it over to their table. Her badge said her name was Cindy.

"Hello, Cindy," Bethanne said warmly. "This is Paul. He's single and available."

Cindy smiled shyly in Paul's direction and added a quarter inch of coffee to their mugs.

"Would you be interested in dating a man like Paul?" Bethanne asked.

"Ah, sure."

Cindy had proven Bethanne's point. "What did I tell you?" she cried triumphantly.

"Cindy, what are you doing tomorrow after five?" Paul asked.

Disappointment flashed in her eyes. "Working, but I get off at nine."

Soon Paul and Cindy were discussing where they'd go.

She left, smiling, and Paul leaned closer. "I want a contingency plan. I'll do as you suggest, but if it doesn't work out, I want you to know I'm coming back for you."

"Paul," she chastised, and then just gave in. "Oh, all right."

"Good." He grinned and lifted his mug in silent salute.

CHAPTER 40

"I do love a good yarn, fiction and fiber. The only thing that equals my joy in knitting is the pleasure of reading!"
—Priscilla A. Gibson-Roberts, author of *Simple Socks, Plain & Fancy* and *Ethnic Socks & Stockings*.

LYDIA HOFFMAN

I visited Mom Sunday afternoon, and it was such a lovely autumn day that it seemed pointless to go back to an empty apartment. Sundays were the hardest for me. This particular Sunday, for some reason, felt lonelier than most. My love for Whiskers can take me only so far.

Mom looked better than she had in months, and seeing her smile cheered me considerably. Leaving her home of nearly fifty years must have been painful. I was grateful she'd accepted the upheaval in her life without an argument. After two weeks in a nursing home, the assisted living facility probably seemed like an extended vacation.

I think Mom understood, once she entered the hospital, that everything would change from that moment on. I could tell she was grateful to have less responsibility, although I don't expect she'll ever admit it. I know she missed her rose garden; I did, too.

We had lunch together in the dining room, and she introduced me to her new friends. I didn't have the heart to tell her I'd already met Ida and Francine last week and the week before that, too. Interestingly enough, Ida and Francine don't appear to remember me, either.

Before leaving work on Friday evening, Margaret had invited me over for Sunday dinner but I'd declined. We see each other nearly every day and frankly, as much as I love my sister, I needed a break. I think she felt the same way since she readily accepted my explanation of "other plans."

A number of subtle and not-so-subtle changes had taken place in the relationship between my sister and me. Margaret was knitting more, and I'd begun crocheting. It was almost as if we were both anxious to prove our willingness to see the other's point of view.

With Sunday afternoon stretching before me, I drove to Green Lake. I'd missed walking the three-mile path around the lake with Brad and Cody and Chase. A dozen times or more, I'd stopped myself from driving there, but I decided not to stay away any longer. If Brad and Janice were on the path, I'd smile and greet them and simply keep going. Physical exercise is good for me and I refused to be deprived of an enjoyable walk just because there was a chance of an awkward encounter. I'd have to deal with it—and so would Brad.

It was a perfect day with the leaves just starting to turn and a light breeze coming off the water. I changed into my tennis shoes in the parking lot and stowed my purse in the trunk of my car. Carrying my car keys, I headed down the path.

I hadn't gone more than a quarter of a mile when a golden retriever shot past me, dragging his leash. Unfortunately, I wasn't quick enough or alert enough to grab it. Somebody would be frantic about this runaway dog. For an instant I thought it was Chase, Cody's dog, but it couldn't be. Chase wasn't that big. But within a few seconds, I heard Cody's voice and I knew I was wrong.

"Chase! Chase! Get back here."

I turned to look over my shoulder and saw that Cody was fast gaining on me. When he noticed me he halted abruptly, looked back, forward and then back again.

"Lydia," he shouted and ran toward me, his arms open wide.

I caught him and hugged him close.

"I have to catch Chase," he said, his eyes pleading with mine.

"Go," I urged.

"Don't leave, okay?" he pleaded, half running.

"I won't," I promised, but I wasn't convinced, despite my earlier determination, that I was ready to see Brad and Janice together.

If I did come face to face with Janice, she'd probably gloat. It hadn't taken me long to discover that she was completely self-absorbed and had little interest in being a mother. I suspected that if I did find her with Brad, she'd be delighted to let me know she could have her husband and son back any time she wanted. She'd certainly proved *that* to be true. One snap of her fingers, and Brad was there.

I hated myself for being so negative. I felt like returning to the parking lot and making my escape, but I didn't want to break my promise to Cody.

Before I was ready to deal with it, I heard Brad shouting for his son. "Cody!" He didn't sound too pleased to be chasing after him.

I glanced over my shoulder, surprised—and grateful—to see that he was alone. Janice was nowhere in sight. Intent on catching up with Cody, Brad jogged past me, eyes straight ahead, and had gone two or three feet before he looked back. Like Cody, he stopped, mentally debated what to do, then started toward me. But his arms weren't open and waiting for a hug.

"Lydia." My name was breathless as if he'd jogged a lengthy distance.

"I assume you're looking for Cody and Chase." Polite conversation was all I could manage.

"What are you—"

"Doing here?" I finished for him. "Walking," I said, answering my own question.

He seemed dumbstruck.

"Cody's about three minutes ahead of you, and Chase about half a minute ahead of Cody," I said, pointing down the path. He didn't need to waste time chatting with me when he had a son and a dog to catch.

Brad continued walking backward, facing me. The way he stared made me uncomfortable. I looked away, almost wishing Janice would hurry so we could get this whole awkward scene over with.

"Chase got away from him," Brad stated, as if I hadn't figured that out.

"He's grown," I murmured.

"Chase or Cody?"

"Both." I was walking at a clipped pace; he'd begun to walk parallel to me along the narrow path.

He nodded. "Cody's grown a full inch this summer. His jeans are all high waters. When I took him school-shopping, I—" He stopped abruptly.

Sure enough, Chase was loping toward me, with Cody behind him, holding tight to the retriever's leash.

"Lydia," the boy cried, almost too excited to speak. "I was afraid you'd leave."

"I wouldn't do that," I told him.

"I wish no one would ever do that again." Cody ran up to me and wrapped both arms around my waist. Brad was now holding the leash; he had far more control over the dog. Chase was actually sitting quietly, tongue lolling.

"Where's your mother?" I asked, not wanting to be caught unawares. If Janice walked up now, there might be some explaining to do.

Cody shrugged. "You know Mom."

I didn't, not really.

"She's out of our lives again." Brad filled in the blanks for me.

"When did this happen?" He hadn't mentioned it earlier, and that hurt. If he'd cared even a little for me, the fact that Janice had changed her mind was worth a mention, even casually.

"Not long ago. I planned on letting you know."

"But you didn't." I kept my tone as cool and even as possible.

"Dad felt bad," Cody said. "And I did, too."

Bad that Janice had left? Or—

"I suppose you'd like to know what happened," Brad said, his voice defiant.

"No—you don't have to—"

"Let's talk," he suggested.

"Perhaps later," I said, my head spinning. "I need to think about this . . ."

"We can walk with you," Cody inserted, eager to be with me. "Did you come here every week? We didn't," he said. "Mom thinks the wind and sun aren't good for her skin, and she didn't think Dad and I should come without her."

"No, I stayed away, too." This wasn't the first time Cody had alluded to his mother. "Maybe you *should* tell me what happened," I said, looking at Brad.

"Cody," Brad said to his son, handing over the leash. "Go on ahead with Chase. Make him heel, okay?"

The boy showed his disappointment. "I want to talk to Lydia, too, Dad. I missed her."

"You'll get your chance, I promise."

Cody looked at me, and I nodded in agreement. He gave a boyish grin and took off, walking sedately. "Heel, Chase. Heel!"

We both watched them for a minute and I smiled at Cody's earnest effort to restrain the dog.

"It didn't work out," Brad said flatly. "Janice is gone."

That was a pretty minimal explanation. "Could you give me a few details?"

Brad pushed his hands into his pants pockets. "You were right. Janice didn't want me back, nor was she particularly interested in being a mother to Cody. She just didn't want you and me together."

I nodded.

"Cody once told her he wanted you to be his mom, and Janice got all bent out of shape. She went into panic mode and decided she couldn't let that happen."

"I see."

"I stopped loving Janice a long time ago."

I didn't feel qualified to comment.

"I had to try to make a go of the reconciliation for Cody's sake. A child deserves a mother and a father."

"I love Cody, too," I cried, "and I understood why you did what you did. But you completely discounted my feelings."

"Be angry with me if you want," Brad concluded, quickening his pace. "The thing is, I'm sick to death of women and their demands. I loved Janice and she pulled every string she could to manipulate me, using my son."

"And that's *my* fault?" I was a second away from reminding him that he'd been the one to shove me aside. As I'd told him, I knew why he'd done it and I loved the way he loved his son, but I had a hard time getting past the pain it had caused me.

"Now you want your pound of flesh."

"I beg your pardon?" I certainly recognized the allusion but didn't understand how it applied to me.

"You heard me," he said. "What you want is for me to come

crawling back to you because Janice decided she needed her freedom, after all."

I swallowed down my pent-up anger.

"I notice it didn't take you long to find someone else."

"What did you expect me to do?" I asked, even though it had been a lie. "Did you want me to sit at home and pine for you?"

He hesitated. "No, and you didn't, which is just perfect." He made a sweeping gesture with his hands. "You know what? I've had it with women and relationships. It's just too damned hard."

"I was the one you dumped," I pointed out. Whether he wanted to admit it or not, Brad had hurt me badly. Now I was supposed to pretend nothing had happened? None of my concerns appeared to interest Brad.

He shook his head. "It's over, Lydia. With Janice, with you, and with every other female on the planet. I don't understand women. I never have and I doubt I ever will. Living the rest of my life alone would be easier than dealing with an irrational female."

"I'm not irrational!"

"Whatever you say. But I'm not crawling back to you."

"Well, I'm not chasing after you, either." I wanted to make that clear right then and there.

He smiled sardonically. "I know, and frankly that suits me just fine."

41

CHAPTER

COURTNEY PULANSKI

According to Grams, Courtney wouldn't be able to ride her bicycle much longer. Two or three weeks at the most. The autumn rains would start in mid-October, and it wouldn't be safe to ride on slick roads. Soon it would be dark by midafternoon.

Courtney would miss riding as part of her exercise and weight-maintenance program. It helped her vent her frustrations and stay out of the kitchen. She'd managed to maintain her twenty-five-pound weight loss, which was no small feat. Making better food choices had become easier, but her gaze often lingered on sweets and on the candy machine. That stuff was pure poison for her.

The best development since school started was that she'd made a few friends, including Mike, her chauffeur. That was what he called himself, and with great flair. He was shy but she'd discovered that he had a subtle sense of humor that seemed to come out of nowhere. Every now and then, always unexpectedly, he'd crack a joke that was hilarious. Until recently, she'd hoped Mike would ask her to the Homecoming Dance, but it was plain he'd set his sights on someone else.

She was only now becoming acquainted with the students in her classes. Most days, she hung around with Monica and Jocelyn, girls from her trigonometry class. Jocelyn and Mike liked each other and were perfect together, so Courtney played the role of matchmaker.

Annie was her closest friend. They talked on the phone often and saw each other at school, but they didn't have any classes together. Courtney liked Andrew, too. A lot.

Taking a sharp corner on her bike, Courtney rolled onto her grandmother's street and coasted to a stop. She climbed off, wheeling the ten-speed around to the garage. Helmet looped over her arm, she headed toward the kitchen door.

"Is that you, Courtney?" Grams called from the living room.

"It's me," she shouted back as she stopped at the sink to get a drink of water.

"You've got company, dear."

Courtney set the glass down and tried to remember whether she'd noticed any cars parked out front. She couldn't imagine who'd be visiting.

When she walked into the living room and saw Andrew sitting on the sofa, she nearly dropped her helmet. "Hi," she said, hardly able to find her voice.

"Hi," he said, grinning back at her.

"Look, dear, he's wearing the socks you knit him." Grams seemed utterly delighted by this. "Well, I'll leave you young people to discuss whatever you want to talk about."

"Thank you, Mrs. Pulanski."

Vera hesitated on her way to the kitchen. "I have some oatmeal cookies in the freezer I can defrost if you're interested, Andrew."

He shared a look with Courtney. "Thanks, anyway, Mrs. Pulanski. Maybe another time."

"You don't need anything, do you?" Grams turned to Courtney.

"Nothing, thanks," she said.

Her grandmother nodded and, good as her word, she left the room.

"What are you doing here?" Courtney asked. No need to beat around the bush. She was hot and sweaty, and if he'd let her know he intended to come over, she would've stayed home instead of riding her bike.

"I came to talk to you."

"When did you get here?"

He checked his watch. "About ten minutes ago. I had fun chatting with your grandmother. You were a cute baby."

Courtney rolled her eyes. "She showed you baby pictures of me?"

"Naked ones."

"No!" Courtney would never forgive that.

Andrew chuckled. "Just kidding."

"It isn't funny." Maintaining a suitable distance, she sat down on the ottoman and hoped she hadn't perspired too much.

Andrew released a deep sigh and then sent a quick look in her direction. "Did you hear?"

She thought about recent gossip that had circulated around the school. Unfortunately, she didn't hear many rumors, and even when she did, she rarely knew the people involved.

"Hear what?" she asked.

"Melanie and I aren't going out anymore. We haven't in quite a while, but it got a little complicated over the summer and—well, let's just say it's over."

Andrew seemed to be waiting for a comment from her. Courtney wasn't sure what to say. "I'm sorry," was the best she could come up with.

"You are?"

Not really, but… "Breaking up is hard."

"Not on my end. Melanie and I don't have a lot in common."

"What does this mean for Homecoming?"

Andrew shrugged. "Doesn't mean anything. If I'm crowned king, I'll have my date and if Melanie's named queen, she'll have hers. No big deal either way."

Being new at the school, Courtney wasn't sure how this worked.

"Are you going to the Homecoming dance?" he asked.

She shook her head.

He seemed surprised. "I thought Mike asked you."

Courtney stretched the truth just a little. "I think he's building up his courage, but he hasn't yet." She immediately felt bad for overstating the likelihood of his asking her, but she didn't want Andrew to think she was entirely without prospects—which at this point, she was—or that she was angling for an invitation from *him*.

"It's getting down to the wire, don't you think?"

The dance was a week away, and almost everyone already had a date. Courtney was convinced Mike would ask Jocelyn. Monica agreed and suggested that rather than be left out, the two of them attend the dance together, dates or not. A lot of girls did that, and guys, too.

"Why are you asking?" she asked curiously. "In fact, why are you here?"

"Can't a friend come by without getting the third degree?"

Suddenly Courtney felt a knot in her stomach. "Your mother put you up to this, didn't she?" She got to her feet and started pacing. No wonder he was so vague! Courtney remembered that it was Bethanne who'd suggested Andrew find her a ride to and from school. She'd also coerced him into taking her to the Mariners' game that first time.

"My mother had nothing to do with this."

"Fine. Whatever."

"Don't go all psycho on me," he muttered. He vaulted to his feet, raking his fingers through his hair. "Listen, there's probably a better way to ask you to the Homecoming dance, but—"

Courtney's head reared back. "You're asking me to the dance?" She hadn't dared to even hope for this. Was he serious? He wasn't teasing her, was he? That would be too cruel.

He nodded. "But listen, there might be a bit of a problem with Melanie."

"What do you mean?"

His shoulders rose in a sigh. "She's the jealous type."

"So the breakup wasn't mutual?"

He shook his head sadly. "No. Not exactly. She's pretty upset and, well—I felt I should warn you."

Courtney frowned. "Why didn't you tell me this earlier?"

Andrew smiled apologetically. "I was afraid if I did, you might refuse to go to the dance with me." He studied her, an expectant look on his face.

This wasn't a joke. He *was* serious. Andrew wanted to take her to Homecoming. "Oh, Andrew," she whispered, trying to keep her voice from trembling. "I'd be honored to be your date." She didn't have a thing to wear—oh, if she'd ever needed her sister, it was now.

Andrew brightened. "Annie said you would."

"*She* put you up to this?"

"No way, but she did give me some advice." Andrew grinned, raising one foot. "She suggested I wear the socks. Did it work?"

Courtney laughed. "Tell her it did," she said, smothering a laugh.

42

CHAPTER

BETHANNE HAMLIN

Bethanne was in the midst of party preparations for an eight-year-old boy. Todd was a fan of old-fashioned Western movies and TV shows, the cowboy and Indian shoot'em up kind. Bethanne had developed a party for him revolving around his favorite hero, the Lone Ranger. The invitations were out, and everyone was asked to come dressed as a cowboy. Bethanne planned to bring her guitar and she'd made arrangements to have a few bales of hay delivered. The parents had agreed to a campfire in their large backyard, and after various games, the boys would eat sitting around the fire and then she'd lead a singalong. In order to get in the mood, she'd tie a red bandanna around her neck and wear her cowgirl boots. She'd even bought a tin sheriff's badge to pin to her plaid shirt.

Humming to Reba McEntire, she stirred the pork and beans warming on the stove. They were canned, but she'd added liquid smoke to give them the flavor of having been cooked on a campfire.

The games were more involved, since she wanted to stick

to the western theme, and she planned to talk over her ideas with Andrew when he got home from school. Everything else was settled, including the menu.

Bethanne liked Elise's idea of making a schedule of standard party ideas, so she wouldn't need to start from scratch with every child. Who would've believed her creativity would get her this far? Her one drawback was the lack of start-up cash. It was hard to balance all her expenses and still make the house payments, but she was learning the importance of following a budget. Money was tight, but both her son and daughter understood that this was important. They all had to sacrifice if the business was going to survive.

The telephone rang, and Bethanne reached for it. Tucking the portable phone against her shoulder, she continued stirring. Pork and beans was the least expensive grocery item on her list, but she didn't want to risk scorching them.

"This is Bethanne," she said. When she could afford it, she intended to get a separate line for the party business.

"Ms. Hamlin, this is Gary Schroeder from Puget Sound Security."

"Yes?"

"We talked briefly a few weeks ago about a loan application you'd submitted," he said. "I hope I haven't caught you at an inconvenient moment."

Bethanne tried to remember this particular loan officer, but drew a blank. She'd been ushered in and out of each financial institution in record time, so it was little wonder she didn't recall meeting him.

"This is fine." The timer on the oven told her the birthday cake was finished.

"Perhaps it would be better if you stopped by our loan department at your earliest convenience," he suggested.

"Ah." Bethanne rationed her gas usage and preferred not to take unnecessary trips. "If you could tell me what this is about, I might be able to manage that," she said. With the phone still pressed against her shoulder, she opened the oven door, slid out the top rack and tested the cake by inserting a toothpick into the center.

"There's a check waiting for you, Ms. Hamlin," the loan officer replied warmly.

"A check? The bank reconsidered?"

"We can discuss that when you arrive."

"I'll be there in thirty minutes," she said, her heart pounding hard. This was incredible! She couldn't imagine what had convinced the bank to finally approve her loan. Whatever it was, she was ready to throw her arms around this man she couldn't even remember meeting.

With the cake cooling on the counter and the beans in the fridge, Bethanne drove to the bank and parked in their nearby lot.

She found the desk with Gary Schroeder's name and approached him, thrusting out her hand. "I'm Bethanne Hamlin," she announced, then realized she still had her apron on. "Oops," she said, untying it. "As you can see, I left in kind of a hurry."

He gestured toward the chair. "Please, have a seat."

Bethanne sat, perched on the edge of the chair.

"Thank you for coming so promptly," he said.

"No problem. I did understand you correctly, didn't I?" She gazed at him earnestly. "You did approve my loan?"

His mouth thinned. "Actually, no."

"No," she gasped. "Then why did you drag me all the way down here? I'm a busy woman, Mr. Schroeder. I have a business to run and—" The disappointment was so overwhelming she couldn't finish. Not only had she wasted her time, but the gauge on her gas tank was hovering at empty. Raising her hopes like this was unfair! She stood up, ready to walk away, but Mr. Schroeder stopped her.

"You don't have an account with our bank," he began. "And—"

"Trust me," she broke in. "I have no intention of opening one now if this is the kind of trick you pull on your customers."

"Ms. Hamlin," he said, lifting one hand in a conciliatory gesture. "I apologize for upsetting you, but this is a rather… unusual situation. Please, sit down."

Bethanne reclaimed her chair and tried to swallow the lump forming in her throat.

"Early this morning, I received a call from a man who asked if you'd applied for a business loan with our institution. I can assure you it isn't our policy to give out such information."

"I should hope not."

"The man, who requested not to be identified, said he'd like five thousand dollars deposited into your account."

"But—as you said—I don't have an account here."

"Which I explained. He then asked if it would be possible to get you the loan amount you'd requested."

"I'm afraid I'm confused," Bethanne said.

"I don't blame you. I was confused myself."

"So, what does this mean?"

"It means that this person, who again asked that his identity not be revealed, wants to give you the money."

"*Give* me the money," she repeated.

"That's right."

Bethanne leaned forward in her chair. "Let me see if I understand this. Someone I don't know wants to hand over five thousand dollars cash—to me. What's the catch?"

"There is no catch."

She still wasn't sure she could believe this. "You're positive about that?"

He nodded. "With the proviso that if the opportunity arises, you will do the same for someone else."

"I see—well, I think I do. Sort of."

"In other words," he continued, opening a file. "I have a cashier's check for you in the amount of five thousand dollars."

Her jaw sagged open as the reality set in. She stared at Gary Schroeder, unable to comprehend who would do such a thing. Then it came to her. She knew of only one possible person who'd want to help her like this, and while she couldn't be sure, she felt she had to ask.

"I have a friend…. The money doesn't happen to come from a man by the name of Paul Ormond, does it?"

Mr. Schroeder shook his head. "As I explained earlier, your benefactor has requested anonymity."

"But it isn't Paul?"

He smiled kindly. "No."

Bethanne tried to think who else her benefactor might be. It didn't seem at all likely that Grant would do this. She realized he had regrets about the divorce, but if he'd found it in his heart to give her this money, he'd certainly want her to know what he'd done.

"Grant Hamlin?" she asked, just in case.

Again the loan officer shook his head. "I can't tell you any more, but I will let you know this. The man who contacted us is not related to you in any way. I suggest you put your questions about his name out of your mind for now. Invest these funds wisely and validate this person's faith in you."

With the check clutched in her hand, Bethanne nodded and got slowly to her feet. "I will," she promised. "I most certainly will."

She couldn't guess who had such faith in her ability, but she would take this gift and use it wisely, as the loan officer had advised. And, in keeping with her benefactor's proviso, she'd pass on his generosity when she had the chance.

CHAPTER 43

COURTNEY PULANSKI

"Grandma, I don't understand," Courtney said, staring at the express mail envelope. It was addressed to her with no indication of the sender's identity. As soon as she'd seen the contents, she'd forgotten that Grandma had become Grams months ago.

"What is it?" her grandmother asked, standing next to her in the foyer. The letter had been waiting for Courtney on the stair railing.

Courtney handed it to her grandmother as she slid her backpack from her shoulders and let it drop to the floor.

"It's a cashier's check," Vera Pulanski murmured, sounding as shocked as Courtney.

"You didn't do this?" Courtney asked, unable to think of anyone else who might be responsible.

"Me?" her grandmother exclaimed. "My goodness, child, if I had that kind of money, let me tell you I wouldn't be spending it on a dress. Let's see the card again."

Courtney reached for the envelope and pulled out the type-written note. It read: BUY A DRESS AS BEAUTIFUL AS

YOU ARE AND HAVE A WONDERFUL TIME AT HOME-COMING. It was signed YOUR FAIRY GODFATHER.

Vera shook her head hopelessly. "I have no idea. It's got to be someone who knows you… Could it be your dad?"

"No, it was sent locally. Dated yesterday—Wednesday. And why would Dad do something like this anonymously?"

Vera merely shrugged.

"I've got to tell Andrew," Courtney sank down on the bottom step and picked up the phone. She was so excited she couldn't dial the number fast enough. Grams, of course, had that old-fashioned rotary phone, black and cumbersome. Annie was the one who answered.

"Annie!" she cried. "You won't believe what just happened!"

"What?"

"Someone sent me money for Homecoming. It's a huge sum of money. Huge."

"How huge?"

"Five hundred dollars."

Annie released a low whistle. "You've got to be kidding."

"I'm not. Is Andrew home?" She wasn't sure why it seemed so important to tell him about this. She supposed it was so he'd know she planned to do him proud. Since he'd asked her to the Homecoming dance, they'd talked several times a day. Just last night, they'd spent almost two hours on the phone.

Once word got out at school that Andrew Hamlin had asked her to be his date, she'd attracted a lot of attention. Some of the most popular kids were talking to her now—the very ones who hadn't seen fit to even acknowledge her a couple of weeks ago. She wasn't taken in by their interest, which struck her as false and opportunistic. While she was friendly and polite, these were not people she wanted as friends.

"Sorry," Annie said, sounding as disappointed as Courtney.

"Andrew isn't back from football practice, but I'll tell him to phone you the minute he walks in the door."

Courtney should've realized Andrew would still be at school. "I'm so *excited*." She had a dress, but it was a hand-me-down from her sister, who'd mailed it as soon as Courtney told her about the date. Rather frilly, it was a pretty pale-blue, much better suited to Julianna than her.

"It's so cool that you're dating my brother."

"We aren't dating," Courtney reminded her friend. "We haven't even gone out on a single date, and there's nothing to say we will after tomorrow night."

"You will," Annie insisted. "Andrew and I talk, you know."

Courtney bit her tongue to keep from questioning her about anything Andrew might've said. She knew that wouldn't be right, despite her curiosity. Maybe she'd have a clearer sense of her future with Andrew after the dance.

Annie would be there, too, with a good friend of Andrew's from the football team. Everything had worked out so well. Courtney could hardly believe it. Monica had been asked by a friend of Mike's, and all four couples intended to go out after the dance.

"As your grandmother would say," Annie continued, "Andrew's smitten."

Smitten. What a perfectly lovely word. "Oh, Annie, I think he's just…wonderful." No adjective satisfactorily described her feelings about Andrew Hamlin. Being with him made leaving Chicago for her senior year almost worthwhile.

"Who'd send you that kind of money?" Annie wondered.

"Your guess is as good as mine." Courtney was beyond conjecture.

"Your dad?" Annie suggested. "Or your brother?"

Courtney automatically shook her head. "No, neither of them," she said.

"Then who?"

"I don't know, but it's the most fabulous gift I've ever received." The doorbell chimed just then. "There's someone at the door. Grams is in the kitchen, so I'd better get it."

"Okay. I'll tell Andrew you called."

"Thanks." She could hardly wait to talk to him.

Hurrying to the door, Courtney opened it and gasped out loud when she saw her sister, suitcase in hand. "Julianna!"

"Aren't you going to let me in?" her sister asked. "Courtney, my goodness, look at you! You're gorgeous. Who would've thought those pounds would make such a difference."

Tears of joy sprang to Courtney's eyes as she threw open the screen door. "What are you doing here?" she asked, hugging her tightly.

In seconds they were both laughing and weeping simultaneously. The commotion was enough to bring their grandmother out from the kitchen. Soon her squeals of delight mingled with theirs.

"My, oh my, this is lovely," Grams said, pulling Julianna into the living room. "But—how did you get here?"

"By plane. The most amazing thing happened. I got an express letter that said my baby sister's been asked to Homecoming by the star football player. Which I knew, of course. The letter suggested Courtney might need a little help getting ready for the big dance."

Her grandmother raised both hands. "I'm telling you right now, I had nothing to do with this."

"There was an airline ticket in the envelope," Julianna explained. "Also included was a long list of instructions. The first was that a car service would arrange to drive me to O'Hare, and that another car would be waiting to pick me up at Sea-Tac. It would then drive me to Grams's house, but I was warned I couldn't say anything to either of you in advance."

"Well, I, for one, am surprised," Courtney whispered, her cheeks still wet with tears.

"I was given a cashier's check for my expenses, but it's far more money than I'll need. I'm thinking we should make an appointment for your hair and your nails as soon as we can."

"My hair and nails, too?" Courtney whispered, so overwhelmed she could barely speak.

Grams looked utterly perplexed. "I wish I'd thought of it, but even if I had, I never would've been able to afford all this."

"Our carriage awaits," her sister announced grandly. "Well, the car. But the driver's in livery." She giggled. "I mean, a uniform—but isn't this just like *Cinderella?*"

"Why's the car waiting?" Courtney felt as if she had, indeed, been dropped into the middle of her favorite fairy tale. At the good part, though, when the godmother materializes and waves her wand around. Or *godfather,* she corrected, and it was a check, not a wand.

"The car's going to take us all to dinner," Julianna said. "We have reservations at Morton's on 4th Avenue. From there, the driver will drop Courtney and me at the mall and take you home, Grams. We're supposed to arrange a time and place for him to meet us when we're finished."

"I can't *believe* this," Courtney shrieked, giving way to her excitement. "I just can't believe this."

"I must admit this is some Fairy Godfather you've got," Julianna teased.

"Let me grab my sweater," Vera said. "I didn't feel like cooking tonight, anyway."

Courtney led her sister upstairs so they could leave her suitcase in one of the spare rooms. "How long can you stay?" she asked.

"Just until Saturday afternoon. I have to get back, and whoever arranged this seemed to know that, too."

"Have you talked to Jason?"

She shook her head. "It isn't him," she said with a laugh.

"He doesn't have a dime to his name. In fact, he's always trying to borrow from me—as if I had anything extra."

The phone rang just as they were leaving the house. Courtney debated whether she should answer it, and then decided it might be Andrew. With her grandmother's ancient phone, Caller ID wasn't an option, even if she'd been willing to spring for it. So phone calls were always a mystery.

"Hello," she answered, hoping it was Andrew.

"You called?"

"I did. Oh, Andrew, the most wonderful thing's happened! But I don't have time to explain everything right now."

"Why not?"

"Because," she laughed, giddy with joy, "my sister's here and there's a car waiting to take me shopping for a Homecoming dress, and Andrew—oh, Annie can tell you about it."

"This must be the day for good news."

"What do you mean?" Everyone was waiting on the porch, but she *had* to know.

"It won't be official until tomorrow, but I've been elected Homecoming King."

"Oh, Andrew! Congratulations."

"Nothing in this world would make me prouder than to have you with me on Friday night."

Running light-heartedly out to the car, Courtney couldn't stop smiling. She didn't know what she'd done that could have merited such generosity, but she'd be forever grateful to whoever had decided to become her Fairy Godfather.

She didn't think she'd ever been happier in her life.

44

CHAPTER

"When in doubt, grab a ball of yarn and Get Creative!"
—Sasha Kagan, Sasha Kagan Knitwear.

LYDIA HOFFMAN

It was more than a week since I'd seen Brad. My anger had cooled and I wished I could take back some of what I'd said. I hoped he felt the same way. Tuesday morning when I removed the Closed sign from my door, I took the opportunity to glance up and down the street. It was too early to see Brad's UPS truck but I was hopeful nonetheless. I hadn't figured out what I'd say but I knew I'd be far less emotional than last week at Green Lake.

It had been an incredible few days. Friday afternoon, Courtney came by to introduce me to her older sister. They had a fantastic story about a fairy godfather who'd stepped in to ensure that her date for Homecoming would be as perfect as it could possibly be. I couldn't imagine who'd do anything like that. I think Courtney somehow expected me to know, but I didn't.

On Saturday it was Bethanne who arrived with an equally fantastic story of a mysterious benefactor who'd given her th money she needed, no strings attached. A gift, not a loan. The only stipulation was that she help someone else if she was ever in a position to do so.

Exuberant, she dashed across the street with a business idea that involved Alix—a contract to provide birthday cakes and other desserts for the various events Bethanne arranged.

I was thrilled for both Bethanne and Courtney. If this fairy godfather had any extra fairy dust available, I could use some myself—not that I expected any magic in my life.

The bell chimed, and Margaret walked in promptly at ten. "Good morning," she said cheerfully.

"Morning," I responded. I thought of asking her about her good mood but hesitated, wondering if she'd volunteer the information herself. Often it's still difficult to know how best to approach my sister.

"It looks like you had a good weekend," I finally ventured, somewhat cautiously.

"We sure did." She was practically skipping as she entered the store. I trailed behind her to the office.

"Did you do anything fun?" I asked. I was thinking maybe dinner out or a movie.

"Better than anything you can imagine!" She gave me a huge smile. Not a typical Margaret smile, either, which often seemed more of a grimace, but a wide, unstinting smile that changed her whole face.

"Oh?" I said, dying of curiosity.

She opened her purse and removed an envelope, which she handed me with a dramatic flourish.

"What's this?"

"Open it and see."

I'll admit I was eager enough to tear it open. Inside was a card and a check. I noticed the amount and gasped—it was for the entire bank loan of ten thousand dollars. The card was a thank-you note written to me by my brother-in-law and signed by both Margaret and Matt.

"What...how—" I stammered, hardly able to form a question.

"Matt has a wonderful new job."

My guess was that this new job had nothing to do with painting houses. "The money..."

"A signing bonus."

"But..."

"We talked it over, Matt and I, when you first gave us the money. Matt was so touched that you'd do this for us. I can't even begin to tell you what a difference it made to be able to keep the house. We—we've never gotten this far behind, and it was a blow to both of us. We're terribly grateful for what you did, but we always felt the money had to be a loan."

"But..." I couldn't seem to get out more than one word at a time—and it takes a lot to leave me speechless.

"The truly astounding part is that Matt hadn't even applied with this particular engineering firm. Their Human Resources department contacted him on Thursday and asked him to submit an application immediately, which he did. They didn't have it longer than a day before he heard back and the negotiations began."

"That's marvelous!"

"It is—more than you know. I've hardly ever seen Matt so excited. He was like a little kid when he got the news. He started work yesterday. I wanted to say something on Friday, but we decided to wait until everything was in place—and we could give you this." She pointed to the check.

"Margaret," I said, hugging my sister. "Are you sure? I mean, there must be a hundred things you need. Keep the money, repay me when you can."

"No," she returned sternly. "This is yours, and neither Matt nor I will hear of anything else."

"Wow," I whispered, "the fairy dust is flying all over the place." I don't think my sister realized what a turning point that loan was for me, in more ways than one. Perhaps for the first time since I became an adult, I'd truly stepped outside myself. I know that sounds odd, but it has to do with the rather insular life I'd lived for so many years. What I mean is, when I was a teenager and in my twenties, my whole life revolved around my sickness and consequently around me. Not until I opened the shop on Blossom Street did I begin to understand how self-absorbed I'd become.

This had been an especially difficult summer for me as I learned to consider needs and concerns other than my own. It was a financial stretch to help Margaret and Matt, but I badly wanted to give back to my sister and her family for all the sacrifices they'd made on my behalf.

Later, with Mom, I came to understand that our roles were now reversed. It was time for me to take care of her. The paperwork, finances and everything else involved in getting Mom settled in assisted living had been time-consuming and often frustrating. But my parents had always handled those details for me, during my bouts of cancer. I received the very best treatment available because my parents fought for me. Now it was my turn.

My third emotional lesson was perhaps the most painful. It came when Brad told me about Janice. I'd just about dissolved into a puddle of self-pity because the man I loved had broken off our relationship. Only later, when I looked past the pain I was suffering, did I understand that Brad had done this out of love for his son. Reconciling with Janice wasn't what he wanted, but he loved Cody enough to put aside his own wants in an effort to give him the family he needed. I failed to be as noble. Granted, once I recognized his motives, I felt less hurt, but I wasn't nearly as gracious or understanding as I could have been.

The bell above the door jangled and I had my first customer of the day. I half expected Margaret to rush out. She seemed occupied with order forms, so I placed the check on my desk and hurried into the shop.

Brad stood just inside and my heart seized at the sight of him. Margaret's smile had nothing on mine. "Hello, handsome," I said.

"Hello, beautiful."

We stood there smiling at each other for the longest moment, until he held his arms out to me. I didn't need a second invitation. My feet barely touched the ground as I ran into his embrace. Anyone who happened to be strolling past my shop window would've seen two people in love. Brad and I were entwined, arms around each other, kissing, kissing, kissing.

When we finally managed to break apart, it was with reluctance. "You're so right," I cried, running my hands over his face, needing to touch him. "I behaved like a jealous fool, and I lied, I *lied*. There's no one else. Brad, forgive me. I'm sorry."

"I am, too—for what I said last week. I could no more walk away from you than I could one of Alix's chocolate éclairs."

I laughed and poked my finger into his ribs. Then because it felt so *good* to be with him again, I wrapped my arms around him and held on tight.

"So there isn't another guy?" he murmured. "There never was?"

"No one. You're the one and only love of my life."

"Forever?" he asked.

I looked into his eyes and whispered, "That could be arranged."

His shoulders relaxed. "I was hoping you'd say that. It's time, Lydia. Time for you and me. I came too close to losing you. I love you, Lydia. I've never stopped. Cody loves you. Chase loves you, I—"

I brought my lips to his, interrupting him. He didn't need to say another word.

His hold around my waist tightened as he lifted me from the floor. "Does this mean you'll marry me, Lydia Hoffman?"

"It does." I wanted to qualify my response with a warning or two. The cancer could return. I wasn't sure I could have children or that it was advisable. But I said none of this. Our marriage wasn't about me—it was about Brad, Cody *and* me. Chase, too, for that matter. We were going to be a family.

"Lydia?" Margaret said, stepping out of the office, her voice tentative.

I smiled over at my sister. "How would you feel about being my maid of honor?" I asked her.

She turned to Brad, then to me. "You're getting married?"

I nodded. "Are you up for a wedding?"

"You bet I am!" she cried.

I draped my arms around Brad and pressed my head to his shoulder.

I swear there was fairy dust floating all over that room.

45
CHAPTER

ELISE BEAUMONT

Maverick had, according to Aurora, returned from the poker tournament in the Caribbean, but he'd made no effort to contact Elise. She didn't ask, but she thought Aurora had told her father that Elise knew about his cancer. Countless times in the few weeks before their last encounter, Maverick had invited her to come to his apartment, but she'd repeatedly refused.

In light of that conversation, he didn't invite her again, and she didn't blame him. She regretted that outburst now. When she could stand the silence no longer, Elise decided to go and see him.

The building was a new one, in a lovely area close to Aurora's, as well as Seattle's downtown area. She noticed that it was also close to a number of medical facilities.

The heaviness that had settled over her once she'd learned of Maverick's leukemia grew more burdensome each day. She felt hurt that Maverick had kept this information from her and yet she understood why he'd been so reticent. Late at night, as they'd cuddled up together in her single bed, Elise had often sensed that he wanted to tell her something. A dozen times she'd felt it, but she'd suspected that he wanted to confess he'd been gambling again. She hadn't been willing to hear that, so she'd pretended to be asleep. Their private nighttime moments were too precious to ruin.

The doorman was kind enough to show her where to press the button connected with her ex-husband's telephone. Maverick answered on the second ring, sounding tired.

"It's me. Can I come up?" Elise asked in a subdued voice.

"Of course." A buzzer rang and the lobby door opened. Maverick's condo was on the fifteenth floor. When she stepped out of the elevator, he stood in his doorway, waiting for her.

She nearly faltered when she saw his welcoming smile. All she'd done for weeks was harangue him with her bitterness. She felt such guilt, such an awareness of opportunities missed. Seeing him now, knowing he was dying, she burst into uncharacteristic tears. She couldn't help it. Her shoulders quaked and she covered her mouth with both hands.

Her emotion had an immediate effect on him. Maverick wrapped his arms around her and brought her into the apartment. He closed the door with one foot, still hugging her.

"Elise, Elise," he whispered, cradling her face between his large hands. "What's wrong with you? My gutsy girl doesn't weep."

"I…feel…so…bad." His sympathy, his soft crooning, only made her feel worse.

"About what?" His gaze searched hers.

"Everything—oh, Maverick, I've been so bitter and so spiteful toward you."

"I gave you plenty of reasons."

"I was never the right wife for you and—"

"Nor was I the right husband for you."

"I love you," she sobbed. At one time she'd tried to deny

it, but she loved Maverick, heart and soul. When she'd learned about his visit, she hadn't wanted to see him because she'd recognized the truth—and it had terrified her.

Gathering her close, Maverick kissed the top of her head. "I've always loved you. Always."

She looked up at him through tear-filled eyes. "I know, but—"

"Why do you think I never remarried?"

She'd wondered and had never wanted to ask. His question implied that he'd had opportunities, and maybe other romances; she had no difficulty believing it. But none of that mattered. Not even the gambling mattered anymore.

"All those wasted years…all those empty, empty years," she said brokenly. "Now…now it's too late…. Aurora told me—she told me you're…dying." It was difficult to say the word.

A deep sigh expanded his chest. "I was afraid she would."

"No, no, I needed to know." But she'd made it impossible for Maverick to tell her himself.

"I'm so sorry." Her sobbing increased. She couldn't tolerate the fact that she was about to lose Maverick so soon after finding him again.

His hold on her tightened. "I'm not dead yet."

If she hadn't been immersed in grief she might have smiled at his wry tone.

She took a long, shuddering breath. "I know…but I regret so much. I'm not sure where to start."

"We both have regrets, my darling."

Elise clung to him. That he could refer to her as his "darling" after the way she'd treated him said a great deal about this man she loved. This forgiving, passionate and often reckless man. A man who saw the best in others, who laughed at himself—a man who loved *her*.

"I…do want to move in with you," Elise announced. "If you'll have me."

She felt his smile before she saw it. "I'd rather you married me again," he said.

"Yes," she whispered. "Yes."

He tilted her chin and gazed deeply into her eyes. "I'll probably keep gambling as long as I'm able to."

She agreed with a half nod. Gambling was an important part of his life. She loved Maverick; loving him meant accepting him for the man he was.

"I'm sorry you lost the poker tournament," she whispered. "For your sake."

"You saw me on television?"

She shook her head. "Aurora and the boys told me."

"Second place wasn't so bad."

His spirits were unusually high. "You have a good attitude about it," she murmured. But then, he'd always been an optimist.

"Let's get married as soon as we can," he said. "Next month? Maybe over Thanksgiving?"

When she nodded, he said, "We have a lot to do to get ready for the wedding. I want to buy you a diamond ring."

"Maverick, no! "

He frowned. "Are we going to start our marriage with an argument?"

"No, but a plain gold band will do nicely."

He shook his head. "Let me take care of that. I also want to hire Bethanne to arrange everything for us."

"I don't know if she's equipped to manage that yet," Elise said, although she was grateful he'd thought of her friend.

Elise offered no resistance when Maverick silenced her with a kiss. In his arms, she had no doubts or questions. If he wanted to hire Bethanne, then that was what they'd do. After all, their wedding was really just a party—wasn't that what Bethanne had said about weddings? A celebration. She smiled at the image of a dinosaur-shaped wedding cake or Alice in Wonderland decorations.

"Yes, let's ask Bethanne," she agreed. "And I'll have Aurora be my maid of honor," Elise said, arms around his middle and smiling up at him.

"I want you to invite your knitting group."

"What about my reading club?" she asked.

"As many of your friends as you desire."

She frowned. All this expense was an extravagance. "It isn't necessary," she insisted one last time. "I'd be happy just to—"

"It is for me," Maverick said.

With that she acquiesced. However, she did feel it was only fair to remind him that she came with encumbrances. "Maverick," she began, "don't forget I'm in the middle of that lawsuit and—"

"What's that got to do with anything?"

"It's a legal and financial mess."

"It'll work itself out. Just promise me you won't worry about it." He studied her intently.

Elise walked farther into the apartment and collapsed onto the edge of a brown leather sofa. "How can I not worry? You have no idea how much money I've lost. I can't just forget about it."

"No, but you can't worry yourself sick over it, either. What will be will be. Nothing you do now is going to change anything. It's in the hands of the courts—isn't that what you told me?"

She nodded.

"From now on, I'll take care of your financial concerns."

At her automatic protest, he said, "Elise, I *want* to help you. I'm a rich man."

She blinked twice. Rich? Maverick?

"Don't look so shocked."

"You're a gambler, Maverick. No one makes money gambling."

He sighed deeply. "I wasted too much of my life seeking that pot of gold, I'll admit that now. There were plenty of other occupations I could've been successful at—but nothing interested me in the same way." He gave an amused little shrug. "I was born with card sense."

Elise remembered that he'd made every single child-support payment on time. She'd often wondered how he'd been able to manage it. She'd been willing to acknowledge that he must've had moderate success—but rich?

"You lost that poker tournament in the Caribbean," she murmured.

"True. But the money for the second-place prize was eight hundred thousand dollars."

Elise gasped.

"No matter what you say, those socks you knit brought me luck."

If she hadn't already been sitting, Elise's knees would've gone out from under her. "Eight hundred thousand dollars?" she repeated in a voice that resembled a squeak. "You've *got* to be kidding." She had no idea there was that kind of money in gambling.

"Apparently you aren't aware of the recent popularity of poker."

Dumbfounded, she shook her head.

"I've placed the majority in a trust fund for Aurora, David and the boys. Plus, I did a bit of what my mother called planting seeds of faith."

Her head snapped up and she looked at him with wide eyes. "It was you," she whispered. "You're the one who gave Bethanne the money she needed."

"If you say so." His voice was nonchalant but his lips were curved in the slightest of smiles.

"I do. It had to be you." Everything fell into place. Maverick had waited for her during each knitting class and on the way home she'd given him an update on each of her friends.

"You flew Courtney's sister out here for the Homecoming dance. How did you ever find her?"

A twinkle flashed in his eyes. "Pulanski isn't a name you hear every day, now, is it?"

"And Margaret's husband?"

"He got that job on his own merits," Maverick insisted, but the smile was growing as he continued. "Taking advantage of an old connection. A word dropped in the right ear. Although the signing bonus is another story."

Elise knew nothing about any of that. "You do this sort of thing often?"

"On occasion. I like to practice what people refer to as random acts of kindness."

"Only these weren't so random, were they?"

"Perhaps not, but I figure whatever I give to others comes back tenfold. Not necessarily to me but to people who need it. People Bethanne or Matt or Courtney meet, maybe tomorrow, maybe ten years from now. Kindness is something that should always be passed on."

Elise regarded him with open admiration. "Have you always been this wonderful and I just never noticed? Or is it a new development?"

He chuckled. "You don't expect me to answer that honestly, do you?"

She brought her palm to his face and let her love shine through her eyes. "Oh, Maverick, I love you. Rich or poor, I love you. We're going to have a very good life together—for however long God gives us."

"The way I feel right now," he whispered, "that'll be a very long time."

Elise hoped he was right.

46

CHAPTER

COURTNEY PULANSKI

The Next Year

Courtney hurried from her last class to her dorm room, hoping there was a card in the mail from Andrew. They e-mailed at least once a day and sometimes more. In their last communication, he'd suggested she check her mailbox in the near future. That was a sure sign he'd dropped something off for her at the post office. He was attending Washington State University on a football scholarship and Courtney was a freshman at the University of Illinois at Chicago.

To Courtney's amazement, her senior year had proved to be the best part of her high-school experience. She'd arrived in Seattle overweight, lonely and miserable, certain she was destined to have a wretched year.

Over the next thirteen months, Courtney had developed a close relationship with her grandmother. She'd learned a lot during the time her father had spent in South America. Grams had shared bits and pieces of family history that no one else knew. At first Courtney had thought Grams's house was full of old things, and it was, but some of those things were family treasures. They weren't antiques that would sell for big cash on eBay or interest the appraisers on *The Antiques Road Show*. But each object had the power of family history behind it. Every now and then, Grams would dig out something to show her, like the cute outfit she'd knit for her father as a baby or his high-school graduation announcement.

Grams had introduced Courtney to her friends, and it was like having ten grandmothers. To this day, whenever she was in a women's change room, she never took the middle shower, in honor of Leta. She still swam two days a week.

Perhaps the most significant change her grandmother had brought to Courtney's life was signing her up for that knitting class. Courtney had been feeling abandoned and alone, and within weeks, she'd made three friends. Three *good* friends. The other members of the class were older, but the bonds they'd built were strong even now, more than a year later. She had an extended family of knitting friends, too, with Jacqueline, Carol and Alix, as well as Margaret. They'd all been supportive and encouraging at the time she'd needed it most.

Courtney walked across the lawn and hurried up the steps to the dorm. She stopped long enough to collect her mail and quickly sorted through the envelopes. Sure enough, there was a card with Andrew's distinctive handwriting and the WSU return address. She was proud of him, proud he'd been awarded a major scholarship. She didn't really expect their long-distance romance to last. They were both young, as her grandmother often reminded her—too young to be serious. Grams was right about that. Andrew, however, was her connection to that wonderful year. First and foremost, they were friends, and she wanted to maintain that closeness. Forever, she hoped, even if their romantic interest waned. Andrew said he felt the same way.

Inside her room, Courtney tore open the envelope and discovered a humorous card with a cat sleeping in the sun on a bed of roses. The cat resembled Lydia's Whiskers, who often slept in the shop window. Opening it, she read: *Wake up and smell the roses.* Below that, he'd scribbled a few lines of encouragement about an upcoming test.

This was one of the reasons she liked Andrew so much. He was so thoughtful, and unlike other star athletes she knew, he wasn't stuck on himself. He regularly did little things to let her know he was thinking of her.

Courtney stayed in touch with Annie, too. It was just Annie and her mom at home this year, and the changes in the family dynamic had required an adjustment, according to Annie. Courtney missed her a lot. When they'd first met, Annie had been angry and bitter. The brunt of that anger was directed toward the woman whose name Annie refused to mention—her father's second wife. Annie had blamed this woman for everything. Oh, she'd been plenty pissed at her dad, too, but they seemed to be working that out. At least she saw him every week for lunch or dinner, which Courtney was glad to hear. Annie's father had made a big mistake, as far as Annie was concerned, and now he had to live with it. Annie claimed he and "that woman" deserved each other— but she still loved her dad.

Sitting on her bed, Courtney read Andrew's note a second time, then logged on to her computer to leave him a message. She discovered an e-mail from her father waiting for her. He'd rented out the house in Chicago for a second year, and Courtney felt fine about that. She'd kept some things of her mother's but she no longer thought of the place as *home*. He was still in Brazil, working on another bridge project, and seemed to be enjoying the adventure. The money didn't hurt either. She answered him, and then e-mailed Lydia about the progress her friends had made knitting.

Once the girls on her floor discovered that Courtney could knit, they'd wanted her to teach them. Soon every girl in the dorm had a pair of knitting needles in her hands. Actually, two circular needles, since the most popular pattern so far had been socks. Courtney had knit a dozen pairs in the last year. Her father loved his and wore them constantly. Even her older brother bragged about his socks, and Andrew had three or four pairs now. Annie was knitting, too; Bethanne had taught her.

A knock sounded at her door. "Court, do you have a minute?" Heather, one of the other girls on her floor, peeked inside.

"Sure," she said and stood up from her computer, leaving the e-mail to Lydia unfinished.

Heather stepped into the room with a ball of fingering weight yarn tucked under her arm and her knitting in her hands. "I hate to bother you," she said guiltily.

"It's no bother." They sat on the edge of the bed while Courtney examined the other girl's project.

"I think I dropped a stitch," Heather murmured.

Courtney could see that she had. "Don't worry. I've got a crochet hook in my desk. They work wonders." After retrieving the hook, she sat down with the half-completed sock.

"I can't look," Heather said, turning her head to stare in the opposite direction.

Courtney smiled. "I did the same thing to Lydia the first time I dropped a stitch. She told me we all lose a stitch now and then. Just like life, don't you think?"

"It is," Heather agreed. "We get so busy that it's easy to let some things slide. We can either pick them up again, or let them stay lost…. I never thought about knitting like that, though."

"I didn't either," Courtney confessed, "until I took Lydia's knitting class."

"You're right."

Courtney caught the loose stitch and carefully brought

up through the rows until she could slip it back on the thin needle. When she'd finished, she returned the sock to Heather.

"You learned a lot from those other knitters in Seattle, didn't you?"

"I did," Courtney said. More than she could possibly explain to anyone who hadn't taken part in those weekly sessions.

Elise was close in age to her grandmother—certainly older than anyone else she called a friend—yet that was how Courtney viewed her. They all kept in touch, and Elise phoned her every few weeks. Bethanne did, too. Courtney almost wished her father had stayed in Seattle longer so she could've introduced the two of them. She knew, from Lydia and Elise, that Bethanne was seeing men from time to time; it wasn't something Annie talked about. Bethanne's booming party business kept her busy these days, which Annie *did* like to mention.

All her Blossom Street friends—Bethanne, Lydia, Elise and the others—had helped Courtney deal with the grief of losing her mother. Five years had now passed since her mother's death, and while the pain wasn't as raw as it had once been, Courtney had never completely filled the emptiness in her life. But she'd seen how Bethanne's love for Andrew and Annie had carried her through the divorce. Maybe, years from now, when she had children of her own, she'd find that same kind of strength and completeness. Bethanne's love for her kids, Elise's for Aurora, Lydia's for Cody—these mother-child bonds reminded her of what she, too, had once had. That feeling was one of gratitude as well as sadness. Courtney recognized anew how deep her mother's love had been.

Lydia and Margaret reminded Courtney of her relationship with her own sister. She was close to Julianna in much the same way Lydia and Margaret were close. They supported each other and they bickered. Courtney found it entirely natural. She'd once heard Lydia explain that it hadn't always been like that, but seeing how well they worked together now, this was difficult for Courtney to believe.

After a couple of months, when they'd all considered each other friends, Lydia had talked about her experience with cancer. Courtney would never have guessed that Lydia had gone through chemotherapy and radiation. When she'd said this, Lydia had been absolutely thrilled and claimed it was proof she had "stepped outside herself." Courtney wasn't sure what that meant but was happy about Lydia's reaction.

"Thanks, Court," Heather said, collecting her knitting and leaving the dorm room.

"Glad to help," she said and sat back down at her computer.

She read over her e-mail to Lydia. "I realized again that living in Seattle was a blessing in more ways than I could count. A Good Yarn—" That was where she'd stopped when Heather came in. But she knew exactly what to say next.

47

CHAPTER

BETHANNE HAMLIN

"Mom, phone!" Annie shouted from the top of the stairs.

"Which line?" Bethanne called from the kitchen, her hands buried in hamburger.

"Business line. Do you want me to take it?"

"I'll get it." Bethanne nearly groaned. The party business was doing so well that she was booked months in advance. She washed her hands, then walked into the room that had once been Grant's office—her office now—where she kept the schedule for the upcoming parties.

She answered the call, scheduled an appointment for a consultation and went back to the kitchen, where she was shaping small meatballs around green olives for a six-year-old's Halloween birthday bash. Not long afterward, Annie drifted downstairs.

"You need any help with those?" she asked.

"Not now, but I will later." Annie had been a valuable asset the previous summer and still was, even in her senior year of high school. Bethanne had hired her on a part-time, as-needed basis, which was good for both of them. She had several other assistants, but working with Annie kept them close and connected. "That's why I pay you the big bucks, you know."

"Very funny, Mom."

The phone rang again and Bethanne looked from her hands to her daughter. "Do you want to get that for me?"

"Hey, I have to earn those high wages you're supposedly paying me, don't I?" Annie joked. She reached for the receiver and answered "Parties by Bethanne" in a professional tone.

Her daughter was almost an adult; every once in a while Bethanne realized that with a jolt of recognition—and pride. A year from now she'd be alone, with both her children in college. The thought no longer terrified her. When the time came she'd be able to afford it, which thrilled her. And she certainly wouldn't be lonely or at loose ends.... In fact, she'd been giving some thought to expanding her business in untraditional ways. One plan involved Lydia—a knitting party, in which Bethanne would serve food and drinks, and Lydia would teach everyone how to knit. The idea was still in its infancy, as was another idea for a children's storytelling party that Elise would help her with.

"It's Paul," Annie told her. "Do you want to phone him back later?"

Bethanne still saw Paul on occasion, but it had been a couple of months since they'd talked. "Tell him I'll call him back. I've got an errand to run and I'll be home after six."

"Where are you going?"

"Lydia's," she answered, finishing up the meatballs and arranging them on a baking tray.

"Here." Annie held the phone against Bethanne's ear. "*You* tell him all that."

Bethanne quickly agreed to meet Paul for coffee at the French Café across from A Good Yarn. "See you at six," she said.

"What was that about?" Annie asked.

"I think Paul's going to tell me it's serious with Angela," she said, and the news cheered her. His relationship with this new woman in his life sounded promising.

"How come you're going to Lydia's?" Annie asked next, eyeing Bethanne suspiciously.

"You're certainly nosy," she teased.

"Inquiring minds want to know."

Bethanne laughed and shook her head. She should've realized that keeping anything from Annie was an exercise in futility. "If you must know, I need another ball of yarn for my current project."

"And your current project is?"

Bethanne heaved a sigh of resignation. "A sweater for my daughter."

"That pink cashmere sweater is for *me?*" Annie cried, absolutely delighted if the smile on her face was any indication.

"Yes, for you, but no longer a surprise."

"Mom, I *love* that sweater and I'm so excited you're knitting it for me."

Bethanne knit almost every night; it was her one true relaxation. At the same time, she was practical enough to like the fact that she could produce something both useful and beautiful. It seemed like a hundred years ago that her teenage daughter had taken the initiative and signed Bethanne up for the knitting class. She'd graduated from socks to sweaters and was planning to knit an afghan to give Andrew for Christmas.

Bethanne left the meatballs baking in the oven, instructing Annie to take them out in half an hour. As she drove to the yarn store, she found herself thinking about the day Grant had walked out. That had been the worst moment of her life, but every day since had been better than the one before. She was independent and happy; her children were doing well.

Both Andrew and Annie had worked on improving their relationships with their father, and they were at peace. She knew

Grant wasn't happy, and in many ways she felt sorry for him. However, he'd made his choices, and she couldn't and didn't concern herself with him anymore. She had her own life to live.

Luckily there was a space directly in front of A Good Yarn and Bethanne took it, hopped out of her car and placed the appropriate coins in the parking meter. She only had a few minutes before Lydia closed the store.

"I was afraid I wouldn't make it in time," she said, walking through the door.

"Bethanne!" Lydia sounded delighted to see her. Coming around the counter, Lydia hugged her, then brought out the skein of pink cashmere she'd put aside. "It's the same dye lot as the original," Lydia assured her. She stepped back to the cash register. "It's so wonderful to see you."

"I feel the same way," Bethanne said. "I've got a free Friday afternoon next week, so I'll drop in for the charity knitting session. How's everyone?" She hadn't been in two weeks and missed seeing the women who'd become so special to her.

"Everyone's great," Lydia told her. "Jacqueline is still in seventh heaven over her new granddaughter. She brought pictures."

"*More* pictures?" Bethanne said with a laugh. She paid for her wool, glancing around the store. It was easy to see that the little shop on Blossom Street continued to thrive. She loved the new designer yarns and the increased inventory. Lydia had scored a success, and Bethanne hoped her own fledgling business would emulate it.

"Can I tell everyone you'll be by next week?" Lydia asked, handing Bethanne her purchase.

"With bells on," she promised and tucked the skein in its A Good Yarn bag inside her large purse.

Lydia smiled. "You look really good."

"Thanks," Bethanne said, and blushed a bit at the attention. She'd gotten plenty of that lately and wasn't quite sure why. She felt good and suspected it showed. *Life* felt good. He world had been thrown into upheaval, and had taken a long time to right itself.

When she left the yarn store, she saw that Paul had arrived at the café and had a table. He stood when she entered, waving. She waved back, saw Alix at the counter and sent her friend a smile before joining Paul.

"Angela will be here in a few minutes," he explained, indicating the third mug on the table.

"How is she?" Bethanne asked, pulling out her chair and sitting down.

"She's engaged."

"Angela's engaged," Bethanne repeated in shock—before she comprehended his meaning. "To you!"

"I should hope so," Paul said with a laugh.

"Congratulations." Bethanne half stood to hug him. "That's just fabulous!" Her instincts had been right, and this news was all the validation she needed. Falling in love with each other would have been easy, but it would've been like taking refuge in a safe harbor rather than venturing out into riskier seas. She'd needed courage to take the stand she did. Paul hadn't wanted to get involved with anyone else, and in the beginning he'd found the transition from potential lover to friend difficult. Time and distance had helped.

"I didn't think I'd ever fall this deeply in love again," he confessed. "In fact, it's better the second time around."

"Oh, Paul…"

"It's your turn," he said.

"Perhaps, but I'm in no hurry." And she wasn't.

The door opened and a tall, lovely brunette walked into the café. Her eyes scanned the room; when she saw Paul, her face relaxed into a smile.

Paul stood and held out his hands to her, and Bethanne watched as Angela approached him. Paul kissed her on the cheek and she sat down next to Bethanne. She'd met Angela briefly a couple of months back and it had become obvious to her then that this woman was special to Paul.

"I understand congratulations are in order."

Angela nodded. "We've decided on a winter date, and it would mean the world to both of us if you'd plan our wedding."

Bethanne smiled. She'd only arranged one other wedding—Elise and Maverick's—and if this one went half as well… Nothing would give her greater joy than to be involved in the wedding of her dear friend.

"I'd be delighted," she told them both.

"And like I said," Paul insisted with his arm around Angela's shoulders, "you're next."

Still smiling, Bethanne shrugged off his words. The divorce hadn't disillusioned her about love and marriage. If anything, it'd confirmed the importance of family and commitment. Remarrying wasn't a priority, but an option—something that might well be part of her future.

In the meantime, she had her children, her friends, her work. She'd rediscovered herself, become the woman she wanted to be, and found new pleasure in the things she loved to do—like gardening and reading and above all, knitting.

It was enough.

48
CHAPTER

ELISE BEAUMONT

Elise glanced at the recipe again, adding flaxseed and blueberries to the mix. She'd taken it upon herself to see to it that Maverick ate healthy, nutritious meals. She believed this would help in his fight against leukemia.

So far, his progress had been encouraging. Maverick was quick to credit her and the meals she so carefully planned. Elise, however, demurred at his praise; yes, a proper diet played its part, but it was love that had kept Maverick alive this long.

"What are you baking now?" Maverick asked from where he sat in the condo living room, the newspaper on his lap. The view of Seattle was spread out before them.

"Goodies."

"The boys love your goodies, you know."

Elise grinned. He wasn't referring to their grandsons, although Luke and John were quite impressed with her baking skills. The minute they walked into the condo they went directly to the cookie jar, anticipating a treat.

"What time will the boys get here?" she asked, and slid the

muffin tin into the preheated oven. These "boys" were Maverick's cronies, who stopped by two and sometimes three times a week for a friendly game of poker. He'd met them at the local poker parlor where he'd first played in order to win a slot in the tournament.

"They'll be here at three," he said. He was apparently well-known in the gambling world. His initial failures, during their marriage, had made her angry and fearful. In her fear—and self-righteousness—Elise had preferred to think of him as living from hand to mouth. In reality, he'd become a success. But he didn't encourage anyone else to choose the life he'd lived, and in fact, dissuaded others from becoming professional gamblers. In retrospect he wished he'd made a different choice.

Elise joined her husband in the living room and sat on the arm of his chair. He held her around the waist and sighed, his eyes closing. He was tired, she knew. A session of tests at the doctor's office that day had drained him, but the most recent news had bolstered both their spirits. The progression of the leukemia had slowed considerably. They'd gotten a reprieve. Elise didn't know how long this would continue, but she figured every single day with him was a blessing she hadn't anticipated.

"Why don't you take a nap before the game?" she suggested.

"I think I will."

She slipped off the chair and sat across from him as Maverick lay back in the recliner. Reaching for her white wicker basket, Elise unfolded her pattern. She was knitting Maverick a lap robe for times like this. The needles made small clicking sounds. Comforting sounds.

They'd been together a year now, and not once had she regretted remarrying Maverick. Every day since then had been a honeymoon. She loved the way he loved their daughter and their grandchildren. He'd seen to Aurora's future and David's and to those of Luke and John with trust funds.

The matter of Elise's lawsuit had been resolved. A portion of her down payment had been refunded; it was more than she'd expected and less than she would've liked. The money she'd received was currently invested. That chapter of Elise's life was closed, and she was grateful to have survived it financially.

She'd never told her knitting friends that Maverick was the one responsible for their good fortune. It'd been tempting, but she'd kept quiet. As Courtney described her beautiful dress and shared the details of the Homecoming dance and the visit with her sister—thanks to the generosity of her fairy godfather—Elise had listened and silently cheered. Tears had gathered in her eyes as she tried to remember each and every word so she could repeat it to Maverick.

The difference his gift had made to Bethanne was even more striking. She'd told Elise privately about the stranger who'd given her a head start on her business, and how much those few thousand dollars had meant to her. That money had changed everything and had come to her when she most needed it.

Bethanne had an impressive business vision. Elise wouldn't be surprised by anything she undertook. A few years from now, Bethanne's party business could well become a franchise. Her ideas were original, fresh, inventive. Maverick's generosity had contributed to Bethanne's success, and someday her friend would give a similar gift of money and encouragement to another struggling entrepreneur. Elise found pleasure and pride in knowing that.

Not once in all the weeks afterward had Bethanne breathed a word about the money to the women in the knitting group. That was just as well. If Bethanne had said something in addition to what Courtney had already mentioned, their friends might have figured it out. Maverick didn't want any thanks or displays of appreciation; he preferred to remain anonymous, unacknowledged.

Elise smiled to herself as she continued knitting. She suspected Lydia knew. She'd never come right out and asked Elise, but she'd casually said one day that there seemed to be a fairy godfather at work in their group. Elise had tried to suggest it must've been Courtney's dad, but Lydia just shook her head. Thankfully, she didn't bring it up again. Elise didn't want to mislead a woman she considered one of her best friends.

She heard the timer on the stove and set aside her knitting to check the cupcakes. Turning off the oven, she took out the muffin tin and placed it on a cooling rack. The scent of warm blueberries filled the kitchen. She intended to slather the cupcakes with a cream cheese frosting and serve them to Maverick and his friends. Little did the "boys" realize how healthy these desserts were.

A half hour later, Maverick woke, looking noticeably rested. He glanced at his watch; the game would start in less than twenty minutes.

Predictably enough, the phone started to ring at three o'clock and Bart, the first of the boys, arrived. He was quickly followed by Al and Fred.

"Smells mighty good in here," Bart said, sniffing the air. He winked at Elise. "No one bakes better'n you, no sir. I'll bet those taste as good as they smell, too."

Elise smiled at the blatant flattery. "I'll see what I can do to make sure you get one, Bart."

He grinned. "I do appreciate that, Mrs. Beaumont."

Al and Fred weren't far behind, staggering playfully toward the kitchen, led by their noses.

"You been baking again?" Al asked, hat in his hands, eyes comically wide.

Maverick shared a secret smile with her. "You're spoiling my friends," he murmured.

"Those for us poor old men?" Fred rubbed his hands together. "Us poor *hungry* old men..."

"Would you three stop it," Elise said, halfheartedly attempting to hold in a laugh. "You know darn well I always bake on Tuesdays."

Bart poked his elbow in Al's ribs. "That's the reason we're here, remember?"

"I thought you came for the poker," Maverick teased.

"That, too."

Chuckling, they gathered around the kitchen table. Maverick pulled out a deck of cards and shuffled. Each one bought in for twenty dollars; the winner of the "tournament" took home the pot.

Within minutes, they were involved in their game. Elise frosted the cupcakes, then went back to her knitting. When the men had finished, she served coffee and cupcakes to the accompaniment of much praise and fulsome thanks.

Maverick caught her eye and she smiled at the man she loved. Her husband smiled back. Being in love did something for a woman, she decided. There was no feeling, no experience, to equal it.

CHAPTER 49

"Sock knitting teaches us to take one step at a time—
cuff, heel, foot, toe—and not to be overwhelmed by the
big picture."

—Kathy Zimmerman, Kathy's Kreations,
Ligonier, PA. www.kathys-kreations.com

LYDIA HOFFMAN

There's a lull at the shop, and after a busy morning, I've decided to take a break in the office. Margaret will handle the customers while I put my feet up. It's been rush, rush, rush all
morning.

A Good Yarn is doing well—so well—and I'm grateful.
sometimes feel as if I'm living in a dream. I know I'm not
because the diamond on my finger sparkles and my heart i
full of love for Brad and Cody. I'm quite possibly the hap
piest woman in the world. I'm engaged to marry the hand-so
mest, most wonderful man alive. Within a couple of months
I'll be living with Brad and Cody and Chase. Whiskers, thank
fully, tolerates Cody's dog and will probably teach him som
discipline.

I don't think my life could get any better than it is right at this moment.

When I first opened the doors to A Good Yarn, it was my affirmation of life. Little did I realize, two years ago, what would happen and all the friends I would make. Jacqueline, Carol and Alix have become very dear to me. They were the three who gave me my start.

I've held several classes since the baby blanket class. All of them were good, but none of those relationships matched the closeness I felt with my first three students. Until recently, with the sock class. That was when Elise, Bethanne and Courtney entered the shop and my life. I didn't think it was possible to feel as close to another class as I did my original one, but again life has taught me a valuable lesson.

I recall how difficult Elise was that first day, fretting over her ex-husband's coming visit. And Bethanne, with her self-esteem shattered by her divorce, and Courtney, a lonely, overweight teenager struggling with a loss of her own. The four of us connected through knitting—who would've thought a pair of socks could change your life? I treasure each one of these women as a true friend, the same way I do Jacqueline, Carol and Alix.

Then there's my sister. I never thought the day would come when I'd claim my sister as my very best friend. Well, that day has arrived. We're closer now than at any other time in our lives. And that special understanding started when she first came to work at the shop.

My sister and I are sharing the responsibility of looking after Mom. Her health is declining rapidly and I suspect we won't have her with us much longer. That makes each day we have her all the more precious. She's still lonely without Dad, still a bit lost.

Both Margaret and I work hard at keeping her busy. We make sure she has lots of small things to look forward to each week—a visit, an outing, shopping, a new book. Anything that we know will bring her joy.

Mom is knitting more and Margaret's been picking her up on Friday afternoons so she can join the other women who do charity knitting. She enjoys these occasions and feels part of the knitting community. My mother is a fast knitter and she's contributed enough patches to make an entire blanket for Warm Up America, plus another for the Linus Project. I think Dad would be very pleased to see the three of us working together, knitting.

I've been so caught up in my thoughts that Margaret's standing directly in front of me before I notice her. "I'm leaving to pick up Mom," she announces.

"Great." I lower my feet. I'm generally not this tired on a Friday morning, but Brad, Cody and I were at a Mariners' playoff game last night and it went into extra innings. I didn't get to bed until after midnight and had to be up early to meet with a yarn sales rep. Brad and Cody, my two sweethearts, are real baseball fans and I've learned to love the game, so it wasn't any sacrifice to be out so late.

Soon after Margaret's departure, Elise comes into the shop, carrying her knitting. The changes in Elise since she remarried Maverick would make anyone a believer in marriage! She's so much more relaxed now and genuinely happy.

I've pretty much figured out that Maverick was our fairy godfather, although I've never asked her directly and she hasn't volunteered the information.

"Where's Maverick?" I ask. He almost always accompanies Elise on Fridays. I've purchased a special chair for him, so he can read while the rest of us knit and talk. Maverick's face might be hidden behind a book, but he's listening. He always was a good listener, or so Elise tells me. Each one of us has more or less adopted Maverick. I know his condition is stable, and although we're all pleased by that, we worry, too.

His immune system has been compromised by the treatments. But Elise is taking good care of him. Those two are so happy together, so accepting of each other. It almost seems that love is what they're living on now.

"He's parking the car," Elise says. "He'll be along shortly."

"How is he?" I ask.

"Doing really well." From the look in her eyes I know she's telling the truth, and I'm relieved. "Bethanne's here, too, and I saw Jacqueline and Carol over at the French Café, chatting with Alix. I imagine they won't be long."

"Great."

A small package had arrived from Courtney earlier in the week, with several patches for the Warm Up America blanket we're currently working on. She has a whole group of girls in her dorm knitting now. Inside was a long letter that I plan to read to the entire group.

According to Bethanne, Courtney keeps in touch with Annie and Andrew. It'll be interesting to see if Courtney and Andrew can maintain a long-distance relationship. I know Bethanne has encouraged both of them to date others and I believe they do. Above all, they're good friends; I hope they stay friends.

Speaking of Bethanne, I don't see her as often as I'd like. We're all so proud of her. And not just because of her success with the business, either. Let me add that she's planning Brad's and my wedding, and I wouldn't trust that to anyone else.

No, the real reason for my pride in her is the way she's virtually reinvented herself, the way she's found confidence, in herself and in others. As I remember it, she didn't even sign up for the class on her own. Her daughter made the phone call on her behalf.

And I feel that we in the class—but especially Elise—can take some of the credit for encouraging that transformation.

The bell rings above the door and Brad strolls into the

shop. We see each other nearly every day now that the date for the wedding's been set. Alix has volunteered to bake the cake and Jacqueline insists we have the reception at the country club, but Bethanne is the one organizing it all. Margaret has agreed to be my matron of honor, and I have six bridesmaids. Six! It wasn't hard to decide who I wanted to stand up with me—my dearest friends. My knitting friends.

"Hello, gorgeous," Brad greets me, wheeling his cart with an expert hand. "How are you this beautiful afternoon?"

I smile back. Fine, I tell him. Better than fine. Happy and very much in love with him and with life in the shop on Blossom Street.

* * * * *

Debbie Macomber's next MIRA hardcover novel,
Susannah's Garden, is a story that will have meaning
for all women, of all ages.
At fifty, Susannah Nelson is coping with teenage children
and an aging mother; she's feeling burned out as a teacher
and vaguely dissatisfied with her marriage and her life. Her
father's recent death brings back memories of the year she
turned eighteen, the year she lost her brother and the boy
she loved, the year that changed everything...
Turn the page to read an excerpt from this emotional—and
surprising—novel.
Susannah's Garden is available in May 2006.

CHAPTER

2

Susannah Nelson dumped the leftover broccoli salad into a plastic container and shoved it inside the refrigerator, closing the door with unnecessary force. Brian, her seventeen-year-old, had mysteriously disappeared after dinner, leaving her with the dishes. She shouldn't be surprised. He had a convenient excuse every night to get out of doing his assigned chores.

"Is something bothering you?" her husband asked from his perch in the family room. Joe lowered the newspaper and all Susannah could see were his dark brows and his eyes behind the steel-rimmed reading glasses.

She shrugged. "I don't suppose you've noticed, but this is the third night in a row that Brian hasn't done the dishes," she said, more sharply than she'd intended.

"I'll do them," he offered.

"You shouldn't have to do that," Susannah told him. "Nor should I."

Joe set the newspaper aside. "This isn't about Brian, is it? You're upset about something else."

"Well, I *am* annoyed about the way he's been skipping out on chores, but you're right, that isn't everything." What concerned her most was her inability to identify a specific reason. She'd been on edge for weeks, feeling vaguely dejected.

It didn't help that she'd dreamed of Jake again last night. Her high school boyfriend had been making nightly appearances, and that unsettled her as much as anything. Susannah was happily married and despite the abrupt ending to her teenage romance, there was no good reason for her to dwell on Jake. Her marriage had survived the crises that any successful marriage does. Her children were nearly grown; her daughter was in college, ready to start her own life. Brian had summer employment, working for a construction company, and would earn enough to pay his own car insurance. The school break would officially begin in a day's time, and she'd be free for nearly seven weeks. Why, after more than three decades, was she dreaming of Jake? It made no sense whatsoever. There he was, big as life, filling her head with memories of a long-lost love.

"School's almost out," Joe reminded her. "That should cheer you up."

He was right; it should. Today was the last day of classes and her fifth-grade students had been overjoyed at the prospect of summer vacation. Susannah was equally ready for a break. Maybe for more than a break—a change. What kind of change, she didn't know. She supposed she could think about it over the summer—after tomorrow, anyway, when she'd be finishing her paperwork.

"You've been restless since your father died," Joe commented in a mild voice. He glanced at her across the family room. "Maybe you should talk to someone."

"You're saying I should talk to a counselor?" She hated to think it had come to this. Yes, her father's death had been a shock, but at the time her grief had seemed...formal. Almost abstract. As though she'd mourned the *idea* of losing a father more than the man himself. She'd never gotten along with him. They'd tolerated each other, at best. As far as Susannah was concerned, her father was dictatorial, overbearing and arrogant. The moment she turned eighteen, she couldn't get away from him fast enough.

"He was your father, Susannah," Joe reminded her gently. "I know the two of you weren't close, but he was still your father." He removed his glasses. "In fact, maybe that's why you're feeling like this. Now that he's dead, there's no opportunity to settle your differences—to work things out."

Susannah shook her head, dismissing the suggestion. Her relationship with her father had been difficult. Complicated. But she'd accepted that reality years ago. "This has nothing to do with him."

Joe looked as if he wanted to argue, but she didn't let him. "Yes, his death was unexpected, but he *was* eighty-three and no one lives forever." The truth of the matter was that while they weren't completely estranged, they rarely spoke. That didn't seem to bother him any. Over the years, Susannah had made occasional efforts to bridge the gap between them, but her father seemed incapable of deepening their relationship.

Whenever she'd phoned or visited, Susannah talked to her mother. George Leary was a decent grandfather; she'd say that for him. Both Chrissie and Brian thought the world of her father. As for her—well, it was better to not think about the way he'd interfered with her life, especially during her teenage years. Yes, she was sorry he'd died, especially so suddenly, but she discounted the possibility that his death was the cause of this discontent she felt. If she was going to blame anyone, it would be Jake. But it wasn't as though she could mention this to Joe, her husband, her wonderful husband. *Hey, honey, I've been thinking about another man lately.* That wouldn't go over too well, no matter how understanding Joe was.

Her husband continued to study her. "Even though you don't agree," he said slowly, "I suspect your father's death had a strong impact on you. Don't you remember what it was like when my parents died?"

She did remember and was embarrassed to admit that she'd grieved for her father-in-law more than she had her own dad. When Joe's mother died ten months later, they'd both been devastated. It had been a rough time for them as a family. Susannah had envied Joe's close relationship with his parents when her own, particularly with her father, was so distant.

"Of course it was a shock to lose my dad," Susannah went on, "but I don't think this mood—"

"Depression," Joe inserted. "Low-grade, garden variety depression."

"I am not depressed." Even while she denied it, she knew Joe was right.

Her husband raised his eyebrows. "If you aren't depressed, then what is it?"

Joe was a solid, strong, self-assured man. Honorable. After twenty-four years together they'd grown accustomed to each other, so alike that they often ordered the same thing from a menu, read the same books, voted for the same candidates. She didn't understand how she could lie beside him in the same bed night after night and dream about another man. This wasn't like her. Not once in her entire marriage had she even *considered* looking at another man.

She'd be crazy to risk her marriage by searching for a high school fling. The episode with Jake was long over. She hadn't seen or talked to him since she was seventeen, and that was…oh, more than thirty-three years ago now.

Joe replaced his glasses after polishing the lenses on his shirt.

"You've had a lot going on in the last six months. Your father's death, your fiftieth birthday, a demanding year at work and everything else."

He wasn't telling Susannah anything she didn't know. Perhaps those *were* the reasons for this discontent, this need to find out about Jake, but she doubted it. Even gardening, her passion, didn't soothe her—or distract her. While she was quick to deny that anything was wrong, Susannah felt certain it all went back to her high school boyfriend and the way their relationship had ended. What she needed was *closure*—that irritating, overused word. And yet nothing else quite explained it. Jake was an unfinished part of her life, a thread left hanging, a path not taken.

In that sense, her father's death *had* triggered her unease, her recurring memories of Jake, since George was the one responsible for breaking them up. As always, he'd been so sure he knew best. The problem was that he sat on his high and mighty judgment seat in court during the day and didn't step down from it when he came home to his family at night.

Susannah refused to dwell on thoughts of her father, refused to let herself nurture these negative feelings toward him. But tonight, for reasons she didn't understand, her memories of Jake wouldn't leave her alone.

"It might be a good idea for you to spend a few weeks with your mother this summer. Perhaps then you'll find some resolution concerning your father."

"Maybe," Susannah agreed, although she didn't really believe it. They'd already decided she should visit Vivian once the summer holidays started, to check up on her and assess the situation.

The phone pealed in the distance, but neither Joe nor Susannah hurried to answer it. With a teenager in the house, there was no need.

Brian stuck his head out his bedroom door and shouted her name at an ear-splitting decibel. "Mom!"

Susannah wanted to ask him who it was, but he'd retreated into his bedroom so fast she didn't have a chance. Walking over to the kitchen phone, she lifted the receiver and waited for him to hang up.

"Hello."

"Susannah, is that you?"

The female voice was familiar, but she couldn't immediately place it.

"It's Martha West. I'm sorry to bother you."

"Oh, that's okay." Susannah tensed. Martha had been the family housekeeper for years. The only reason she'd be calling was to tell her something had happened to her mother. "Is everything all right with Mom?" The last time Martha phoned had been with the news that Susannah's father had dropped dead of a heart attack.

"She's just fine," Martha assured her. "I did want to talk to you, though, before you drove here. Vivian mentioned that you planned to visit soon and, well…" She hesitated. "There's no easy way to say this." Again she paused. "Susannah, your mother seems to think I'm…taking her things. I hope you know I'd never do anything like that. I swear I had nothing to do with those missing teaspoons."

"Teaspoons?"

"Your mother accused me of taking four of her matching teaspoons when I was there to clean this afternoon."

"Martha, I know you'd never do anything like that." The woman was completely trustworthy.

"I would hope not," she blurted. "And let me tell you that if I was going to steal, it wouldn't be teaspoons."

"Makes sense."

"Then she said I hid her purse. I searched for an hour and

found it tucked behind the sofa cushions. When I showed it to her, she said I was the one who'd put it there."

Susannah groaned. "Oh, Martha, I'm so sorry."

"I don't know what's wrong with her," the housekeeper said, sounding exasperated. "Nothing's been the same since your father died. One day she's her normal self and the next, well, I hardly know her anymore. She asked me why I'd take her things. I would never! You know that. Teaspoons? She believes I walked away with her teaspoons and God help me, even though I looked everywhere, I couldn't find them. But I didn't take them!"

"I'm sure you didn't. I'll talk to her," Susannah promised.

"So she hasn't said anything to you about me supposedly stealing her things?" Martha asked.

"No." This was a half truth. In their last conversation, her mother had said she wanted to have a talk about Martha once Susannah arrived. Susannah had assumed that the housekeeper was planning to retire. As it was, Martha cleaned the house only twice a week now. She was getting on in years, too.

"I'll talk to her," Susannah said a second time—although she had no idea what she'd say.

"Please do, and if you can't convince her that I'm an honest and loyal employee then…then maybe I should look for work elsewhere."

"Don't do that," Susannah pleaded. "Give me a chance to get to the bottom of this."

"Good." Martha seemed somewhat appeased.

"I'll be in touch when I get there," Susannah said.

After a few words of farewell, Martha ended the conversation and Susannah replaced the phone.

"What was that all about?" Joe asked as he refolded the evening paper.

Susannah sighed deeply and told him.

"You did say your mother seems awfully forgetful these days."

Susannah nodded. "I talk to her almost daily, but there's only so much information I can get over the phone." She sighed again. "Mom keeps telling me the same things over and over, but I thought that was simply old age. Maybe it's more than that." Many of her friends faced similar concerns with their aging parents.

"What about asking one of her friends?" Joe came into the kitchen and stood beside her. Gazing down at her, he clasped her shoulders, his eyes serious.

She looked up at him with a resigned smile. "I'll give Mrs. Henderson a call. She's been Mom's neighbor for years."

After finding the Hendersons' phone number, Susannah reached for the phone again. When the initial greetings were dispensed with, she was quick to get to the reason for her call. "I'm worried about my mother, Mrs. Henderson. Have you talked to her lately?"

"Oh, yes," Rachel Henderson told her, "she's often out puttering in her garden—not that she gets much done."

"How is she…mentally?" Susannah asked next.

"Well, to be honest, she just hasn't been herself since she lost George," the neighbor said thoughtfully. "I can't say exactly what's going on…but I'm afraid something isn't right with Vivian."

"How do you mean?" Susannah asked. Joe walked over to the coffeepot and poured himself a mug while watching her.

She knew. Deep down, Susannah had known for weeks that her mother was having problems. She'd sensed changes in Vivian even before her father's death.

"I realize you talk to your mother a lot and I don't mean to be putting my nose in where it doesn't belong. Al said I should mind my own business, but then this evening…"

"What happened this evening?" Susannah asked, suddenly nervous.

"I'm sure you're aware that Vivian hasn't adjusted well to losing your father."

"I know." Her mother was often weepy and sad, talking endlessly about George and how desperately she missed him. Susannah had driven across the mountains to visit over spring break but had only been able to stay four days. Vivian had clung to her, pleaded with her to remain in Colville longer, but Susannah couldn't. Driving there and back meant the better part of two days, and that left only one day to prepare for school.

Susannah had tried to talk her mother into moving to Seattle, but Vivian had stubbornly refused to consider it. She didn't want to leave Colville, where she'd been born and raised. Her surviving friends all lived in the small town sixty-three miles north of Spokane.

"Something happened this evening?" Susannah repeated, wanting Rachel to get to the point.

"I know this may shock you, but your mother asked me to help her find George."

"What?" Susannah's eyes shot to Joe. "She thinks my dad's alive?"

"She claims she saw him."

"Oh, no," Susannah muttered.

"She was wandering down the street, looking confused. I got worried, so I went after her. Then she started talking all this nonsense about George—how he brought her home and then disappeared. When was the last time you saw her?"

"March." Susannah *knew* she needed to visit Colville more often, but she hadn't been able to make it during the last few months. Between Brian's sports, other commitments, including teaching workshop, and social engagements, there hadn't been a single free weekend. Guilt felt like a lead weight dragging her down. "I planned to drive over this weekend. School's out for the summer and I'm going to spend a couple of weeks with Mom."

"That's wise," Mrs. Henderson said. "She's lost weight, you know."

Her mother was barely a hundred and ten pounds when Susannah had seen her in March.

"I don't think she cooks anymore," her neighbor went on.

During her visit, Vivian had asked her to make dinner every night. Susannah hadn't minded and the shelves certainly seemed to be well stocked. Although Susannah had noticed a number of gourmet items her mother had never purchased before. Like fancy mustards. And sun-dried tomatoes in pesto which Susannah had used in a pasta sauce.

"You mean she isn't eating?" Susannah clarified.

"Not much, as far as I can tell. I keep inviting her over for dinner, but she refuses every time. I'm not the only one she refused, either. She seems to be holed up in the house and barely comes out, except to work in her garden."

"But…why?" Her mother had always been social, enjoying the company of others, hosting parties for George and their friends.

"You'll have to ask her that."

"But on the phone she talks as if she sees you quite a bit," Susannah said. It wasn't like her mother to lie.

"Oh, yes, we chat over the fence, but I swear…" Mrs. Henderson paused. "Sometimes I'm not sure your mother knows who I am."

"Oh, dear." This was what Susannah feared most. Her mother was losing her memory, and it seemed due to more than the erosion of old age.

"Another thing," Mrs. Henderson said, hesitating again.

"Go on," Susannah urged.

"The other day when I went to check on her, I found h

sitting in the dark. Turns out she forgot to pay the electric bill. She felt embarrassed about it, and I don't think she'd like me saying anything to you, but I felt you should know."

Susannah groaned inwardly. These were the very things she'd worried about. Bills unpaid, the stove left on, meals and appointments forgotten.

"Not to worry," Mrs. Henderson rushed to add. "I helped her get it straightened out and her lights are back on. Like I said, she told me you'd be visiting soon and I thought I'd talk to you then, but this business with her seeing George—now, that's got me worried."

It worried Susannah, too. She wished Mrs. Henderson had contacted her earlier. "I tried to talk to Mom about moving into assisted living when I was there in the spring."

"Yes, she told me. It upset her something fierce that you were going to kick her out of her own house."

"She said that?" Susannah's stomach tightened. She was hurt that her mother would even think such a thing, let alone voice it to a neighbor.

"Yes, but quite honestly, Susannah, I don't feel she should be on her own any longer."

Susannah should've insisted back in March, but she hadn't felt she could take her mother out of her home so soon after a major loss. She'd had enough upheaval in her life. Evidently it'd been a mistake not to act sooner.

Susannah ran one hand through the soft curls that had fallen onto her forehead.

"It might be best if you came right away," Mrs. Henderson suggested. "I would've phoned you myself, but Al said I should keep out of it. Seeing that you phoned me, well, I figured I'd better tell you what's going on with your mother. I hope that's okay?" she asked anxiously.

"I'm grateful you told me," Susannah said. "I'll drive over as soon as I can make arrangements."

After a brief farewell, Susannah replaced the receiver. Joe leaned against the counter, still watching her, coffee mug in hand.

"I'm afraid it's worse than I thought," she said, answering his unspoken question. "Apparently she's wandering around the neighborhood looking for my father."

Joe released a low whistle. "You're going over right away, then?" Originally Susannah had intended to wait for the weekend.

"I guess that would be for the best." Then, thinking out loud, she added, "I don't have any choice but to put her in an assisted-living facility."

"I agree."

Susannah pinched the bridge of her nose, dreading the approaching confrontation. Her mother would fight her on this. She didn't doubt that for a minute.

"Do you want me to go with you? Perhaps the two of us will be able to talk some sense into her."

Susannah shook her head.

"You're sure?" He frowned as though disappointed. "You were wonderful when my parents died, Suze. I want to be there for you."

For a moment Susannah was afraid she'd cry. "No... I need to do this on my own. I've decided," she said, the idea taking shape in her mind as she spoke, "that I'll stay in Colville for a while." Although it was crazy to even consider the idea, she might be able to find out where Jake was living. She had to talk to him, had to find out what had happened and why. Susannah knew her father had something to do with the breakup she just didn't know the details. Maybe, once she learned the truth, she could put an end to this fantasizing about Jake.

"Okay." Joe sighed heavily. "But after you convince her to move, you'll have to make a decision about the house."

Susannah hadn't even thought of that. All at once the task seemed overwhelming.

"How long do you think it'll take?" Joe asked.

She didn't meet his eyes while she contemplated spending time in Colville. "Three weeks should do it, I imagine. Possibly a month."

"That long?"

"It isn't going to be easy to talk my mother into leaving her home," she said. "And there's the matter of arranging assisted-living accommodation for her. And cleaning the house. Whether I decide to rent it or put it on the market, either way it'll need to be cleared out."

"I could help. Brian, too."

"No, I can manage." She appreciated the offer, but she wanted to spend time with her mother—just the two of them. Not only that, she had a private agenda concerning Jake, an agenda she couldn't confide to her husband. She had to resolve *that* problem on her own. If Joe and Brian were there, she'd be torn between her present and her past. "Perhaps on the weekends, if you want." As a dentist, Joe couldn't change his appointment schedule at the last minute.

"Brian and I have our fishing trip scheduled for next weekend, but we can cancel that."

"No, don't," she protested. It was hard enough for the two of them to find time together.

Joe nodded. "Then we'll try to come one weekend after that." He put down his coffee mug and glanced at her, a half smile on his face. "I have a feeling you're going to learn a lot more than you expected from all of this."

Susannah suspected he was right.

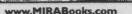

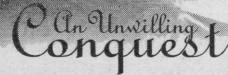

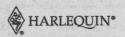

If you enjoyed what you just read,
then we've got an offer you can't resist!

Take 2 novels FREE!
Plus get a FREE surprise gift!

Clip this page and mail it to The Reader Service

IN U.S.A.
3010 Walden Ave.
P.O. Box 1867
Buffalo, N.Y. 14240-1867

IN CANADA
P.O. Box 609
Fort Erie, Ontario
L2A 5X3

YES! Please send me 2 free novels from the Romance/Suspense Collection and my free surprise gift. After receiving them, if I don't wish to receive any more, I can return the shipping statement marked "cancel". If I don't cancel, I will receive 4 brand-new novels every month, before they're available in stores! In the U.S.A., bill me at the bargain price of $5.24 plus 25¢ shipping and handling per book and applicable sales tax, if any*. In Canada, bill me at the bargain price of $5.74 plus 25¢ shipping and handling per book and applicable taxes**. That's the complete price and a savings of over 10% off the cover prices—what a great deal! I understand that accepting the 2 free books and gift places me under no obligation ever to buy any books. I can always return a shipment and cancel at any time. Even if I never buy another book, the 2 free books and gift are mine to keep forever.

185 MDN EFVD
385 MDN EFVP

Name	(PLEASE PRINT)	
Address	Apt.#	
City	State/Prov.	Zip/Postal Code

*Not valid to current subscribers of the Romance Collection,
the Suspense Collection or the Romance/Suspense Collection.*

**Want to try two free books from another series?
Call 1-800-873-8635 or visit www.morefreebooks.com.**

* Terms and prices subject to change without notice. Sales tax applicable in N.Y.
** Canadian residents will be charged applicable provincial taxes and GST.

All orders subject to approval. Offer limited to one per household. Credit or debit balances in a customer's account(s) may be offset by any other outstanding balance owed by or to the customer. Please allow 4 to 6 weeks for delivery.
® and ™ are trademarks owned and used by the trademark owner and/or its licensee.

BOB06R   © 2004 Harlequin Enterprises Limited

DEBBIE MACOMBER

32208 50 HARBOR STREET	___ $7.50 U.S.	___ $8.99 CAN.
32160 THE SHOP ON BLOSSOM STREET	___ $7.50 U.S.	___ $8.99 CAN.
32110 ON A SNOWY NIGHT	___ $6.99 U.S.	___ $8.50 CAN.
32073 44 CRANBERRY POINT	___ $7.50 U.S.	___ $8.99 CAN.
32028 CHANGING HABITS	___ $7.50 U.S.	___ $8.99 CAN.
66674 BETWEEN FRIENDS	___ $7.50 U.S.	___ $8.99 CAN.
66930 A GIFT TO LAST	___ $6.99 U.S.	___ $8.50 CAN.
66929 204 ROSEWOOD LANE	___ $7.50 U.S.	___ $8.99 CAN.
66891 THURSDAYS AT EIGHT	___ $7.50 U.S.	___ $8.99 CAN.
66830 16 LIGHTHOUSE ROAD	___ $6.99 U.S.	___ $8.50 CAN.
66800 ALWAYS DAKOTA	___ $6.99 U.S.	___ $8.50 CAN.
66719 311 PELICAN COURT	___ $7.50 U.S.	___ $8.99 CAN.
66576 DAKOTA BORN	___ $6.99 U.S.	___ $8.50 CAN.
66974 MOON OVER WATER	___ $6.99 U.S.	___ $8.50 CAN.
66976 PROMISE, TEXAS	___ $6.99 U.S.	___ $8.50 CAN.
66975 MONTANA	___ $6.99 U.S.	___ $8.50 CAN.
66973 THIS MATTER OF MARRIAGE	___ $6.99 U.S.	___ $8.50 CAN.

(limited quantities available)

TOTAL AMOUNT	$ _____
POSTAGE & HANDLING	$ _____
($1.00 FOR 1 BOOK, 50¢ for each additional)	
APPLICABLE TAXES*	$ _____
TOTAL PAYABLE	$ _____

(check or money order—please do not send cash)

To order, complete this form and send it, along with a check or money order for the total above, payable to MIRA Books, to: **In the U.S.:** 3010 Walden Avenue, P.O. Box 9077, Buffalo, NY 14269-9077; **In Canada:** P.O. Box 636, Fort Erie, Ontario, L2A 5X3.

Name: _____
Address: _____ City: _____
State/Prov.: _____ Zip/Postal Code: _____
Account Number (if applicable): _____

075 CSAS

*New York residents remit applicable sales taxes.
*Canadian residents remit applicable GST and provincial taxes.

MIRA®

MDM1105BL